SEPTIMANIA

SEPTIMANIA

A NOVEL

Jonathan Levi

OVERLOOK DUCKWORTH
NEW YORK • LONDON

This edition first published in hardcover in the United States and the United Kingdom in 2016 by Overlook Duckworth, Peter Mayer Publishers, Inc.

NEW YORK
141 Wooster Street
New York, NY 10012
www.overlookpress.com

For bulk and special sales, please contact sales@overlookny.com, or write us at the address above.

LONDON
30 Calvin Street
London E1 6NW
info@duckworth-publishers.co.uk
www.ducknet.co.uk

Library of Congress Cataloging-in-Publication Data

Names: Levi, Jonathan, 1955- author.
Title: Septimania : a novel / Jonathan Levi.
Description: First edition. | New York, N.Y. : The Overlook Press, [2016]
Identifiers: LCCN 2015044768 | ISBN 9781468312485 (hardcover)
Classification: LCC PS3562.E8878 S47 2016 | DDC 813/.54--dc23
LC record available at http://lccn.loc.gov/2015044768

A Catalogue record for this book is available from the British Library.

Book design and type formatting by Bernard Schleifer

Manufactured in the United States of America

ISBN: 978-1-4683-1248-5 (US)
ISBN: 978-0-7156-5096-7 (UK)

FIRST EDITION

1 3 5 7 9 10 8 6 4 2

To my parents,
Judith and Isaac Levi,
who lifted me onto their shoulders

PART ONE

Comfort me with apples, for I am sick with love.

—*Song of Songs*

1/0

One garden. One tree. Two backs against the trunk, two bums on the grass, two mouths sharing a pipe after dinner.

London is burning. Plague is riding flame and smoke, and the early August sun radiates death north to Cambridge. Henry VIII stands in stony guard over the silent Great Court of Trinity College, students dismissed until further notice. Further north still, in the garden of Mrs. Hannah Newton Smith, one of these students, her strange scholar of a son, sits with a friend. I am that friend, a foreigner—some traits cannot be disguised. But a foreigner who can think of no better way to weather the closing of the university than to share a pipe and a tree with friend Isaac.

"I was a posthumous child." Isaac blows a puff, the smoke mixing like China tea with the granules of sunlight, and passes the pipe to me. "I never knew my father, and the feeling was mutual. I was born Christmas morn, so small, I am told, that I fit in a quart pot, and so weakly that, when two women were sent to Lady Pakenham at North Witham for some herbal strengthener for my struggling spirit, they sat down on a stile by the way, certain there was no occasion for making haste as I would be dead before they could return."

"That would explain your healthy appetite." I take the pipe from Isaac.

"And yet," Isaac watches the smoke rise towards the fruit in paisleys and curlicues, "I am certain that—my mother's bitterness notwithstanding—I must, at one time, have had a father."

"And a Holy Spirit?"

"Fuck the Trinity," Isaac grabs the pipe from me and puffs again.

"The college," I ask, "or the concept?"

"Father, Son, Holy Spirit—for an orphan like me, there is but one Father, one God—finitum—and all that we know, all that we are radiates forth from the One like the rays of the Sun. I suppose at heart," he smiles a smile that at sunset gives me courage, "I must be a Jew."

"It isn't the heart that interests this Jew." I smile back with a glance at Isaac's thighs.

"A true Christian, like a true Jew, believes in the single God."

"The God of Abraham?"

"And Isaac."

"That's two gods right there," I laugh. "Never mind Trinity College and your Trinitarians. You'd be surprised to know how many of my circumcised brethren are Quarternarians."

"Quarternarians?"

"They believe, quite openly, in four deities. Some students of the Kabbalah even hypothesize the existence of seven Gods!"

"Heresy!"

"Septimaniacs," I tell him. "Septimaniacs—with a God for each of the seven heavens, for each day of the week, for every direction of space, every planet, every Pleiad, every color, every virtue . . ."

"And every deadly sin," adds Isaac. An apple falls and lands between my legs.

"Take a bite," I offer without moving.

"After you," Isaac demurs. "There are plenty of apples."

"Precisely," I say. "Welcome to Septimania."

NE SHAFT OF LIGHT.

Louiza.

Louiza's golden head around the side of the Orchard Tea Garden, Louiza's pale chin lifting upwind, deciding direction, scenting the surprisingly balmy air of mid-March in 1978. Louiza crossing the Cambridge Road, elbows at her side, shoulders a marble channel for the faded straps of her flowered dress. Louiza's teeth-bitten fingers lifting the latch of the churchyard gate, Louiza's raspberry calves disappearing from view.

Malory.

Corduroyed Malory. Bell-bottomed Malory. Beatle-haired Malory.

Malory up in the steeple of St. George's Church, Whistler Abbey. Hesitant Malory, five-foot-six-point-five Malory perched on the tips of his boots on a stack of abandoned hymnals, his Book of Organs in one hand, his breath in the other.

Looking.

Malory looking for the demon that was throttling the church organ, keeping it out of tune and him from his lunch. Malory climbing up the steeple, looking out through the slats at a girl he had never seen, never suspected.

Louiza looking for the loo, but drawn across the road from the Orchard towards a church and a ladder.

"Hello up there!" Louiza.

"Yes?" Malory's own voice in the pinched register of a six-inch reed.

"May I come up?"

Louiza and Malory.

They took refuge from their embarrassment in the view of the dappled fire through the windows of the Orchard. Then, from the far side of the steeple, the specter of the blasted yew—planted four thousand years ago, the vicar claimed, twice as old as our Lord—in whose hollowed trunk Malory had been known to conduct the younger nose-pickers of the parish in elementary hymns. Malory pointed Louiza to the northern reach of Whistler Abbey, and in the distance, the reclaimed marshland and hamlets of Rankwater and Silt, beginning to thaw in the early spring sun. Malory fought valiantly not to be discovered examining the corona of sunlight around Louiza's jaw, the dusting of wheaten hairs that softened the rims of her ears, the way her nose in profile, as she followed the direction of his finger towards some distant Norman church, pointed towards a narrow upper lip and a chin thrust slightly more forward than classical beauty might have recommended. Malory wrestled with the magnetic attraction of Louiza's left breast, its silhouette refracted by the prism of her cotton dress, its parabola hard with the defiance of youth, refusing to acknowledge gravity and raising the nipple towards an astonishing and hopeful zenith. Most of all, Malory struggled towards intelligence, realizing that the more he talked to this girl about the history of Cambridgeshire and the draining of the fens, the more his own voice fell out of tune.

"May I ask you a question?" Louiza turned away from the view and fully into Malory's face. Her eyes drew the blue of the afternoon into the steeple for a moment, with a force Malory had never imagined possible—not, at least, within the universe of Newtonian physics, which was, after all, his universe. The power of her eyes, the unity of their focus, as devoid of color as they were full of hope, convinced Malory of what he had already decided. Louiza was the most beautiful girl he had ever seen, or at least the most beautiful girl he had ever seen at such proximity. And this discovery rendered Malory incapable of saying anything other than—

"Yes?"

"What are you doing up here?"

Malory told Louiza how he had bicycled down from Cambridge, how he had arrived at St. George's just after eight in the morning, intending to tune the organ and return to the Tea Room of the University Library for the first scones of the day. He was the Organ Scholar at Trinity, he mumbled, without going into great detail about the cold matins and inconvenient vespers he had to play, the acrobatic rehearsals whenever the Trinity Choir decided to premiere some optimistic composition by the Choirmaster.

Tuning the nineteenth-century organ of St. George's Church was a private arrangement, normally the job of a single hour. But fifteen minutes into the tuning that morning, Malory found something wrong with the D-sharp in the six-inch reeds of the organ. He slipped the rod a quarter-inch and brought the pipe into tune, only to find that the problem migrated to the G-sharp. Solving the G-sharp only spread the oddity to two other pipes. Sometimes it was a defect of pitch, sometimes it was complete strangulation. All morning he chased the blockage, from pipes to stops, from bellows back to console. The six-inch reeds were only fifteen feet above the paving stones of the nave and easily examined by means of a wooden A-frame that the warden kept with the mop and bucket behind the safe in the Lady Chapel. But as scones lost out to lunch and Malory still hadn't left the church, the demon of the organ continued to elude him.

It was after three when Malory climbed from the chancel, by way of a staircase behind the reeds and then up a vertical ladder, fifty-two rungs—so he told Louiza as she twisted a strand of hair around a wheaten ear—to the bell tower. He wasn't certain what he'd find up there among the webs and guano. There was no clear link to the organ twenty feet below. Certainly the bellows drew air from up here through the four sets of slats cut into the sloping steeple, although it drew air, one might say, from everywhere. He needed a change of scene but wasn't prepared to leave St. George's until he had slain the dragon. Perhaps if he did not play, the demon would not appear.

"It's like Schrödinger's cat," Malory said.

"Don't know him." Louiza bowed her head, casting a tangle of gold over the front of her eyes in an embarrassment that Malory immediately regretted.

"No, no. Schrödinger was a physicist, German, back in the 1920s. He tried to describe why looking for things was, well, difficult.

How looking changed what you were looking for." Malory was so flummoxed by his own attempts at explanation that he could barely look at Louiza. "Schrödinger presented a problem—a cat is in a box along with a bottle of poisonous gas and a tiny piece of uranium. The uranium spits out radioactive particles at random, like a popcorn popper at Strawberry Fair. We can never tell when a particle will come whizzing out, or in which direction it will fly. But when enough uranium particles finally hit, the bottle of poisonous gas will explode."

"And then?" Louiza asked.

"The cat will die," Malory said. "Painlessly," he added, although he was pleased to see that Louiza was more interested in the intellectual problem than in feline sensibilities. "So we make our experiment—we put the cat in the box with the gas and the uranium and seal it tight and let the clock tick. After a minute or so, we ask the question, is Kitty dead or alive?"

"Yes," said Louiza.

"Yes!" Malory whooped. "That is the answer of the old physics. Yes, the old physics would have said—the cat is either dead or alive."

"Hmm," Louiza hummed.

Hmm? Was Louiza making fun of him, or did she already know the joke, or was she simply bored and he was losing her? "The new physics," he continued, "quantum mechanics, says until we open the box, the cat is possibly dead and possibly alive."

"Or nibbling on popcorn at Strawberry Fair?" Louiza smiled, and Malory felt the pipes in his chest rise up half a tone.

"Anything is possible," he whispered, "until we look."

"And afterwards?" Louiza asked.

"What do you mean?" Malory hadn't reckoned on questions, only a little sympathy for an organ tuner who had missed his scones in search of a dead cat.

"After the box is opened," Louiza said, as simply as Pandora. "Once we look inside, is anything still possible?"

"Well," Malory said, "some physicists believe that there are two worlds that exist after the box is opened. In one world is the cat we see, in the other the cat we don't. In one world, the cat is being chased by worms. In the other, he is raring to catch mice. The only problem is, neither world knows anything about the other. Live Felix doesn't know Dead Felix exists. But they both do."

"Ah!" said Louiza, and clapped her hands. "That's what I hoped."

"You did?" Malory said, pleased if confused by his ability to provoke such delight in this angel.

"Yes!" Louiza said, jumping up and reaching for the high beam of the steeple. "You see, that's where I come from, a world of half-dead cats."

It was then that Louiza explained to Malory what she had never explained to others. She told him of the soggy schools and playgrounds of the Norfolk marshes, where the teachers and children insisted on reading and writing in a language of letters that made no sense to Louiza. She talked of her mother, who tried to drill the rudiments of language into her uncomprehending daughter, while her father grumbled over reheated shepherd's pie. Finally, Louiza told Malory about mathematics, how mathematics connected her to the world.

"It was very simple," she said. "If I could link a word with a number—say, the word *cat* with the number negative 57—if I could turn a word into a formula, then I could read the world."

"Why negative 57?"

"Because the world of my teachers, my enemies, my own father was all so negative. 'Louiza can't read'—negative. 'Louiza can't write' —negative. 'Doesn't focus in class'—negative. 'Never amount'—negative. My whole life, one big negative. Naturally, when I began to think in numbers, I made z negative 1, y negative 2, up to negative 26 for a. So *cat* is negative 24 plus negative 26 plus negative 7—equals negative 57."

"I am negative one," Malory said, aiming at wit with sympathy.

"No," Louiza said, "i is the square root of negative 1." Her eyebrows rose to emphasize the italics.

Even Malory, flustered by Louiza's parry, knew that mathematicians since the time of Newton have written the king of imaginary numbers as a lowercase, italicized i. The force behind Louiza's pronunciation of the letter was, perhaps, born from the vertigo of those early mathematicians as they pondered the square root of –1, afraid themselves of tipping over with the effort of imagining such a thing. The square roots of negative numbers, after all, did not exist in the real world any more than half-dead cats. What number, times itself, would give you a square with an area of –1? When you squared a number, a positive number or a negative number, it gave you a positive answer. +2 times +2 equals +4. –2 times –2 equals +4. That was how it went. That was cricket. Those were the rules. All numbers, when you squared them, when you multiplied them by themselves, gave you a positive number. So the question, *What is the square root of –1?* was just, well, clearly not a question you should ask. Nevertheless, it was easy enough, with a piece of chalk and a board, or a pencil and paper, to scribble down equations like:

$$x^2 + 1 = 0$$

For many people, these scribbles, these equations not only existed but demanded answers. Subtracting 1 from both sides of the equation, whether in the smoky, chintz parlor of Louiza's Norfolk farmhouse or the drafty, gothic classroom of Malory's King's College Choir School led to:

$$x^2 = -1$$

and then:

$$x = \sqrt{-1}$$

which a sixteenth-century mathematician decided to baptize with an italic *i*, perhaps to keep it from infecting the real numbers, the ones you could see and touch and chew.

$$i = \sqrt{-1}$$
$$x = i$$

"I was eight," Louiza said, "when I asked my father what was the square root of negative 1. He thought the question was nonsense. Negative numbers he could understand, as years on a timeline, as negative *befores* in contrast to positive *afters*. But the square root of negative 1? I might as well have asked him what was the square root of the Magna Carta or a sugar beet. It was my mother who couldn't be bothered with her own ignorance and asked the maths teacher at school.

'Louiza, meet i,' he said to me. 'i, Louiza.' And after i, the brothers of i, the distant cousins, the family tree of imaginary numbers built around i. Suddenly i became my escape. I found a home in a world peopled with histories and futures and pets dead and alive, a nook in the universe where reading and writing made sense."

"And that's what you're studying for your BA?" Malory asked.

"PhD actually," Louiza looked down. "Studied. I passed my *viva* this morning."

"This morning?" Malory steadied himself with a hand on the rough boards of the roof.

"Would you like to hear my thesis?" Louiza reached up to Malory's belt and pulled him down into a conspiratorial squat, her cotton hem riding up above a pair of knees that Malory thought might just fit in his mouth.

"Of course," Malory said, still dizzy at the thought that this young woman—could she even be twenty?—was about to graduate with a PhD and had just happened to climb up the steeple of St. George's Church, Whistler Abbey, and find him, Malory, who had spent the past ten years avoiding his own doctorate on Sir Isaac Newton with an alternating diet of organs and scones.

"$i = u$"

"I equals you?"

"$i = u$." Louiza took Malory's Book of Organs and wrote the formula on a blank page in a sharp, decisive hand. "$i = u$," she repeated, slowly tracing the letters on Malory's receptive chest. "In *italics*."

"Italics," Malory repeated in idiotic rapture at the touch of Louiza's finger on the flannel of his shirt.

"I," Louiza said, "Louiza. You?"

Malory told her. He told her about his rooms in Great Court next to the chapel; as Organ Scholar of Trinity College—on call from matins to vespers, from baptisms to funerals—proximity to the chapel was essential. He told her about his sitting room, which looked out onto Trinity Street and the apple tree planted in 1966 in honor of the three-hundredth anniversary of Newton's *annus mirabilis*, the year the great man ran from the Plague back to his mother's garden in Lincolnshire and discovered the law of gravity, the nature of light, calculus, and half a dozen other Promethean treasures. He told her about the summer mornings when he would awaken to the desperate cramming of field mice in his rubbish bin and winter mornings when a prism of thawing ice rode the bobsled of gravity from the window-pane to his head. As a graduate student writing a doctoral thesis on the great Sir Isaac, it was foregone and fitting that Newton's rooms, if not his genius, should come to Malory.

"But you," Louiza said. "Who are you?"

Malory told her that his own Christian name was Hercule (his mother Sara being French-born) and that the last name on his birth certificate was Emery (being his mother's alone). "But everyone calls me Malory, with one *l*," Malory said to Louiza, whose eyes widened in what Malory could only believe was the usual astonishment. "I know what you're thinking," he rushed on. "Malory as in Thomas Malory who wrote about King Arthur and the Knights of the Round Table. You know, Lancelot and Guinevere, Galahad the Pure?"

"No," Louiza whispered, "it's not that." But Malory didn't hear her message, eager as he was to confess something he'd never told anyone else. That Malory was the name of a father who had never seen his son. That Malory, like the great Sir Isaac, was posthumous at birth, his fisherman of a father having died after failing to judge the proper speed of the Irish ferry on which his mother was arriving to marry him. That was as much as he knew of the old man—the sur-name, the fatal eagerness with which he'd loved young Sara—and that much he had gleaned from his mother only after it was clear, shortly before his tenth birthday, that she too would be leaving him, and with-out much more than this one story.

"Malory," Louiza whispered again and looked at him, Malory thought, as if she were really, really interested in him, his name, his history. And he also thought, hoped, dreaded that Louiza would kiss him—his first kiss, he was ashamed to even think, his first girl. Twenty-six years old and he would finally kiss a girl. Not that he'd been a man's man. There had always been something too homuncular about him to make him a target of the older boys at King's College

Choir School or later. There had been dozens, millions of times, actually, from childhood through to the present, when he would have gladly cuddled up to anything human: male, female, or child. But there had never been occasion. He had to content himself with pencils, small rocks, horse chestnuts, the edges of worn sweaters that, with their smells and their textures, kindled enough of an image of affection to stave off his hunger. But now, this girl, this Louiza, of imaginary numbers and cats—

"Is this it?" Louiza reached around Malory.

Malory sat for a moment, still waiting for the kiss, still trying to make sense of the brief equation Louiza had traced on his chest and his equally brief confession. And then he focused, with an attempt at equilibrium, on the lightly dusted hand holding an apple pip in front of his face in the slanted light of the steeple. An apple pip. Between two perfect, if nail-bitten, fingers, Louiza was holding an apple pip that she had pried loose from between two slats of the shutters. And although Malory needed ten minutes of chromatic variations on Bach's "Come Now, O Savior of the Gentiles" to prove that this singular Pip was the demon that had asphyxiated the organ, the demon he had chased from one key to the next, he knew, beyond a doubt, that Louiza—in any of her many possible worlds—could solve all problems without looking.

The kiss, the undressing of flannel shirt and cotton dress, the exploration and all the rest followed with calm, with passion and a sense of musical inevitability. Yet there was so much that was unpredictable in Louiza's movements, such a matrix of unsuspected jumping-aways and lunging-togethers that it wasn't until afterwards, with the afternoon sun casting a final five-line shadow on the eastern wall of the steeple, that Malory stopped to wonder why. Why him? Why now? Why here in the steeple of St. George's Church, Whistler Abbey?

"Your name," Louiza said. "Malory, your name equals negative 78." Louiza traced the unitalicized equation on Malory's unshirted chest. "So does my name, Louiza. Negative 78. I equals you."

He did the maths. Of course she was correct—m plus a plus l and so on equaled l plus o plus all the gorgeous things that had just happened, that had just happened to him. But being Malory, being a student of Isaac Newton and a tuner of organs with an ear that wouldn't be satisfied, he had to ask.

"What does it mean, my equation?" Louiza's cheek was resting on his thigh. Her voice was soft, but it resonated through his body as if she were whispering in his ear. "How can my equation, how can $i = u$ change the world?"

"Yes," Malory said. "Something like that."

"The applications," Louiza began. "The applications are extraordinary. And quite possibly dangerous."

"Dangerous?" Malory sat up.

"I'll explain next time," Louiza said, springing to her feet and stepping to the ladder.

"Next time?" Malory said, in some desperation that this time seemed to be drawing to a close. "Where? When?"

"Wherever you find that cat," Louiza said. "Whenever." She handed him the Pip with those slender, teeth-bitten fingers. "Remember: $i = u$." And disappeared.

1/2

WHY DID MALORY LET LOUIZA DISAPPEAR? WHY DIDN'T HE JUMP up? Why didn't he play Galahad and leap, or at least slide down the ladder from the steeple and out to wherever the breath of late afternoon had borne her?

The sun was in his eyes. Or rather, there was a vision, a curtain between the floor where Malory sat and the trap door down which Louiza had disappeared. A curtain, or better still, a gentle waterfall of light flowed down from the beveled slats of the roof to the wooden planking of the steeple floor. A dusty host of angels climbed up and down that mid-afternoon sunbeam, flapping their wings to the back-beat of a Hosanna over Malory's Kit Bag, his Book of Organs, his Universal Tuner.

There was nothing unusual about any of the three. They were as worn and discolored as any of the million keepsakes that other solitary adolescents have adapted to adult use over their own histories. The Universal Tuner was a foot-long piece of twisted metal the ten-year-old Malory had found lying on a cairn in the hills outside Narbonne, that last summer he had spent with his mother. He had never been curious enough to ask about its composition, although it was clearly harder than the lead that made up the better organ pipes. He was thankful for the Universal Tuner's angular eccentricities, its ability to scratch and bang and pry and cajole thousands upon thousands of pipes into harmonic precision, and its singular economy, as compact as a Swiss Army knife and as ingenious as a Geiger counter for diagnosing and curing the many ailments of the pipe organ, in their multitudinous variety. The Book of Organs was as near a diary as Malory had ever possessed—listing the name, the location, the birth date, baptism, and every subsequent tuning and idiosyncrasy of every organ he had played, tuned, cleaned, or vacuumed free of dust and mouse droppings, going back to the organ of the cathedral of Narbonne.

Both Universal Tuner and Book of Organs had special pockets in Malory's Kit Bag, which was not lacking in the pocket department. It could hold half-eaten sandwiches, cake wrapped in waxed paper, music folios, and shoe polish. The Kit Bag was the only souvenir Malory possessed of his dead fisherman of a father, although why his father had the bag was a mystery. As far as Malory knew, his father had never been a soldier. In any case the bag was too small to be useful either as a duffel bag or a serious daypack. Green canvas was hardly the kind of waterproof material for a fisherman carrying bait and tackle and a fish or three, no matter how many pockets it had. But the Kit Bag, the one true link to his paternity, was stenciled on the flap in broken capitals:

MALORY

Tenuous and puerile as Malory realized such attachments were, there were moments in the drafty organ lofts of East Anglia when tracing the letters with his fingertips brought a certain warmth. All three—Universal Tuner, Book of Organs, and Kit Bag—were Malory's constant companions. Yet something had happened to Malory in the steeple of the church of St. George's, Whistler Abbey. And in case Malory was too dim to understand the significance, the seraphim of Nature were mobilizing to focus his eyes on the obvious.

The obvious sat in its own pool of atomized afternoon, atop the pebbled and abused cover of the Book of Organs. The Pip, the Pip that Louiza had pried from between the shutters of the steeple, the Pip that had brought Malory's life into tune. The brown-husked mini-ovum of a Pip that drew the afternoon light into its brownness at the new center of Malory's expanding universe. The Pip was the obvious cause of Malory's change—or at least obvious to Malory, who could interpret the beating of his heart, the coursing in his veins, the dizziness of what others simply call love, only through the light and the gravity of his Newton. The Pip brought Louiza and Malory together, the Pip witnessed all that had gone between them. The Pip was the Sun that drew the Moon to the Earth and spun them around one another. The Pip would bring them back together for all time. The Pip would keep company with the Universal Tuner and the Book of Organs in his Kit Bag. The Pip would be his guide.

Malory packed the Pip into a plastic 35-millimeter film canister that he normally used for resin, wedged it safely into a pocket of the Kit Bag, added the Universal Tuner and the Book of Organs, and let gravity pull him back down the ladder to the nave. He was twice as tall when his feet touched the paving stones of the nave as when he had ascended that morning. He was certain that Louiza would be waiting for him outside St. George's, or in the Orchard, or if not there, then not far away.

"Good afternoon."

Not Louiza. In the cooler light of the second pew sat the Old Lady.

"Good afternoon, Hercule," the Old Lady said again.

"Good afternoon—"

"Please," the Old Lady said. "Come sit for a moment."

Malory had no desire to sit, had no desire to talk to any old lady—this one, perhaps, in particular.

"Please," the Old Lady said again. "I will not bite." The crumbs of French at the edges of the Old Lady's accent gave the invitation a certain force that Malory—being Malory and therefore incapable of giving offense—could not ignore. Malory sat. "You know who I am, I suppose."

She was covered in a dusty blue and gray, although the dust, to Malory's eye, was neither the dust of the angels nor the dust of neglect but more of a powder that softened the threads of her woolen suit, molded the silk at her neck into the ancient pockets of her skin and blended the powdered white of her hair into a hat that Malory would only remember as expensive in the way that history must be. But the sensation that struck Malory with the sharpest power—a power that he was soon forced to recall on many occasions—was the scent of pine and sun, the scent of the four-thousand-year-old yew in the churchyard, one he hadn't smelled on a human being since the death of his mother nearly twenty years before.

"Mrs. Emery," Malory said. "Good evening." He knew she was Mrs. Emery. Old Mrs. Emery who lived alone, it was said, in the gothic pile of Whistler Abbey, a manor that overlooked the yew. Old Mrs. Emery, who for as long as Malory could remember had said nothing to him, but had placed a shilling in his palm following every service. Given the choice, Malory would have sooner spent a night in the churchyard than in Whistler Abbey with Old Mrs. Emery.

"Mrs. Emery," she repeated. He saw another church, in the Cathar South of France when his mother was still alive, a land as hilly as the fens were smooth, the church where a younger Malory ran for the warmth and all-consuming vibrations of the organ, where he danced on the pedals because his feet could not reach from the bench, while his fist relaxed into a Bach prelude or a Saint-Saëns fantasy. "Hercule," Mrs. Emery repeated. "I know that we have complex relations."

Malory had survived by avoiding complexity, by seeking simplicity, in Newton, in Bach. But complexity was clearly the motif of the day—first Louiza with her $i = u$, her complex nature bound up in a web of numbers built from the square root of -1, and now Mrs. Emery, whose every breath reminded Malory that he had never known his father and had lost his mother at an age when the world was beginning to seem unbearably complex. Both Louiza and Mrs. Emery had found him at St. George's Church, Whistler Abbey. Malory needed tea. Badly.

"Hercule," Mrs. Emery said. "You are in a rush, I can see."

"Yes," Malory said. "Sorry."

"Don't let me keep you." Mrs. Emery didn't move, and it was clear that she did not mean what she was saying. "But perhaps you can spare a moment for your grandmother."

His grandmother. Mrs. Emery. Ahh. Malory's mind began again. Mrs. Emery was his grandmother. There was the word. The Old Lady in the second pew was his grandmother. Like the discovery that goosed Archimedes out of his ancient Sicilian bathtub, the realization that Old Mrs. Emery was his grandmother had a touch of Eureka to it. But the surprise was tempered by a recognition that this was something he had always known. His mother had never spoken of her family. Malory had assumed a chorus of disapproval. Disapproval of his mother, disapproval primed by Sara's choice of Irish lover, Malory *père*, a man whose judgment was in inverse proportion to his love.

Was it malice that Old Mrs. Emery felt towards her daughter Sara, towards the Irish lover, Malory's father? Was it malice on Sara's part that denied her own mother the knowledge of her grandson? For the first ten years of his life, Malory was only too willing to worship the decisions of his mother. And nothing he learned after her death induced him to develop the faculty of inquiry. Someone arranged for him to study and room at King's College Choir School. He never asked who. He was at an age where he accepted everything, accepted the academics, the music, the bullying, although his posture was so naïvely open that the worst of the thugs felt it beneath their dignity to bloody a boy who didn't know how to cower. And he never wondered why he was there.

Was it to this Mrs. Emery, this grandmother, that Malory owed—as unthinkingly, perhaps, as he owed God—his four A levels and subsequent Organ Scholarship to Trinity College, Cambridge? Was it to her he owed the request of the Master of Trinity that, for a small additional stipend, he play the ten o'clock service at the tiny Norman church of St. George, Whistler Abbey, every other Sunday morning (in such a depleted parish, the church had to share a preacher with Lesser St. Arnulf's in Cambridge)? It was from the organ loft of St. George's that Malory saw the gray-haired lady in the second pew every other Sunday. When later he had learned that, like his mother, her name too was Emery and that his stipend was directly transferred from her weekly donation to his pocket, he began to guess at her identity, or rather at his own. With the weight of that possibility, at the height of the organ loft, he felt his abandonment most keenly.

Instead of acknowledging the word *grandmother*, he made up a fiction to justify his abandonment. He had inherited his love of the organ from Mrs. Emery. Her piety, like his, was merely a stop that she could push in or pull out to create the desired effect, an unspoken linkage of two notes. It was part of a secret they shared. He'd always known and refused to think it odd that the old lady who smiled up at him from her seat on the aisle in the second pew never spoke to him and never approached him save to place a shilling in his palm at the close of service.

"You have known, Malory," Mrs. Emery said, "I hope you have known for a long time that you had a grandmother who loved you very much, but loved her daughter more."

Knowledge, Malory thought—tricky business, that.

"It was out of respect for my poor, dead Sara that I never approached you directly when I saw you in St. George's, or the many times I traveled into town on visiting days at school and ordinary times, and watched and felt the loneliness I had brought upon you and your mother. I expect it was your own love and loyalty to your mother that kept you away from me, stronger than any loneliness imaginable."

Malory said nothing, holding onto a gothic refusal to degenerate into a Dickensian Pip. But he remembered that final summer in the South of France.

"Whose garden is this, Mother?"

"What do you mean, Hercule?

"Does it belong to Charlemagne?"

"Not everything belongs to Charlemagne," she smiled. "Not much, in fact. Any more."

"Then who?"

"It's yours, Hercule. The garden, the house."

"It isn't yours?"

"Some things," she said, "are just for boys."

"But this garden is just for me?"

"If you like."

"Do we like it here?"

"You like the organ in the cathedral, don't you?"

"Oh, yes."

"And the old lady next door? Do you like her?"

"In the big house? I thought this was her garden, her cottage."

"No, Hercule, it's yours. The old lady and I are just looking after it for you. Until you are bigger."

"And the medallion of King David in the cathedral? The one that you say looks like me. Is that mine?"

"One day, perhaps. Who knows?"

"The boys in the market make fun of my name. They say there is a giant Hercule who's asleep beneath the hills."

"How do you know what they're saying if they speak another language?"

"Is it true, Mother? About the giant?"

"If I told you, would you believe me?"

"They say he stood in the ocean and pushed Europe away from Africa. Then he got sleepy and lay down."

"Not surprising after such hard labor."

"They say he rose up, the giant, and chased away all the Saracens."

"The Saracens! Did he?"

"Is he my father? The giant Hercule?"

"I thought you wanted to go to the cathedral, to play the organ."

"It's out of tune, mother."

"Oh, Hercule. You and your ears!"

"But it is. The whole world. England, France, Europe, Africa. Out of tune."

His mother paused. She tried to smile.

"Then you must tune it, Hercule," she whispered, *"the way the giant Hercule tried to adjust the Strait of Gibraltar."*

Malory said nothing to Mrs. Emery, sitting in the second pew of St. George's Church, Whistler Abbey. He shifted the Kit Bag on his shoulder, the canvas of the strap brushing a light B-flat against the corduroy of his jacket. There was nothing to be said, zero. But not an uncomfortable zero. It was a zero stuffed full of history—addings and subtractings, the products of time and experience and the gain that fills the vacuum of loss.

"I've brought you a gift, Hercule," Mrs. Emery said.

"Ah."

"No," Mrs. Emery smiled. "Not the usual shilling. A book." She handed him a parcel covered in brown paper and string. "An old book. It's been in the family, which, after all, is your family, at least—" She smiled again at her own inability to disguise her wistful distaste. "At least your mother's side of the family."

"Thank you," Malory said, ever polite, finding a convenient slot for the parcel in the depths of the Kit Bag. "But why?" he asked. "Why today?" He didn't know why he said it. But in a day of mysteries, it was the question of Pips and fair-haired girls and grandmothers.

"To celebrate your discovery, of course." Mrs. Emery stood and handed him a coin, her fingers as cool as the paving stones. "Now run across the road and get yourself a cup of tea."

IT WAS GETTING ON TOWARDS THREE O'CLOCK. BENEATH THE FIRST BUDS of the apple trees, a dozen green-striped lawn chairs were scattered as bait for the hardened tourist who might bicycle or motor or even punt the three miles from the urban towers of Cambridge in hope of the first bucolic pleasures of spring. But Malory needed to warm his brain. He opened the garden door of the Orchard and chose a small table inside near the fire. The single customer, a tall, red-bearded man, was chatting at the till in what Malory guessed was some sort of American accent. He nodded at Malory, but Malory turned to the fire, pretending not to see—not keen to give offense, but not prepared for a third new encounter.

"For you." The Brazilian wife of the proprietor—Malory had let her twins crawl on the pedals on the organ during several of his tunings—set a cup of tea and a plate of scones in front of him.

"Thank you," Malory said, "but I only have a shilling."

"A gift," the Brazilian said.

"But—"

"Not from me," she added, and turned back to the till. But the red-bearded American was gone. The Brazilian matron, too, moved away from Malory to clear the remains of what looked like an extensive three-bottle celebratory luncheon.

The parcel, the tea, Malory thought. And above all Louiza. Three gifts in one strange day. One was in his Kit Bag, one was quickly disappearing down his gullet, and one may have vanished forever.

He chewed, he swallowed.

Antonella, he thought. Antonella would know. Antonella would be at the Maths Faculty at the Sidgwick Site. Antonella would do anything for Malory, even search in the records and find clues to lead him to Louiza. Although Malory preferred cycling along the footpath by the river, March was a month of mud, and he was in a hurry. Though Antonella seemed to live at the office, Malory knew that even lonely Italian girls had their limits and he had better hurry.

The favor was not an issue. Antonella was clearly disposed—had been disposed for the better part of the three years she had worked as departmental secretary—to do more than just about anything for Malory. While Malory was only vaguely aware of his power over Antonella, he did know that in the Kingdom of Mathematicians, he as a Historian of Science, with his Beatle hair and bell-bottomed trousers, bestrode the River Cam with the charisma and stature of a Colossus. He couldn't fail to notice her at the occasions where he was called upon to speak about Newton—at an introductory lecture for promising students or a social for curious old-age pensioners. Antonella was all copper curls and Botticelli bosom packed into a bit of Laura Ashley smocking—impossible to ignore, particularly at the departmental teas when Antonella with her biscuit tin was at her most solicitous. It was Rix, the Head Porter at Trinity—and therefore privy to the dozens of invitations to teas and coffees and esoteric mathematical functions that Antonella delivered by hand—who had first noticed Antonella's interest.

"Mr. Malory," he said one severely rainy afternoon, "you'll forgive my saying so, but there is a new film by Bertolucci at the Arts Cinema. He's Italian," Rix added when Malory stared up at him blankly from the crumbling foam of the Senior Common Room sofa. "As such, it might interest a certain young Italian lady."

"Ah," Malory said, comprehension swimming to the surface of his embarrassment. "Antonella, you mean?"

"I believe that is the young lady's name, yes," Rix answered. "Although I have difficulty with Italian names."

Malory's embarrassment disappointed Rix, disappointed Antonella, and failed Bertolucci entirely. Nevertheless, he was sufficiently sussed to know that if Antonella was still at her desk at 4 p.m. of a March evening, he could ask her to search for Louiza in the files of the Maths Department, and she would give him another cup of tea—undoubtedly with two biscuits. But when Malory locked his bicycle and unclipped his trouser cuffs by the red-brick and glass optimism of the Sidgwick Site and ran two flights up the concrete and veneer stairwell to the Maths Faculty, he found Antonella weeping in the corona of a battered black-and-white television set.

"Oh, Malory!" She jumped up and ran to him, shaking in spasms that Malory quickly realized meant he might get neither his answers nor his tea as quickly as he had hoped.

"Antonella!" Malory said, trying to pat helpfulness into her expansive shoulders. "What happened?"

"*Guarda*!" she sobbed and pointed at the TV. The large-lipped, puppy-faced Anna Ford, whom Malory had always wanted to invite to High Table at Trinity if only to listen to her voice, was just turning to the camera.

"Good evening," she said. Antonella pulled Malory down onto the edge of her desk, dislodging a stapler and a stack of pencils. "Former Italian prime minister Aldo Moro has been kidnapped in Rome."

"*Capisci?*" Antonella turned her eyes, freshly teary to Malory. But Malory didn't *capisce* a bit. He couldn't even understand how he had ever been attracted to the newsreader, no matter how doe-eyed or thick-lipped. He had been pierced by Louiza's $i = u$ and that was it.

"Mr. Moro's escort of five police bodyguards were killed," Anna Ford continued, "when he was snatched at gunpoint from a car near a cafe in the morning rush hour."

"What is this all about?" Malory asked.

"This morning," Antonella sobbed anew. "Aldo Moro—he is like your John F. Kennedy."

Not my John F. Kennedy, Malory wanted to say but let her continue.

"They took him. Kidnapped."

"They?" Malory asked.

"I do not know," Antonella said. "Terrorists, *Brigate Rosse*, Red Brigade. Or maybe not. Maybe just politicians, maybe even the Americans."

"Americans?" Malory asked. The only American he could picture at the moment, besides John F. Kennedy, was the red-bearded giant at the till of the Orchard.

"There is a war, Malory," Antonella said. "In my Rome, a war." She took his left hand in both of hers.

"Ah," Malory said, with as much sincerity as he could muster. Her eyes really were very pretty, magnified by the lens of tears. And he would have liked to make her feel better, independent of his own need to scan the departmental records. But the best he could say was, "Sorry, I've never been to Rome."

"But I am the one who is sorry!" Antonella jiggled off the edge of the desk and wiped her eyes with the backs of her hands. "You came to see your Antonella, and she is crying."

Malory reached into what he hoped was the cleaner of the pockets of his corduroy jacket and handed her a handkerchief.

"Antonella," he said. "I know this is a bad moment. But there is a bit of information. It really would be most helpful."

"*Ma guarda, tesoro*," Antonella said and ran to the bookshelf next to the television. "I am forgetting my Malory." She flipped on the electric teakettle and reached up to the cupboard for mug, sugar bowl, and biscuit tin in such a way that Malory momentarily forgot what he was so delicately preparing to ask.

"I'm not bothering you?"

"*Figurati!*" Antonella said, swishing the hot water around the bottom of the teapot in a way that suggested an infinity of other activities. "The old men are all meeting an American. They think he is about to win the Fields Medal and are giving him some sherry. I was about to go home when I thought just a peek at the news, and I saw . . ." And she shook against Malory as the tea steeped.

"Antonella." They were now seated comfortably, knee to knee, or rather knees interlocked like the inlay on a backgammon board, Malory biting into a semi-molten chocolate digestive biscuit. "I am looking for—" He began again. "I need to get in touch with one of the faculty's PhD candidates. Just passed the viva today."

"Today?" Antonella said. "What is his name?"

"Her," Malory said. "Her name, actually. She's a woman. A girl, really. Very young."

"Oh, Malory!" Antonella laughed and offered the biscuit tin again. "*Scherzi!* You are playing games with your Antonella."

"Games?" Malory stopped, biscuit halfway to mouth. "Why games?"

"Because Antonella is the only girl, the only female in the Department of Mathematics. You know that!"

"Yes," Malory said. "Of course. But Louiza distinctly told me she passed her viva today. For her PhD."

"Louiza?" Antonella put the biscuit tin behind her, on top of the TV, more in curiosity than in jealousy. "So, you are on the first-name basis with this PhD Louiza?"

"Only first name," Malory said. "I was hoping you might supply me with a surname, if not an address."

"Poor Malory," Antonella said. "But I tell you, there is no Louiza with viva today or yesterday or tomorrow, with or without surnames."

"No Louizas?"

"No girls. No women. Only Antonella."

"Ah," Malory said. "Perhaps," he pondered, "it wasn't the Maths Department. Perhaps I need to ask—"

"Perhaps Antonella could find out for you? Perhaps Antonella could help you?"

"Would you?" Malory didn't realize he was holding Antonella's hands until she squeezed them with a digestive warmth.

"For Malory?" Antonella said. And if Anna Ford hadn't interrupted with a fresh bulletin on Aldo Moro, Malory would have been constrained to kiss a second woman in the same day.

"Thank you!" Malory slung his Kit Bag across his shoulder as Antonella drew a full, Roman lip between her teeth at the photo of Aldo Moro on the television. A nice-looking man, Malory thought, as he pressed open the door to the stairwell.

In response, a vibration stopped Malory at the top of the landing, a buzz that came from inside his Kit Bag. The Pip, in its 35-millimeter canister, was announcing something far more than was dreamt in Anna Ford's philosophy.

"LOUIZA, DARLING . . ."

The words came from her father's mouth. But they were so unexpected, and half of Louiza was still up in the organ loft of St. George's Church, that it took two repetitions to make her see that indeed her father had spoken.

"Louiza, darling," her father repeated, "there's someone I'd like you to meet."

Louiza blinked again and noticed that there was a fourth person at the table in the Orchard and that she had completely missed her own celebratory lunch.

"Where were you, darling?" Her mother. The Shetland cardigan, soft gray. "I checked the loo. We were so worried."

It was a man, the fourth at the table, a large man. A large man in a double-breasted suit with a thick head of red hair slicked back full of bear grease or motor oil or who knew what men put in their hair.

"Hello, Louiza." Deep, the voice. American. Big teeth, especially the left one in the front. And radiating positivity. Supremely positive, with a red beard.

"Darling—" Her father again. "Mr. MacPhearson is an American—what would you call your profession?"

"Congratulations on your degree," Mr. MacPhearson said. He looked at Louiza so positively that she had to turn away.

"Oh," she said, which passed for modesty. She wondered what Malory was doing back in the church.

"I understand that you're at loose ends," MacPhearson added.

Loose ends? Louiza wondered what that meant, loose ends. She touched her hair. Her elastic band must have disappeared somewhere between the Orchard and the organ loft.

"Mr. MacPhearson has an interesting offer, darling," her father smiled. He too was positive, had turned positive for the first time Louiza could remember, but in a way that only pushed her anxiety higher. "He's from America."

"You were gone over an hour," her mother said.

"America." Louiza didn't want to acknowledge the red-bearded addition to the table, but wanted even less to tell her mother about her walk past the loo of the Orchard and across the road to St. George's church and her climb up to the loft and the strange little man who equaled the deepest algebra of her identity.

MacPhearson and her father took her single "America" as encouragement and launched into a lengthy explanation. MacPhearson had tried to attract her attention at the Maths Faculty following the viva. But failing that—Louiza's father in particular had been intent on reaching their car before time expired—he had followed the family out to the Orchard and waited at a discreet distance until they had finished their celebratory lunch.

MacPhearson's explanation of why he had followed her out to the Orchard, what company he worked for, and how he wanted to hire her on "very generous terms" in the words of her father, filtered only vaguely into Louiza's consciousness. What was vastly clearer—to her at least—was that MacPhearson had waited until she had left the table, perhaps until she had disappeared safely into the shadows of St. George's Church, to approach the table and flatter Louiza's parents with his offer.

She caught certain words—complex, negative, equation—that made her suspect that MacPhearson, far from being a mathematician, was merely an agent for someone or something else that wanted Louiza. But she also caught other phrases that made her think that perhaps mathematicians were only agents for the MacPhearsons of the world. She had told Malory that the applications of $i = u$ were many and potentially dangerous. Lucrative, too.

"Mother," she said. Perhaps it was in the middle of the explanation, but it didn't really matter. "Do you want me to do this?"

"Darling," her mother said.

And since Louiza would do anything for the mother who had introduced her to i, Louiza soon found herself living in a thatched cottage by the river, perhaps only a mile or so from the Orchard itself along the towpath towards Cambridge. Her mother had wanted to outfit her room—there were two others in the house, and Louiza had a small bedroom in the back of the second floor. But the "secrecy" phrase in MacPhearson's explanation and the papers they all signed at the Orchard and the cash advance MacPhearson placed in care of Louiza's father, meant that Louiza would be saying goodbye to her parents at the door of MacPhearson's Morris Minor and would not be permitted to communicate with them, or anyone outside the company, whatever it was, for the first twelve months of her employ.

There was no way, clearly, that Louiza could know the effect of this prohibition on her mother. The problems that MacPhearson asked Louiza to solve the next morning—or rather the problems that appeared on the kitchen table every morning at breakfast, delivered by one or another of her Cottagemates—were fascinating enough to distract Louiza from memories of home and even that funny little Malory in the organ loft. Her life consisted of descending for meals and problems and ascending to the desk under the eaves for solutions. As the weather grew into summer, a lighter duvet appeared on her bed. Fresh clothing arrived, the washing up was done. Her curiosity about the ripening foliage, the music of the river, was satisfied by an open window. All other questions were satisfied by the mathematics of negativity.

And the growth.

The first morning at the cottage, Louiza knew she was pregnant. It had been the first time for her, and obviously the first time for Malory. Her basic knowledge of biology had prepared her for the possibility. Her belief in mathematics had acquainted her with certainty. Malory = Louiza. $i = u$. From identity came multiplication, and now exponential growth.

Louiza could have checked with a doctor. Her Cottagemates could have alerted MacPhearson, who could have alerted Malory, who could have—it was easier to avoid the dark woods of human behavior and retreat into the world of negative numbers. Young and thin as she was, the channel of her shoulders let the straps of her summer shifts hang loose enough that no one would have noticed a change, and in any case, no one was looking. Morning sickness never struck. Her nipples, although they darkened, never called attention to themselves.

Louiza knew there was something alive inside her by the gradual swell and the occasional rumble. But whatever the something was, it shared its mother's ability to lose itself in concentrated activity and generate few ripples. Summer turned to autumn. A heavier duvet appeared on Louiza's bed along with a set of jacket-length knit cardigans that easily camouflaged her metamorphosis.

Until the morning of the kick.

Louiza had finished her egg and had just ascended the stairs to her room with fresh problems and a second cup of tea, when she felt the kick. More than a kick, it was a full-fledged riot that pulled her stomach towards the window, leaving a wake of spilled tea and damp papers. She had felt the baby's presence before, but more as friendly companionship. Now it was announcing itself as an independent life, urging her closer to the window, forcing her to put down her tea cup and take a look outside towards the river.

"Malory!" she said. There he was, the little man from the organ loft. He was on the towpath by the river, wearing the same brown corduroy jacket, with the same military bag slung across his shoulder, atop a bicycle. Or, rather, under. Malory had fallen off.

IT WAS ONLY A FEW HOURS EARLIER THAT MALORY HEARD HIS OWN KNOCKING. Waking from a rare, dreamless sleep, he thought that the knock belonged to Louiza, who had found him, who had observed his quest and finally deemed him worthy of rescue.

"Mr. Malory?" No, the fruity baritone was not Louiza. "Rix, sir. I've brought your breakfast."

"What time is it?" Malory opened the door to the porter. The electric light was still on in the stairwell, and the small window that opened onto the Great Court of Trinity was too full of the greasy residue of some ambitious fresher's late-night grill to give much of a clue.

"Just gone seven, Mr. Malory," Rix said, the tray of tea and scone balanced on his left hand. "A telephone call in the Porters' lodge, just now," Rix continued.

"Breakfast?" Malory said.

"Rather urgent, sir. The vicar, St. George's Church, Whistler Abbey. Very sorry to bother, but he wondered whether you might play a service this morning."

"This morning?" Malory's left eye was just beginning to open.

"In one hour, eight o'clock."

"Ring him back and say you couldn't find me. Please." Malory turned to close the door.

"He was quite insistent." The tray was inside his rooms. Malory was forced to retreat as Rix set it down and poured him a cup. Malory wasn't particularly fond of the vicar at the best of times and was still shrouded in the disappointment of finding Rix rather than Louiza outside his door. But his inability to offend gave him the energy to pull on yesterday's clothing as Rix buttered his scone—there was no need for fancy dress; he'd be up in the loft, hidden by the balustrade and a robe—brush his teeth and do his best with his hair, grab his corduroy jacket and Kit Bag, and stumble to the door.

"And Mr. Malory." Rix handed him the scone with one hand and slid an envelope into the outer breast pocket of his jacket. "This came for you. From the Master." Another dinner. Malory chewed and stumbled towards the bicycle shed. More Americans at High Table.

Malory pushed his bicycle through the arch of the college, beneath the gaze of Henry VIII holding a leg of mutton or a scepter in his stony hand. The light was graying towards eight o'clock by the time he reached the towpath by the river. It was that hopeful hour of dawn that encouraged him to rise each morning and resume his search for Louiza, as he had every morning for the past seven months. Louiza's disappearance had coincided with the Easter Holiday, which emptied Cambridge of any student or fellow with even half a family and a lamb chop. Malory stayed if not happily then with determination in the depopulated cave of Trinity College, intent on pushing the rock of his stupidity up the cobbled slope of his loss. But his search for clues in the shadows and echoes of the new spring turned up only a lost Iranian student or a freshly widowed fellow, caught in the perplexed limbo of embarrassment and grief. As Easter Term led through the May Balls of June into the empty twilights of summer, Malory paid regular visits to the Maths Faculty and Antonella's teakettle. Although every time he did, it seemed that Antonella's beloved Rome had suffered another disaster.

At the beginning of May, Aldo Moro was discovered lying on his back in the boot of a cherry Renault 4 behind the Caetani Palace—dead, shot ten times. Pope Paul VI's death in early August didn't release an equal flow of tears but still provoked in Antonella the terror of a fast-approaching Day of Judgment. And when the newly crowned Smiling Pope John Paul I failed to awake on September 28 after only thirty-three mornings on the throne of St. Peter, Malory had to spring for a pair of kebabs and half a carafe of retsina at the Eros for the poor, distracted Italian girl.

Of course, there were quieter, less dramatic times with Antonella, when she would pull a shoebox of photos and postcards from a Heffers carrier bag and give Malory a guided tour of her Rome, from the mosaics in Santa Prassede to the oak-paneled door of the Basilica of Santa Sabina, where Antonella had spent much of her girlhood in battle with the Dominican nuns. Malory's favorites were the frescoes in the Carafa Chapel of Santa Maria sopra Minerva.

"There was an ugly cardinal," Antonella told Malory, opening up her biscuit tin. "I mean really ugly. *Bruttissimo*, as ugly as a mathematician. Sorry," she said immediately, but Malory the Historian of Science couldn't imagine why she would apologize, since calling Louiza something as simple as a mathematician had never occurred to him. "Cardinal Carafa hired a poor Tuscan bastard named Lippi to decorate the family chapel." Antonella propped three postcards up against the tin. St. Thomas Aquinas seemed—as best as Malory could tell—to be the subject of each one: a pale man in a dun-colored cloak, who was overly familiar with the insides of the biscuit tin. "My favorite," she said, picking up one card between two magenta nails, "is the *Annunciazione*."

Antonella was correct. The cardinal was ugly. The patron behind every Annunciation always got pride of place, kneeling before the Virgin. But the patron kneeling in the scarlet robes, with little hair and an unfortunate nose, must have been truly hideous if this was how Lippi had idealized him. Aquinas stood behind Carafa, introducing him to the Virgin Mary, while a Florentine angel frantically tried to point out to the young lady that the Holy Spirit was on the cusp of bringing her some very good news.

"But see how the Virgin tells the angel to wait," Antonella said to Malory, "like that news lady you like so much on the BBC—"

"Anna Ford?" Malory looked at Lippi's virgin and thought, in fact, how much more she reminded him of Louiza than of the Italian with the biscuit tin or the British rose of the TV screen. The pale skin, the wheaten hair, the eyes turned down below nearly invisible eyebrows, as Louiza turned down hers when she announced the formula that won her the PhD and the everlasting devotion of Malory.

Malory accepted Antonella's hand across a biscuit tin, her arm in the Arts Cinema as a fair trade for her help in his quest for Louiza. And as it was, Antonella uncovered quite a bit, even if Malory was uncertain how to interpret the discoveries. Malory hadn't disclosed any of the more tender portions of his afternoon with Louiza. But he had shared with Antonella the academic characteristics of Louiza's work, chief among them, of course, the equation $i = u$. Familiar as she was with the form if not the substance of the work of her mathematical charges, Antonella immediately recognized the complexity condensed within that simple equation.

"Old news," she told him. "No one in the Faculty is interested in complex numbers. They put their noses in the air and walk around talking about K-theory and Z-algebra. They snort and say only Americans and Russians are obsessed with imaginary numbers."

"Americans and Russians?" Malory asked, diving without invitation into Antonella's bottomless biscuit tin.

"It has something to do with silly secrets," Antonella said. "Secrets the Americans want to keep, secrets the Russians want to keep."

"Secrets?" Malory asked. "Secret codes? Encryption?" Louiza had suggested that the ramifications of her simple equation were astonishing, perhaps even dangerous.

"*Forse sì,*" Antonella said. "None of my old men are interested in the Americans. *C'era una volta,* once upon a time my Mama, back in Garbatella. She too was interested. After the War, she had the *voglia* to wash and cook for Americans, twenty-four hours a day. Now—"

"Yes," Malory said, wondering more about the Americans than Antonella's mother. He had met Americans, of course, during colloquia at the Physics Faculty or when the Master insisted he sit next to one at High Table—most recently an animal behaviorist from Harvard talking of Africa and pygmies and spare parts for his Land Rover. "But which Americans in particular disinterest your old men?"

"I don't know their names," Antonella said. "They come in so full of smiles and laughing and cologne, and I am embarrassed to ask why they are here."

"But they never have a young girl with them?" Malory asked. "A young, British girl?"

"Yes, yes," Antonella said, making Malory blush at her annoyance. "A young, fair-haired British girl, who picks the skin from around her finger nails and has skinny, little shoulders and likes fuzzy organ tuners in corduroy jackets. I think," she said, flicking a piece of lint from the lapel of Malory's own corduroy, "that you have described Louiza well enough that I would recognize her in a crowd of a thousand fair-haired girls—even Americans."

Malory had enlisted Rix as well, whose familiarity with the comings and goings of the students and fellows of Trinity—not to mention the porters and the porters' families of the other twenty-odd colleges that made up the University of Cambridge—gave him unparalleled access to the secrets and practices of virtually the entire academic community. Malory attended colloquia and seminars and conferences with an eye out for wisps. He dined at High Table with the Master who, although an economist, dabbled enough in numbers and money that Malory could drop the phrase $i = u$ into casual conversation and watch for a reaction. But after seven months of searching and questioning, he was no closer, no surer that he was even searching in the right corner of the right steeple.

Of course Malory haunted the environs of St. George's Church, Whistler Abbey, the Pip in a plastic 35-millimeter container in his pocket, the sole companion and proof that something remarkable had happened, that the search for the lost Louiza that occupied the greater part of his waking thoughts and all of his nocturnal dreams was not complete lunacy. So, early and unexpected as the call from the vicar had been, Malory was not entirely displeased to be riding his bicycle along the towpath to Whistler Abbey to the rhythm of i (down with the left pedal) *equals u* (down with the right).

He was halfway along the towpath—whether on i or u he couldn't remember—when suddenly something knocked over his bicycle. Malory fell to the ground, more confused than hurt. He hadn't felt a gust of wind. There was no large dog or early morning jogger who might have plowed him over. But as he lay under his bicycle, he felt a vibration from inside his Kit Bag. He unstrapped the flap and looked inside. The Book of Organs, the Universal Tuner were in place. But from the secret pocket where he had squirreled away the 35-millimeter canister and the Pip came the unmistakable hum of a low C, the vibration, he was sure, of the Pip, the Pip Louiza had found in the steeple. Had he been knocked over a second time by the Pip? Could such a small thing have such a force?

BY THE TIME LOUIZA PULLED ON A PAIR OF WELLIES AND RAN OUT THE back door of the cottage, Malory had righted his bicycle and was disappearing around the curve of the towpath. It was the first time Louiza had been out of the cottage in, well, perhaps since MacPhearson had brought her there that March afternoon after lunch at the Orchard. She didn't look back to see whether the Cottagemates were following her. She merely began to walk to the rhythm of the kicks in her cardigan-beshrouded belly.

She had no idea, really, where her cottage was in relation to the Orchard or Cambridge or for that matter the rest of the world. But in an animal way, she knew that Malory was cycling to St. George's Church. The identity $i = u$, Louiza = Malory, included the world in which they had first met and conceived this new life that, in the mysterious way that numbers propagate numbers, was becoming an integral part of this equation.

MALORY PARKED HIS BICYCLE BY THE SOUTHERN WALL ON THE YEW SIDE of the church and entered through the chancel. He was pulling on a robe in the shadows of the narthex when the vicar approached.

"Much obliged, Malory. Sad occasion, what?"

Malory looked up towards the altar and noticed the blond pine of the coffin lying on a pair of sawhorses.

"Yes," Malory said. Rix had said "service," hadn't he, not "funeral," but no matter. Music wasn't the problem. Malory only wondered why the rush? There were only half a dozen people in the church. Not a state occasion. Had another organist canceled? "Bach?" he asked the vicar. "Albinoni?"

"The deceased requested simply that you play what you wish," the vicar said. "I'm certain you'll do what is right. And Malory—"

"Yes?"

"Do stay for the graveside. I need to speak with you after."

Malory flipped one switch, and the light over his keyboard illuminated the fine moondust of the windless organ loft. He flipped another, and the electric motor twenty feet away behind the pipes began to pump air into the lungs of the instrument. The hum of mechanical power vibrated confidence through the organ bench, up Malory's body, and into his fingers. He knew this organ, knew its tranquility, its quirks. His Book of Organs memorialized the tunings of all the organs he had tended, all the services he had played, the weddings, the funerals, the christenings and communions, the hymns and psalms and Indian ragas and Procol Harums from the more esoteric ceremonies that the charismatic members and observant hippies had introduced in recent years. The record of the organ of St. George's, Whistler Abbey, was no different from the rest—except for the Pip, the demon that bedeviled that scone-less March morning and continued to confuse and exhaust and rattle a lost harmony in the sleepless hearing of Malory's ear. The Pip was mentioned briefly in the Book of Organs: "16 March 1978. 8 a.m.–2 p.m. tuning. Pip in steeple." But encoded in the ink was the full meaning and direction of Malory's life, a description and a story as full of promise and potential danger as Louiza's equation.

Malory glanced in the rearview mirror that gave him a view of the coffin at the altar and the vicar at the pulpit. The vicar gave a nod.

It was time for music. The deceased had left it up to him. It was time to play. It was time to play what he had played every time he had cycled out to St. George's in the past seven months in the hope that Louiza would be waiting for him in the organ loft.

It was time to play *i = u.*

Louiza = Malory. As set to music, of course.

Bach and Schubert and plenty of less-inspired composers, after all, had turned letters into numbers and numbers into music, into points on the twelve-note scale. Louiza's own peculiar calculus of names gave Malory a system of composition, an initial theme to rise off the launching pad and into the stratosphere of improvisation. Setting middle C at −1, as Malory did, then −2 equals B-natural. −3 equals B-flat, 4 equals A-natural, and so on.

He believed that if he played his melody, their melody, the melody of unity and identification, Louiza = Malory, Malory = Louiza, the girl of the golden head and the pale chin would reappear from around the Orchard and lift her eyes to the sound of Malory and his organ.

The melody began with Louiza's name, the drama of a diminished triad in first inversion—B-flat, D-flat (since D-flat equals C-sharp as surely as *i = u*), G—resolving with a perfect fourth to the key of C, before dropping a half step, with ominous portent, to a cliffhanger of a B-natural. It was a phantom-of-the-operatic bit of drama that promised tears, sweat, more tears, but eventually the full-throttle, stops-out consummation of an entire life of smiles and kisses with his beloved, if Malory only followed Louiza's name with his own:

M   A   L   O   R   Y

Amazing, if he thought of it—as he had, of course, every morning when he awoke and every evening in the tentative hour of dusk—that his name, Malory, was connected to Louiza's by a perfect octave. And he could even reverse the notes, since identity is reversible.

LOUIZA = MALORY

as sure as

MALORY = LOUIZA

and

$$u = i$$

follows absolutely from

$$i = u.$$

Malory glanced into the mirror—the few parishioners with their heads bowed in silent prayer or morning exhaustion, the vicar at the pulpit, the coffin immoveable at the altar. Not all melodies, Malory knew, not all science was reversible. Not all toothpaste could be unsqueezed back into the tube. Time, for one, was not reversible. There was a grave in the foothills of the Pyrenees where his mother lay that could not be undug. Even the lid on this particular coffin would not open. But Malory believed in the power of music, in a melodic magnetism that would not only bring back the memory of that afternoon with Louiza, retrace her climb down from the organ loft, her exit from the church, her walk down the flagstone path of St. George's Church to the Orchard, but would bring back Louiza herself, draw her close enough that he could hold out his hand and lead her into a life of eternal identity.

His improvised prelude led to thoughts of Americans and Antonella's suggestion that Louiza's interest in complex numbers might have something to do with codes more useful than the musical ones that generated Malory's prelude. The thought of Americans reminded Malory that Rix had handed him a note from the Master, an invitation undoubtedly to another duty at High Table. So as the vicar began the first reading—Malory had expected Ashes to Ashes, but the vicar jumped straight to Revelations, I am the Alpha and the Omega, the Beginning and the End—Malory winkled the envelope from his pocket and slid open the flap.

It was not an invitation. Rather the opposite.

12 October 1978

Dear Mr. Malory,

I regret to inform you that, according to the provisions of Parliamentary Act #1096 (1954, revised 1976) the term of your doctoral dissertation, which commenced 15 October 1971 and was renewed on the same date severally of 1974 and 1976, will expire 15 October 1978. The College expects your rooms to be clear, your keys returned to the Porters' lodge, and all bursary charges paid by the end of that day. I wish you success in whatever future occupation you may pursue.

Sincerely,
A.J. Potts
Master

Malory had received letters like this before, full of Parliamentary numbers and historical dates, from a succession of masters before Aubrey. This letter was different. After seven years of working on his dissertation, it was over. Not finished, over.

He wasn't surprised. It wasn't as if he were three weeks away from dotting the final footnote and a brief stay of a month or two would mean the difference between doctorate and death. Malory was miles, light years, lifetimes away from finishing his thesis. The reprieves of "the same date of 1974 and 1976" were not the optimistic glimmers of light at the end of a short polish or the obsessive edits of a perfectionist, but the rewards of conversations, friendships, and free organ-tunings for influential vicars in the Cambridge vicinity.

But hadn't those reprieves also been the fruit of incisive questions he had asked in packed lecture rooms to the Feynmans and the Westfalls of the world, the impromptu disquisitions he had delivered in select colloquia? Weren't they the postprandial cordials of brilliant High Table epigrams, the perfect demitasses of wit with a dash of wisdom that had sent contemporaries and elders to their rooms with a nightcap of a chuckle and a shake of the head? And his Sunday morning improvisations on the organ, his ability to remember and, even more, improvise upon the full archive of organ music, from Bach to Saint-Saëns to King Vidor, Messiaen, and—if the mood was right for a bit of Rolling Stones—even Billy Preston? Hadn't they all said, professor, praelector, and priest alike, "Malory, you're a genius!"

Well, sure. Malory shifted on the organ bench. They'd also said, "*Simplex sigillum veri*—the simple is the sign of the truth." They said, "Simplify," followed by another word: "Write."

As if it were that simple.

Louiza could simplify. But that was mathematics. And hadn't Dr. Gödel or Dr. Who proved that maths wasn't the whole story, that no matter how much you tried to boil the universe into a few mathematical rules, there was always one little spare bit of leek or potato floating in the corner of the pot, running away from your ladle and spitting soup in your face? And then there was the ladle and the pot. They couldn't be part of the mathematical stew, could they? And what about the Cook?

It wasn't that Malory couldn't think, and it wasn't that he couldn't talk. Reading—wahaay! Piece o' cake! There was no reader like Malory, and no corner of the university's collection of Newtonia that hadn't seen the thumb and barcode of Malory's reader's card. The Gules Collection at the Museum of the History of Science on Lesser St. Giles, the Rankin Collection at the Newton Center itself. The great Wren Library, with its tesseracts of sandstone and Pauline vaults, owed the very organization of its catalogue to Malory's ingenious system of division and hot-cross-reference. He had read—and he could say this without fear of hyperbole—everything that had been written on the subject of Sir Isaac Newton. But more than that, he had read everything that *could* be written.

It was writing. Writing evaded him. Massively. Even with a lever as long as the Peloponnese, Archimedes could not have lifted Malory's writer's block. At night, it loomed above him like the barnacled hull of the Flying Dutchman or the endless crenellations of the Death Star. During the day, it concentrated its way into a ball that rolled around his mouth with a taste of old coffee, metal filings, and airplane fuel. But at all times it had the bulk, the heft, the specific gravity of seven years' devotion, as massive as the Kaaba, and Malory took as many ritual strolls around his Block as the most devoted pilgrim. Malory knew he had something to say. He just couldn't open his pen and write it.

Malory folded the letter and returned it to the envelope. He unbuckled the flap of the Kit Bag and searched for a suitable burial place for the envelope, far away from the pocket of hope and the 35-millimeter canister with the Pip. But as he was rummaging, he felt the unfamiliar crinkle of tissue paper. The vicar was stuck in his exegesis, so Malory investigated some more and pulled a packet out of the Kit Bag. With the packet came a scent—the scent of the four-thousand-year-old yew in the churchyard, the scent of his mother, of Old Mrs. Emery, that reminded him of that brief interlude half a year ago in the cool light of the second pew, when he had descended from the organ loft and his discovery of Louiza to find his grandmother waiting for him. The packet was his grandmother's gift to him, a gift that had lain dormant and undisturbed in the bottom of his Kit Bag for seven months.

Pulling back the tissue paper, Malory saw that the gift was a book.

It was a book, a book bound in leather that had cracked and faded into a light black, of a size and shape that felt immediately of another age and place. It was a notebook, Malory saw, not more than a few inches to each side, perhaps fifty pages deep, with a musty smell, distinct from the damp of the organ loft. Embossed on the front cover of the notebook in a faded gold no bigger than a thumbprint, there was a seal. It was a capital *S* within a seven-sided border. There was something ancient about the sign, older than the notebook itself, smacking of troubadours and damsels: the *S* fenced in the heptagon like a unicorn that had escaped from some medieval tapestry. Like the white-haired Mrs. Emery.

Malory opened the notebook. It was filled with an ink whose antiquity nearly melded with a paper that had browned with the centuries. At first blush, the writing seemed to be Italian in a hand too ornate for Malory to read. Every page or so was headed by a date, although the dates were scribbled in a way that made it difficult to tell numbers from letters, sixes from *b*'s or *g*'s. A diary, a journal of sorts.

Malory turned the pages slowly, and then he began to turn faster. One word stood out from the others within the ornate scrawl. It was a word sometimes alone on a page, sometimes repeated. A word that was a name, a name that occasionally didn't appear for many entries. But it was a name that he knew well enough that no manner of scribbled hand could disguise it.

"Isaac!" Malory whispered. One of the parishioners looked up from a back pew, but the vicar went on rumbling.

Malory continued turning the pages. He looked at the dates at the tops of the entry pages, at the numbers of the dates again. Yes, it was possible, it was very possible that the numbers began with a "1" and then a "6," and, if so, that the diary or journal—since that is what the notebook most nearly appeared to be—was written in the 1600s. That the Isaac was his Isaac, his Newton.

"*Un giardino, un albero.*" Malory read the first words of the first entry with some effort, and then further down the page, "Isaac." But Newton was no gardener, Malory thought, flipping randomly through the rest of the Chapbook. What garden? Whose tree?

And then he saw it.

The last page. The final page of the diary was written in a different handwriting from the rest of the journal, a hand he recognized in a language he understood. It was the hand of the Old Isaac Newton, the Old Man, long after the youthful discoveries of 1666, his *annus mirabilis*, long after the triumphs and the celebrations, the paranoias and the lawsuits against Leibniz and Boyle, long after his term in Parliament and his stint at the Mint, his leadership of the Royal Society, his descent into alchemy and the Book of Revelations and his calculations of the End of Time. There was no disputing the identity of Isaac now. This last page was written in English by Isaac Newton in his hand, the hand of a man close to death.

This was a diary, a journal written in Italian by a friend of Newton's, so it seemed. A friend who had known Newton all his life, perhaps until the end. And on the final page of the journal, a sentence written in Newton's own hand—and no one knew Newton's handwriting better than the Newton Scholar (*ex*-Newton Scholar, Malory thought with a pang) of Trinity College, Cambridge.

"*I have found the One True Rule that guides Mathematics,*" Malory read, "*the One True Rule that guides Science, that guides the Universe.*"

Malory read again. And again. Newton had found a single rule? Had refined his Laws of Thermodynamics and Optics and Calculus and Gravity into a single rule?

"*I have found the One True Rule,*" Malory read. "*But the Rule is too weighty to fit on one page of this Chapbook.*"

Malory looked at the top of the page. There was no date written in Newton's hand. The last entry in Italian was dated sometime in 1692. Malory knew 1692. He knew it was the year before the fifty-year-old Newton suffered what was clearly a nervous breakdown. Malory had read the correspondence left by the Master and Head Porter of Trinity from that year. He knew that Newton was incapable of writing in 1693. This was not the handwriting of the Newton of 1693. This was the shaky penmanship of a much older man, perhaps of the Newton on his deathbed in 1727. And the rule? If, before he died, Newton had actually found the One True Rule that guides the universe, then he had found something even Einstein couldn't find, the Holy Grail of modern mathematics and physics, the Unified Field Theory. It would be the single point from which all science follows, the single cause for all that came after Creation. It would be God. Not the three-part God of the Trinity that Newton despised, but the One God in whom Newton believed the way Malory believed.

Malory wasn't entirely certain what he believed. But he saw himself laying the Chapbook down on the desk of Aubrey Potts—he must ask Antonella to translate the Italian straight away—and not only winning a PhD, but also finding Louiza as part of the equation. Mallory rubbed the Chapbook like an oil lamp and pondered the research ahead, the papers he would publish, the books, the Nobel Prize in Physics. The scientists of the twentieth century had turned their backs on Newton as they searched for a Unified Field Theory. Now Malory would show them that his Newton had beaten them to the punch. Newton knew something, Malory was sure of it, that would turn gravity on its head, that would bounce the apple back up from the ground to its nostalgic stem. *Simplex sigillum veri*—the simple is the sign of the truth. No more High Tables. No more colloquia. One work. One girl. Find the One True Rule, and he would find the One True Girl.

And then he heard the vicar.

"All ends are good ends. All ends are bad ends." The vicar had put away the received wisdom and was improvising his own eulogy.

Malory sat up on the organ bench, set the Newton Chapbook beside him and wondered what improvisation of his own would suit this discovery. Perhaps something based on Newton's name?

"Although not technically a member of this congregation," the vicar continued, "and although born on distant shores, our dear departed cousin chose to make Whistler Abbey her home and the Church of St. George her resting place."

But what other name could he use, Malory wondered, as a counterpoint to Newton. Perhaps—

"Mrs. Emery—"

And at the sound of that name, the part of Malory's brain that was digesting his dismissal from his PhD, from his Organ Scholarship, from the Newton Rooms next to the gate of Great Court, Trinity College; the part that had barely begun to taste the discovery of the Newton Chapbook with its possibilities of redemption and salvation, emptied in one great sluice and filled with the even greater wash of his own stupidity.

That was his grandmother in the box, his grandmother in the coffin at the altar. His grandmother was dead. No amount of looking or not looking would bring her back to life. His last surviving link to any family—gone, and he'd never known her. Never even known enough to understand that no one else would have requested that he be awakened to play whatever he liked at her funeral. His improvisation had been all about himself and Louiza. No rationalization could expand to identify Malory with his grandmother and make LOUIZA = MALORY = EMERY. The Old Lady, late of the second pew, added up to considerably more than either he or Louiza.

IT WAS ENTIRELY WITHOUT SURPRISE THAT LOUIZA FOUND HERSELF LEAVING the towpath and ducking around the fading branches of the Orchard, across the road, and up a flight of leafy steps to St. George's Church. The nave was empty. Two sawhorses stood forgotten at the altar. Louiza took a seat in the second pew and looked up at the Byzantine mosaics of gold and scarlet and aqua. The English sun had leached much of the pigment from the stained glass. But one ray shone through to Louiza's feet, to a lone cushion, a hassock stuffed with straw, perhaps from a recent cutting. The weaving on it was unlike the others. No sign of crosses or lambs. Only a tree, a single tree, a single northern apple tree, green foliage spread out in full against a golden background of late-summer barley.

A kick from her belly roused Louiza from contemplation of the hassock in the second pew. Her eyes lifted. There was the ladder she had climbed seven months earlier. It was a challenge, at the very least, for Louiza to climb to the organ loft. Yet foot over foot, sidesaddle in respect for the belly, she ascended one rung at a time.

"Come," she said to her belly, "let's see if we can find your father."

Of course Malory was no longer at the organ. Nor was he up in the steeple. But when Louiza followed the murmur of voices and took her belly over to the churchyard side of the steeple and peered down through the slats, she saw Malory at the head of a grave, standing next to the vicar.

"There he is." She rubbed her right hand around the dome of her belly. "That's Malory. Can you say *Malory?*" Another kick in answer. Malory looked thinner than when Louiza had seen him last, his hair a little longer. She thought, even from the height of the steeple, that he could do with a bath. The vicar was speaking to Malory. Malory's eyes were fixed on the pit before him, on the spade of the gravedigger, whose chunk and clink made it difficult for Louiza to hear their conversation. But there was one word Louiza heard, that the baby in her belly heard.

"Rome."

"Rome?" Louiza repeated out loud.

Malory looked up at the steeple. The baby kicked.

The vicar handed an envelope to Malory.

"Everything is inside," the vicar said. "Instructions, explanations, a note of introduction to the Do-mi-ni-cans—" The vicar pronounced the syllables, each tasting worse than the one before. "And of course, the train ticket to Rome."

"Rome," Malory said, shocked by his own shock.

Louiza knew he couldn't see her between the slats, but it seemed that he was looking straight at her. She took a step back and glanced out the slats to her left. Two people were walking from the towpath by the river through the Orchard. Two. The Cottagemates.

"Come," she said to her belly, lowering herself down the ladder. The baby kicked. "Rome."

1/4

3 September 1666 10 p.m.

"I'd like to return to a subject you raised before dinner."
Darkness had fallen. Isaac's mother had long since cleared away the mug of soup and loaf of bread. Once more the pipe, once more two backs against the tree. Isaac had been distracted throughout the meal. I knew what he would say.

"Septimania," he said, and let the smoke from the pipe rise into the hesitant moonlight. "Earlier, you mentioned Septimania."

"I did." I smiled and took the pipe from his distracted hand. I had, indeed, planted the seed.

"Prithee explain," Isaac said. "Is this Septimania a place or a disease?"

"Judge for yourself." I handed the pipe back to Isaac and looked up to the moon for guidance. I had traveled for the better part of a month from Rome to England in search of a savior for my kingdom. All I needed was the right story to water the seed of Isaac's curiosity.

"In the first years of the siege of the Franks," I began, "the year of Our Lord 752, Order still held the innocent hand of Hope in the market town of Narbonne along the northwest coast of the Mediterranean Sea. All was in balance between the Muslims and the Jews. There were two of everything—two houses of worship, a mosque and a synagogue; two ritual baths, one for Muslim women, the other for Jewish; two schools; two markets; two guilds of craftsmen; and two houses of slaughter. Ibn Suleiman at the eastern gate facing Mecca was the Muslim butcher. And at the western gate, Yehoshua ben Gabriel chopped for the Jews.

"From his father, the young Yehoshua had learned the laws of kashrut, how to slaughter animals in the manner the Jews called kosher. His father *taught him about the rope around the hind hooves, the quick slice at the throat. His father taught him to measure a knife, to balance a cleaver, to check the lungs for scarring, to separate the permitted organs and reserve the kidneys and intestines for the Franks, to name the joints, the cuts, the sirloins, the brisket. The profession of shochet went back in Yehoshua's family to the Temple of Solomon, when butcher and priest were the same man, holy and filthy all in one.*

"From his mother, Yehoshua learned to wash away the blood and the shit. From his uncle, he learned explosions, the gases that expand the unpunctured abdomens of frightened animals. He learned that the bladder of a stillborn lamb made the sharpest sounding bombs. Even louder were the discarded udders of a dairy cow that had milked her last.

"The explosions scared his sisters and annoyed his mother on the airless Sabbath afternoons when the smell of the shore, salt mixing with the rotting bodies of forbidden crustaceans, rose over the walls of Narbonne along with the adolescent laughter of Yehoshua's Muslim and Jewish friends, all ringing on the same pitch, musically indistinguishable.

"From the Frankish children in the distant countryside, he learned a song:

> *Butcher kills the cattle,*
> *Butcher kills the flocks,*
> *Butcher, Butcher keep your knife*
> *Away from Christian cocks.*

"From the dogs he learned survival.

"The western gate in front of Yehoshua's slaughterhouse was the best-traveled entrance into and exit out of the city, facing Toulouse and Carcassonne and the paths through the mountains to Sepharad. It was the first stop for the shepherds, the final stop for the soldiers of the Muslim Caliph of Cordoba who ruled Narbonne. There were many times that Yehoshua fried a last supper of sheep's liver with fermented apple for the quartermaster and his whore, as his father loaded the army wagon with the hindquarters and tripe that were permitted the Muslims and their soldiers but not the Jewish people. Yehoshua became rich, within the limits of Jewish wealth. He married, fathered three girls and a boy. His father died. He became richer still.

"His son Moses was born the day the Caliph of Cordoba ordered the gates of Narbonne closed. It was in the 4513th year since the creation of the world according to Yehoshua's Jewish calculator, which the Caliph calculated as 133 years from the flight of his Prophet from Mecca to Medinah, and Pepin the King of the Franks reckoned at 752 after the death of his God. This same Pepin also reckoned Narbonne would make a good seaport for his kingdom. For a while, the soldiers of the Caliph dissuaded this Frankish inclination, and the family of the Jewish farmer Solomon Ben David, who in the summer grazed his cattle along the salt marshes to a distance of several leagues to the west and in the winter fed them only apples in the belief that the wisdom of the Tree of Knowledge would filter through the several stomachs and udders of his cattle into the Jews of Narbonne, was able to bring its animals to Yehoshua's slaughterhouse. But within a few months, it became clear to the Caliph of Cordoba that Pepin had designs upon his city and that closed gates saved lives. The family of Solomon Ben David brought his herd into Narbonne, where he bedded down fifty head of cattle and twice that number of sheep and goats in pens attached to Yehoshua's house that he had erected and stocked with apples and grain with the foresight of someone who believes that all adversity is temporary.

"Even when Pepin's soldiers surrounded the city and it became clear that the Franks were not going away soon, Yehoshua managed to provide the Jews of Narbonne with fresh kosher meat and still leave enough fertile livestock to replenish the supply. Ibn Suleiman at the eastern gate did the same for his Muslims.

"In the second year of the siege, Yehoshua's son Moses began to accompany his father on his rounds.

"In the third year, as the Franks torched the fields around Narbonne and the grain, and even the apples gave way to rot and evaporation, Solomon Ben David looked the other way, and Yehoshua began to slaughter the younger animals. In the fourth year, in the words of Yehoshua, there was nothing left but coitus. But so joyless were those unions, so empty of the essential juice of life, that they produced no babies, only wormlike spirits that slithered along the cracks in the earth then found their ways out the gutters or through the air past the wretched Moors. By the fifth year, Yehoshua's family was eating rats. By the sixth year, Solomon Ben David was dead.

"As the shochet, the ritual butcher for the Jews of Narbonne, Yehoshua had long been familiar with death. Not his son. From the time he could talk, Moses asked why the animals had to die. There was nothing accusatory in his questions. More a desire to learn all the angles, all the curves, all the possible rationales so he could separate out the excuses for death in a search for something that Yehoshua never had time to ponder—the truth. Moses knew enough, six years into the siege and his own brief life, to hold his tongue on the mornings when he woke to find strangers whispering in the dawn shadows, or on the nights when other shadows came to purchase half a dozen gas-filled bladders that Yehoshua larded with small stones and nails for use as bombs against the Franks. By the age of six, Moses had already figured out that humans shared a common ancestor with cattle. Putting the combustible bladders of dead villagers to use against the enemy was only an admission of the universal goal of survival.

"As the seventh year shone upon a changed Narbonne, Yehoshua—his wife, his daughters, his sons—found themselves thigh high in the filth and decay of siege. The little food that managed to bribe its way past the sentries never went out as shit, in fear that the Franks might use it as fuel or pile it up against the outer walls of Narbonne to weaken or surmount them. Before the siege, there had been two thousand Jews in Narbonne and five times that number of Muslims. By the seventh year, only one quarter of the population remained.

"And then the morning came when Yehoshua rose and Moses did not. Yehoshua let his dead son lie, told his wife and daughters not to disturb him. By then, his wife's movements were limited and her thoughts shifted only when Yehoshua could barter his bomb-making skills for a cup of flour or a fistful of radish greens and pour a spoonful of the gruel into her devastated mouth. Two nights later, Moses's belly began to swell with a stench more familiar to her nose than all the other perfumes of death. Yehoshua began to wrap him methodically with sharp little things that found their way into his empty mangers on dark nights. It was then that his wife rose from the straw. She didn't have the strength to yell with the force of protest. But her eyes reflected Yehoshua's own pain, magnified his own doubt, and generated a new thought. In its clarity, its crystalline purity, the message was simple. Enough. Thou shalt not turn the *corpse of thy son into a weapon. It was time to stop making money from death. It was time to sell the living. It was time to sell the Muslims to the Franks.*

"And that is how it came to pass, in the seventh year of the siege, in the years 4520, 140, and 759, respectively, that the trust of Ibn Suleiman and the Muslims of Narbonne and all the shadowy figures who had passed over the years through Yehoshua's slaughterhouse was butchered in one night of betrayal, one moonless opening of the western gate to the Frankish soldiers, one hour of soundless slaughter—for how can a starving people, even Muslims, inured by religion to fasting, scream? But Yehoshua's people, the Jews, his wife, his daughters, were spared."

"But Septimania?" Isaac remonstrated. "Why should I care about your bomb-making butcher, your Judas of a Jew? I asked about Septimania."

I winced, but in the dark Isaac noticed nothing. Methodically I packed a fresh pipe with tobacco, lit it with the candle Isaac's mother had brought to the garden, and continued.

"The next morning, Yehoshua found himself in the presence of the son of the Frankish King Pepin. Charles was merely a prince at the time, a few years older than Yehoshua's poor, dead son Moses, and a decade away from his future baptism as Charlemagne, Carlo Magno, Charles the Great. And it was to be another forty years until Pope Leo III crowned Charles Holy Roman Emperor in the Basilica of St. Peter's in Rome. But on this particular morning, in exchange for his treachery, in thanks for delivering Narbonne to the Franks and ridding the kingdom of the Moors, the young King Charles gave Yehoshua a gift. The King promised the Jews royal deeds to Narbonne, and to the cities of Béziers, Elne, Agde, Lodève, Maguelonne, and Nîmes."

"Seven cities!" Isaac said.

"Yes," I said. "This, Isaac, is the Septimania of which I spoke. The Jewish Kingdom of Septimania arose from Yehoshua's betrayal."

"Hmm," Isaac said. "Couldn't have been much of a kingdom if Charlemagne gave it to the Jews. Certainly I've never read of it in any of the histories."

"There are kingdoms that exist just outside the periphery of our vision," I replied, "as surely as there are more heavenly bodies in the sky than have been seen by Signor Galileo's cannocchiale. And there are

rulers who guide the affairs of men and women with a wisdom as clear and invisible as the Laws of Nature."

"As the Laws of Nature?" Isaac laughed. "Who was this invisible King of Septimania who was such a force of Nature?"

"Charles and Yehoshua agreed that the kingdom of the seven cities of Septimania would be ruled over by a Jewish prince. He would be the ally of the Franks, but an independent king over an independent people."

"An interesting definition of independence," Isaac scoffed.

"More interesting than your independence from God?" I shot back. "Or from your mother?"

"Or from you?" Isaac smiled. "Prithee continue."

"When the sun next rose," I went on, "three days later than required by Jewish law, Yehoshua buried his son. In the afternoon, he sent a letter to Baghdad."

"Why Baghdad?" Isaac laughed. "And with what form of post? I thought your Jews of Narbonne had eaten all the carrier pigeons?"

Isaac's mother looked over at me at every mention of the word Jew. Cromwell had only recently invited the Jews to return to England after an absence of three hundred years and replenish the nation's war-torn coffers with continental gold. The few other Jews I had encountered in Cambridge trod lightly on the strange soil. While God may have feared Isaac's mother more than she feared Him, clearly she was nervous about my effect on her son.

"Baghdad in those days," I continued, "was ruled by Haroun al Rashid, Caliph of all the Persians, from a palace that was known more for its gardens than its wars, and for its dedication to science more than its application to the law."

"Haroun al Rashid?" Isaac asked. "I've heard that name before."

"Perhaps as the hero of many of the Thousand and One Nights, *the tales the young and inventive Scheherazade told her husband Prince Shahryar on her wedding night and for three years of nights following to keep him from hacking her in two, the way he had divided his adulterous first queen and her paramour."*

"Yes! That's it!" Isaac said. "Sinbad, the Magic Bag of Judar. There was a time when I read more than mathematics and dreamed of more than stars."

"One night," I continued, "Haroun al Rashid dreams that he orders the palace gardeners to find him the sharpest axe in all the city of Baghdad. Armed with this handle of summer ash and this blade of winter steel, the Caliph marches into the garden, determined to cut down every standing tree, from fig to cherry, from oak to walnut. One by one, he hacks and hews, until the garden is nothing but kindling and dust. All that remains is an apple tree, a tree as unremarkable as the one supporting our backs, a beardless sapling with its promise still to come. In his dream, Haroun grips the handle and raises the axe above his head and prepares to strike. Suddenly an old man appears before him. Snatching the axe from Haroun, the old man lifts it above his own head—as King Shahyar would over his faithless queen—and hurls it at the noble brow of the Caliph with such force that blood spurts all over his face and beard and flows down onto his ivory robes.

"Haroun al Rashid recognizes the old man as a djinni of the wood, a sacred forester, and falls upon his knees praying for mercy and swearing to nurse the sapling, to water it himself, to prune its branches, that it might shoot up into a leafy tree. No sooner has the oath left his mouth, than the Caliph awakes. Touching his brow, he sees that there is, indeed, blood on his face. Haroun is certain, with the absolute certainty of a Caliph, that the dream was far from ordinary.

"Even though it is the middle of the night, Haroun rings for a servant and summons a Jew named Benyamin, known for his skill in interpreting dreams. Benyamin asks for ink and quill and transcribes the dream of the Caliph. He calculates the value of each word according to the Jewish system of gematriya, assigning a number to each letter of the alphabet, a sum for every word, and then makes a complex analysis of the sentences and the formula of the dream as a whole. But while he is calculating, searching for the number whose abstract power will unlock the secret of the Caliph's dream, Benyamin is thinking of his grandson, a remarkable boy of fifteen years, who is also susceptible to bad dreams."

"They both have my sympathies." Isaac puffed once, twice.

"The grandson," I continued, "was the son of the King of the Jews in Exile. What the Hebrews of Baghdad called Resh Galuta, the Exilarch. It had been several hundred years since the Babylonians drove the Jews out of the land of Israel. They had settled more or less comfortably in Persia, *where the rulers, pagan and Muslim alike, gave them free rein in matters ranging from the preparation of food to the celebration of death. King of the Jews was a hereditary title that traced its ancestry, as did Jesus Christ himself, back to King David, the musician and adulterer."*

"Very good!" Isaac handed me the pipe and smiled. "David was always one of my favorites."

"'My Prince,' Benyamin explains to Haroun, 'in the house of the Exilarch my daughter lives with her husband and her son. One day, insha'allah, my grandson, now the youngest of the princely house of David, will follow the path of his father and become King of the Jews himself. But my daughter worries. I myself worry that this sapling already has enemies among your people, among my people, among people we cannot yet imagine, who are sharpening their axes, waiting for the right moment to chop him down.'

"'Enemies?' the Caliph asks. 'What enemies? You are as an uncle to me.'

"'My Lord,' Benyamin answers. 'This very night, before your guards came to my door and requested my presence at the palace, my grandson awoke from a troubled sleep and ran to my bed.'

"'Another bad dream?' Haroun asks.

"'The very same dream that Your Excellency related to me,' Benyamin answers and bows low.

"'This boy, your grandson,' the Caliph asks, clearly moved. 'What do they call him?'

"'Your highness,' Benyamin answers. 'They call him by a name whose gematriya equals the sum total of your dream. They call him Gan. Which in Hebrew, as you know, means garden.'

"Immediately, without making his own calculations, Haroun al Rashid orders his guards to bring Gan to the palace. Over the course of days and weeks, the lad distinguishes himself before the Caliph and his grandfather with his learning and displays extraordinary powers of intellect and courtesy. One afternoon, though stung by a wasp while in the presence of the Caliph, Gan forbears to drive it away by so much as the movement of a finger, in deference to his royal master. The Caliph showers gifts upon the boy. Then and there he installs him above and beyond his own father—though Gan has yet to attain his sixteenth year—as King of the Jews in captivity, as the Exilarch."

"While his father was still alive?" Isaac says, passing me the pipe for the briefest of moments. *"A rather Republican concept."*

"Yet even as Haroun al Rashid is setting the seven-jeweled crown upon the youngster's head," I continue, without relinquishing the pipe, *"a messenger arrives in Baghdad from the South of France."*

"The letter from your Jewish butcher!" Isaac shouts. Unamused, his mother shuffles back into the cottage.

"The letter comes with the seal of Prince Charles and his father King Pepin. They ask Haroun to send them a king for their new kingdom, a gardener to tend their garden a thousand miles away."

"Gan!" Isaac smiles.

"Precisely," I smile back. *"Haroun al Rashid turns pale at the request and touches his forehead. His dream, his young sapling, stands before him in the full light of day. He knows that to cut the tree means disaster. Yet Haroun's sense of diplomacy and politics shake his certainty. And so he prepares to go . . ."*

"To Septimania?"

"Ah! Now you are curious." I offer the pipe back to Isaac, but he is in the full flow of the distraction I intended. He is the one, I have no doubt. *"Shall we make the journey?"*

"*BUON GIORNO, DOTTORE.*"

Malory opened one eye. A shaft of pre-dawn light. A grizzled buzz cut, a twisted nose, a tortured breath. One friar, a Roman friar, backed by stone and shadow—Fra Mario, was that his name? Malory closed his eye. Through one ear he heard the shuffle of feet in the cloister, the polyphony of baritone virgins.

"*È tempo,*" Fra Mario said. More chanting, more shuffling.

Tempo for what? But the Roman friar was gone.

THE VICAR HADN'T SAID MUCH AT THE GRAVESIDE.

"I am merely a messenger," he said, wiping his hands with a handkerchief that mixed the scent of lavender with the fenny pong of the loam that covered his grandmother's remains. "Mrs. Emery, you may know, was not technically a member of the parish."

"Yes," Malory said, with surprise at his own anti-clerical passion.

"Whistler Abbey itself belongs to some distant foundation. But there is an inheritance for you—what it is, I haven't a clue. Your grandmother gave me this envelope some time ago. To hand over to you on the event of her death."

The vicar reached into an obscure pocket and handed Malory a cream-colored envelope. The flap was embossed with the same *S* fenced in by the seven-sided box that graced the cover of the journal belonging to the seventeenth-century friend of Isaac Newton. On the front, a single name in purple ink: Hercule.

"A train ticket, Mr. Malory. You are to go to Rome. Those were her instructions. You are to go to Rome and stay with the Dominicans"

—the vicar couldn't help his sneer—"and await instruction from a Signor Settimio. Name ring a bell?"

"The Dominicans?" Malory asked.

"Santa Maria sopra Minerva," the vicar said. "I understand there is a monastery next to the basilica. You can walk from the train station."

"And then?"

"You might inspect their organ," the vicar smiled. "I'm certain it needs tuning."

Rix had offered, in a spirit of soldierly camaraderie, to pack up Malory's books and store them in a corner of Trinity where they wouldn't be bothered for a century or two. Antonella had wept and left Malory with a complex kiss and a simple tinfoil packet of biscuits that Malory packed into the rucksack along with three changes of clothing and a Tesco bag of toiletries. If Malory brought little with him it was not with the expectation that he would follow his grandmother's instructions and then return to Cambridge in a few days. It was with no expectations whatsoever, or with the minimal expectations of the stunned.

By train from Cambridge to London, London to Rome; by foot from the station. As Malory walked with only the dimmest directions from Termini towards Santa Maria sopra Minerva, sensation returned to his brain, and he wondered whether this journey was taking him nearer to or farther from the Louiza he had last seen on the same day he'd last seen his grandmother alive. There were a few late-night drinkers on the steps of the Pantheon. A pair of wistful buskers were scraping out "Limehouse Blues" on fiddle and guitar, leaning on an ancient brick wall beneath an even more ancient arch that once, in an even more ancient past, must have led through a grand opening to some palazzo, some temple, some somewhere full of hope. The façade of the church of Santa Maria was so uninviting, so graffiti-free, so plain that merely a single gypsy, hidden beneath sacks of muslin and crepe, had thought to camp out on its steps. Not even the music of the buskers penetrated the midnight air. Only Bernini's statue of an elephant retained its sense of humor, standing quizzically with its half smile, a lonely ornament in the center of the piazza, an arbitrary pink obelisk balanced on its howdah. An act of vandalism or pity had decorated the animal—the elephant shone, even in the moonless night—a rich enamel blue as deep as Louiza's eyes.

Sì, Fra Mario said, answering Malory's bell, they had received his grandmother's letter. *Sì*, they had been expecting Malory. *Sì*, he knew Signor Settimio well and would alert him in the morning to Malory's arrival. *Sì*, they were giving Malory a special cell at his grandmother's request—*la cella di Galileo! Galileo, lo conosce?*—and Fra Mario wiggled his fingers next to his head in a way that made Malory wonder whether his entire journey were an act of madness. *No*, Fra Mario said, no one had said that the organ was broken. If indeed Malory could fix the organ—for which he, Fra Mario, being a fallen-away Neapolitan, had no real ear, although, come to think of it, the organ was clearly *rotto*—it might be a good thing. This, at least, was how Malory, with his little Italian, deciphered the stream of language that flowed from Fra Mario's smile before he sank in exhaustion and incomprehension onto the bed that had once borne Galileo.

MALORY SAT UP. IN PAIN. WITH A BURN IN HIS RIGHT SHOULDER AND AN ache in his left thigh, his neck bent like an over-tuned crumhorn, and the back of his skull throbbing as if some Old Testament barber had taken vengeance on the wilderness of his scalp. Had the Dominicans slept any better? Did these monks, whose bowels and prostates sang their flatulent matins as they passed Malory's cell, did these outdated old men, great-grandsons of the Inquisitors, vestiges of a time when the one true God inspired a singular terror through the hearts and across the shoulders of the religiously nervous, did these pious men really sleep on beds made of rope and straw? Did torture focus the mind? It had been 350 years since the Inquisition had invited Galileo to Rome, invited him here to the monastery of Santa Maria sopra Minerva for his trial. Malory couldn't quite remember if it was dropping balls off the Leaning Tower of Pisa or inventing the telescope that got the Florentine into trouble. With his eyes half-conscious, Malory could only conjure a fuzzy image of Galileo in stringy beard and long robe and a kind of squinty velvet hat that reminded him of

Jethro Tull. Legend had it that it only took a few days for the Inquisition to persuade Galileo that he wasn't 100 percent certain that the Earth revolved around the Sun. It wasn't the days that changed Galileo's mind. Legend had it wrong. Legend hadn't spent a night in Galileo's bed.

"*Forse oggi*," Fra Mario said, returning to Malory. Malory stood. There was no need to dress as he had fallen asleep in the jeans and corduroy jacket that had borne him from Cambridge the day before. He had no idea whether Fra Mario was taking him to Signor Settimio or the organ or, more hope against hope, to breakfast. Leaving his rucksack on Galileo's bed of inquisition, Malory slung his Kit Bag over his right shoulder and followed Fra Mario into the corridor. "*Forse oggi*," Fra Mario said again. And Malory gradually understood that the Dominican activity around him was the vague optimism of a New Era in Rome. Fra Mario and the dozen Dominican monks of Santa Maria, and indeed all of Rome and much of the rest of Italy and, for all Malory knew, much of the world were expecting the College of Cardinals to announce a successor to poor John Paul I, who had just died after barely a month in office.

"*Forse oggi*," Antonella had smiled at him through tears and biscuits, "you will arrive in Rome and there will be a new pope. You will see the white smoke up the spout of the Sistine Chapel. They say he was poisoned," she'd whispered to Malory, biting her soggy bottom lip to stop the flow of tears. "I have a cousin who works at the Banco Ambrosiano in the Vaticano. Nobody talks very loud there, but these days, he says, they are talking faster and softer. They say John Paul I was the wrong pope. A mistake was made. The way Aldo Moro was the wrong politician. Malory,"—Antonella had grabbed his corduroy arm in a fistful of painted nails—"you are a scientist. Tell me, if the pope is chosen by God, how can there be a mistake?"

Kit Bag across his shoulder, Malory followed the outline of Fra Mario's muscular brush cut through the sacristy into the church. A vague glow from the windows high in the apse and at the piazza end of the long nave met at a Christ the Savior that stood to the left of the altar, carved by Michelangelo but dressed much later by some nineteenth-century critic frightened by naked marble. Next to Jesus and below the altar, illuminated by her own electricity, a sarcophagus held the complete remains of Santa Caterina of Siena—minus head and right thumb, which had found their ways to Siena, and a foot, which wandered occasionally around Venice. Off to the side in the chapel of the Torquemada family, a colossal cousin of the more famous Spanish Inquisitor sat on his cardinal throne judging these abused ancients. High above them all, golden stars filled the blue firmament of the ceiling of Santa Maria sopra Minerva, but failed to give off any light of their own.

Fra Mario turned a key. A door opened across from Michelangelo's Savior. A staircase appeared, next to it a pegboard holding the business end of the bell ropes. Malory followed Fra Mario—one flight of steps, two flights, back and forth up the shaft of the *campanile*. The tower smelled of damp and the droppings of small things that scurried just out of sight through the cracks and holes and nests in the walls at their approach. The corkscrewed spire of San Ivo appeared through one slit of the tower, the saucepan lid of the Pantheon through another. The more Malory climbed, the more he began to wake up, and both were torture. He wondered what he was doing following Fra Mario, who kept murmuring *forse oggi* and climbing like William Tell. He wondered, as he turned a corner up the narrowing staircase, whether some Inquisitor, or perhaps the ghost of Galileo himself, was waiting to push him and Fra Mario off the top of the *campanile* in a scientific auto-da-fé, and which one of them would hit the gypsies first.

But as he turned the corner, the sun shot a ray through the window and fractioned the morning into the seven colors of the rainbow. The full spectrum spread across the wall of the staircase in front of Malory, a sign as powerful as the vision of St. Michael with his sword that converted the Roman Constantine to Christianity.

Light, Malory thought. Prism. Newton.

The pot of gold at the end of Malory's rainbow, however, was merely a door into the dusty choir room. The hall was broad and high-ceilinged, lit through a rank of dusty and leaded windows, furnished with a pair of upright pianos and an opened trunk of water-stained surplices, a room that had clearly not been used in some time or, if used, set aside as storage for rancid hymnals guarded by poorly painted and forgotten bishops. At the far end, Fra Mario held open a tiny Wonderland door. Malory stepped through the opening.

"*Forse oggi*," Fra Mario said, "*ma adesso l'organo.*" With the finality of real hope, he retreated into the choir room, pulling the door shut.

The case was a fluffy bit of baroque *panna cotta*, a gift from a Borghese prince who was more aesthete than musician. The organ itself, like the one Malory had advised Trinity College to purchase, was a Metzler, built by a Swiss burgher who believed organs were created to play Bach and not Iron Butterfly. Swiss organs, like Swiss watches, trains, knives, and, for all Malory knew, fondue burners, ran fine as long as they were tended by fastidious Swiss organ tuners or confused British organ scholars. Leave them for a few years in the variable humidity and smog and waxy perfume of a Roman church and, well, they would need work.

Still, without playing the organ, without backing it out of the garage, driving it around the corner, and listening to its particular purr as it ran the preludes and fugues, it was impossible to know the soul of the organ and prescribe the appropriate therapy. A faded *cinque-cento* case with its birthmarks long dissolved by years of damp and pigeon shit might disguise an instrument of genius, as well-tuned now as it was the century it was installed. A sparkling canary and forest-green façade, on the other hand, could mask a scrapyard of rusted pipe and moldy wood fit more for a Duchamp fountain than a Dominican church. Malory had a fondness for these mismatches, the puzzles, the illegitimate offspring of budget and architecture. It was time to tune his attention and speak to this particular bastard.

He emptied his Kit Bag one weight at a time onto the music stand. First the Book of Organs, next the Universal Tuner. Finally, Malory pulled out a 35-millimeter reliquary that had no mass, but which still contained the weight of Malory's hope. Malory flipped one switch, and the light over his keyboard warmed the neglected ivory. He flipped another, and the electric motor twenty feet away behind the pipes began to wheeze air into the lungs of the instrument. The hum of power vibrated confidence through the organ bench up Malory's body and into his fingers. The organ of Santa Maria sopra Minerva might be broken, but chances were it was playable. There was no point in gentling up to the keyboard, testing it with a tentative finger, one note at a time. Not when the stops, the manuals, the pedals, the pipes, the very bellows themselves were crying out for release. It was time for music. It was time for improvisation. $i = u$. Malory = Louiza. Malory raised his left hand six inches above the keyboard and brought it firmly down on the first letter of Louiza's name.

"*Fututi pizda matii!*"

Malory pulled his hand off the keyboard. The note faded to silence. He raised his left hand and brought it down on the B-flat once again.

"*Fututi pizda matii!*" The noise came from the organ case. The bottom rank of pipes, the sixteen-footers. Right register, wrong language.

"*Scusi?*" One of about twelve words Malory knew in Italian. But there was no response. He looked over the parapet of the organ loft. The church was empty. Malory turned back to the bottom manual and pressed the B-flat again.

"*Cazzo!*" No doubt about it. A human voice. Not a voice or vocabulary he associated with Fra Mario or the aged Dominicans.

"*Chi è?*" Malory slid down the bench, his eye on the door to the choir room and the spiral stairs. "Hello?" No answer, just the muffled sound of movements behind the pipes.

And then Malory saw the handle on the door to the pipe case turn, the door open. A figure stepped out of the pipe case and around the corner of the 16-footers. There was such a stoop to the man's appearance that Malory at first imagined he was one of those Victorian creatures from Dante's *Inferno*, damned for some sin Malory could hardly remember, swinging his head by the hair like a lantern at waist height. The man's hair itself was medievally long, bog dark, and streaked with darker still, matted, nicotined, uncombed, and tangled past the shoulders, circling like a wet dog into a beard that seeped into the vague middle of his chest. He was dressed entirely in black—black t-shirt, black jeans, black jean jacket, black boots, all as wrinkled as the hair and as menacing as the hobnails of the bovver boys who hung around the clove-scented exit of the Taboo Disco Club on St. Andrew's Road back in Cambridge and threw uncomprehending foreign students into oncoming traffic. Exhausted by Galileo's bed, confused by Fra Mario's Italian, Malory's brain was without the oxygen to register fear, surprise or much of anything.

"*Che cazzo fai?*" The man pushed himself off the organ case and cracked his back, sending a rifle shot of an echo through the arches of the church. Erect, the man stood at least six feet tall, Malory thought, maybe double that. "*Che cazzo fai qui?*" and the apparition stumbled away from the pipes and towards Malory on the organ bench.

The only exits available to Malory were between the giant's legs or over the balustrade of the organ loft, fifty feet to the stone nave of Santa Maria sopra Minerva. Malory slid carefully down the organ bench as the man approached. But the closer the man came and the more Malory slid, the further he put himself from any reasonable solution. At the end of his options, Malory grabbed his Kit Bag and his Universal Organ Tuner and stood.

He hadn't meant to hold the Universal Tuner, a piece of metal nine inches long—pointed and ridged of course—in a threatening pose, as if he were, in fact, one of those very bovver boys in front of the Taboo Disco Club. And he hadn't meant to tread with his own boot on the low C pedal of the organ. But in one movement, Malory's theatrical gesture and the low C of the organ, which let forth a roar like the unleashed menagerie of Noah's Ark, so surprised and so overwhelmed the giant, that he fell against the balustrade of the organ loft and began to pivot backwards over the edge. And that equal and opposite reaction so surprised Malory that it wasn't until the last rumble of the low C died away in the fissures of the church that Malory realized he had somehow lunged forward and caught the giant by the belt with the Universal Organ Tuner. He was stretched out at full length, the toes of his own boots caught painfully, if securely, by the bench. His two hands gripped in agony the rough metal that had served all sorts of other purposes in the twenty years since he had found it in a field near Narbonne, but never to hold two men away from certain death on the floor of a Dominican church in Rome. *Forse oggi*, Malory thought. *Forse oggi*, gravity will have its way. And the sadness that he would die without seeing Louiza again was unimaginable. But just as Malory felt the last of the Universal Organ Tuner begin to slip through his hands, the giant pivoted his torso up with another echoing crack, and fell onto the floor of the organ loft, with Malory somehow on top of him.

"Sorry," Malory apologized, worming his body off the stranger's and fiddling uncomfortably to disentangle the Universal Organ Tuner from the man's waistband. "*Mi dispiace, ma . . .*"

"American?" The man was breathing heavily.

"Sorry," Malory apologized again, wishing he wouldn't. "No. British. English."

"So—" The man pulled himself into a sitting position on the floor, back against the balustrade. "You British come all the way to Rome to play organs and wake me up at . . . what the fuck is the time?"

"Not exactly," Malory said.

"Not exactly?" the man said. "*Fututi pizda matii!*" The man laughed and wiped his eyes with thumb and forefinger.

"Sorry," Malory said, "I don't speak much Italian yet."

"Not Italian," the man said. "Rumanian. It means 'fuck the . . .'" He stopped and turned to Malory. "Do you have a mother?"

"Actually," Malory said, "she died some years ago."

"In that case," the man said, "I won't waste the explanation, or curse the private parts of a dead woman."

"You are Rumanian?" Malory asked.

"Not exactly," the man said with an actor's attempt at sobriety that quickly gave way to more laughter. He reached into the breast pocket of his jacket and pulled out a pair of rimless glasses. "What are you not exactly doing up here?" He tweezed the glasses over the back of his ears and onto his helpless eyes. Malory realized that the apparition breathing heavily and laughing lightly next to him on the organ loft floor was essentially harmless.

"I was planning on tuning the organ, actually."

"Actually?"

"This piece of metal"—and Malory held up the Universal Organ Tuner—"is what I use to scrape and bend the pipes. Put them in tune."

"Not to rescue Rumanians?" The man took the tuner from Malory and scratched the end of his nose.

"Not exactly," Malory laughed. And he thought that it had been a while since he had laughed and a long while since he had laughed at himself. "What does it mean to be not exactly Rumanian?"

"So," the man began, "you have heard of Dracula?"

"Mmm," Malory said.

"Don't worry," the man said. "I'm not a biter. It's just to give you a geographical idea of how fucked my part of Rumania is—fucked by the Ottomans, fucked by the Hungarians, the Austrians, the vampires, and, most recently, the Red Star Pioneers of the Soviet Union and its finger puppets, Monsieur and Madame Ceauşescu." He handed the metal back to Malory. "I come from a place that has been scraped and bended, but is not exactly in tune."

Malory had little grasp of Eastern European history. But it occurred to him that the man's voice itself was out of tune. In the months that had followed his discovery of Louiza and the Pip, Malory's own internal tuning had become so acutely wired that he felt the need—like Charlie Chaplin with his spanners in *Modern Times*—to take his own bent piece of metal and tune the horns of cars, the cries of seagulls, the whistle of the wind, to tune the world. And the voice that came to him first from the organ case and now from beside him on the floor of the organ loft of Santa Maria sopra Minerva was out of tune in a way that was unsettling.

"But you didn't come here, I mean to Rome, for a tuning."

"Not exactly," the man said, but this time he didn't laugh. "Back in Rumania, I was a little bit of a big shot. Which means Ceauşescu let me direct Shakespeare and Chekhov three or four times a year, and I had enough friends in the Securitate to keep me tranquilized with Carlsberg and Camels."

"But you left."

"I left," the man said, "because I followed *La Principessa*."

"*La Principessa*?" Malory asked. "Is she living inside the pipe case, too?"

"Living?" the man looked full at Malory. "You think I am living there?" It seemed to Malory that he was on the verge of laughing, but something more painful arrested the impulse. "I only came up here to get a little sleep. *La Principessa*," he continued, "at this moment is in the Ospedale Fatebenefratelli, preparing to give birth."

"Congratulations," Malory said, "I mean, I assume . . ."

"That the baby is mine? I assume too," the man said. "It is no consolation." The man pulled himself standing and turned to face into the vacuum of the church. "I told her," he said in a whisper mixed with a low bass undertone, "if it is a girl, you must give her away before I fall in love with her. If it is a boy, I will strangle it with my own hands."

"*La Principessa* is your wife?"

The man pulled Malory to his feet.

"You tune organs. You also play?"

"Well . . ."

"You will play something for me. Something for *La Principessa* and the baby."

Malory sat once more on the bench, the Rumanian beside him. Once again, he brought the little finger of his left hand down on the B-flat and introduced the theme of $i = u$, MALORY = LOUIZA, this time without interruption. Lucky Rumanian, Malory thought. In the seven months of absence, the seven months of searching, Malory had named not two, but three of the children he would have with Louiza. If he ever found her.

But as he played, another note crept into the improvisation, a note that hadn't been part of the melody in any of the many variations he had played over the past seven months. It was a low F-sharp, two octaves below middle C, a note that had its own force, its own gravity. The note came from a different scale, and added a discordant voice, especially when played with the toe of Malory's left boot on the far reaches of the pedals. As surely as the Rumanian had taken his place on the bench next to Malory, so had the low F-sharp taken its place in the music. MALORY = LOUIZA was unimaginable without this note.

Malory finished. His hands sat in his lap, his feet dangled from the bench. Only the whir of the motor for the bellows could be heard in the distance.

"Tibor," the man said softly. "My name is Tibor."

"Malory," Malory managed to breathe, even though his lungs were exhausted.

"Malory," Tibor said, placing his large palm on Malory's shoulder. "Malory, you saved me this morning."

"Saved you?"

"Come with me to *La Principessa* and save my child."

Malory had left Cambridge and traveled to Rome against all reason, thrown himself across Europe with only the vague instructions in the letter from his grandmother and the dim light of a single afternoon's memory of Louiza to guide him. He had spent a restless and ultimately torturous night in the very cell where Galileo had endured the worst of the Inquisition. And yet, at this very moment, with the touch of the man's hand, with the touch of Tibor's hand, all the pain in his neck and back, all the uncertainty about Louiza drifted away from his body and out the drafty walls of Santa Maria. Tranquility replaced terror.

Tibor. Even the man's voice changed with the sound of his name —Tibor. It came into tune, on that low F-sharp. That low F-sharp reminded Malory of another sound, a note he remembered from fifteen years before, a sleeping giant from the foothills of the Pyrenees, a note that Malory identified with a care and affection he had heard only a few times and long ago. In the organ loft, Malory felt that he had found someone who might take seriously his quest for the lost Louiza. Maybe, even, a friend.

"Come, Malory," Tibor said, and turned towards the door to the organ loft. Malory thought he should make an excuse. He had an organ to tune. There was an appointment with a lawyer, Signor Settimio—his grandmother's letter had been vague. There were reasons why it made sense for Malory to stay in the organ loft of Santa Maria sopra Minerva and continue to do what he was doing before this Tibor appeared. Instead, Malory let himself be pulled by this new acquaintance, this new sensation. He stood up from the organ bench. He opened the flap of his Kit Bag, put the Universal Tuner back in its place, and swung it over his shoulder.

But Malory had forgotten the 35-millimeter canister. At the moment he stood, either Malory knocked the Pip off the music stand of the organ or the Pip, of its own volition and magnetic charge, flew in search of the Kit Bag but miscalculated. Hitting the floor of the organ loft, the 35-millimeter canister rolled slowly along the tiles towards the opening of the balusters and off into the darkness below.

"The Pip!" Malory's shriek, louder than the first note that had awakened Tibor, louder than Tibor's own awakening roar, echoed in the church, bounced off the stone columns and the painted chapels, off Michelangelo's statue of Christ the Savior at the altar and the more pedestrian bulk of Cardinal Torquemada in the right nave, and performed a ski dive of an arabesque off Bernini's funerary marble in the near apse in the tones of a crumhorn. As the highs and the lows settled, Malory leaned over the railing, searching into the black for an answering sound from the canister hitting the paving stones. But the echo that returned was in a softer pitch. It was a voice he remembered from another church, a voice he had never forgotten.

"Malory?" Something moved below. "Malory?"

Next to the tomb of the headless and thumbless Santa Caterina, a figure shifted in the dawn shadows and called his name again.

Malory ran.

The corkscrew of the spire of San Ivo unwound, the saucepan lid fell back onto the cauldron of the Pantheon. The colors of the rainbow drew themselves back off the wall of the tower into the white light of the sun to the clang of Malory's footsteps—one, two, then four at a time—his ear and his heart harnessed to gravity in the singular desire to reach the ground floor of the church before that voice died away. Seven infinite months had passed since he had last heard it. But he had no doubt that, even through the confusion of his meeting with the giant Rumanian, the overturning of the 35-millimeter canister and the vacuum of the church, it was—

"Louiza!" Breathing hard but not shrieking, Malory ran out of the door of the staircase and into the nave. Although he slowed down the panic of his legs, it took a moment for his blood to catch up with him. Here she is, Louiza, here in Rome, where he'd least expected. Here she is, *oggi*, risen from the tomb of Santa Caterina below the altar and sitting on the second pew to the right of the aisle, the position Mrs. Emery took every week in a different church in a different time.

Malory walked as calmly as he could, tugging at Kit Bag and lapel, conscious suddenly that his own unwashed and rumpled appearance might be important. Because something else was different, different about Louiza. Even in the dawn shadows, with his heartbeat searching for escape through his eyeballs, Malory could see how tightly Louiza's cheeks clasped her face, the red at the edge of her lobeless ears, softened only by a fine pale down. The shadows of pre-Mass dawn draped a shawl of care around Louiza's neck, as if all nourishment, all strength had leached away in the past months, flown south to sustain a fullness, a roundness of the belly that pressed to bursting through her gray jumper. Louiza was pregnant. Louiza. Pregnant.

"I thought," Louiza began.

"I knew," Malory continued, and then corrected himself, "or at least I think I knew." Because although he had come to Rome in the trance of the instructions that his grandmother had left with the vicar, Malory knew that something was pushing him off course, as surely as it had pushed him off his bicycle on the towpath by the river. He had felt the same pull, the same gravitational tug that he had felt since arriving in Rome, since that March afternoon with Louiza in the organ loft of St. George's Church, Whistler Abbey. A pull he felt most strongly now, a pull he recognized that dropped him to his knees in adoration. He wanted to touch Louiza's face, to pull her lips, swollen and chapped as they were, to his.

"So . . ."

Malory had forgotten the Rumanian.

"Is this what you dropped?" Tibor held up the canister. Malory broke his gaze from Louiza's belly and stood.

"Yes," he said. "Thank you."

"And this is your *Principessa*?"

"Louiza," Malory said, confused as always with introductions. "This is Tibor. I met him . . ."

"So," Tibor said, "you did not come to Rome just to tune an organ. Not exactly."

"What is that?" Louiza said, standing and reaching for the canister in Malory's hand.

"The Pip," Malory answered. "Do you remember?"

He knelt down beside Louiza in the narrow trough between the pew and the rail in front of it, and opened the lid and held the Pip between his thumb and his middle finger. And as he did, a magnetic force teased the fingers with the Pip closer to Louiza. A magnetic force that made resistance impossible, a magnetic attraction drew Malory's hand towards Louiza's belly and drew towards the Pip the unmistakable shape of another hand, a tiny hand from within Louiza's belly, a hand that rose to press and touch the Pip.

"*Fututi pizda matii!*" Tibor's voice joined Malory's amazement, but in a timbre more attuned to the phenomenon at the second pew to the right of the aisle in Santa Maria sopra Minerva. The Pip was caught in a perfect intersection between Malory and Louiza and that tiny hand. Malory's gaze floated up beyond Louiza to the dimly lit Madonna of Filippino Lippi's *Annunciation,* the fresco he had seen in postcard miniature propped up against Antonella's biscuit tin. Louiza was—there was no doubt about it—Malory's pregnant Madonna. And Malory—and Tibor too, for that matter—would have stayed motionless in worshipful wonder of this Madonna if an unholy cry hadn't, at that moment, erupted from Louiza's mouth, accompanied by a splash of water on the paving stones of the church.

"Malory!" she screamed, and fell into his arms, her teeth—fine and white and sharp—digging through the corduroy sleeve of his jacket as Louiza clamped down during the first contraction.

Malory knew enough to know that Louiza was going into labor. He knew enough to know that there were better delivery rooms in Rome than the nave of Santa Maria. And he knew that it might have been easier for all concerned if Malory had led the way and his new friend, the giant Tibor, had provided the muscle and heft to the gasping weight of Louiza. But Malory also knew that his arms alone should wrap themselves around the back and thighs, should press Louiza's damp hair beneath his chin and lift her up from the paving stones of Santa Maria sopra Minerva.

And yet the weight—

"The Pip," Louiza whispered into his ear as the contraction eased and her jaw released his jacket. "By your foot . . ." Sure enough, there on an uneven square of marble, illumined by the morning, the Pip glowed with anticipation of the journey. Malory bent to retrieve the shining seed.

And *mirabile dictu*, with the Pip in its canister in his Kit Bag, Louiza's body, sweating and panting in temporary relief, felt no heavier to Malory than a bottle of claret or Isaac Newton's *Principia* as he followed Tibor towards the door out of the church and into the piazza.

"Fatebenefratelli!" shouted Tibor, striding ahead. "We take your *Principessa* to meet my *Principessa*."

"*Principessa*?" Louiza mumbled into Malory's left ear.

"And maybe," Tibor roared, "we save a few lives!"

1/6

THERE WERE MANY THINGS THAT LOUIZA WANTED TO SAY TO MALORY. It had been a long time since Louiza had spoken to anyone about anything. During her months by the river in Cambridge, she rarely saw the Cottagemates. The problems she picked up and the solutions she returned so occupied the many studies and corridors and niches of her mind that she was well-insulated against what her father called "the universal human need for conversation." But the pull from the cottage to the church of St. George, the sight of Malory, first on the towpath by the Cam and then graveside with the vicar, the journey to Rome and the church of Santa Maria sopra Minerva by train, plane—how and with what she could barely remember—the necessity of the trip as strong as the kick of life inside her, made Louiza realize that for months she had been holding mouthfuls of vowels and consonants for him, for Malory. As if she had been frightened that if she wasted these words in public conversation, she would lose the air in her lungs, the chords in her throat, the lift in her tongue, that special language only she and Malory shared that had first led her to talk about *i* and *u* in the dusty afternoon rays of the organ loft.

There were many things that Louiza wanted to say to Malory.

Not about the cottage, which was boring and, in any case, she couldn't understand. Not about the Cottagemates either, or the change in the seasons along the river, or even the change in her own season.

She wanted to tell him about the problems. Not the solutions, the problems.

She had begun to feel, particularly in the past few months as her own secret had grown inside her, that she was seeing something, becoming aware, recognizing a pattern in the problems they were bringing her in the mornings, the problems that were left for her on the kitchen table.

They were all problems about origins: equations about sources, about where things came from. Louiza knew, of course, from a life in the countryside of East Anglia, about chickens and eggs, about the grunts of sows birthing in straw and muck, about lambs born in forgotten ditches and discovered only after the thaw in the recovered memory of lone sheep. She knew that the movement inside her was generated by something more biological than a chance meeting one spring afternoon in the organ loft of a village church. She even knew something about the various theories of the origins of the universe, about the physical forces unleashed by the Big Bang. And her father had an Anglican word to explain all origins.

What she wanted to tell Malory was more elemental than God.

"I saw—" she began.

Malory stopped just outside the door of the church on the piazza of Santa Maria sopra Minerva as Louiza's contraction dug into the back of his neck and an exposed piece of his left wrist. He wanted to tell Louiza that it would be all right, that she was going to be fine, that he was with her, that he would stay with her, that he would never leave her again. But half his body was resetting its muscles after the run down the nave of the church into the piazza, and the other half was wincing at the pain in his own neck and wrist. What little attention he had left was surprised by the statue of the elephant carrying the obelisk in the center of the piazza. Malory could have sworn that the night before, when he had knocked on the door of the Dominican monastery, the elephant had been painted an enamel midnight blue, as rich as the ceiling of the nave of Santa Maria sopra Minerva. But now—there was no question, even though he was half-starved of oxygen—the elephant was the crimson of the cardinals whom Fra Mario believed *forse oggi* would choose a new pope.

"I thought—" Malory began.

"Make no mistake, Malory," Tibor said. "There is a war going on."

"War?" Malory asked.

"Three hundred and something years ago, Fra Domenico Paglia, the Grand Poo-Bah of Santa Maria sopra Minerva, found an Egyptian obelisk buried in his blessed cloister, a scrap from the time of the Romans. So, Fra Domenico decided to erect this *puli* in front of the piazza and held a competition to design an all-purpose obelisk holder. One of the finalists was Gian Lorenzo Bernini, Mister Baroque, the drinking buddy of four or five popes and a couple of dozen cardinals. The other—surprise, surprise—was Fra Domenico himself. Bernini won, of course. Fra D. was an amateur who only had time for a bust or two when he wasn't condemning heretics. But that didn't stop him from showing Bernini who's boss. He offered Bernini some divinely received structural advice, how the weight of the obelisk would fracture the thirteenth and fourteenth lumbar vertebrae of the elephant. Bernini knew Fra Domenico was weak on the anatomy of pachyderms. But he also knew that the Dominicans were the Hounds of God and would bite hard if he didn't lend at least one ear to this inquisitorial engineer.

"So, Bernini put a little stone box beneath the elephant's gut, to make Fra Domenico happy. And then Bernini led his elephant into the middle of the piazza. Now, a lesser artist might have faced the elephant's trunk towards the church and another might have faced him away, as if pulling the weight of the cathedral towards Heaven or the Tevere, whichever came first. But Bernini was a genius. He parallel-parked Dumbo with his left flank against the church and his head facing the lobby of the Hotel Minerva. And then he lifted the tail of his beast ever so daintily to the port side, so he could aim his fragrant marble farts through the window of the study of the Dominican friar."

Louiza's contraction subsided, her grip on Malory's neck and wrist loosened. She giggled.

"I like your girlfriend," Tibor said.

Malory smiled down at Louiza, trembling and chapped, her hair, damp from exertion, pasted to the whiteness of her cheek, but smiling up at him all the same.

"Showtime, kids!" Tibor squeezed Malory's shoulder and set off at a jog towards an alley at the far corner of the piazza. With the new-found strength of an elephant with an obelisk on its back, Malory lifted Louiza once again and ran. From Piazza Minerva, Malory followed Tibor down the narrow Via dei Cestari, past the windows of the liturgical boutiques, where ecclesiastical dandies ran up diocesan expense accounts with accessories for their altars and sacristies. Malory pressed Louiza's face into his chest away from some of the more explicit artifacts—the portraits of Jesus straight off the covers of romance novels and body-building mags, the altar cloths woven with raised scarlet threads as if freshly washed in the blood of the lamb, the crowns of thorns, the boxes of 14-karat nails.

At Largo Argentina, Tibor stopped the cars and *motorini* for Malory to ford the rush hour traffic and then raced ahead down a narrow *vicolo* to the massive door of the Palazzo Caetani on the Via delle Botteghe Oscure. Caetani, Palazzo Caetani—Malory knew the name. When the vicar mentioned something about an inheritance, Malory's inheritance, he'd named property in Rome. A villa, or was it a palazzo? It couldn't possibly be something this cold and massive, with an entryway ten, twenty, maybe thirty feet high, the name Caetani etched in testamentary capitals above the door. But the name Caetani, Palazzo Caetani troubled Malory's memory as he hefted Louiza around the side of the building and followed Tibor down a narrow slalom of Cinquecentos and Citroens. He knew the name.

"Malory?" It was Louiza struggling to say something against his chest.

"Yes?" Malory said, pausing halfway down the alley, where a drainpipe bled a green stain of neglect on the side of the palazzo. "Tibor, wait!" he called, and crunched his ear down towards Louiza's mouth. "What is it, Louiza?"

"Biscuit," Louiza said.

"Biscuit?" Malory leaned in closer, wondering what he had heard.

"Biscuit," Louiza repeated. But before Malory could ask whether she was really hungry and he should stop at a café on the way to the hospital and was this really wise, Louiza screamed and writhed in another contraction. Malory held onto her as she opened and closed and squirmed and changed shape and form like—which one of the Greek water gods was it, Malory tried to remember, in which one of the Greek myths?

And in his own struggle to remember, another memory shot its way to the surface of Malory's sweating brain. Biscuit. Biscuit tin. Antonella's biscuit tin. Caetani. Palazzo Caetani and Antonella's biscuit tin and the small black-and-white television set in the Maths Faculty on Selwyn Road and the voice of Anna Ford.

"Aldo Moro." But now it was the voice of Tibor, who had run back from the bottom of the alley and stood with Malory. "This was where they found him. Like I said, there's a war going on."

Malory remembered the TV footage he'd watched with the sobbing Antonella—the crowd in the alley, the Palazzo Caetani, of course. And the cherry Renault 4, boot open, the assassinated Prime Minister curled up in his own fetal drama.

"Louiza wants a biscuit," Malory said. Louiza's body slowly relaxed, and the moisture from the latest contraction left a stain against Malory's corduroy lapel.

"And I want a coffee," Tibor said, "and half a bottle of grappa. But there isn't time." And Tibor put a large paw on Malory's shoulder and propelled him forward, down the alley.

"Biscuit later, Louiza," Malory murmured. He felt her nod, or at least felt her nose bury itself between two buttons of his shirt until it pressed its wet, friendly intimacy into his chest.

She wanted desperately to talk to Malory, to tell him about the problems. But she couldn't, weak with the pain and the effort and needing sleep and a biscuit, maybe two, and some tea, and a way to ease this thing, this problem out of her womb and into this world. But what world? The world in her vision was Malory's damp shirt, the walls of Renaissance palazzi as Malory carried her through the streets of Rome, the occasional bit of sky. Broken columns, amalgamated brick and stone of crumbling houses, a square block of roof, and then a sky that opened up as Malory carried her towards the river, figured more as variables in an equation than as points on a guided tour of Rome. They were all part of another problem of origins, like the problems they had brought her in the cottage. If she could only solve this problem, Louiza thought, then maybe, just maybe, the pain would go away.

There would be time, she was sure of it. There would be time to take pencil and paper and sort it all out. As blurred and bumpy as the journey was, Louiza felt a comfort in Malory's arms. She was rescued. Malory had come and rescued her, even if she had been the one who had traveled—she still couldn't remember how—across the Channel and half of Europe to find him in Rome. He was with her now, carrying her past elephants and down alleys, carrying her and their child. Had she told him? Of all the many questions, the one that had an answer was whose child she was carrying. It was Malory's, could only be Malory's. They would be together, the three of them, she and Malory and the child, bound in that indelible equation $i = u$.

But where in that equation was there space for the baby? Louiza raised her face towards Malory, Malory of the determined eyes, Malory of the unfailing plod and steady breath, who was trotting after Tibor, following him past the buzz of motorcycles and the rush of water mixed with the diesel of autobuses. The equation was perfect with Louiza and Malory, but with Malory and Louiza alone. Louiza = Malory, Malory = Louiza. Maybe that's why this baby inside her was causing such pain, up, down, inside and out. It didn't fit. The baby didn't fit in the equation.

There was another equation that troubled Malory.

October minus March equals seven. Seven, not nine. Not the nine months of human gestation, but the seven months since he had made love to Louiza in the organ loft of St. George, Whistler Abbey, which, although they seemed like an eternity to Malory, didn't add up. Wasn't twenty-eight weeks much too early? Was Louiza's baby premature? Or worst of all, had some other organ tuner climbed into Louiza's loft two months before him?

"There it is," Tibor shouted at Malory as they shuffled across the Lungotevere through the fallen leaves of the plane trees. Malory saw an island in the middle of the river, a fortress of an island, a stone boat floating, against the rules of all physics, in the middle of the river.

"What is it?" Malory puffed after.

"L'Isola Tiberina. The island of the Tiber!" Tibor shouted into Malory's uncomprehending face. "The best goddamned place to have a child on Earth. Follow me!"

"Ah," Malory said. And armed with little more knowledge than before, Malory struggled over a stone bridge to the Isola Tiberina following Tibor as he turned right beneath an Art Nouveau awning: *Ospedale Fatebenefratelli.*

"*Buona sera.*" A nun nodded at him. "*Sua moglie?*" Malory was on the verge of stopping and asking which way it was to the maternity ward, when he saw the sign *Maternità* and turned left.

"Malory!" Tibor shouted at him from the opposite direction. "Forget the signs, this is Italy." At a slightly slower pace, Malory carried Louiza into one courtyard, full of visitors squatting on plastic benches or stretched out on old newspapers along the wall. They jogged around a makeshift bar of charcoal burner and clothesline holding pages of the day's *L'Osservatore Romano*, through another arcade and into a second courtyard that turned back in the direction of the bridge. Malory looked hopefully to the signs on the left-hand staircases, but most of them were either unintelligible or prefixed with pessimistic *onco*'s and *cardio*'s.

"I told you," Tibor said, running for a staircase in a far corner, "no signs! This way." Malory followed Tibor up a staircase one flight, then two.

"Almost there, Louiza," he whispered her name, setting his courage to the verge of overheating with the thought that he, Malory, was on the cusp of fatherhood.

"Malory," Louiza said, "you'll stay with me, won't you? You'll stay?" She had forgotten about the equations, forgotten about the problems. The contractions had focused her mind on this miraculous man who was carrying her—was he really big enough to do that?—carrying her in his arms.

And Malory—Malory didn't know what the rules were, barely knew where they were, but he pulled Louiza tight, his cheek pressed to hers, her breath hot and wet in his ear. And if it were possible, he felt the Pip in the Kit Bag pull her in even tighter as he floated, yes floated with the long-sought Louiza in his arms down the hallways of the Ospedale Fatebenefratelli.

"*Fututi pizda matii!*" Tibor shouted for the fifth time that morning. "*Eccoci qua!* Here we are!" Tibor stopped at a door much like the others. A variety of nurse-like nuns or nun-like nurses kept a steady flow down the slow lanes of the corridors as Malory tried to catch his breath. And with that announcement, Tibor turned the handle and pushed the door wide open.

Breathless as he was, Malory stopped breathing for more than a moment at the radiance that embraced the three of them. Even Louiza raised her face towards the glow that came from inside. The room that opened up to them was at the forward-most point of the Ospedale Fatebenefratelli, the prow of the ship. It was a triangular room of sunlight and marble; an altarpiece window on starboard and another on portside made the room seem like it was carving a wake of light through the Tiber towards the Ponte Garibaldi and, in the far distance, the dome of St. Peter's. And the sun from the windows made it nearly impossible to see the few contents of the room—an armchair, a low table, a pair of beds.

A nun appeared from behind the door.

"We've been expecting you, my dear." An English accent. The sister guided Malory to the bed on the left. She pulled down the covers and smiled. Malory, in his exhaustion, accepted both accent and invitation as he would a pair of scones and a cup of tea. He met the sister's smile and set Louiza gently on sun-warmed sheets.

"Don't go," she whispered through the sweat and the matted hair.

"No one's going anywhere," the sister said, easing Louiza's grip from Malory's neck. "We're just going to clean you up and help you into something more comfortable. You'll want to look your best to greet your new baby, won't you?"

In the Roman sunlight, filtered only by the umbrella pines outside the window and a bit of curtainy lace, Louiza was as angelic as any of the creatures he had seen dancing in the dust of the organ loft that afternoon back in March. Some might say Louiza needed a serious wash-up after her cross-continental *hegira*. But to Malory, there was no more best than how she looked.

"Thank you."

Not Louiza's voice.

Malory turned. He hadn't seen anyone else in the room when he'd entered, but now he turned to the new voice, and saw on the other bed a figure intercepting the force of the sun from the far window.

The figure, a woman, didn't so much deflect the current of light from the window as draw it inwards. A long braid wrapped around one shoulder onto her breast, she was a vision in gray—gray hair, gray eyes as if she had captured all the color of the sun, determined to transform herself into the black-and-white heroine of a movie by Fellini. It was a gray that shone like the scales of an enchanted fish, a half-seen mermaid, a transparent stream, the hidden, veinless back of an autumn leaf. The hair was pulled away, back from the cheekbones, as impossibly sculpted and Slavic as any Pietà. At the heavenward end of her left cheekbone, a soft mole led Malory to the woman's eyes, which waited in serenity for Malory's full attention. Gray-haired as she was, the woman could not have been more than twenty-four or twenty-five years old.

"Thank you." The woman smiled at Malory with a softness that pushed the corners of her eyes into Siamese feathers, although it may—Malory thought later—have been only the smoke from a Gitane between her fingers that she handed up to Tibor. Could you really smoke in Italian hospitals, and just before you were due to give birth? But what stopped Malory short was the sound of the woman's voice. It shared not only the same Eastern European tones as Tibor's, but also its uncomfortable dissonance. The sound that came to Malory's right ear was gentle with undertones, he thought, of lavender and ambrosia, though he was only vaguely aware of what ambrosia might be. But at the same time, the "thank you" that came into his left ear was nasal and unsettling, like a sorceress from a Brothers Grimm tale scratched out in Cyrillic.

"You're welcome," Malory said. "But thank you for what?"

"For rescuing my husband."

"Ah," Malory said, "you are *La Principessa*."

"And I am the Count of Monte Cristo!" Another voice entered the room, another accent—American, a male voice. The man belonging to the voice was tall. Red-haired, in a full-bodied lupine way that made him seem twice as tall as Malory, with red hairs protruding from his cuffs and running down onto his knuckles. He was wearing tan khakis, a pink-striped shirt, a blue blazer, and a pair of soft, expensive moccasins that seemed out of place with the white coat draped cavalierly over his shoulders. Malory hoped that this was the standard uniform for obstetricians in Rome.

"Are you Louiza's—" Malory began to ask, but the nurse jumped in.

"Doctor, I thought the fathers might go down to the *cortile* for a coffee, while we prepared the ladies."

"Excellent!" the red-haired American boomed. And the vibrations of the boom had an effect on Malory's knees and drew him to his feet. "You gents grab a coffee while I check up on your wives."

"Malory!" Louiza called. He could see that something about the red-haired doctor clearly terrified her. But it was time for Malory to be a man, to be a father, to do the manly thing and let the professionals take charge and he would be back for the birth and the life and Louiza in the five minutes it would take for the nurse to run a washcloth across her pale skin and change her into something more appropriate for new beginnings.

"It will be all right," Malory whispered to Louiza. He bent down and scooped a strand of hair, black with sweat, behind Louiza's ear. Her lips were chapped with exhaustion. But the warmth of her kiss removed all doubt. Louiza was here, the child was here. The equation was balanced. But as he followed Tibor into the hall and the red-haired giant of a doctor winked and closed the door behind him, a jerk from his Kit Bag made Malory turn. The red-haired American, the plate of scones at the Orchard. Was it the same red-haired American who had bought him tea at the Orchard when he'd first lost Louiza, Malory wondered? Had a demon followed him? Had he once again played a false note?

1/7

"SIGNOR MALORY?"

A new man took his elbow in the corridor. Tall, tight-fitting dark suit, sunglasses, good shoes, hair combed back in ranks of well-oiled centurions. Italian, Malory thought. The director of the hospital, or maybe a chauffeur.

"Please," the man said, "you must come with us."

"Us?" Malory said, turning back to Louiza's room.

A second man appeared from the same nowhere as the first. He wasn't barring Malory's way back to Louiza's room, but he was present in a way that rearranged Malory's center of gravity. Even shorter than Malory, he was dressed in a long, night-blue woolen coat. The hint of cufflinks and a double Windsor at the collar suggested a formality that Malory hadn't seen in either the Master and fellows or the porters that served at High Table at Trinity. The afternoon light from the far end of the corridor sprinkled the man's face with a Roman dust that softened his silver hair. The maze of lines and shadows that ran from eyes to smile, made Malory think the man was as ageless as his grandmother, Old Mrs. Emery.

Of course! Malory shook off the anesthetic charm of the maternity ward. This was the man his grandmother had written about, the man who would tell him about his inheritance. Malory looked again. The clarity of his eyes, pale, past blue, a color nearly newborn in its transparency and openness, led Malory to understand that the man, the men came from a world where numbers and ages were counted according to a different system, a system that might prove invaluable to Malory, with an uncertain future and a new family on the other side of the door.

"Signor Settimio?" Malory said, thinking—how fortunate! He and Tibor could have a coffee in the *cortile* with Signor Settimio and his Driver. Signor Settimio could hand over whatever bank account and safe-deposit trinkets that Mrs. Emery had left to her neglected grandson. And then Malory would be free to welcome his child into the world and spend the rest of his life with Louiza.

"Settimio. Simply Settimio," the man said, the words almost sung in a tenor accent, somewhere between Puccini and Britten. "Eternally at your service." He bowed his head and, it seemed to Malory, also his right knee as his left hand went to his heart. Malory looked to the younger man with the sunglasses to see whether the appropriate response was a laugh or a giggle. But the other man's head was also bowed. Towards Malory.

"Please," Malory said. "*Prego*, thank you, *grazie*," running through his full vocabulary of Italian. "You are, you were a friend of my grandmother's, of Mrs. Emery. May I offer you a coffee down in the *cortile*?"

"There is not time for a coffee. I have much to tell you, *mio Principe*," Settimio said—the *Principe* flummoxing Malory as much as the rejection of the coffee. Was everybody in Rome a *principe* or a *principessa*, like Tibor's gray-eyed wife? Settimio raised his head and turned to the man with the gloves. "We must go."

"I'm sorry," Malory said, "I need to stay close by . . ." He paused, searching for the word to most accurately describe Louiza and his necessity. "If this is about my inheritance, certainly it can wait until tomorrow. I'm staying at Santa Maria . . ."

"There is a certain urgency," Settimio said. "For you and for many others. *Prego*." And with that *prego*, both Settimio and the man in the sunglasses touched Malory on the elbows—lightly, but with an electricity that began to move Malory's feet down the corridor.

"One moment," Malory shook himself loose and turned back to Louiza's door. This time it was Tibor who stopped him with a gentle palm to the shoulder.

"Go," Tibor said.

"Let me speak with the doctor." Malory eased Tibor's hand away and stepped towards the door. Tibor wouldn't be budged.

"I'll wait here and look after your Louiza. Come later, when you're finished with your business." The palm again on Malory's shoulder. Comfort and assurance. "We will celebrate."

"We must hurry," Settimio said, his childlike eyes icing into something barely warmer than insistence. "The Driver will take you. I will follow."

"The Driver? Where?" Malory said again. "I really have only five minutes. Ten minutes maximum." But Malory felt his feet begin to jog down the corridor, down the staircase with a sense of urgency, the two Italians at his elbows, the confidence of Tibor behind him. Louiza was in good hands—a doctor, a hospital, a new Rumanian friend who owed Malory his life. Perhaps the bank was closing. Perhaps there were papers that he needed to sign by the end of the day. Malory's Cambridge had effectively been sealed by the death of Mrs. Emery and the dismissal from Trinity College. Whatever Settimio was leading him to in Rome was, of necessity, the key to new beginnings with Louiza and their new baby. Louiza would understand. He would hurry. Determination, Malory whispered to himself. Courage.

At the entrance to the hospital, the tall man helped Malory straddle the passenger seat of a Vespa. Settimio turned to another *motorino* by the fountain.

"I'm sorry," Malory said. "You must tell me where we're going. What is so important at this very moment?"

"All shall be clear," Settimio said, as he steadied Malory's elbow on the narrow cushion behind the Driver. "Prepare yourself"—and Settimio started up his own Vespa—"prepare yourself to become a king."

King? King! Had he heard Settimio correctly? He wanted to shout, Wait! Or, What! But the Vespa took off beneath him, over the bridge and onto the Lungotevere, leaving all courage and most of his breath behind. King? Organ tuner, yes. Possible father, possibly. But King? Hadn't he told this man, this Settimio that he only had a few minutes to spare? What had induced him to take Settimio's hand, to follow these men and leave Louiza when she was on the verge of giving birth? What had persuaded him to climb onto the Driver's Vespa? What did Malory know of Vespas, how to stop a Vespa, how to jump off a Vespa? What did Malory know of the streets of Rome? What could Malory know about the one-way systems of the future that, in any case, would do little to assuage the panic of any hapless passenger on the back of a *motorino* speeding down the narrow cobblestones of the Lungaretta, veering off to the right just before the peeling, neglected mosaics of Santa Maria in Trastevere, past the *pasticcerie* of the Via del Moro and the smells of lunches just finished and the sounds of dishes drying almost drowned out by the unmuffled hum and denatured smell of the engine? How could Malory know that Settimio, riding ahead of them on an identical machine, was no lunatic but merely serving the function of regal processions in centuries past, going back to the times of Renaissance princes, medieval warlords, Roman emperors, and consuls before them, who first built the streets leading from the Tevere to higher ground, who haggled and bartered and even killed in order to out-dazzle their neighbors with the splendor of the processions that brought them from this place to that. How was Malory to know that Settimio and the Driver and their matched Vespas were the economical evolution of the equine consorts of yore? Indeed, at the speed of the Vespas, which slalomed past the mothers with prams and grandmothers with canes and dodged the traffic spewing from the tunnel beneath the Gianicolo like stuntmen, at such a speed, how was Malory to identify this breakneck, hair-raising, flesh-crawling dash as anything other than the final lap of the race of his own life? How could he have possibly thought that these men, these Italians who had introduced themselves into Malory's universe only a few minutes before and then motorinoed him off in the opposite direction from where he wanted to be, were leading him to the modest bank account that he hoped might finance his new beginnings? He had whispered prayers over the past few months, usually upon waking and again at that hopeful moment of dusk when just one more ray of sunshine might bring Louiza's bright face into his vision before darkness fell—prayers that his quest for his Louiza might quickly be done so that he might embark on the project of the rest of unconscious mankind: life.

Life. Malory wanted life, a life, with the love of a real woman. He had never suspected it would require a gruesome death at the intersection of a speeding Vespa and a piece of Renaissance masonry.

Malory saw nothing of St. Peter's Dome, as the Driver turned the Vespa into the great piazza, nothing of the massive saints waving their stony salutes from atop Bernini's arcade, nothing of the long avenue of the Via della Conciliazione stretching down to his left. But he knew enough to pray. Malory prayed as they sped past the harlequinade of the Swiss Guard, through the portcullised arch of the Papal Palace. Malory prayed with the last breath in the bellows of his lungs, merely to live. And with that prayer, the Vespa came to a halt at a small wooden door where, already parked and groomed, Settimio stood, ready to escort him inside the Vatican.

"Bloody hell!" said Malory, who had been known to swear on very few occasions.

"*Mio Principe*," said Settimio, steadying Malory's elbow as he unwrapped his thighs from the clammy vinyl of the Vespa. The Driver opened the jump box of the motorino and withdrew a small whisk broom and gave Malory a quick brush to remove the most obvious layer of dust. "I'm afraid we haven't time for much more," Settimio added. "But you shouldn't worry, my lord. They don't stand on ceremony."

"Who don't?" was the question Malory thought to ask, but only much later. Two Swiss Guards presented themselves to Malory with the same hand to the heart and bend to the knee with which Settimio and the Driver had greeted him.

"No need for concern," Settimio said. "I shall accompany as far as possible."

"Where?" Malory asked. But as his escort moved forward and Malory walked with Settimio half a step back and to the starboard side, Malory's wit and geography guessed he was somewhere between St. Peter's and the museums in the few acres of the Vatican City. The corridors down which he trotted within his peculiar committee were lined with plaques and bas-reliefs of crossed-keys and pontifical hats and the kind of adornments that he reckoned stood in for the family snaps and framed posters of Hay Wains in the households of normal families.

Another rank of the Swiss Guards appeared at the base of a corniced staircase of foot-polished marble, silent, still, eyes forward, except for a single Alpine novice who seemed as curious about Malory as Malory was about the procession and its destination.

"Settimio?" Malory asked.

"You look splendid, *mio Principe.*" Settimio's answer—although not to any questions at the top of Malory's mind—cauterized Malory's anxiety. He would be fine. Louiza would be fine. Settimio—Malory turned and smiled at Settimio. Settimio he could trust. This must be one of the governmental buildings, he thought. What had Antonella said about the Vatican bank? Perhaps this is Immigration and I'm entitled to a Vatican passport as part of my inheritance, which would be cool, but why the rush? And maybe, Malory thought, part of my grandmother's will provides for servants, and these men, Settimio and this Driver, are my employees. And yet, in that case, shouldn't I be the one giving them orders, not vice versa? Shouldn't I be the one telling them to take me back to Louiza, perhaps with a Swiss Guard or two to help me question the red-haired American obstetrician, or whoever he was?

At the top of the staircase, the Guard turned right and then left with the Windsor-knotted Settimio and corduroyed Malory in their midst. They marched through a chamber of battle scenes before turning left past burning Troy and a host of other Raphaels. Malory stared up at The School of Athens. There were Aristotle and Plato out for a stroll, there was hemlock-swilling Socrates lying on the stairs and next to him a bewigged friend—could that be Newton? Isaac Newton popping up again today, this time in a Raphael painted over a hundred years before Newton's birth? A second look was impossible. The phalanx moved forward into another corridor and then stopped. A door opened. The Swiss Guard stood aside.

"*In bocca al lupo,*" Settimio said, patting Malory—with the proper fraction of respect—on the shoulders and propelling him across a threshold into the beginning of an explanation.

There were a hundred of them, men. And Malory knew immediately—it was as impossible not to know as it was impossible to believe —from their scarlet capes and scarlet caps and generally ancient composures, that they were cardinals, well before he looked up at the shadowy figures on the ceiling and realized he was in the Sistine Chapel. There was a moment of awe approaching tranquility—a moment, looking back, that Malory wished he could have prolonged into a minute, an hour, a lifetime of gawking. There was a moment when the splendor of the caps and capes and frescoes and marble made him feel immaculately invisible, shielded and safe in a bottomless curiosity, alone with his corduroy jacket and Kit Bag in the Sistine Chapel without busloads of tourists but with a hundred-odd scarlet-beanied tour guides, each of whom Malory was sure had his own peculiar but culturally stimulating Unified Field Theory, his own cardinal interpretation of the origins of the universe. Instead, Malory felt immediately and literally drenched in a deluge of biblical embarrassment. It was worse than his first day of school. It was worse than his first mass, his first organ concert, and far worse than his first, very recent lovemaking. It wasn't that Malory was embarrassed by his lack of familiarity with the frescoes that lined the walls—the story of Moses on one side, the story of Jesus on the other, and the Last Judgment behind him. He had been brought up believing that Moses and Jonah, whose huge portrait peered down on him from the ceiling, were merely Jesus in disguise—that the Savior was waiting until just the right moment to reveal himself. This, after all, was the bread and butter of the sermons he had sat through for decades as he waited to play the organ. No, the embarrassment was at the cardinals. These are cardinals, Malory thought. These are *the* cardinals. The College of Cardinals, all the cardinals of the world. And they are all looking at me, sweaty and unbathed, smelling of Dominicans and Louiza and hospital, as if they'd been waiting for me, as if they are waiting for me, waiting for me to do something.

And then the thought entered his head, he didn't know how, although in the embarrassment of the moment he might have readily voted for divine intervention—the organ! The organ! The organ, of course! Fra Mario had said—what was it?—*Forse oggi. Forse oggi*, perhaps today. Today the cardinals were going to make the decision, perhaps they had already done so. Today they were going to choose the next pope, and they couldn't do so—how could they?—without a freshly-tuned organ on which to proclaim their Hosannas and Alleluias. There is a certain urgency, Settimio had said. Little wonder. Forget this business of his grandmother's inheritance. He was who he was, what he always had been—if not the best, well then, a damned-fine organ tuner. Word had got round, through Fra Mario and Settimio, that he was in town. The Vatican network moved in strange ways, and presto here he was and, lucky for them, he had his Universal Organ Tuner in his pocket, fresh from its triumphal rescue of Tibor. He looked up—the Last Judgment loomed before him. And on the ceiling above, the finger of God touched the finger of Adam just as he had touched that tiny finger through the translucent belly of Louiza an hour before. Malory pulled his Kit Bag snug around his shoulder and turned to look for the organ.

At the time, he had no idea what that turn meant. He had no idea that the turn, far from being innocent, was the decisive moment in the *oggi* that Fra Mario had mentioned only a few hours earlier. It was only later that Malory discovered that a key part of his inheritance, along with Settimio and the Driver and the Chapbook with Newton's declaration of his discovery of the One True Rule, was the rank of cardinal. It was only later that Malory discovered that the honor came with neither church nor notoriety, but with the right to wear the same scarlet cap and cape, although since the title was shrouded in secrecy, Malory was only allowed to wear them in the privacy of his own room and not even in the presence of Settimio or the Driver.

Much more importantly, Malory had inherited the unique power to cast the deciding vote in a deadlocked conclave. After seven ballots, the papal conclave was still unable to decide on a successor to poor John Paul I. They had called Settimio. Settimio had brought Malory. And Malory's turn, the turn of the unknowing, untutored Secret Cardinal towards what was, in fact, a perfectly tuned organ, would in the future be known as The Turn and become enshrined in legend and archive of Vatican history. As he turned, Malory found himself looking into the sympathetic face of the Polish cardinal, who had the great good fortune to be standing between Malory and the organ. Malory's turn, his pivot, his awkward pirouette, his random ecclesiastical spin-the-bottle, chose this Polish Cardinal Wojtyla as the new Bishop of Rome, the soon-to-be John Paul II, as neatly as Louiza had found the Pip.

Such knowledge only came to Malory gradually. His official work done, Malory's innocent walk to the organ was gently deflected towards a door in the back of the chapel. Another set of arms, these ones clad in the somber shade of deepest black of the Vatican functionaries, now put in motion the machinery designed to trumpet the announcement of the new pope to the visible world. They led Malory down a marble passageway and around to an ancient lift. Malory stepped forward into the cage and once again turned to find the chosen cardinal, the smiling Pole. The rest of the old men, the cardinals, stayed behind, or, as Malory was to discover later, went directly to the balcony of the basilica overlooking the piazza to await their new pastor.

The Pole smiled. Malory smiled back but looked over his shoulder, searching for Settimio. Alone, the two men descended through a hole in the floor that gradually became the hole in a cupola of another chapel. The elevator stopped. Another black-clad functionary opened the gate. Together, still smiling, Malory and the Pole walked from the elevator. He knew where he was, he recognized this statue, this Michelangelo, knew this mother, this boy, this dead child cradled in his mother's arms. He stood for a moment, stripped hopeless with love and memory. The memory of Louiza, the warmth of her body against his as he dashed from basilica to hospital, mixed with a longing for another lap. He imagined a return to a lap and a mother that he must, once upon a time, have known, a beginning when there was no difference between the familiar and the unfamiliar, the mundane and the miraculous. Malory's longing for this original enlapment pierced him so thoroughly that he could have wished for death if death were the requirement for such a peace.

But the functionaries had other plans for him. Two of them brought a cape, a green cape in a color that reminded Malory of that childhood garden in the South of France. Two others reached to remove his corduroy jacket and his Kit Bag. But Malory was not going to be parted from the Pip again and tugged back. It was the struggle of a second. But in that struggle, it wasn't the Pip, but the book, the Newton Chapbook, the strange diary that Malory had received from his grandmother on that March afternoon in the second pew of St. George's Church, Whistler Abbey, that flew from the Kit Bag into the hands of the smiling Pole.

Gently, the Pole examined the book. Malory wondered what the Pole made of what he read—wondered whether he read Italian? Whether he read English? Did he know enough maths, enough physics, did he know enough history and even religion to realize the importance of Newton's declaration:

I have found the One True Rule that guides Mathematics, the One True Rule that guides Science, that guides the Universe. I have found the One True Rule. But the Rule is too weighty to fit on one page of this Chapbook.

Gently the Pole led Malory, in green cape and hiking boots, from the *Pietà* into the center of the nave of the basilica. And gently the Pole placed one of Malory's palms upon the Newton Chapbook and raised the other.

"I'm afraid," Malory whispered to the Pole.

"I too," the Cardinal said. "I am also afraid."

"I'm afraid," Malory continued. "I don't know what I'm supposed to do." The Cardinal smiled. Malory felt a moment of calm. "I hope that if I make a mistake, you will correct me."

The Polish Cardinal thought for a moment. And then, with a gentle touch on the shoulder, he pressed Malory down onto his knees, onto a purple stone set into the floor of the basilica, into the center of a perfect circle of porphyry.

It was only later that Malory discovered that the perfect circle of porphyry just inside the entrance to St. Peter's was the very stone on which, nearly twelve hundred years before, his great-great ancestor, Charlemagne, had knelt before Pope Leo III. It was only later that Malory learned all the various titles that his inheritance, leading from his grandmother back to Charlemagne, and through Charlemagne's son-in-law back to King David himself, had brought upon him, including Holy Roman Emperor, King of the Jews, and King of Septimania. For now, as he listened to the Polish Cardinal, the man whom he, by his innocent Turn, had crowned Pope John Paul II, as he repeated oaths in several unintelligible languages, one hand on the Chapbook and the other in the air, Malory merely felt that this extraordinary day must, in some way, be a prelude to a new life, with Louiza and her—could it really be their?—baby. Somewhere, he hoped, if not in the vastness of St. Peter's or the howl of the crowd waiting in the piazza, his mother, his grandmother, and Sir Isaac were watching him.

"Mazel tov," the Polish Cardinal said, raising Malory up and kissing him on both cheeks.

"Excuse me?" Malory said.

"Ah, my poor boy," the Pole sighed. "I know very little. But you know even less."

And thirty minutes later, when Malory arrived at the Ospedale Fatebenefratelli and, despite the assistance of Settimio and the Driver, could find no trace of Louiza, *La Principessa*, Tibor, or the red-haired American, Malory—the newly crowned king of kingdoms he never knew existed—knew even less than that.

PART TWO

As many as the fireflies a peasant has seen

(Resting on a hill that time of year when he
Who lights the world least hides his face from us,
And at the hour when the fly gives way

To the mosquito) all down the valley's face,
Where perhaps he gathers grapes and tills the ground:
With flames that numerous was Hell's eighth circle

Glittering.

The Inferno, Canto XXVI

2/0

What is the first thing one wishes to see upon waking and the last before closing one's eyes?

My love? My loved one?

The simple is the sign of the nearer truth.

Light. We wish to see the light. In the beginning, if we are believers, there was light. Before the end, even if we believe not, there is light as well.

In the early morning, when the light hurdles the Tevere and joins me in my solitary bed, and in that hour before dusk when I stand alone in the garden, hidden from the nuns of the Aventino, and the sun is at nearest sympathy with the horizon, I have often had cause to ponder on the nature of light. There is no element as quick and powerful. Yet no element as easy to deflect. A mirror crazed with age, a summer lagoon dusty with neglect, an eyeball moistened with solitude, or a boot polished with spit will shift the direction of the swiftest ray of light without breaking a sweat.

I was bending light with a simple glass prism when Isaac descended to breakfast on the fifth morning of our journey. We had stopped in Troyes for the night in an inn attached to the Broce-aux-Juifs where I had a few friendly connections and knew the meat would not upset Isaac's Lincolnshire digestion. I had picked up the toy in Cambridge before the Plague—a piece of glass carved into two triangles connected by three narrow rectangles. As I waited for Isaac, the morning brightening the steam from my coffee, I twisted the prism in the light from the doorway and watched the colors form, the seven colors of the spectrum, on the wall above the innkeeper's bar.

"*Richard Of York Gave Battle In Vain!*" I looked up. Isaac was beaming on the stair, as happy as I'd seen him since we'd quit his mother's garden.

"Good morning!" I said, putting the prism down on the table and rising to greet him.

"No, no," he said and jumped from the stair to the table. "Once more!" And he picked up the prism and caught the morning in a practiced motion. Again the light divided and cast its rainbow upon the wall. "*Richard Of York Gave Battle In Vain!*" he crowed again.

I looked perplexed, as sometimes I do when these English schoolboys play history games with me.

"It's how one remembers the trick of the prism—the seven colors that it paints the light," Isaac laughed, happy to have an audience that needed a lecture. "Red, Orange, Yellow, Green, Blue, Indigo, Violet . . . *Richard Of York Gave Battle* . . ."

"But, Isaac," I interrupted gently.

"*R* for Richard and Red, *O* for *Of* and Orange . . ."

"I understand," I said. "But surely you don't believe that this clear piece of glass gives color to the light."

"Of course it does," Isaac said, twisting the prism again. "Look! *Richard Of York* . . ."

It was then that I removed a second prism from its hiding place in my jacket pocket. Intercepting the seven-colored band from Isaac's prism, my new prism captured the color and projected the light into a single, clear, colorless beam on the innkeeper's wall.

Of the many virtues that attracted me to the multi-hued Isaac Newton, my favorite is his desire to know the truth. In an instant, all thoughts of Richard, Duke of York, vanished. Isaac sat at the table, the first prism in his left hand. He took my wrist gently between his fingers and moved my hand closer to his and then farther away. He laid the prisms down on the table while he reached for the eternal chapbook in his own jacket pocket and a stub of pencil and drew a rough sketch. Coffee and breakfast gave way to experiment and measurement.

I knew the truth before Isaac descended. Still, I was happy to watch him in the flight of discovery and description, calculating angles, drawing rays, holding my wrist oblivious to the rising temperature of my blood, the *beating velocity of my heart. "The prism does not color the light," Isaac declared finally with the light-giving pride of conquest in his eyes. "The light is made up of colors!" Meanwhile, I had made a deflection of my own.*

We would no longer head south to the Septimania of the past, the kingdom that the shochet of Narbonne had long since abandoned. I needed more than light. I needed life. Septimania needed life. I would take Isaac to the city where my family, for over eight hundred years, has ruled its quiet empire from a villa hidden from the world beneath the crest of the Aventino. The Aventino Hill of Rome, with its view of the River Tiber and St. Peter's Basilica—I would take Isaac to the Villa Septimania. All roads, all colors lead to Rome. And Isaac had seen the light.

2/1

W ITH SETTIMIO ACTING AS GUIDE AND TRANSLATOR, MALORY searched all the rooms in the prow of the hospital, where he had last seen Louiza and Tibor's wife. From ward to ward and office to office, he asked about a young English woman named Louiza, a young Rumanian woman, her tall, long-haired husband, a red-bearded American obstetrician. By 10 p.m. it was clear that the Ospedale Fatebenefratelli had no more record of Louiza than the Maths Faculty at Cambridge University.

"The police," Malory said. "Let's go ask them."

"Which ones, *mio Principe*?" Settimio answered. "The *polizia,* the *carabinieri,* the *vigili?*"

"Whoever can find Louiza, of course!"

"The *carabinieri* are in charge of missing persons and they have a few dogs. But you are not even convinced that Signorina Louiza is missing."

"Then the British Embassy."

"Which is closed for the night and undoubtedly will be very busy congratulating the new pope in the morning."

Malory sat very slowly down on a bench in the courtyard of the hospital. The lights had gone out, the televisions were cold. "*Mio Principe.*" Settimio stood in front of Malory. "There are many things you will learn about Rome in the coming years. And many things about your new kingdom."

"I've lost her again." Malory's porphyry solidity evaporated. "My new kingdom is nothing."

"Your new kingdom is Septimania," Settimio said with the firmness that had first led Malory out of the hospital. "You have not begun to know her."

"Her?"

"Your new home. If you will allow us, we will take you to the villa, to your new home."

"We can't," Malory began. "I won't," he stood, "leave without Louiza and the baby." Even standing, Malory felt as small a child as at any time in his life.

"There is one more person who might interest you here," Settimio said. "She will be awake, even at this hour. And if there is a baby, if your child was delivered, she is the only woman who could have delivered it." Settimio turned and crossed the courtyard back towards the entrance.

Malory sat for a moment.

If there is a baby.

She is the only woman.

Malory followed Settimio. He had little choice.

The little man in the Windsor knot and the midnight blue coat receded along the long pier of Fatebenefratelli in waves of sulfur shadow from lamppost to lamppost. Malory followed across the piazza, past a gothic shrine that rose like a miniature Albert Memorial in the middle of the island. An ancient Roman slept rough on the cobblestones, a significant hound beside him, jowls on paws, neither aware of the celebration at the Vatican, neither interested in Malory's search. Settimio didn't look back, but headed for a squat little church at the back end of the island. No more priests, Malory pleaded, no more friars, no more popes. But Settimio was too far off to hear.

Instead of walking straight into the church, Settimio turned to the left along the façade, to a corner where a long, low building lay like a breakwater against one rush of the divided Tevere. Malory entered. The stairwell was ill-lit, but he followed the cue of Settimio's steps, neat and methodical despite the late hour and Settimio's advanced age. Along the walls of the stairwell, yellowed frames held photographs from early in the century: colorless, long-bearded men, women tented in black—travelers in an antique land, posed in front of the repositioned columns and lintels of the Forum. In the shadows of the stairwell, Malory couldn't make out the exact descriptions, typed on index cards. But at the top of each of the frames a few words stood

out. Above, the words were in Hebrew. Below, the presumed translation—OSPEDALE ISRAELITE. Not a hospital for Israelites, or Israelis for
that matter, Malory thought as he climbed, but a Jewish hospital.
Although why Settimio should lead him there at midnight in his search
for Louiza was beyond his limited linguistic powers.

At the top of the stairwell, a pair of windowed doors was still
swinging. Malory followed into a long hall, a refectory perhaps, with
a high ceiling and a cool floor speckled with marble meteorites, empty
except for a row of polished benches that lined the walls—one set of
windows facing into the center of the island, the piazza with the
miniature Albert Memorial, the other lit by the sulfur lamps across
the river by the synagogue. A Jewish hospital without any patients.
Without any inhabitants, Malory thought.

"Settimio!" Malory heard a low alto, the rustle of movement
behind him. "You've come to visit. And you've brought company."
He turned and saw a woman sitting at the end of the wooden bench,
a nun perhaps. Yet there was nothing in her appearance, speckled by
the shadows from the lamppost through the window, to assure him
that the voice had come from her. No motion from the mouth. And
in the vastness of the hall, sound came from everywhere.

"Permit me to present—" Settimio began. He walked over to the
nun and bent to kiss her cheeks.

"*Tesoro*," the old nun murmured, "you forget. I know the boy."

"*Il Principe*," Settimio bent by her ear in gentle correction.

"Ah, she has finally died," the woman said. All was black and
yellow and shadow, but Malory saw the delicate creases of her eyelids
flutter like the leaves of the poplars behind the Wren Library. "I never
liked your grandmother." The old woman raised her chin towards
Malory. "If it had not been for Settimio here, she would have denied
me the privilege of delivering you, and you would have been born in
some distant swamp in France."

"Suor Miriam believes all of France is a swamp," Settimio said,
with no effort at discretion.

"It was one thing for your grandmother to fight against the laws
of heredity," Suor Miriam continued. "She was born a fighter."

"Laws of heredity?"

"I have not yet informed the *Principe* of the special nature of his inheritance," Settimio said to Suor Miriam with an apologetic turn at the corner of his mouth. "You see, *mio Principe,* while a woman like your grandmother may take up the title, only a man may inherit the kingdom."

But Malory was more struck by his calculations.

"Did you deliver my grandmother too?"

"*Figurati!*" Suor Miriam laughed, and her eyelids fluttered again, but in a way that Malory could only think had a bit of the coquette in them. "I was a girl then, a novice, barely fourteen, twelve even. But I assisted. I was there. I saw the sorrow of the *Principessa,* I heard the disappointment of the *Principe* through closed doors—he was nearly seventy years old, after all, and it was his final opportunity to produce a *maschio,* an heir. I heard the first screams of your grandmother, her refusal to be decorous in the face of the disaster that was her birth.

"I was too young to have an opinion. Perhaps I am still too young." Her eyelids fluttered again but didn't wait for a gallant response from Malory. "Later, I was sympathetic. My friend Settimio agrees with me, I know. The church, and perhaps your kingdom, would benefit from the participation of women in more than childbirth." Of the two of them, the nun seemed clearly older—ten, perhaps twenty years. In another life, or perhaps in this one for all Malory knew, their familiarity might have been connubial. Perhaps the nun was all the family Settimio had. Perhaps her enforced celibacy provided suitable companionship for Settimio. Malory had known him, after all, for less than three hours and had no idea whether there was a Signora Settimio, half a dozen Settimio sons, and a brace of junior Settimini.

"Come, Hercule," the old nun said, and patted the darkened slice of bench next to her. "Sit. You didn't come to hear me talk of your grandmother or the swamps of France. Or the birth of you or your mother, for that matter. Tell me why you have come to see me when there are more important people, I imagine, waiting to meet you."

Malory sat. He spoke. He told Suor Miriam everything—the first discovery of Louiza, the meeting with his grandmother, Old

Mrs. Emery. The funeral, the instruction to go to Rome, the loss of his fellowship, and everything that had happened in the past twenty-four hours, from the moment he'd arrived in Rome to the fantastical few hours in the Vatican. But most of all, he spoke about the redis-covery of Louiza in the second pew of Santa Maria sopra Minerva, the dash to Fatebenefratelli, Tibor's gray-haired and very pregnant *Principessa*, the kind nurse, and the red-bearded American obstetri-cian. Malory spoke, but he watched the eyelids of Suor Miriam for any sign that might indicate intimate knowledge that would unite him with Louiza. When he'd finished speaking, she sat in silence, her eyelids motionless.

"Suor Miriam," Malory murmured, wondering if she had fallen asleep. "Did you hear me?"

Again silence. Malory stood. He looked out at the mini Albert Memorial. He turned to the other set of windows and the synagogue beyond. Enough. Enough of the little man in the long coat, the blind and perhaps deaf nun, whether or not she was the midwife who had delivered him. It was time to go to the police, the *carabinieri*, to camp out in front of the British Embassy and shine a little rational English light on the disappearance. He was not about to let Louiza become a second Aldo Moro. He walked back across the speckled marble con-fusion to the foyer doors and stairwell.

"Come back at four tomorrow afternoon." Suor Miriam's voice stopped him at the door.

"Excuse me?" Malory said, turning. "Why should I come back tomorrow afternoon? What do you know? And if you know some-thing, why can't you tell me now?"

"Poor boy." Malory could feel Suor Miriam's eyelids fluttering, even at ten paces. "I know nothing. Suor Anna, the young nun who was with you and your Louiza and the Rumanian and his wife, she will return to the hospital at four tomorrow afternoon to begin her shift at four-thirty. She comes to me first for my blessing. She may know something. Come here and we will ask her what happened. Together."

"But if you know Suor Anna," Malory walked back, barely con-trolling his own alto register, "why can't we go see her now? Time . . ."

" . . . is immaterial." Malory had forgotten about Settimio. This was the Settimio of authority. Although in the state Malory was in, authority was suspect.

"What do you mean immaterial? The longer we wait, the farther away she might be."

"Come home, *mio Principe*," Settimio said, in a more gentle register.

"Home?"

"I brought you here to meet Suor Miriam. I thought it would give you some comfort to talk for a moment with the woman who first touched your head, who first dislodged your shoulders from captivity and brought you into the air of Rome. But the visit has only added to your agitation."

"Do not be so hard on the poor boy," Suor Miriam murmured. "This is a place that has seen great drama. It concentrates anxiety."

"Indeed," Settimio said. "I know."

"How do you know?" Malory found himself standing over Settimio as other bullies at school had stood over him. He felt ashamed, but he felt too far gone to retreat.

"This room," Suor Miriam said, "this ward has a history. I myself have been here for only a fraction. Most recently, it has been a hospital for the Jewish people—for many years, many decades. This is a place of injury, of recovery."

Malory looked around. There were none of the overtly Jewish symbols he had seen in the stairwell. But there was something precarious about the two rows of windows, as if crossfire were the normal state of affairs.

"Settimio is too modest to admit to the role he once played here," Suor Miriam continued. "The Germans left the Ospedale Israelite alone for much of the war. Why? Who knows, there is rarely an answer. But when the Gestapo finally came to the hospital in 1943 to gather up the patients and send them north along with the rest of the Jews of Rome, Settimio received the information first—don't ask me how. He ran down from the Villa to the hospital, to this very ward, just minutes before the Germans arrived. We had a young doctor at the time—very attractive, the kind of Italian the Germans liked:

thick-browed, clean, vegetarian. He spoke to the Germans while Settimio hid behind the nurse's cabinet and whispered his lines to him, like that Frenchman with the long nose."

"Cyrano de Bergerac?" Malory was in awe of the woman's voice and answered in as automatic deference as in any oral exam.

"'You are welcome to take the patients,' the doctor said, repeating Settimio's whispers. 'But they are all suffering from Syndrome K.'

"'Syndrome K?' the officer said.

"'Highly contagious,' the doctor explained. 'Inevitably fatal.' I was standing right there where you are now. Forty-seven Jews Settimio saved. That day."

Malory turned to Settimio, unmoving in his Windsor knot and his midnight blue coat, but changed nonetheless. Strange, Malory thought. Settimio seemed younger, at least not as old as Old Mrs. Emery or the nun sitting on the polished bench.

"Go home with Settimio, my poor boy. Come back and see me tomorrow at four in the afternoon. Tonight you will have to sleep with questions." Suor Miriam reached up with her hands. Understanding the motion, Malory bent forward and let Suor Miriam bless his forehead with her lips, let her kiss take with it the last grains of his energy. The Driver was waiting below with both Vespas. Malory descended into the seat behind him, felt the October night warm on his face as they drove off the island, Fatebenefratelli at their backs, and rose up a winding alley that smelled of night and pine. A gate opened, and the Driver entered, it seemed to Malory, directly into the side of a hill. They dismounted. There were more stairs. A door opened, a light. There was a kitchen, bread-warm. Settimio removed his coat, Malory his corduroy jacket. There was a bed, there were pajamas, a glass of water. Malory lay down in a country beyond exhaustion but with enough strength for a final question.

"Settimio," Malory said, pulling himself up against the pillows to a seated position, his legs following like serpents from a foreign zoo.

"*Sì, mio Principe?*"

"Where am I?"

"You are home."

"Home?"

"Many years ago," Settimio sat in the shadows beyond the lamplight and began to speak, "a Jewish butcher named Yehoshua lived in the town of Narbonne along the coast of the Mediterranean Sea." He spoke with a gentle bass, like the pedals of the great organ of that same Narbonne where Malory had first learned to play, singing him back to the last time he had been told a story at bedtime. Settimio's voice encircled him as securely as the mattress below and the duvet above, floating around Malory's ears at a gothic distance between waking and dream. Later, when Malory opened his eyes in the dark and the silence, he was not only unsure whether he was awake or asleep but even where he was and in which century. For more than a moment, he imagined he was back in the Dominican cell of Galileo Galilei where, only twenty-four hours before, the hempen bed cords had begun to engrave a fresh Roman dissertation into his skull. In the darkness of the morning, Malory reached with his right hand into the air beside his bed and located a cord and a switch.

"Louiza?" he called out.

There was light.

There was more.

Above him a ceiling of a blue richer than the sky of Santa Maria sopra Minerva, as pure and saturated with color as any he had seen through any of the dozens of Newtonian prisms he'd examined over the years. It was a color unknown to the British sky, but an inseparable part of the wood outside Narbonne, where he had lain for hours on his back on a mattress of bluebells, paralyzed by nature.

Malory pushed himself up on his elbows. Around the walls, Malory's own image gazed back at him. In a dozen or so portraits set into the hazelnut panels of the room, Malory's own face—young and old, as a man, as a woman, in costumes as ornate and archaic as any he had seen in the halls and chapels of Cambridge—looked back at him, refracted in mirrors of time and manner. In curling wigs or in flat caps, with beards or rouged cheeks, every portrait had an ear or a chin or a cheek that Malory felt was essentially his own. The perplexed look in all of their eyes as they looked at him lying in the bed, made him realize that his own appearance of general bewilderment had more to do with genes and less with his history of abandonment. The painting directly across from him—the most recent an Edwardian-looking gentleman, perhaps his great-grandfather, the last prince of Septimania before himself—couldn't hide his own confusion behind a starched collar and whiskers. Had all those faces in all the portraits in the bedroom wondered at one time the same thing he was wondering—what am I doing here?

In answer, there was a knock on the door.

"*Mio Principe?*" A knock again. "I saw your light. Do you require something?"

"Ah—" Malory said. Which meant nothing, but was interpreted as an invitation.

Settimio was dressed in dark trousers, a long white shirt, clipped at the cuff by medallions that caught the light from Malory's bedside lamp and shone a touch of comprehension into his awakening brain. Above the shirt and trousers, Settimio wore a smock, long and leathery like the apron of a butcher. It must be morning, Malory thought, or perhaps later.

"Did you sleep well, *Principe?*"

"Were you reading to me all night, Settimio?" Was there really a story about a Jewish butcher?

"Reading?"

"Telling me a story?"

"Until you fell asleep."

"Which was?"

"Almost the moment you lay back against the pillow. Yesterday was a long day. One for which your grandmother did little to prepare you."

"She knew?" Malory pulled his shoulders a little higher above the pillow.

"Your grandmother knew many things. I communicated with her in recent years exclusively by telephone. But she was always a deeply curious person."

"Hunh," Malory said, searching the wall for any portrait that might resemble Old Mrs. Emery. "Not curious enough to introduce herself to me. Until the end. Or almost."

"Curiosity, *mio Principe,* is often best served by discretion."

"Observation at a distance?"

Settimio smiled. Again Malory felt the comfort of a perfect mark on an exam, applause at the end of a concert. With the relaxation that accompanies pleasure came the conviction that he needed the toilet. And that today he would find Louiza. Again. With the same delicate hints and gestures he had used the night before, Settimio guided Malory out of the bedroom and up two short steps to a bathroom no smaller than the bedroom Malory had just left. If Malory had bothered to look up, he would have seen his own reflection multiplied—if not as many times then more accurately than in the portraits of the bedroom. But while one hemisphere of his brain was trying to understand where he was, the other was fixed on where he wanted to be. Since the effort so occupied the brain of Malory, the body was left to its own automatic devices. It urinated, it flushed, it bathed, it shampooed and shaved—Settimio not only ran a bath but set out Malory's toiletries, such as they were, in places where the automaton of his body could not fail to use them. In a robe of velvet and midnight blue, Malory returned to the bedroom.

"Settimio?"

"*Principe?*"

"What time is it?" A fresh pair of jeans and a chamois shirt, brand new but clearly in his style, lay on his bed. Had Settimio set them out while he was bathing? And made the bed? "We should get back to the hospital. What is the name?"

"Fatebenefratelli. But you may recall that the nurse you wished to interview expects you in four hours. Might I suggest something to eat?" The jeans, the shirt fit. So did the ankle boots—in a leather and a toe not too ostentatiously Italian. Not even at Cambridge, where the bedders—under the supervision of Rix's integral wife, Emma—swept and tidied away his bedclothes and tea-droppings, had he been shown such an assiduous respect.

"Then we have time to ring the Embassy." Malory stood. The boots were a miracle. "You mentioned the *carabinieri* last night."

"We have two types of scone." Settimio pinched the shoulders of the chamois and flattened the shirt against Malory's chest. "And there is marmalade. Your own oranges. Breakfast. You will find it immensely restorative." Settimio turned and exited the bedroom. Malory looked up at the portraits, each one a perplexed soul. Was there a Settimio hidden on the reverse of each, face pressed against the wall in discretion?

Malory followed Settimio down a paneled corridor, his boots treading without a sound on a wood of acoustical properties Malory could not plumb. The corridor opened into a low-coffered foyer, a gentle hub leading out into other corridors, a handful of paintings and sculptures punctuating the entrances and exits.

"Settimio." Malory stopped. "Who is that?"

"Borromini, della Robbia, Giotto."

But that wasn't the question Malory was asking. With the same sense of recognition he'd had upon waking to the portraits in the bedroom, Malory saw his mother's cheek in the Michelangelo *Santa Marta*, his grandmother's hair in the Canova *Venus* by the western wall. Settimio walked. Marta smiled down on Malory. Breakfast, she seemed to say. Eat now, we will talk later. Malory followed. Malory sat. Settimio poured his tea. Malory pulled the first scone in two, varnished one surface with a layer of orange marmalade and rind, and took a bite. He chewed. Marta was right—the scone helped. He took another bite. He raised his eyes. He stopped chewing.

"Settimio, where are we?" It wasn't the scone, the tea that confounded him. He knew he wasn't back in Cambridge, although the hovering of Settimio bothered him in the way that had often made him embarrass Rix into sitting down once he'd brought Malory's morning tea to his rooms, to talk about Trinity's recent acquisition of machinery for polishing cutlery or cutting grass.

"The dining room," Settimio said with simplicity. But when Malory failed to respond, he continued. "You are sitting in one of seven chairs of Tiberian oak. The table is Jerusalem cedar. Gifts, all of them. I would be happy to go into more detail if you wish."

"That." Malory swallowed and pointed with the half-eaten scone. "Them."

Across from Malory, on the far side of the table of Jerusalem cedar, a marble statue stood raised on its base. Or rather, two life-sized statues stood on a single base. A man and a woman. Two marble people, in the long hair and long coats of the Enlightenment, were clearly enjoying themselves. The sculptor had caught them in the middle of a game, a ball game. One was tossing the ball to the other—although at the distance of a dining room table and a half-eaten scone, Malory couldn't tell properly which one was tossing to which. Malory put down the scone, wiped his mouth, and pushed back his oaken chair—with the aid, naturally, of Settimio. He walked around the table to the statues. The figures were slightly smaller than Malory and greeted him on their pedestal at eye level. Malory recognized the male statue immediately.

"Newton!" he said.

"Newton," Settimio answered. There was no mistaking the face, the coat. This was the student Newton, the Newton of the great discoveries, the Newton of the *annus mirabilis* of 1666, only slightly younger than Malory. "He posed for the sculptor."

"The sculptor?"

"Gian Lorenzo Bernini," Settimio said. "There are several Berninis in the villa and the garden."

"Bernini went to England?" Malory turned to Settimio. "And sculpted Newton? During the Plague?"

"The ledger for the year shows that Isaac Newton posed for the statue here."

"Here? What year?"

"1666, I believe."

"In Rome?"

"In the garden. I would be happy to show you where."

"The garden?" Malory repeated.

"Perhaps after breakfast, I could take you out."

"You mean here? Newton was here? In 1666?" Malory knew the history, the biography, the writings, the readings, the eating habits of Isaac Newton better than anybody, perhaps even better than Newton knew himself. Malory knew that although Newton was acquainted with a number of European scientists, even had a romantic relationship—it was rumored—with a Swiss mathematician, the world met Newton in London. Newton never left England. Newton never traveled to Europe, much less to Rome. The statue must clearly be an act of the imagination.

But was Bernini's imagination—the great Gian Lorenzo Bernini, favorite of princes and popes—interested in Newton? And the second figure—a woman. Was there ever a woman who was interested in Newton? Newton had never shown any inclination towards females, except of course his mother, Hannah, and the niece who kept house for him in his later years. Who was this second figure, this woman? She was slightly smaller, her nose more aquiline, her eyes larger, her chin with a delicate cleft above a polished neck.

Then Malory saw the ball that the two were tossing. Now that he stood and approached the statue, scone in hand, he could see that it was no ball at all, but a polished marble apple. Malory smiled. Of course. Bernini's imagination had been piqued by story. He had sculpted Newton and the woman and the apple as an allegory for one of his more scientifically minded patrons. The gossip must have crossed the continent, the reports that a falling apple had led the young Isaac to his theories on gravity and the attractions of heavenly bodies at a distance. Perhaps the woman was Bernini's Renaissance approximation of Minerva herself, the Goddess of Wisdom, tarted up in the robes of Lucrezia Borgia or Catherine de Medici or some more intimate Bernini conquest.

Then Malory stopped smiling. He had assumed that the ball, the apple, was attached discreetly to another piece of stone or supported by a thin piece of iron or suspended by a filament from the ceiling or the outstretched hands of one or the other of the apple-tossers. But as Malory ran one hand and then another above, below, to the sides and then around the apple, like a Christmas magician at the Cambridge Corn Market, he could find no support, no suspension. The apple was floating in mid-air.

"Settimio."

"*Sí*," Settimio offered with his usual gentle guidance. "It is quite remarkable, is it not? *Molto particolare.*"

Molto particolare was not what Malory was thinking.

"I am hardly an expert," Settimio said. "I understand that you are an aficionado of Signor Newton and the world of physics in general."

"This is, well . . ." Malory hesitated at his own certainty in either observation or judgement. "This is, impossible." Malory walked around the statue, knelt down below the apple, and peered up.

"And yet, *mio Principe*," Settimio suggested, "the stars remain suspended in the heavens. The Moon itself moves in perfect balance around the Earth, which revolves in its turn around the Sun—all without the aid of supporting wires. From what I understand, Newton himself . . ."

"Yes, yes . . ." Malory's mind was moving with impatience. He knew the astronomy and the physics of the motion of planets. He knew that the Sun drew the Earth towards its center and the Earth drew the Sun towards its own, and that the balance between the two depended on the size of each and the distance between the two, not to mention the speed of the Earth's journey in orbit around the Sun. And he knew that the Moon and the Earth danced a similar tango and that even the Sun flirted with the Moon as it did with millions of hotter Milky Way companions on a somewhat larger dance floor. And he knew that everything was guided by the laws of attraction at a distance between bodies. And he knew, as Einstein and generations of physicists and historians and schoolchildren and BBC commentators, not to mention Anna Ford, knew, that Newton searched his whole life for a simple rule by which the motions of the heavenly bodies of the planetary system could be completely calculated, if one knew where they all were at one time.

And Malory also knew that theoretically—a word that was tossed around colloquia and High Tables like custard and claret—*theoretically* every body had its own gravitational pull. Every body was a magnet. Not just the Moon, but chunky asteroids, Apollo 13, Mount Everest, Moby Dick. Even a man the size of, say, Aldo Moro or Settimio—who was thankfully a few hairs shorter than Malory—had his own power of attraction. But it didn't take too many experiments, with a shard of toothpick or even tissue, to realize that the gravitational pull of the Earth would yank any apple—McIntosh or marble—with a far greater force than a statue, even one carved by the great Gian Lorenzo Bernini, who could carve fingers clutching thighs out of marble and make you believe they were clasping flesh.

"May I?" Malory turned to Settimio, pointing at the apple.

"Everything in this villa is yours, my lord," Settimio answered simply. "But there may be consequences."

And sure enough, as Malory reached out to take the apple, he felt a tug from either side, as if the statue of Newton on the left and the statue of the woman on the right were fighting him—as surely as the Earth—for the piece of fruit. It wasn't that the apple was so heavy or magnetic or sticky or golden. The figures tottered as Malory pulled, and Settimio stood by with widened eyes. It felt to Malory that just a little more effort . . . But no, he just could not move it. Malory let go. Newton and the marble woman and Settimio seemed to take a breath of relief and tottered no more, secure once again in a mutual attraction that had withstood more than three hundred years of dustings and earthquakes and other attempts, since Malory could not imagine he was the first to try to steal the apple.

Malory leaned back on the table and then slid down into one of the Tiberian chairs that Settimio quickly shifted beneath him. He took a fresh cup of tea from Settimio and chewed on the rest of his scone, all the while fixing his gaze on the marble apple.

"Settimio," he said. "I'm ready. Please explain—what is this place you call my home?"

"MIO PRINCIPE," SETTIMIO SAID, "YOU ASKED ME THAT QUESTION last night. I told you the story of Yehoshua the butcher who delivered Narbonne to the Franks. Of Charlemagne's promise to give a kingdom to Yehoshua and his Jews. How Charlemagne sent a request to the Caliph of Baghdad to send him a Jewish prince from the line of David and Solomon to take the throne as the first King of Septimania."

"You mean," Malory asked, "that wasn't just a bedtime story?"

"The statue that attracts you so strongly," Settimio answered, "is it just a statue? This dining room—the chairs of Tiberian oak, the table of Jerusalem cedar—is not only the room where I hope to serve you many meals as my ancestors served a long line of kings before you, but also tells its own story of Septimania, bedtime stories stretching back to King Solomon, King David, and beyond."

Malory's nostrils opened to the barely perceptible but gently hallucinatory honey and clover, balsam and loam.

"The vestibule"—Settimio led Malory back to the Canova and the Michelangelo, Giotto, della Robbia, and half a dozen other Renaissance Italians—"is a poetic reminder that your ancestor Charlemagne was crowned Holy Roman Emperor, the way you were yesterday evening by the new pope."

"I was?" Malory asked, less to Settimio than to the *Santa Marta* that reminded him so strongly of his mother and the *Venus* that had his grandmother's hair—and only that, he hoped—and wondered why those two women hadn't given him a little hint while they were alive that they, and therefore he, were descended from Charlemagne and King David.

"Holy Roman Emperor and King of the Jews." Settimio walked out of an opening at the far end of the hub. "But the true genius of Yehoshua and Charlemagne was to befriend the Caliph of Baghdad. The friendship of Haroun al Rashid and the first King of Septimania is said to have been very great, almost biblical in proportion."

"The Caliph of Baghdad?" Malory followed through an arch topped by a blackened medallion of another familial Virgin. Could she be Mexican?

"Welcome to the *majlis, mio Principe.*"

The long summers Malory had spent with his mother in the countryside outside Narbonne had been filled with illustrated books— the complete *Morte d'Arthur* of Thomas Malory with Aubrey Beardsley's rose-crowned drawings; Richard Halliburton's *Book of Wonders* with engravings of the Library of Alexandria, the Colossus at Rhodes, and other long-gone miracles of an ancient human race. And of course he had spent days, weeks, months in the inky harems and casbahs of Richard Burton's *One Thousand and One Nights.* But to enter the *majlis,* as Settimio called it, was to abandon whatever reality his bath and tea and scone had provided him and give himself over to the storybook kingdom that Settimio insisted on calling his home. The walls were tiled, the ceiling honeycombed in a stone crocheted by a sweatshop of *djinns.* In the center of the room, a fountain of seven bronze lions gargled water into a stone basin.

"These carpets," Settimio was saying, "are from the Caspian shores near Tabriz. The tapestries on the far wall were conceived by the magicians of Shiraz on the Persian Gulf and woven with the lost Kashan art of Infinite Knots that makes it impossible for even the restorers from the Vatican Museums to decipher where the rug begins and where the rug ends."

"Cor," Malory said, sitting down because his legs were finding it less easy than his brain to keep up with Settimio's tour.

"The bolsters cushioning the walls are from Yemen, the censers from Kazakhstan. And the throne you are sitting on . . ."

"Sorry!" Malory jumped up.

"It is yours, *mio Principe,* the throne for the King of Septimania. Please . . ." Settimio took Malory's elbow lightly and eased him back down. "This throne was carved by a single axe from a single apple tree in the garden of a palace in Baghdad. It was transported to Rome in person by the Caliph Haroun al Rashid as a belated wedding present for Gan and his bride Aldana, the red-haired daughter of Charlemagne, on the occasion of Charlemagne's coronation as Holy Roman Emperor in the Year 800."

"Not a bedtime story," Malory said, rubbing his left palm along the armrest.

"No," Settimio acknowledged. "Applewood. One tree."

"But," Malory said, standing up, the scientist in him awakening, "how do you know all this? How do you know it's not just another story cooked up by some younger Scheherazade?"

"Books, *mio Principe*. I believe in books." Settimio smiled, perhaps the first time Malory had seen him smile. "I believe you also know something about books. Would you be so good as to follow me?" Settimio walked to the far end of the *majlis*, where the niche in the eastern wall curved back between the Catholic vestibule and the Jewish dining room. Malory approached and looked inside.

"In here?" Malory asked. There was a passageway. A passageway of tile and wood and light—a light that led up, that led down, that led sideways. They walked. They walked some more. The rooms of the villa that Malory had seen felt like they must be mere anterooms, and yet Malory continued to follow Settimio through the passageway up to a wooden door padded in leather.

"The Sanctum Sanctorum," Settimio said. "The true wealth of Septimania. The Holy of Holies."

The padded leather gave only a hint of how discreetly Septimania veiled its treasure. Settimio opened the door and led Malory into the first room. It was equally modest—a low-ceilinged study, bare except for a seven-sided desk lit by a concentric fixture suspended from a coffered ceiling. The seven books on the seven sides of the desk were anything but simple.

"On the left," Settimio said, pointing to one of seven boxes, "is the oldest manuscript in your collection—a Septuagint, dating from the third century BC, the Greek translation by seventy-two rabbis of the forty-six books of the Tanach, what the pope, as you may know, calls the Old Testament. Next to it is a Codex, complete with the New Testament, or at least many of the books of the Codex are still associated with the New Testament. It was commissioned by the Emperor Constantine shortly after his conversion to Christianity and given by Pope Leo III to Charlemagne in the year 800 on the event of his own coronation as Holy Roman Emperor. It is known as the Codex Septimania, although known as such to very few. Next is the first of the five Korans made around 650 AD by the Third Caliph Uthman, son-in-law of the Prophet Mohammed, the oldest Koran in existence, except, according to believers, for the Koran that was made by Mohammed the Prophet and which the Angel Gibreel keeps in his own Sanctum Sanctorum up in Heaven. The following two boxes hold the writings of Buddha in one, the Vedas of the Hindus in the other, including a fragment of the Rigveda that is thought to be over three thousand years old."

A choked gurgle came from Malory's throat. He was pleased that he was even that articulate.

"The sixth box, at your grandmother's request, is the oldest version of Isaac Newton's *Principia Mathematica*."

"Wait a minute," Malory said, suddenly waking up in a world he knew. "I've seen the oldest edition—Newton's own copy of 1686. It's back at Trinity College, in the Wren Library, with Newton's handwritten corrections for the second edition."

"You may find," Settimio said, with a smile of some satisfaction, "that this copy predates the Trinity copy by some twenty years."

"Twenty years!" Malory was shocked and then alarmed and then shocked again, like some ten-year-old junior scientist not quite convinced that sticking a fork into an electrical socket is a bad thing. "The manuscript?" he asked somewhat more stupidly, although just saying the words tickled his neck. "You have the original manuscript? From 1666? In Newton's hand?"

"*You* have the manuscript," Settimio corrected him. "This is all yours, *mio Principe*."

"And the seventh book? The final book?"

"Is a box," Settimio said, and waited for some type of reaction.

"Empty?" Malory asked.

"Open it and see."

"But if I open it . . ." And Malory was back in the organ loft of St. George's, Whistler Abbey, with Schrödinger's cat and Louiza's Pip and his own indecision.

"*Simplex sigillum veri,*" Settimio said.

"*Simplex sigillum veri?*"

"The simple is the sign of the truth."

"Yes, yes," Malory said, surprising himself that he had developed the haphazard annoyance of someone with servants. "I know what it means. I just don't know what it means in this case."

"Neither do I, my lord," Settimio said mournfully. "But my instructions are to reply in such a manner. Should the new King of Septimania ask me whether the box is empty, my instructions are to reply *Simplex sigillum veri.*"

"Your instructions?" Malory asked. "Instructions from whom?"

"From my father," Settimio answered, "who trained me the way his father trained him."

"May I ask," Malory ventured, a little more calmly, "whether previous kings of Septimania have asked the same question?"

"I have direct knowledge," Settimio said, "of only one prior king, your great-grandfather. The father of your mother's mother, the most recent king of Septimania."

"So this is the first time you've had to say *Simplex sigillum veri?*"

"The first time, my lord, in my knowledge, that any of us Settimios have had to say it. Opening boxes used to be somewhat simpler."

Malory sat at the desk. He rubbed the back of his scalp against the back of the tapestried armchair, as he had rubbed it so often against the crumbling foam of the Trinity College Senior Common Room sofa. So many things used to be somewhat simpler. *Write,* they had said back in Cambridge. *The simple is the sign of the truth.* They had known, all the other kings of Septimania had known what was in the box, or at least hadn't doubted that there was something, one thing in the box. But for him, the first Quantum King of Septimania, the first one in love with a quantum woman whose position he might know or direction he might know but never the same at once, nothing was *simplex*. And the Truth?

"You asked me," Settimio interrupted Malory's reverie, "how I came upon the knowledge of the history of Septimania."

"Yes," Malory said, looking up at Settimio and noticing behind him shelves filled with books—leather-bound folios and quartos, papers held in boards and tied with ribbon, boxes annotated in a faded ink.

"I have spent a great deal of time in the Sanctum Sanctorum," Settimio said, "preparing for your arrival."

"Really?" Malory said. "That was very kind of you."

"Twenty-six years to be exact. Ever since it became clear that your mother intended to raise you outside of Rome and in the English language. And even before then," Settimio continued, flicking one electric switch after another, "I spent a great deal of time cataloguing the books and manuscripts and scrolls in the Sanctum Sanctorum. There was not a great deal else to do while we waited for a male heir to take possession." As Settimio flicked the switches, lights turned on in distant passageways. Seven, Malory counted, one leading away from every corner between the seven walls of the room. Lined, as far as he could see from his position at the seven-sided desk, with miles, perhaps, of bookshelves.

"You catalogued all this?" Malory said.

"What might interest you most, *mio Principe*," Settimio said, "as you contemplate whether or not to open the box—although I would not presume to give you advice—is an English translation that was the labor of much of the past twenty-six years. You will forgive my mistakes, I trust."

With that, Settimio laid a book in front of Malory—a good thousand pages of typescript on whose marbled binder was engraved:

THE COMPLETE HISTORY OF THE KINGDOM OF SEPTIMANIA

Malory opened the cover. He began to read.

> *In the first years of the siege of the Franks, when Order still held the innocent hand of Hope, I kept my head down and slaughtered whatever came my way.*

"The letter, *mio Principe,* from the butcher Yehoshua to the King of the Jews in Baghdad requesting that he send a prince to rule the new land of Septimania, as stipulated by the deed of Pepin, the father of Charlemagne. It is the first recorded document to mention the Kingdom of Septimania. I took the liberty of photocopying the original, which I have stored elsewhere, for safekeeping," he added with the hurried apology that reminded Malory of the librarians at the University Library whose expectations of themselves far outreached those of their clients.

"You did all this?" Malory said. "For me?" He turned a few more pages. There were letters between Ambassadors with their ornate courtesies and catalogues of gifts.

> *Seven days from the shores of Palestine. It was nothing.*
> *We lost only three parrots, and that was due to a faulty*
> *latch on the cage of the jackal.*

Then Malory came upon something different. A story recounted by a Jew in Baghdad who served in the unusual capacity of Dream Counselor to the Caliph. Haroun al Rashid had a bad dream and called upon his Dream Counselor for interpretation. One thing led to another, and the Counselor introduced Haroun to his grandson, Gan, the sixteen-year-old son of the King of the Jews of Baghdad. Haroun invited Gan to live with him in his palace. His dream—or rather his Dream Counselor—had convinced Haroun that his own safety rested on the safety of this young boy. He not only took Gan under his wing but showered him with all the comforts and delights that were his daily milk and honey.

"*In the name of Suleiyman, son of David, I swear,*" the young Gan wrote.

> *Paradise.*
> *A fucking paradise is what it was.*
> *Shami apples and Omani peaches for breakfast.*
> *Mutton rubbed with limes from Egypt and stuffed*
> *with myrtle berries and Damascene nenuphars.*
> *Dates from Al Ahsa.*

Soap-cakes and lemon-loaves and Zaynab's combs and
Kazi's tidbits and more wine every evening than my mother ever
placed on our table for all our Purims combined.
And served by . . .
In sixteen years of sitting at the feet of my father and my
grandfather and learning Torah and Talmud and the histories of
the people of Abraham and the stories of philosophers and trav-
elers who had journeyed to places where the birds of the trees and
the insects of the ground and the air and the fish of the deep and
their cousins who crawl on land and the animals of the plains and
the forests and the frozen wastelands of the north and the humans
draped in skins and the ones who run all day naked as on the day
they were cut from their mother's cords—in all the stories of all
the places of the Earth where the light of the Sun and the Moon
colors every living thing in every shade of color, I had never heard
of sirens as gut-squeezingly ripe as the ones who brought me my
breakfast in the morning and my supper in the evening, who drew
my bath and wiped me dry. Yemeni houris and Syrian nymphs,
Babylonian naiads and purple-haired Khazars from the savage
ravines of the Caucasus, with throats like antelopes and navels
that would hold an ounce of olive oil, half a dozen purple-veined
grapes, or a featherweight of frankincense from the caravans of
the Sudan. Solomon sang of a Sheba as black as the tents of Kadar,
with eyes like doves and breasts like gazelles that feed among the
lilies. My Grandpa Benyamin, Master of the Caliph's Dreams,
told me that imagination is the daytime seed from which grows
the Tree of Fantasy. I have never been to Kadar, have never seen
a gazelle among the lilies, have never met the Queen of Sheba. Yet
I am sure that the dreams primed by my dark-nippled companions
were as vivid as any of Solomon or my savior Haroun al Rashid
and need no interpretation.

"This boy," Malory looked up to Settimio, who continued to
stand, "this Gan is the Gan who sailed across the Mediterranean?"

"*Certo, mio Principe.* He married Aldana, the daughter of
Charlemagne, produced an heir, who produced generation upon

generation of heirs to the Kingdom of Septimania, down to you your-self, *mio Principe*."

All from a dream, Malory thought. His own dreams—while devoid of Yemeni houris and Syrian nymphs—had been remarkably vivid during the months since he had first met Louiza, full of medieval damsels and organ music. Reading Gan's entry in the *Complete History*, Malory thought that, with only a single afternoon's passion to show for himself, how much more like a sixteen-year-old princeling he was than King of the Jews and Holy Roman Emperor. Charlemagne alone must have polished off three or four virgins before break-fast, even back in the days before cappuccino. And Haroun—

"Settimio?"

"*Sì, Principe?*"

"The *majlis*. That's quite a room, isn't it?"

"Without overwhelming you, *Principe*, with the size and variety of the rooms within the villas and palaces and office blocks that make up the holdings of Septimania, I would venture to say yes, the *majlis* is a jewel of the eye and the imagination."

"It certainly made me wonder," Malory said. "I mean, I can understand that Septimania, whatever kind of kingdom it is, has ancient connections back to Charlemagne. Rome makes sense, a villa in Rome makes sense."

"I am delighted you approve, *Principe*."

"Okay," Malory said, "perhaps I don't know enough yet to make proper sense of anything. But Haroun al Rashid—what did he have to do with Rome? Was the *majlis* another diplomatic trinket, from one emperor to another?"

"If you will permit me?" Settimio leaned over Malory's shoulder and found a photocopy of a document in the *Complete History*. The translation was dated 10 September 789. "You will find this fragment from Haroun's private journal was written a few weeks after Gan's rhapsody on the Yemeni houris. I trust you will find the translation instructive."

Allahu akbar
Allahu akbar

The entry began:

I have traveled South from Baghdad to the Desert of the Ethiop,
North to the Steppes of the Khazars,
East to the Poppy Fields of the Indies,
Last night the elephant turned blue. The night before, yellow.
This is a voyage of transformation.

Malory remembered a drafty schoolroom and the story of an elephant, of Charlemagne's elephant. It was named Abu-something and was a gift from the East, maybe even from Haroun al Rashid. Reading the memoir of Haroun, Malory also thought of Bernini's elephant in the piazza in front of Santa Maria sopra Minerva. The night he arrived in Rome, hadn't Bernini's elephant also turned blue?

"If I am remembered by history," Malory turned back to Haroun al Rashid's tale in *The Complete History of Septimania*:

it may not be as the wisest of caliphs who ruled in the name of Allah the Almighty. There are many times I have been betrayed by a brother I trusted, cuckolded by a wife I adored, and surprised by an argument or a punch line that others have seen coming from a league or two away. My weakness is known throughout my empire. I am a sucker for a good story. Any beggar, any cripple, any criminal, any heretic can win himself a bowl of soup, a set of crutches, or any of a thousand and one pardons if he can spin a good yarn for Caliph Haroun al Rashid. And if I am remembered, it will be for the box I used to store these stories, as carefully transcribed as the words of Allah in the Holy Koran.

I hope I may be forgiven for seeking a solution in both an affair of state and an affair of the heart by throwing myself, for the first time I hasten to add, into the center of a tale. By climbing into my own box of stories, by stowing away on the ship sent to bring the spark of my soul, the young Jewish boy Gan, to the shores of Septimania.

I expect the reader will understand that, from the beginning, neither Gan, nor his grandfather Benyamin, nor my Vizier Ja'afar had any inkling of my plan. A box, after all, is not such a large thing to smuggle onto a ship, particularly one already laden with dozens of trunks of jewels and carpets and exotic fruits and even an elephant that I fancied might entertain the great King Charles to the west. The evening before the journey, I bade Gan a sad farewell and retired to my rooms with strict instructions not to disturb my melancholy. Gan, his grandfather Benyamin, his mother, sisters, and the entire Jewish community of Baghdad were wrapped in a shroud of dockside mourning. No one expected to see Gan return to Baghdad. Neither did anyone expect to see me return to the port, climb into the chest and restore its lid. Therefore, nobody did.

The first day at sea brought a tranquility I hadn't known since the death of my father marked the beginning of a life ruled, in truth, by the calendar that man uses to stumble after the relentless plan of Allah. By the second day, I felt my mind float free from the second guesses and anxieties of leaving Baghdad so precipitously unprepared for my absence. By the third, I felt the tingle of fantasy—not the sensation that excites me every time I feel myself in the presence of a master storyteller, but the anticipation of the birth of my own imagination. So that by the fourth night, when I climbed out of my chest to walk in the fresh air of the deck, while all the crew, save the pilot, slept below, I was not surprised to discover that the elephant I had ordered aboard the ship as a gift to the Frankish king, my prize elephant, had turned blue.

Nor was I surprised, on subsequent nights, to feel the tears of Gan in the mist of the sea spray, to hear the song of the pilot on the bridge take the voice of the innumerable unintelligible tongues of the dreams of his sailors, or to see the elephant's leathery coat change from blue to green and eventually red, through the seven shades of the spectrum. The tears, the moans, the trumpets of rainbow exuberance from the elephant, not only transported me from the lazy throne of a listener to the uncertain crouch of an actor, but bolstered my conviction that I had acted well. I was not, as I suspected many of Gan's family believed, chopping down the apple tree of Eden. I was preserving that tree, preserving my friend, by transplanting, exporting, marketing, managing, grafting him onto a Frankish trunk that—from what I could tell in the tone of the letters and the weight of the presents—was at least as well-rooted and powerful as mine.

We made port on the morning of our seventh day at sea. The chest in which I lay curled as a baby in the womb was transported with adequate care, from what my senses told me, to the unventilated back stall of a Jewish butcher. I would have waited until nightfall, once again, to open the lid and free myself. But the story itself took control of my destiny.

"I thought I might find you here," Gan said, opening the chest with less surprise in the discovery than mine in being discovered.

"You did?" I looked up at him, an unusual angle.

"It was," Gan said, "one of two possibilities."

At the time, I was too stiff with astonishment and inexperienced confusion to wonder about the other possibility. I had very literally thrown myself onto a ship of which I was not the captain and onto a shore of which I was not the King. I had climbed into the box a mere Caliph and climbed out a human being. Possibility, at that moment, seemed infinite.

"Quick," I said to Gan, "find me some clothes, some disguise." It would have been unwise, of course, to let anyone else in on the secret of the contents of my box. Even the most selfless Charlemagne would have to be a fool not to capitalize on the potential ransom of a captive Caliph. But so many of the storytellers who came searching for my favor had dressed me up in one disguise or another in order to place me more centrally in their tales, that my imagination immediately leapt to this hackneyed recourse. I looked around the stalls, but the racks of tools and pens of fodder were strangely bare of fancy dress.

"My friend and former master," Gan said, steadying me with a hand as I climbed out of the chest. "You are already *clothed. No one in this country has the slightest idea what you look like. The only disguise you need is a good story." With the patience of a true prince, Gan told me what I had, of course, known back in Baghdad. None of the Franks expected to see the Caliph Haroun al Rashid. Therefore, none would see the Caliph Haroun al Rashid.*

"I will introduce you as the Ambassador," Gan said. "Ambassador from the Caliph of Baghdad. As the Ambassador from your own court," Gan proceeded, and I could see the story taking on weight and flesh, "you will be welcomed into every home that welcomes me. We are, in fact, expected for dinner, upstairs in the home of the shochet Yehoshua."

"Twenty-four hours off the boat and already you know the butcher?" I asked, although I was not unhappy at the thought of a meal after a fast of a day and a half.

"Yehoshua is a very wise man," Gan said. "He has read none of the books I have brought with me—he is not, in fact, a reader by inclination nor ability. But he is wiser, perhaps, than both of us put together. You understand the price of maintaining power. He has learned the price of attaining it. And it has worn canyons of a measureless depth. In his face and in his soul."

"And what is that price?"

"Sacrifice."

"The shochet, in the days of the Temple, lived up to his elbows in the business of sacrifice. The unlettered shochet could not read the rules of sacrifice, the ones written by Moses for the use of those of us who crossed over to the Promised Land. But when, every week, you sacrifice half a dozen cows, thirty or forty sheep and goats, hundreds of chickens and assorted birds of the wild, who has time to read? You learn from your father, the way he learned from his father before him."

We were sitting at table, just the three of us. Yehoshua had shown no surprise when Gan ushered me forward as the Ambassador from Baghdad. He spoke a fluent Arabic, tinged, of course, with the Moorish accent of our distant cousins who had once been his neighbors. There was a woman of sorts who appeared with an extra plate and knife, an extra cup. Yehoshua pointed to our seats, sang the prayers over the bread and the wine, and then began the explanation of his craft. It sounded to my ears like he was making excuses, excuses for his betrayal of his Muslim neighbors twenty years before in Narbonne. But that could be the fault of the Moorish accent.

"The first father," I said, "of course was Ibrahim. The father of Ishmael."

"And Isaac," Yehoshua added, before I could be so dull as to forget. "Yes, he was the first shochet, ready to slit the throat of his own son,"—Yehoshua smiled benevolently over at me— "no matter what his name. Thankfully, the Lord chose that moment to inform Abraham that the days of human sacrifice were over, that slicing the throat of your first born was not only no longer required, but no longer acceptable in polite company. From Abraham, the path led to Isaac and Jacob and Levi and, after Solomon built the Temple in Jerusalem, to the descendants of Levi and their divinely measured knives. After the destruction of the Temple in Jerusalem, when our people went into exile, even animal sacrifice began to look bad."

"Perhaps to your people," I sniffed. Gan winked at me in memory of the sheep we had sacrificed before he sailed, before we sailed from Baghdad. There were whole eggs, and handfuls of raisins, and even a brace of quail stuffed inside. I had given him the eyeball of a lamb, wrapped in rice that tasted of cardamom and anise. How could he forget?

As if in answer, the woman entered the room, a full leg of mutton on a wooden platter. Yehoshua took up his knife.

"With what shall I approach the Lord," he asked, addressing the leg as much as us, his guests.

"Do homage to God on high?
Shall I approach Him with burnt offerings?
With calves a year old?
Would the Lord be pleased with thousands of rams?

With myriads of streams of oil?
Shall I give my firstborn for my transgression?
The fruit of my body for my sins?"

Gan treated the prayer as a real question and gave a real
answer and a glance in my direction. "Study and good deeds
have replaced sacrifice, don't you think?"

"I wouldn't know about study," the shochet said, and
began to carve the lamb.

Gan said, "You knew enough to save the Jews of Narbonne."

"Please!" Yehoshua stopped carving but gripped the knife
as tightly as his guilt. "I don't think I will ever be forgiven for
my good deeds."

I touched the arm of Yehoshua, the arm of the hand holding the knife. "If you are not willing to be a sacrificer, then you
are doomed to be the sacrificed."

"That is the other possibility," he said, and returned to his
carving.

At that moment the woman returned to the room and
hurried over to Yehoshua. The shochet smiled, but I had already
guessed the origin of the new tightness in his lips, the tension in
his cheeks. I had heard the sound, as muffled as it was, of three
pairs of boots approaching the door of the Jew.

"My son," Yehoshua said, standing. "We have a visitor. I
am afraid we must interrupt our supper to entertain him. I am
also afraid," he said, turning to me, "that you must excuse us."

"Do not worry," I said, holding up my hand. "I will be
content down in the stables and will await your call." I smiled
at Gan, who had not yet guessed that the visitor was the Frankish King. Years of wrapping myself up in cloaks and capes and
touring the city of Baghdad on similarly quiet afternoons accompanied only by my equally disguised Vizier Ja'afar had accustomed me to the tricks of monarchs.

And so I descended a ladder at the far end of the shochet's
bedroom, directly into a stable that smelled of hay and elephant,
where my crate and dozens of others sat ruminating in the shadows

of late summer. I expected a half hour's leisure, a chance to lie at my ease in the straw and let my imagination wander like a lazy peasant at the hour when the sun announces the end of work but the moon has failed to prod him homewards. What I didn't expect was the sight of a young girl, perched on the edge of my crate.

"Salaam alaikum," she said, clearly amused by her superior knowledge of my language. But the red hair that wouldn't be stifled by her woolen cape reminded me of Ja'afar's stories of the daughter of Charlemagne.

"Wa alaikum salaam, Princess," I saluted her back.

"How do you know who I am?" she asked, clearly ruffled.

"The story of your birth is famous in our court," I replied, with as much of an avuncular smile as I could muster.

"My Uncle Roland," the girl said, "told me that your court was famous for its storytellers."

"He was a gentleman," I answered, disguising my pride as best I could. "I know he was closer than a brother to your father. The Caliph was pained to hear of his death."

"On the day that I was born," Aldana continued, "an ambassador from your Caliph arrived at Marseilles, where my father had come to join my mother in anticipation of my birth. My Uncle Roland told me that on the anniversary of my first week of life, my father carried me from my mother's chamber into the monastery of St. Guillaume, where your ambassador was resident. It had not been a happy week, or so said Roland. I had cried more than smiled, and agitated more than slept. None thought I would survive the week. Some, Roland told me, prayed that I would get on to Heaven as quickly as possible and allow them to regain their wits. Nevertheless, my father carried me in to the Ambassador. One look at his turban and my wails redoubled, so that all Marseilles could hear me. But then your Ambassador reached over to my father and took me from his arms and onto his lap and began to tell me a story."

The Story of the Crying Princess was one I knew well, that Ja'afar had told me many times. Of how first he, as my father's Ambassador, took this red-haired and red-faced infant onto his lap and quieted her sobs by reciting the Story of Khalifah the Fisherman. No sooner had he finished, however, than the baby's wails resumed at twice the volume. And so the Treasurer, my uncle Aziz, took the baby onto his lap and told her the Story of the Hunchback. Once again the girl quieted, bewitched either by our Arabic tongue, the story itself, or a desire that one day, she too might become part of a story. But it shortly became clear that Charlemagne, his Queen, his court, his army, and the population of Marseilles and its environs, would make our entire embassy, ten strong, recite all night and into the next days and weeks as long as this infant daughter wailed at the finish of each story, crying for another. Ja'afar and my uncle and all the rest had sailed from Baghdad across the sea, so it seemed, to become a chorus of Scheherazades, doomed to death should the music of their stories ever cease.

"I no longer cry," the Princess said. But I could see liquid anxiety at the rims of her eyes. She had been brought like a sacrificial lamb to the stable of the shochet and left alone while her future was weighed above.

"And after today," I said, "you shall have further cause for rejoicing. Your father has come to marry you to our young Prince."

"I heard he was a Jew," Aldana said.

"Not just any Jew," I cautioned her.

"Are there different types?" she asked.

"There are even types that contain other types," I said.

"Like crates that contain other crates?" She leaped off the side of mine with a lightness of step and a quickness of mind that made me look again at that shock of red hair peering from under her cape.

"I know what you want," I laughed.

"And that is?" she laughed back.

"You want a story, greedy girl."

"Perhaps," she said, suddenly aware that it was not entirely appropriate for the daughter of Charlemagne to flirt in a stable with the Ambassador of the Caliph of Baghdad, like a milkmaid with a blacksmith.

"Do you remember the Tale of Judar the Son of Omar?" I asked.

"*I was only a few days old . . .*" *she protested.*

"*Do you remember?*" *I pressed her.*

"*Of course I remember!*" *She lifted her pale chin upwind, scenting the air of mid-September, deciding direction.*

"*So you remember how Judar, the poor fisherman went casting his net in the Lake of Karoon?*" *I asked.*

"*And how the three brothers, the Three Moors came to him, one after the other on three successive days, with instructions to bind their arms and legs behind them and throw them into the lake?*" *she answered.*

"*Very good!*" *I congratulated her.* "*So you remember how the first two Moors drowned, but the third survived and brought Judar with him back to the Maghreb . . .*"

"*Because the Moor knew that only Judar the Son of Omar could open the Treasure of Al-Shammardal that lay below the sea, the treasure that had been stolen from the great magician, the father of the Moor, by the Red and the Black Princes, and that had already cost the lives of his father and two of his brothers.*" *Her eyes were glistening even brighter with the excitement of the story than with fear of her upcoming betrothal. I knew, with a mixture of both anticipation and sadness, that all I needed do was spin out the story and she would do with me what the girl in the chest did with Shahryar and his brother. And that the remorse I would feel at falling in love with the Princess and allowing her to fall in love with me would be worse than the punishment of any djinni. So I cut the story short.*

"*Do you remember,*" *I asked her,* "*what present the Moor gave to Judar in return for his help?*"

"*The Bag,*" *the Princess answered immediately.* "*The Magic Saddle Bag. All Judar had to do was to ask the djinni hidden inside the Bag for any dish to eat—chicken with prunes, lamb with steamed rice and dates, pheasant in a sauce of tamarind and honey eggs—and the dish would come out on a silver plate, steaming hot and ready to eat.*"

"*A silly choice, perhaps,*" *I added carelessly.*

"*Silly?*" *she said.* "*I cannot imagine a better gift!*"

"Then you will be very happy," I said. "Your Jewish Prince is just such a Magic Bag."

"I don't understand," she said. Indeed, my shift in direction had pulled the carpet out from below her feet and left her struggling for balance. Little did I know how my glib metaphor would also unbalance me. During my seven-day sea crossing, even as the elephant changed from blue to green to red, a truth cast a clear, steady light through my own milky waters: the Jewish Prince is, in fact, the perfect gift. Gan contains my stories, all my stories. All the stories I have imagined, all the stories I might imagine, and even the ones I cannot. He is not only the garden, he is the apple tree. He is the fruit and he is the leaf and he is the seed. He is the Pip. I was giving away this Pip to a girl who would rather have the axe. And I was the double loser.

"Aldana!" a voice called from the stair.

"Coming!" she called back but made no move to go.

"Go now," I said. "Insha'allah one day I shall return to ask what you have learned."

"Please," she said, "I need to know the answer to one question. Now."

"Yes?"

"If I reach my hand into the bag and ask for a dish from Baghdad . . ."

I am the one who is leaving and returning to Baghdad.

I am the axe.

I have uprooted him from the garden.

I uprooted the tree from the garden.

Why?

For a Frankish king who sent me nothing I did not have already?

To graft my Prince to this red-haired Princess, this crying baby who softens only at the sound of a Muslim voice and a good story? To uproot this Princess, to show her that a single bag can hold many dishes, many gods, many men?

Before I grafted her to myself?

I uproot my own heart. I carry it back onto the ship bound for Baghdad lest my right hand awake like a djinni of my own creation and slice my own self into a thousand pieces. I leave behind an elephant, turning all shades of the rainbow, large enough to move mountains, small enough to fit in the Bag of Judar the Son of Omar.

Malory looked up. Settimio was still standing by his chair.

"Who has read this book?"

"From the beginning, the key to Septimania has been discretion," Settimio said. "When Charlemagne heard that his future son-in-law was named Gan, he said, 'What kind of a Frankish name is that? In the future you will be named Aimery. You will be King of Septimania. You will have lands and property and subjects—but quietly, *pian piano*.' Both Charlemagne and Gan understood that a certain amount of secrecy was proper. And as the offspring of Aimery and Charlemagne's daughter continued the dynasty down through the centuries, the marriage of secrecy to power was sanctified in Septimania."

"Aimery?" Malory asked. "As in Emery? As in Mrs. Emery?"

"Both your grandmother and your mother were known to this house as Mrs. Emery," Settimio acknowledged. "But since the Rule of Succession does not permit a woman to reign supreme over Septimania, both women were permitted only the name and certain other rights and privileges. The throne, however, remained vacant until her death. Since a male heir had, after all, been produced."

"As in me?"

"As in you, *mio Principe*."

"I am the product of the marriage of secrecy and power? King of the Jews and Holy Roman Emperor?"

"Neither Charlemagne nor Aimery had any problem with the double title."

"But Charlemagne's daughter . . ."

"Aldana."

"Certainly she wasn't Jewish, so none of her children were Jewish . . ."

"*Mi scusi, mio Principe.* But you will find that none of the books in the Sanctum Sanctorum, including the Septuagint and the many Torahs, insist that Judaism is passed down by the mother."

"Still . . ."

"*Simplex sigillum veri.* The simple is the sign of the truth."

"What is simple?"

"Charlemagne and Aimery decided it was so. Simple."

"As simple as that?"

"You are both King of the Jews and Holy Roman Emperor, *mio Principe.* It all depends on how one looks."

"I would hardly call that simple!"

"Then think of it as useful," Settimio continued, "a trick of the light if all other explanation fails."

"Useful in what way?"

"There was a time," Settimio explained, "when many of the crowned heads of Europe looked to Rome and the King of Septimania to reveal himself and save civilization."

"And what happened?" Malory asked.

"The guillotine," Settimio said. "The French Revolution proved the wisdom of discretion. Better to see all of Rome, while Rome sees nothing of us."

"And now the crowned heads of Europe—what do they expect of Septimania? What do they expect of me?"

"Expect, *mio Principe*?" Settimio said. "You are the one who expects. Nothing is expected of you."

Nothing. Nothing was expected of him.

"Except in fifteen minutes—Suor Anna shall be with Suor Miriam."

FOURTEEN MINUTES LATER, MALORY AND SETTIMIO STOOD BEFORE SUOR Miriam in the long ward, now fledged in late-afternoon shafts of light shooting in through both sets of windows from the sun over the sea at the mouth of the Tevere. It didn't appear to Malory that Suor Miriam had moved since the midnight before. But now there was a younger nun standing by her, small, eager, and undernourished.

"Gentlemen," Suor Miriam said softly, "welcome back. As I promised, I have invited Suor Anna to speak with you."

"*Buona sera,*" Settimio said.

"*Buona sera,*" Suor Anna said.

"It's not her," Malory said.

"Not her?" Suor Miriam repeated. The light intensified around the old nun, or perhaps it just dimmed on Malory in sympathetic annoyance. Still, Malory pressed on.

"I've never seen you before in my life," Malory said. The young nun's eagerness turned into a blotchy confusion. "Have you seen me?"

"*Sì, signore,*" the young girl said and moved a step closer to Suor Miriam.

"*Principe!*" Suor Miriam corrected her.

"Yesterday afternoon, in the hospital. You were carrying a young lady in your arms. You came into the room very quick and put her on the bed."

"Is this not true?" Suor Miriam turned her blinking eyelids up to Malory.

"I'm telling you," Malory said, not caring whether it was impatience or disappointment speaking, "that I have never seen this girl, this nurse before in my life. The nun I saw was English."

"English, *mio Principe*? In Fatebenefratelli?"

"Settimio, you were there. You saw the red-bearded doctor and the English nurse."

"I am afraid I only saw you in the corridor, *mio Principe*. And only the doctor and your Rumanian friend were in attendance."

"But it is impossible," Suor Miriam said. "There are no English nurses in Fatebenefratelli and certainly no English nuns."

"The *Principe* is correct." The little nun with the blotchy cheeks stared at the pavement of crushed marble and waited for a reaction.

"*In che senso*—in what sense correct?" Suor Miriam repeated. "Were you telling a story just now, that you were there in the room with the *Principe*?"

"No, no," Suor Anna said with a firmness that smelled of honesty. "Perhaps the *Principe* did not see me, but I was in the room. He was wearing a jacket the color of . . ."—Suor Anna searched the room and pointed at the lintels of the windows—"of *terracotta* and made out of a funny material that looked as if it had been scratched by a cat."

"Corduroy," Malory said.

"*Sì!* And you had a funny bag across one shoulder."

"My Kit Bag," Malory said, "yes."

"I was standing behind the door. You were in a big hurry. But," she added, looking with more confidence up at Malory, "the *Principe* is correct. There was an English nurse. I did not recognize her habit. She was not a Franciscan or a Dominican, or from Santa Birgitta or Santa Sabina. I thought perhaps that she came from the Colegio Inglese, the English College, on via di Monserrato. She was very firm. As soon as the *Principe* entered the room carrying the young woman, the English nurse told me she would manage. I was very sorry to leave. I spoke only four words with the Rumanian *signora*, but she seemed very nice."

"What a nuisance," Suor Miriam said. "Forgive me, *Principe*, for raising your hopes with this silly girl."

"*Grazie*, Suor Anna," Settimio said. "We are sorry to have bothered you." He inclined his head to both nuns—less a bow than a crumb of politesse frosted with disappointment—and signaled to Malory that the interview was over. But Malory wanted to hear more from this little nun, this nothing of a girl who was born afraid and neglected and reminded him of a young, deserted boy who had learned that survival depended on standing behind doorways and overlooking while being overlooked.

"Suor Anna," he said, holding her gaze. "You saw more, didn't you? You saw what happened to the lady I brought in. And even perhaps to the nice Rumanian *signora*."

Settimio stopped in mid turn. Suor Miriam's eyelids fluttered.

"*Sì*," Suor Anna said. "I did. I saw the doctor, the big doctor enter the room."

"The American doctor with the red hair?"

"*Sì*, I remember the red hair. And he had a beard and he was very tall."

"You are not inventing this, Suor Anna?" Suor Miriam asked.

"Oh, no," Suor Anna said. "He passed me in the corridor. It is easy for me to look up at people. They are always looking ahead at something above me."

"And that's all?" Malory asked.

"The English nurse told me to leave the room. But I had nowhere else to go. My instructions were to assist in the maternity ward. I stood in the corridor, perhaps three meters from the door, and waited against the wall. I saw the *Principe* leave with the husband of the Rumanian woman. I saw this gentleman . . ."

"Settimio . . ."

"*Sì,* I saw him introduce himself to you, *Principe.* I saw you leave with him. I saw the Rumanian man walk down to the *cortile.* I watched him smoke a cigarette."

"And the women?"

"A few minutes later—you had barely gone—the door opened. The English nurse was pushing one bed with the Rumanian woman. The doctor was pushing the woman you brought in. They went down the corridor and then turned towards the back of the building, to Operating Theater Number Three. You know which one I mean, Suor Miriam?"

Suor Miriam nodded, but Malory also saw her take a quick breath, as if someone had surprised her from behind or punched her in the stomach.

"The corridor outside Operating Theater Number Three was in shadows, so I stood a little farther from its door at the edge of the light from the *cortile.* I could see the husband of the Rumanian *signora* smoking his cigarettes. I counted. Ten cigarettes. Ten cigarettes later, I heard one cry, then another. Two babies. Two baby cries. Two different babies. I know, I have heard them before." Suor Miriam nodded, with a smile of shadowed remembrance.

"Finally the door opened. The English nurse came out. 'Good,' she said when she saw me. The Rumanian *signora* was sitting in a wheelchair. I was surprised, of course. It was much too soon for a woman to sit in a wheelchair. But the English nurse insisted that I take the Rumanian *signora* down the lift to her husband in the *cortile.* I thought that maybe the English know better than we Italians about these things. So I wheeled her to the main lift."

"This was one hour after I left?" Malory asked.

"*Sì*. It was seven o'clock, when the lift is very busy with people leaving for the night. And everybody was so excited about the Holy Father in San Pietro—it took me several minutes to get a lift with enough room for the Rumanian *signora*. When the lift doors opened, I looked down the corridor into the shadows by Operating Theatre Number Three again and saw the door open. The tall doctor was wheeling another chair. I was certain he would come in my direction and I held the door. I was about to call to him, but I saw him turn the other way. I don't know why. The corridor ends at that level. But I thought perhaps he just wanted to give your wife some fresh air."

"Ah . . ." Malory wasn't certain how to respond to the word *wife*, but gave the young nun an encouraging smile.

"I took the Rumanian *signora* down to the cortile. Handed her and the chair to her husband. Neither of them spoke to me, neither noticed me. I stood for perhaps two minutes and then excused myself and climbed the stairs back to Operating Theater Number Three. I knocked on the door—I had, after all, done what the English nurse asked me to do—and entered. The room was dark. Only the light from the lamps on the Lungotevere shone through the window. The English nurse was standing, looking out at the synagogue. The two beds were empty, the machines turned off. But in its own shaft of light, not far from the English nurse, I saw a cradle. I walked over. I was eager to see the babies."

"And you saw them?" Malory asked.

"I saw one," Suor Anna answered. "One baby."

"Only one?" Suor Miriam raised her chin. "But you heard two cries?"

"*Sì e sì*," Suor Anna said. "I asked the English nurse where was the other baby. 'Go home,' she said to me. I protested, I'm afraid that I was rude. I wanted to know what happened to the other baby—I assumed, of course, that it was with your wife, *Principe*—and I wanted to know where she had gone with the tall doctor with the red hair and beard. They could not have left the hospital without taking the lift down to the *cortile* and passing me."

"There is another lift," Suor Miriam said. "It is not obvious, but it is where you saw the doctor wheel the young lady. It has been used in the past, when discretion was called for." She lifted her chin to Settimio. He nodded.

"The English nurse asked me where I lived. I told her Santa Sabina with the Dominicans. She said 'Then it won't take you long to get home. Good night.'"

"And you left?" Malory said.

"I left," Suor Anna said.

"And the Rumanians?"

"To walk to Santa Sabina I must cross from the Isola Tiberina across the Ponte Fabricio. As I turned to cross the bridge, I saw the two of them—he was holding her arm, she was walking, I could not believe it, very slowly in the opposite direction, across the Ponte Cestio to Trastevere."

"Without a baby?"

"It is impossible to walk like that with a baby."

"And then you went home?"

"I went to Santa Sabina, sì. I prayed."

A distant bell rang. Twice.

"I am afraid they expect me in the hospital," Suor Anna said.

"May we go with you?" Malory asked, suddenly taken with a plan of action. "We must be able to speak with Suor Anna's supervisor, or the director of the hospital, and find out who is this tall American doctor with the red beard and his English nurse. I mean, can just anyone come into a hospital in Rome and deliver a few babies without permission?" The distant bell rang again. Neither Suor Anna nor Suor Miriam said anything.

"I believe, *mio Principe*," Settimio murmured delicately, "that we might have more success searching for your Rumanians. Or better still—waiting for them to search for you."

As Settimio predicted, it was the Rumanian who found Malory.

The elevation of the Polish cardinal to the Chair of St. Peter magnetized the Eternal City. The kings and queens of the Catholic countries of Europe, the congressmen and senators from the United States who bore Polish names, and tens of thousands of fortunate Poles who found themselves outside the borders of their native country descended on Rome by plane, by coach, by motorcycle, by Volga and Lada, Trabant and Dacia, Polski Fiats and little Maluchs, and even by automobiles with lawnmower engines that ran on potato skins and cabbage leaves for the inaugural Mass of the new pope, John Paul II. Although it would not have been discreet for Malory to attend the Mass, Settimio asked him twice whether he would like to host a small luncheon at the Villa for a select group of guests who were already aware of the existence of Septimania. But not even the temptation of sharing *tortelloni in brodo* with Princess Grace could shake Malory out of his reluctance to be examined by royal invigilators on subjects he had never studied.

Settimio dutifully worked the telephones and called whomever Malory requested—from *carabinieri* to secretaries in the embassies of the United States, England, and even Rumania. But few picked up their phones, and those who did were at best confused and at worst unhelpful. Rome was otherwise engaged. Travel through the streets was nearly impossible, backed up to the rim of the bowl with a holy wash of dignitaries and pilgrims. The city was buried beneath the weight of a machine nearly two millennia in the making, fueled only in the smallest part by religion.

Isolated and besieged, Malory devoted his days to a better under-standing of his inheritance, with the not-so-secret aim that it might reveal to him how he might be reunited with his barely seen Louiza and his unseen progeny. He developed a speedy dexterity with the card catalog of the Sanctum Sanctorum, although the vast bulk of the collection in the dozens of tunnels beneath the villa were in Latin, Greek, Hebrew, Arabic, and several other languages that meant nothing to Malory. Dur-ing his nights in the Sanctum Sanctorum, he read through *The Complete History of Septimania*. He read and read again the story of Haroun al Rashid and his secret mission to bring the first King of Septimania to the West. He read again of his meeting with the butcher Yehoshua and his subsequent encounter with the daughter of Charlemagne. But his imagination was most attracted to the story Haroun spoke of with the red-headed Princess Aldana. "The Tale of Judar Son of Omar" appeared in each one of the fifteen editions of the *Thousand and One Nights* that Settimio was able to draw out of the depths of the tunnel.

"Do you think," Malory asked him one evening, "that these tales are also more than bedtime stories, Settimio?"

"You may recall, *mio Principe*, that bedtime meant something very different to the young Scheherazade."

"Ah," Malory said, wondering how the girl could fall asleep at night knowing that her survival the next day depended on coming up with an A-plus yarn for King Shahryar. "Do you remember the story of Judar—do you remember the Magic Saddlebag? All you had to do was imagine a dish, put your hand into the bag, and voilà! There it was on a silver platter ready to serve. Do you remember?"

"*Certo,*" Settimio smiled.

"And do you remember the Celestial Orb? All you had to do was to turn the orb towards the sun, and you could see into all the countries of the world, all the cities, all the homes."

"The Celestial Orb, *sì*, I remember."

"Settimio," Malory wasn't certain how to ask the question with-out seeming either silly or greedy. "Those treasures—they wouldn't be stored here, would they? They wouldn't be part of my inheritance?"

Settimio's smile softened. "It would certainly make the cook's job easier at dinnertime."

"You've been very kind to me," Malory said. "And the food I like seems to appear at mealtime without my having to do much more than Judar with his bag. But the Celestial Orb . . ."

"You wish there were an easy way to turn a little globe in your hand and find your Louiza? I wish it too."

That night, Malory lay with his cheek kissing the top of the seven-sided desk and slept free of dreams, surrounded as he was by nothing but.

In the morning, Settimio woke him at the desk and led him up to the dining table and the chairs of Tiberian oak for his tea and scones. Outside, it was still dark.

"The streets are empty at this time of the morning," Settimio said, as he guided Malory onto the back of the Driver's Vespa. "The Driver will take you to the *Mattatoio*, the slaughterhouse in Testaccio. Rumanians, Bulgarians, Poles, the illegal workers of Rome line up there at dawn. At seven o'clock, any employer in need of a worker for a day, a week, a month, can drive by and make a selection."

But on this morning, there were no Rumanians at the *Mattatoio* who responded to Malory's questions, who knew the name of Tibor. The Driver took him across the river to Porta Portese, where matrons from Monteverde Vecchio knew they could always pick up cheap day help from Yugoslavia, Bulgaria, Turkey, or Albania when their regular domestics called in sick. Malory waded into the early-morning scent of women, desperate to wash pots in the back rooms of Chinese restaurants, to babysit the children of occasional tourists, to wheel the crippled and demented beneath the Roman pines for a bit of fresh air and a few hundred lire. But no one knew Tibor. No one knew a Rumanian woman who had recently given birth. Malory returned to the villa with no treasure to speak of.

Four days after the Pope's Inaugural Mass—which Malory watched as a favor to Settimio on a small black-and-white television in the kitchen—Malory was leaning over the parapet of the garden, looking down on Fatebenefratelli and thinking how accustomed he was becoming to his anxiety, when Settimio approached him with a message.

"Suor Miriam telephoned from the Ospedale Israelite, *mio Principe*. Your Rumanian friend, he found Suor Anna. He was looking for you."

Settimio was glowing, Malory thought, with radioactive pleasure at his prescience. "He will be at Trajan's Column at five this afternoon."

Malory arrived at Piazza Venezia on the back of the Driver's Vespa. He'd seen Trajan's Column before, or at least a plaster cast of it, in the Victoria and Albert Museum in London, where two dismantled halves stood in a nineteenth-century pavilion built to house the story of Trajan's conquest of Rumania. Two long helixes of chariots and fallen warriors, victorious soldiers and captive slaves as depressed as any he'd seen at the *Mattatoio* or Porta Portese, wound up the V&A columns—a comic strip for the circus-going masses. The message was clear even in London—Victory was in the Roman DNA. The single triumphant shaft of Trajan's Column was the starting point for a display of conquest and power that stretched in an unbroken line of ruins down the Fori Imperiali to the Colosseum. Triumph was as politically complete as it was genetically inevitable.

"*Fututi pizda matii.*"

Malory looked up.

"Organ tuner!" the voice called. "Organ tuner!" One hundred feet in the air, at the summit of Trajan's Column, someone was waving his arms frantically. It was possible, Malory thought, that this someone had a beard. It was possible that the Rumanian had beaten Trajan at his own game.

"Mr. Malory, please?" There was a man beside him, a boy really, in a pair of oversized black eyeglasses like the guitar player he'd seen out his window at the Trinity College May Ball that past June.

"Me?" Malory asked. The Driver turned the Vespa back on, just in case.

"Please," the boy said again, "you are organ tuner man?"

"Not exactly!" Malory looked up from the boy to the shout from Trajan's Column.

"Malory!"

"Tibor!" Malory unstraddled the Vespa and started across the Via dei Fori Imperiali as the Driver stopped traffic as best he could.

"Yes!" the boy said, running alongside Malory. "Is Tibor. He wants you."

"He likes heights, doesn't he?" Malory said.

"He sees better up there," the boy said.

"Maybe he can find somebody for me," Malory said, hurrying down the incline towards the base of the column, although he imagined it would be difficult for Tibor to disappear at this point, perched as he was one hundred feet above the Forum.

"No, no," the boy said, skipping to keep up with Malory. "He is making auditions."

"Auditions?" Malory remembered something vague Tibor said about Shakespeare and Bucharest.

"Don't you know?" the boy's glasses bounced on the bridge of his nose. "Tibor was big shot director in Rumania. National Theater, Shakespeare . . ."

"Ah yes," Malory said, "Carlsberg . . ."

". . . and Camels," the boy added, smiling. "My name is Radu," he said.

"Malory." Malory shook the boy's hand.

"Please, Mr. Malory," he said, "this way."

Malory walked around to the far base of the column. Another boy guarded a door.

"This is Sasha."

"Hello, Mr. Malory." Sasha shook his hand—a skinny version of one of the Monkees, the one with long sewer-streaked hair and spaniel cheeks.

"It's all right," Malory said to the Driver. The two boys, flashlights in hand, led Malory inside.

For a hundred, maybe two hundred steps, Malory climbed a staircase as Radu and Sasha told him how Tibor had received money from the Commune di Roma and several charities to stage a production of Dante's *Divine Comedy*.

"Tibor has a plan. He is going to cast two hundred people," Radu said.

"No pros," Sasha added.

"And lead the audience around Rome."

"Down to the inferno of a shithole of the Cloaca Maxima."

"Up to the paradiso of the altar of the Ara Pacis."

"Orphans as angels."

"Politicians and priests as the Damned."

"Refugees and homeless as refugees and homeless."

"Mostly Rumanians."

"Rumanians have a colorful history with Rome."

"I'm sorry," Radu said, "that we can't take you up the outside of Trajan's Column. The whole history of Trajan's slaughter of the Rumanians . . ."

"Dacians . . ." Sasha explained.

"His battle with the Dacians . . ."

"Two battles, two wars . . ."

"Brought them back to Rome as slaves . . ."

"Like us . . ."

"*Fututi pizda matii!*" Radu stopped and turned on Sasha and continued for thirty seconds in unbroken Rumanian.

"Excuse me," Malory said, taking advantage of the pause to catch what little breath he had. "Who are you?"

Radu stopped. He pushed his oversized glasses straight on the bridge of his nose.

"Tibor didn't tell you about the Bomb Squad?" Sasha asked.

"The Bomb Squad?" Malory wondered whether it was a mistake to leave the Driver below.

"We came out of Rumania before Tibor and Cristina."

"Cristina?" Malory asked.

"*La Principessa*," Radu explained.

"Back in Rumania, everyone was in the army. But because we are artists, we were drafted to clear mines out of the Delta of the Danube."

"Mines?" Malory asked. "Artists?"

"Artists are expendable," Radu explained. "But we are also very good."

"Sasha was very good," Radu said, starting up the stairs again. "He is guitarist. He has good ear. But Tibor was best. His nose . . ."

"Anything," Sasha added. "Tibor can find anything. Music. Women. Just look what he found today."

Malory emerged from the staircase onto the platform at the top of Trajan's Column and looked down onto the rubble below. The sun was thinking about calling it a night, but hundreds, perhaps a thousand people had shown up at the base of Trajan's Column. A host of women in World War I nurse's aprons and starched hats were trying to create some order, corralling the would-be actors into pens.

"Who are those nurses?" Malory asked.

"They are the Nurses." The note was a low F-sharp. The paw landed on Malory's shoulder. "Also artists. And there," Tibor pointed down into Trajan's Forum to a woman sitting on a block of fallen marble like a princess on a camp stool, surveying the triage, "is *La Principessa*."

"Tibor," Malory said. "I've been looking for you."

"And I've been looking for you, Dante."

"Malory, actually," Malory said.

"Dante," Tibor said finally. "You will play Dante in my production. You explained," he turned to Radu and Sasha, "didn't you?"

"We didn't get to that part."

"*Fututi pizda matii!*" Tibor said, but then turned and smiled at Malory. "You and me, Malory. We are both of us, like Dante said, *nel mezzo del cammin*, in the middle of the road of life. When I found you, when you found me up in the organ loft of Santa Maria sopra Minerva, we were both stuck in the middle of the *autostrada* with *Cinquecento* and *motorini* whizzing around us."

"Tibor . . ."

"We were midway between the starry ceiling of Santa Maria sopra Minerva and certain death on the flagstones. You caught me with your metal hook before I fell . . ."

"Tibor . . ."

"But you. I couldn't catch you. You are still lost. Like Dante. *La Principessa* saw it when you arrived at the hospital. You still need to make the journey. You are Dante, don't you see, Malory? You need to be Dante, and I will direct you. I will be your Virgil B. DeMille!"

"Tibor," Malory said, stepping back from the paw to gain perspective. "I've been looking for you for two weeks. Since that night at the hospital, at Fatebenefratelli, with Louiza and your wife—Cristina, is that right? I was only gone for an hour or two. You weren't there when I got back."

"So," Tibor said. The sun dipped below the crest of the Capitoline Hill. Malory saw something dim. Or rather, he saw that he had pushed in the stop that closed off the bellows of the Rumanian giant. "Sasha, Radu," Tibor whispered. "Go down. Send them home. Auditions are over."

"Tomorrow at the same time?" Radu asked.

"Go," Tibor whispered, but it had enough force to send his Bomb Squad down the spiral staircase. Malory waited for the footsteps to fade.

"Tibor, did you and Cristina leave the hospital with your baby?"

"Malory," Tibor said and leaned over the railing, looking down onto the expectant actors and actresses, "does that look like a woman who left the hospital with a baby?" Malory took three steps towards Tibor and peered a little more gingerly. Cristina was sitting immobile on the marble block, her gray head catching the last of the sun, lunar still within the flickering motion among the ruins.

"Suor Anna thought not."

"And Suor Anna is?" Tibor kept looking down, his wrists loose over the railing.

"The nurse who wheeled Cristina down to you in the *cortile*. I spoke with her the next day. She said that as soon as you and I left, the English nurse and the American doctor wheeled Cristina and Louiza to another room, an operating theater. An hour later the English nurse came out with Cristina in a wheelchair. She told Suor Anna to bring Cristina down to you in the *cortile*. She saw you a little while later, walking across the bridge to Trastevere."

"So, you know," Tibor said. "Why all the questions?"

"I don't know what happened inside the room, inside the operating theater."

"You tune organs, Malory. What do you think happened?"

"I think there were complications. I think Cristina had her baby, your baby. I think, perhaps, that there were reasons—maybe Roman reasons, maybe financial reasons why she couldn't stay in the hospital with the baby. I think you went back to see the baby the next day. I think you brought it home a few days later."

"Roman reasons," Tibor said. "Why not Rumanian reasons?"

"What are Rumanian reasons?"

"I told you in the church, in Santa Maria on top of the Goddess of Wisdom, what I told *La Principessa*. If it is a girl, she must go away before I fall in love with her. If it is a boy, I will strangle him with my own hands."

"But you didn't mean . . ."

"Malory," Tibor turned to him. "Go home. Go back and tune your organs in your country where the Theory of Evolution, the Primal Urge to Reproduce, the Social Contract and The Rule of Law and Newtonian Physics are still practiced by honest citizens. In my country—the country I carry with me that makes my back crack with the pressure and the poison—all those were burned a long time ago in a ditch that is still smoldering with a *puzza* that would turn your stomach if you ever visited."

"You left the baby?"

"We saved a life," Tibor said. "I told you at the church. I needed you to come to help me save a life."

"You also told me not to worry," Malory said. "When Settimio"—Malory stopped, part of him already sensitive to discretion—"when I left with those men, you told me you would stay there, you would look after my Louiza, you would wait for me."

"So," Tibor said, "you have come to punish me for putting the welfare of my *Principessa* over a promise I made to an English organ tuner I met only one hour earlier? Wouldn't you do the same with your Louiza?"

"She's gone," Malory said.

"Gone?" Tibor changed key and looked at Malory. Malory nodded and looked down at the platform. "I'm sorry, Malory." Tibor put his palm on Malory's shoulder, but Malory stepped back. "These things happen," he shrugged.

"I don't mean that she left today or yesterday. That day at the hospital—I was only gone for an hour or so," Malory said. "I must have got back just after you left. But she was gone."

Malory raised his head. He saw Tibor's eyes. Tibor was looking into him. There was a new focus, he thought, perhaps anger. "What do you mean gone? Not just in the operating theater?"

"I mean that Settimio and I searched the entire hospital for two hours, spoke with nurses, doctors, administrators. No one had seen her, no one had seen the red-bearded American doctor or the English nurse or the babies. Only the next day, when I met Suor Anna . . ." Malory recounted Suor Anna's story to Tibor, the disappearance of the doctor with Louiza, the single baby in the cradle in the lamplight of the operating theater. "If you and Cristina didn't take your baby, then the baby that Suor Anna saw must have been yours. And Louiza must have been taken away with hers. With ours."

"And the hospital didn't say anything?"

Malory shook his head. "Not one record. Nothing."

There were footsteps in the column, and then Radu's black eyeglasses followed by Sasha's mop.

"Mission accomplished," Radu said, sucking in the evening air as best he could. Sasha had his hands on his knees in the hope that his breath might catch up with him more easily at that height. Down below, the crowd was sifting out towards the Piazza Venezia in one direction and the Colosseum in the other.

"A new mission," Tibor turned to them.

"Really?" Sasha looked up.

"We have to find a girl. And her baby."

"That's not why I came," Malory said. "I've already tried the police, the embassies."

"Please," Radu said, and Sasha straightened up to join him and Tibor at the railing. "We are the Bomb Squad. We know how to find anything and everything."

"You really think?" Malory began.

"It may take some time," Radu said.

"But if they are here, we will find them," Sasha said.

"What can I do?" Malory asked.

"Leave it to us," Radu said. "You are obviously no good at finding things."

"We had to find you, after all," Sasha added, "no offense."

"Tibor," Malory started again.

"I will be your Virgil," Tibor said, "I will guide you. I will help you find your Beatrice, if you will be my Dante."

"What do I have to do?" Malory asked.

"Not much," Tibor answered. "Go through hell, that's all. Otherwise nothing, absolutely nothing." And with that, he stepped into the column and began his descent.

Oh the sheets of roe
Are filled with rubber
Anchovy prints
Are everywhere

TIBOR'S PAW GUIDED MALORY AROUND A FRAGRANT CORNER OF the prison of Regina Coeli in the direction of the music. Tibor had insisted—and now that Malory had found him, there was no real question he would follow—that Malory come home with him for dinner and plan the search for Louiza. They walked at a measured pace—as if Tibor were calculating strategy or counting syllables in a canto—from Trajan's Column through the Ghetto and out the back end of the Teatro Marcello, to the Synagogue and across the Isola Tiborina. Part of the route was familiar from Malory's dash with Tibor and Louiza two weeks earlier. But part was different and new. Even without the weight of Louiza in his arms, Tibor's determination lightened Malory. He let Tibor guide him, be his Virgil, across the Ponte Cestio and into Trastevere, the dome of St. Peter's making the occasional flirtatious appearance according to the curve of the river. He followed Tibor down a set of steps fragrant with rotting leaves and urine into the medieval circle of Rome, past the prison of Regina Coeli up to a high gate that shivered with the sound of drums, an electric guitar, and a Rumanian-accented song he thought he recognized.

Cuttlefish ink
Cappuccino double
With a fork and knife
On the Spanish Stairs.

"Dylan?" Malory asked. It was the soundtrack of garden parties and May Balls along the Cam, but in a less self-conscious key— F-sharp major, perhaps—one whose strings were less taut, whose harmonics were less forced than the madrigals and pantos and practiced frivolity of Cambridge. Tibor pushed open the gate. Seven or so first- and second-tier members of the Bomb Squad, tie-dyed and batiked and bandanaed and bejeweled, and a variety of Danube mädchens, befrocked like Florence Nightingale auditioning for *The Night Porter,* were gathered around Sasha who, guitar draped like a Kalashnikov across his chest and perched on the bonnet of a shipwrecked car, was in full chorus:

Gotta get a bag from my hotel room,
Where I got me some dates from a pretty little girl in Greece,
She promise, she beat and whip me,
When I pain my fututi pizda!

"So . . .Welcome to the Dacia."

Radu handed them glass jars filled with a bubbling, celebratory punch of indistinct origin. Nurses thrust ramekins beneath their chins, full of mozzarella and olive and some impossibly hot Carpathian pepper. More of them, dozens of them, Nurses and Bomb Squad, danced through the gate and in and out of the shadows of Christmas lights hanging like Babylonian grapes from the iron struts of the Dacia. Smudge pots of citronella lit the dying moments of quixotic mosquitoes who had slouched over to the Dacia from the neighboring Botanical Gardens. The Dacia, as Malory discovered over the succeeding weeks of punch and grill, had once been a nursery of fig and pear and apricot and apple trees for princes and cardinals who lived at the fecund base of the Gianicolo, two healthy spits away from the Vatican. The Nurses and the Bomb Squad took over the ruins of a house and garden from impatient families who used it as a rest room around the corner from the prison of Regina Coeli. They fixed the holes in the roof, put locks on the doors, ran the whole thing through with industrial brooms and whitewash, and baptized the compound as the Dacia, not because of any romantic memories of the summer *dachas* of Pasternak or Akhmatova or the Bucharest *nomenklatura,* but because Brendushka's diminutive Dacia 1300 finally dropped its gearshaft in the middle of the garden after her flight from Bucharest. It was late October 1978 to Malory, the physics dropout from Cambridge. But to refugees from the other side of the Iron Gate it was still the Summer of Love.

That first night, Malory did little more than sip at his jar of punch as Radu and Sasha—once he'd relinquished his guitar to Dora or Brendushka or one of the other many Nurses Malory eventually came to know—and a handful of other members of the Bomb Squad peppered him with questions. Not just searching for the obvious physical details about Louiza, but for behavioral quirks—the way she walked, the way she talked, the way she thought. Malory gladly told and retold the stories of his two encounters with Louiza to an audience far more demonstrative than Settimio. He told them about Louiza's mathematics, he told them about Whistler Abbey. They were intrigued by the story of negativity and soberly awed by the image of Louiza tracing $i = u$ onto Malory's naked chest in the late afternoon light of St. George's.

"Do not forget the Pip." Tibor pulled at a cigarette and wiped the smoke from his beard. And so Malory told them of the Pip, from Louiza's discovery in the shutters of the steeple of St. George's through its fall from the organ loft of Santa Maria and Tibor's miraculous discovery of the tiny apple seed in the morning shadows of the pavement below the altar. Malory tried not to embellish or editorialize. But Radu in particular encouraged him not to worry himself too much with the effect his own attraction to Louiza had on his description of the girl.

"We need to find the girl you are searching for," he said. "Not just some little blonde named Louiza."

When he was finished, Malory excused himself and walked out the gate. The Driver found him around a discreet corner and drove him on the Vespa back home to the Villa Septimania. Malory returned the next night and the next for an update from this new family of dispossessed. The Nurses and Bomb Squad would wander in at odd moments from their occasional jobs. Some evenings Tibor was already at the Dacia when Malory arrived, some evenings he showed up later or not at all. But Malory always found a Nurse chopping vegetables she had seduced off a *fruttivendolo* in the markets of Campo dei Fiori or San Cosimato, and Radu or Sasha or Vlad scaling and grilling a fish that one or another extra from Tibor's production had donated to the cause. Malory listened to tales of discovery as they chopped and scaled and he experimentally sipped on a glass of whatever was placed in his hand. He listened to stories of escape from the East— Radu and Sasha wrapped in horse blankets in a corner of a refrigerated truck, Dora and Anda less insulated in the boot of an English tourist's Morris Minor. Tibor and Cristina had flown out of Bucharest in style, of course, thanks to Cristina's discovery of an uncle in Ramat Gan, who wangled her an Israeli visa with a flight connection in Rome.

"*Nel mezzo del cammin di nostra vita*," Tibor quoted to whomever would listen. "We got off the plane in the middle of the flight, and that particular yellow line suits us just fine."

Much of the truth of Tibor's story was veiled in cigarette smoke, but no one dared contradict Tibor when he was in voice. The paw that Tibor had first placed on Malory's shoulder, that Transylvanian crag of a hand, was nothing compared to the force that hogtied the Bomb Squad, the Nurses, and any others he corralled into the garden of the Dacia with his stories. Malory was as happy as the rest of them to recline on the paternal speechifying of Tibor.

Cristina, as *Principessa*, held her own court and followed a different protocol. Cristina never had to queue for auditions. She arrived in Rome to three well-paying jobs—cleaning a Canadian journalist's office in Piazza Barberini, wiping the noses and bottoms of four-year-olds in an *asilo* on the Via Sistina, and preparing lunch for a lonely fiddle maker in an *attico* off Piazza Navona twice a week. Cristina never followed Tibor on his evening tours of the garden. Cristina perched gray-eyed on a sprung sofa off the kitchen, smoking a filtered cigarette of exotic origin. Some evenings, she would look over to Malory, and Malory would join her. He didn't smoke. But he shared their loss in a silence that he hoped gave her as much comfort as it gave him. And sometime during the evening—before dinner, during, or most often once the dishes had been piled up in the Dacia bathtub—Cristina would stand up from the sprung sofa. The Bomb Squad, or occasionally a non-Rumanian guest, would strike a guitar or a zither or a drum, and Cristina and the Nurses would throw on costume boas or army greatcoats or strip down to their Weimar nighties and perform a post-Brechtian, pre-Madonna cabaret with a determined chaos that, for at least a little while, helped all of them forget the daily indignities of exile.

Malory expected it would be a matter of days until the Bomb Squad found Louiza and their child. But as the rains of November rose higher up the embankment of the Tevere, overflowing the Isola Tiberina and threatening the trees along the upriver prow and the more untraveled cargo holds of the Ospedale Fatebenefratelli, as the rains of December drove Tibor's *Divine Comedy* rehearsals under sheets of plastic and corrugated scrap, the Bomb Squad returned every evening to the Dacia without a single wisp of fair hair or dyslexic, mathematical clue.

"Sometimes," Radu said to Malory one evening, wiping the rain off his glasses with the sleeve of Malory's jacket, "you get closer to your treasure by figuring out where it definitely is not." Malory put his own palm on Radu's shoulder. Perhaps he had lost, perhaps they all had lost at least as much as Malory and had even less of a chance of recovery. "Some bombs are hidden very deep."

"Accidental discovery, *mio Principe*." Settimio listened every morning at breakfast, as he served Malory his Earl Grey and scones in front of the statues of Newton and the Woman and the Apple, as Malory recounted the previous evening's Tales from the Dacia. "The history of man, and I suspect nature in general, is one of accidental discovery, finding something precious while looking for something else."

"But don't you understand? I don't want anything else."

Settimio knew that the cure for petulance was to be found in the Sanctum Sanctorum. And during the days—while Malory waited for the evening summons to the Dacia and hope of news from the Bomb Squad—Settimio profited from Malory's other passions and cushioned him with manuscripts around the seven-sided desk.

One of those mornings, the day before Christmas, Settimio appeared at the padded door of the Sanctum Sanctorum.

"*Mio Principe.*"

Malory had been examining the manuscript of Newton's *Principia*—although he found himself taking frequent breaks to read back over Haroun al Rashid's encounters with the daughter of Charlemagne. He placed a slip of paper into the book, slightly embarrassed that Settimio might have found him out, and looked up.

"You may recall Fra Mario. From the Dominicans. Santa Maria . . ."

"Of course!" Malory said, climbing up from the stables of the Jewish butcher back to memories of an organ left untuned and a girl left unfound.

"Fra Mario rang," Settimio said, "on the telephone, a moment ago. A young lady, he said."

Malory jumped up—less petulant now—and headed towards Settimio and the padding. He had known, at least he had hoped that, even if his own gravity was insufficient, the bulk of Santa Maria sopra Minerva might pull Louiza back to its pews and end his two months of anxiety and search. This was better than any voyage of transformation.

"Not that young lady, *purtroppo*," Settimio said. "A young Italian lady. Quite insistent. Fra Mario said that she must see you at once."

"Italian?" Malory asked. "I don't know any young Italian ladies."

But when fifteen minutes later the Driver parked the Vespa in the Via del Beato Angelico and escorted Malory through the rear entrance of Santa Maria, past Michelangelo's *Salvatore*, past the tomb of the anorexic Santa Caterina and past the pew below the organ where he had last found Louiza, the copper curls bobbing above the gate of the Carafa Chapel reminded Malory that yes, indeed, he did know one Italian lady.

"Malory," Antonella whispered—but with the same enthusiasm she used to serve him biscuits and tea in the Maths Faculty. Malory hugged Antonella back—not caring that the Lippi Madonna was looking down at him with contempt—happy, grateful at this very fleshy reminder of a life before his landing on the planet of Septimania. "Look at you!" Antonella said finally, releasing him only to hold him at the length of a nose and a little more. "What a change."

"Well, yes," Malory said, "a haircut, a few new clothes . . ."

"No, no," Antonella said. "Your eyes, Malory. They are—they have become so vulnerable. You have seen a few ghosts since the last time you drank tea with your Antonella."

"You're in Rome for Christmas? To see family?" Malory asked, trying to ignore the warmth of both her sympathy and the scent of lavender that came off her hair. I should invite her out for tea or coffee, he thought, without knowing where or how. The Villa Septimania was out of the question, and Malory hadn't ever drunk tea or coffee outside the villa.

"To see you, my Malory. Only you."

"Me?"

"To bring you news."

"About Louiza?" Malory couldn't help himself, although he wished he'd been slightly more discreet and kept up the pretense of interest in Antonella herself for just a few more minutes. Antonella looked at Malory and at Malory's curiosity. His need to know, far beyond any normal curiosity, kept him looking into her eyes. The midafternoon light shone blue around Antonella's red curls. Above that halo, Lippi's *Annunciation* ballooned in illustration—closer than when Malory had looked above Louiza's head back in October and seen her face in the pale oval of the Madonna. Now it was the curls of the Angel, come to give good news to the Madonna, that Malory saw reflected in the hairdo of the Italian girl before him.

"Be careful," Antonella said.

"Careful of what?" Had this been the good news the Angel gave Mary?

"When you left Cambridge," Antonella said, "there were many Americans who stopped by the Faculty."

"Looking for Louiza?"

Antonella kept her gaze fixed on Malory.

"I know this is the last thing you want to hear from your Antonella, my Malory. Forget Louiza. Please, for your own safety."

"What does Louiza have to do with my safety?"

"Please, Malory . . ."

"Antonella, who were these Americans?"

"Americans, Malory. Like the Americans my mother told me about after the War. All smiling and asking innocent questions about imaginary numbers and dividing by zero."

"Dividing by zero?" Malory found himself squeezing Antonella's hand in his excitement. Hadn't Louiza told him about her childhood ambition to divide by zero? And here were the Americans snooping around the Maths Faculty talking about dividing by zero.

"Malory," Antonella said, "these are not ordinary mathematicians. One of them—he looked like a soldier—he came and sat on the edge of my desk. He said he liked my hair, you know, that kind of soldier. He asked me about dividing by zero, and I told him I don't even divide chocolate biscuits. And then, as he was reaching inside my biscuit tin, I thought of my Malory, and I said, 'If you want to know about dividing by zero, why don't you ask Louiza?'"

"And?" Malory knew he was squeezing too tightly but didn't want to break the spell of the name.

"The soldier jumped up from my desk as if my biscuit was poison!"

Malory wasn't certain why he was excited by this news—it certainly supported Antonella's contention that this was dangerous business. But it was the first time since October that the world had deigned to recognize the reality of Louiza.

"I don't know if they are CIA," Antonella whispered, "or FBI or military or top secret some other letters. But if you want to know what your Antonella thinks, I think Louiza is working in another Maths Faculty that doesn't have anything to do with my Sidgwick Site. Some place that is very interesting to the Americans. Some place secret. And dangerous. I know."

Dangerous. If Louiza were, in fact, involved with American intelligence, then there must be a way—Settimio would certainly have the appropriate phone numbers tucked somewhere in the Villa—for Malory to contact them, find her. He had selected the latest pope, been asked to serve dinner to Princess Grace. That must be good for something, for information. "Was there one American?" Malory asked. "Tall? Red beard?"

"Information is dangerous, Malory."

Malory couldn't imagine what Antonella meant. Cholera was dangerous. The Red Brigades were dangerous. Miscalculating the arrival of a Dublin-bound ferry was dangerous. But information had neither bacteria nor trigger.

"But your Antonella has other information that will make her Malory very excited!" Antonella unleashed her hands and plunged them into the unshapen cloth bag on the pew beside her. Malory expected biscuits. Instead, Antonella drew out a Heffers bag holding a heavy binder, the size of a doctoral dissertation. "*Ecco!*" she said. "You see, Malory. All you have to do is ask your Antonella, and . . ." Malory couldn't for the life of him remember what he had asked his—had asked Antonella, except, of course, to help him in any and all ways to find Louiza. Then he opened the binder and remembered.

Before leaving Cambridge, he had shown the Chapbook to Antonella and had asked her to translate the first lines. *One garden. One tree.* That much he remembered. She had offered to make a photocopy and more, a full translation—since all but the final lines were in Italian and Malory's grasp of the language didn't extend beyond *buon giorno* and *forse oggi.*

"My goodness," he said, trying to focus a new enthusiasm on Antonella's dedication.

"Oh, Malory," Antonella said, seeing straight into the heart of Malory's embarrassment. "You have no idea what is inside here. All the travels, all the meetings of your Isaac Newton. I used a marker to highlight all the names of people and places." Antonella turned to Malory until he was almost in her lap, under the gaze of Lippi's Madonna, the divine impregnation coming at her on the wings of a dove, full of a certain kind of portent. She turned the pages. Names jumped up at Malory in yellow—Rotterdam, Münster, the Abbey of Westphalia, Princess Elizabeth of Bohemia, Descartes, Nuremberg, Leibniz.

"Leibniz!" Malory shrieked, perhaps less loudly than when the Pip flew off the organ loft of Santa Maria but no less forcefully. "Leibniz in a journal about Newton? Newton hated Leibniz. Leibniz boasted that he had invented the calculus first, before Newton." And yet, Malory read in the journal of Newton's Italian chum about how the two of them had stopped off in Nuremberg in August of 1666 to visit some Rosicrucian friends of the chum and had met the young Leibniz, who was working as an apothecary and engaged Newton in a discussion of alchemy.

Malory, of course, knew all about Newton's interest in alchemy, his years of research and countless experiments looking for the Philosopher's Stone that would turn ordinary metals into gold and the Elixir of Life, the liquid gateway to immortality. He knew about his calculation of the End of Time based on cranky interpretations of Biblical texts. But Malory, like all other Newton scholars, considered these interests to be the side hobbies at best of a Newton gone ga-ga long after his brain had been pickled by the extraordinary discoveries of 1666.

And yet here, so it seemed, was information—information more precise than the vague notion that Americans were snooping around the Cambridge Maths Faculty trying to divide by zero—that Newton was interested in alchemy from an early age. Perhaps the Newton community had it backwards. Perhaps alchemy, magic, and crackpot religion had been Newton's reasons for waking up in the morning, and the hard science—the work on gravitation, optics, the calculus (and meeting Leibniz in the winter of 1666!)—were at best sidelines, things that Newton whipped off while he was sitting on the loo. Accidental discoveries, as Settimio would say.

Malory looked up at Antonella. The light around her had changed. Beyond the copper curls and blue halo, Antonella was indeed the Angel of the Annunciation. She had brought him great good news, information that, perhaps like the announcement of the Virgin's impending birth, was both miraculous and potentially dangerous.

"Antonella," he said, lifting her up from the pew, "it's Christmas Eve. Would you like to see something spectacular?"

THE PREMIERE OF TIBOR'S *DIVINE COMEDY* WAS SET FOR THAT EVENING. After much back and forth with the Minister of Monuments, half a dozen archaeologists, and the *carabinieri* of eight districts, a 5 p.m.

curtain was scheduled for the *Inferno* in the Colosseum. The *Purgatorio* would begin its procession at midnight, winding out past the Forum, Trajan's Column, Mussolini's balcony in the Piazza Venezia, and up the Corso to the Piazza del Popolo. And then, in the first light of Christmas morning, the finale to Dante's grand trio, the *Paradiso*, would unveil itself in St. Peter's Square.

Malory led Antonella out of Santa Maria as the bell in the spiral of the tower of San Ivo rang four. The elephant with the obelisk balanced on its back looked revived, washed clean of color. Malory also felt the anticipation of renewal, and it drew Antonella's sculpted fingers into the crook of his arm at the top of the steps. Malory knew that the Driver was watching from a discreet distance. He didn't mind. He didn't mind the Driver following them as they walked out to the Corso and past the single pine tree in the center of the Piazza Venezia. He didn't mind him following them down the Fori Imperiali, already overflowing its banks with Romans heading towards Christmas dinners and tourists searching for pre-Christian meaning in a beer or a Negroni.

The Colosseum was an end in itself for Malory, a chance to celebrate Tibor's first Christmas, his first success in the West. The forward guard of Bomb Squad and Nurses greeted Malory at the entrance closest to the Arch of Constantine. They registered Antonella with a care that recognizes fragility. They handed Malory two tickets—he was certain the Driver would find his own way in.

In the two months since he had invited Malory to play Dante, Tibor had stayed true to his word. He hadn't called Malory to a single rehearsal, hadn't given him a single line to learn in either Italian or English. At one point Dora, with her Louise Brooks fringe and omnivorous mouth, had tried to describe Tibor's directorial method; in Bucharest, she had been Tibor's assistant for the first six months of his marriage thanks to a friendship with Cristina forged during hot teenage summers on the Black Sea, with official boyfriends and contraband cigarettes.

"What the audience sees is one thing," she told Malory one evening in the back seat of Brendushka's Dacia. "What Tibor sees is another. He has a dozen actors and actresses and assorted hangers-on

of varying talents playing Dante during the course of the whole production. After all," she said, "from the top of the Colosseum or the
back of St. Peter's, who can see a face, especially if it's wearing one
of those pointy Dante caps with ear flaps. What really matters"—and
Malory wasn't certain whether it was the hand on his forearm or the
weight of Dora's mascara that drew him into the sobriety behind her
eyes—"what really matters is what Tibor sees as he is imagining his
Comedy."

"But the five or ten Dantes," Malory said. "Aren't they confused?
Isn't a single Dante, one actor, one face, one personality better?" And
he told Dora and a few others in the front seat about Isaac Newton,
about Newton's discovery written in the margin of a Chapbook, about
the search for the One True Rule that guides the universe.

"You really believe in this Newton?" Dora asked him, resting a
narrow chin on his shoulder.

"Well . . ." Malory began.

"What he believes"—Tibor stuck his beard through a rear window into the middle of Malory's lecture—"is in the number one. Not
just one Dante, but one rule, one girl, one god."

"Why not?" Radu said. "One is a good number. At least it's
a start."

"So . . ." Tibor said. "My poor friends. You have learned nothing from your childhoods on the dark side of the moon."

"He means Rumania," Dora whispered up at Malory, her chin
still uncomfortably present. "Ceauşescu, our beloved president,
thought he was the only One."

"But I'm not talking about politics," Malory whispered back.

"Then why talk about girls?" Tibor roared. "One girl! One girl!
This sacred search for One! Why not two girls, why not twenty-two?"

"Or seven?" It was Sasha, innocent and inquiring, standing outside in the grass. How had he picked the number seven?

"I like One." Dora breathed garlic into a cloud around Malory,
who knew that she meant something else.

As Tibor predicted, Mastroianni, Cardinale, the pop stars Mina
and Adriano Celentano, the blue suits of the Camera dei Deputati led
by Giulio Andreotti, whose sins would have landed him a choice seat

in any number of circles, all the politicians and movie stars, club own-
ers, and tourists came out for the four hours of the *Inferno*, a chance
to visit Hell on Christmas Eve and still catch mass at midnight.
Heretics, Adulterers—the Proud, the Gluttonous—seven circles, one
for every sin, wound down the inner shell of the Colosseum. All was
flame and music and spectacle. Although there was at least one Dante
and one Virgil, one tiny Beatrice—Dante's unreachable teenage love—
somewhere in the arena, Malory gave up early on trying to point out
to Antonella the difference between the actors and the audience. A
trio of popes, both Abraham and Mohamed, suicides, sodomites, and
false leaders. Francesca da Rimini and her brother-in-law Paolo flitted
by like a pair of starlings—up, down, eternally attached by some unheard
signal. They stopped for a moment on the terrace below Malory and
Antonella and looked up at them:

> *Love, which in gentle hearts is quickly born,*
> *Seized him for my fair body . . .*

Francesca sighed, before flitting away.
"What did she say?" Malory turned to Antonella.
"She's talking about her brother-in-law Paolo," Antonella said.
"They were very naughty." Francesca flew back:

> *One day, for pleasure,*
> *We read of Lancelot, by love constrained:*
> *Alone, suspecting nothing, at our leisure.*

Lancelot, the faithful right-hand of King Arthur, had been as much a
hero to the nine-year-old Malory as the giant Hercules, although at
that age he couldn't possibly have understood quite how naughty
Lancelot was with Guinevere, the wife of his best friend.

> *Sometimes at what we read our glances joined,*
> *Looking from the book each to the other's eyes,*

Looking from the book. Malory remembered the book they must have
read—his namesake's, Sir Thomas Malory's *Le Morte d'Arthur*—and

the illustration of Lancelot kneeling before a queen with long, red, pre-Raphaelite locks.

> *And then the color in our faces drained . . .*
> *That day we read of Lancelot no more.*

Francesca and Paolo flew away in a cloud of immigrant extras, and with them went the attention of the crowd. But Malory felt Antonella's hand in his. A single hand, he thought, will not cast me down into the circle of Hell reserved for adulterers who read books. Anyway, he resolved, it is a hand of guidance not of naughtiness. He let that hand remain in his for the rest of the journey, even as Dante and Virgil climbed to the top of the ruin and upward to the stars.

They filed out in silence, along with the other thousands, too stunned by their private visions to begin to appreciate Tibor's art. And yet very few—only the Bomb Squad, the Nurses, Cristina, a few experimental theater directors from Latvia, and a pair of acting students from Texas on Fulbrights—joined Malory and Antonella on the long hike to the Piazza del Popolo and the late-night limbo of the *Purgatorio*. By the final cantos, when Malory and Antonella followed Virgil up from the purgatory of the Piazza to the Eden of the Villa Borghese to watch the sun rise over Rome and breakfast on apples, there were fewer still.

Malory and Antonella walked arm in arm almost alone in the pre-dawn, back down the winding path to the Piazza. He had invited her to this spectacle without warning her what it might be—since he, in fact, had only the vaguest notion. But she had followed, she had listened, she had understood perhaps even better than he. Was he guiding her, or was she indeed the Angel of the Annunciation, her red curls leading him to his one Madonna, his only Beatrice?

An audience had already gathered in the Piazza San Pietro as they arrived. Canto by canto it increased in size. By the time the *Paradiso* swelled into its grand finale, Malory guessed there might have been as many in the crowd as on the day that the Polish pope first waved to his Italian fans. In the final canto, the velvet ropes of St. Peter's opened and the thousands of lost souls in the piazza surged inside. The grand organ of St. Peter's—a Tamburini from Crema, Malory knew—began to play a tune he recognized dimly and then recognized completely. It was a melody he had played in Whistler Abbey, a melody that had awakened Tibor on the morning they had first met. MALORY = LOUIZA was the tune. Had he sung it to Tibor? Had Tibor really listened to Malory? Did anyone else know?

And then he saw the cast—the Beatrice, the Dante, Virgil, Thomas Aquinas, Paolo, and Francesca, all two hundred actors and musicians and extras—he saw the audience turn as one and begin to sing:

Tanti Auguri a te,
Tanti Auguri a te,
Happy Birthday to Dante . . .

To Dante?

They were looking at him. He was not Dante, but they were clearly singing to him, to Malory. It was his birthday, the way it had been Isaac Newton's 309 years earlier. No one had sung to him since his tenth birthday, his last Christmas with his mother. And now, here in St. Peter's as he stood with Antonella on the circle of porphyry, the Pole walked up the steps to the altar below Bernini's *baldacchino* preparing to celebrate Christmas Mass and waved down the nave to Malory—

Happy Birthday to You!

Malory waved back, with hesitation and pride to his friend at the altar. And as the cheering continued, he turned to the congregation behind him and waved to them. Beyond those thousands in the nave, Michelangelo's sculpted mother sat holding her son in her lap. He wished his own mother, he even wished Old Mrs. Emery could have been here for the cheering. And there was another mother, another child . . . Antonella took his elbow and turned him away from the dream, straddling his biceps with her very immediate breasts.

"Happy Birthday, my Malory." With two gentle hands, she curled the stray hairs of Malory's fringe behind his ears and pulled his lips to hers. And as the fluffy *zabaione* of Antonella's lower lip touched Malory's upper, an elixir tasting of Marsala and the yolk of forbidden eggs and forgetfulness pumped a warmth into Malory. Antonella's lips came briefly away from his and drew with them an anesthetic that had coated his senses for nine long months, releasing a new drug that pulsed through his lips and tongue, across his cheeks, along his jaw to the nerves that sparked his brain, and down his throat to the untapped pipes of his most delicate organs. It unplugged, transposed the key of everything that Malory believed—beyond the skepticism of Tibor or the ministrations of Settimio—beyond everything Malory had worshipped since that first afternoon in the organ loft of St. George's, Whistler Abbey.

Here he was in Rome with another woman, not Louiza. Here was Antonella, tasting of pillow and *zabaione*, and—as she wrapped her fingers into the few bits of gray matter that remained beneath his hair and urged his own hands lower towards the abundant bits of Italian girl that only the nearest celebrants in St. Peter's could see—not only did she seem to want Malory, not only had she worked and traveled hundreds of miles to see Malory, but she had done so while knowing of Malory's single-minded pursuit of Louiza. There was a part of Malory—just how much he was only beginning to sense—that, after a single fragrant kiss, was tempted by Antonella. Not the unseen, veiled Madonna but the very present Angel. Antonella reached up and took Malory's face between her hands and kissed him again, without translation, without tea and biscuits, without Anna Ford or the Carafa Chapel.

"*Fututi pizda matii!*" The paw landed on Malory's shoulder.

"Tibor!" Malory shouted, detaching, recalibrating. "This is Antonella. A colleague of mine. From Cambridge." But it was not only Tibor. Cristina, Radu, Brendushka, Dora, Sasha, and the entire pack of Bomb Squad and Nurses were jumping and flitting around them in a show of Rumanian enthusiasm.

"*Eccezionale*, Tibor! *Complimenti!*" Without releasing Malory, Antonella reached up and kissed Tibor on both bearded cheeks.

"*Grazie mille, bella* . . ." Tibor bowed. "But tonight the *complimenti* are for the birthday boy."

"How did you know?" Malory began.

"We are the Bomb Squad," Sasha said. "Do I need to remind you?"

"And the party is just beginning. Brendushka," Tibor called, "take Malory's colleague to the Dacia. I want to steal our hero for a few minutes."

"Malory!" Antonella held onto his hand.

"Do not worry," Tibor laughed. "The Dacia is my kingdom, and you are under my protection and the care of my Nurses."

Malory kissed Antonella one last time and then let Tibor lead him out of St. Peter's, below the balcony where only two months before the Polish cardinal had been reborn as pope to the world of Catholic believers. They threaded through the remnants of Christmas morning out the arches of St. Peter's into the quiet of Santo Spirito.

"Thank you, Tibor," Malory said at last. "Your *Divine Comedy* was spectacular. And that last . . ." Malory reddened, knowing that he was about to gush. "That was amazing!"

"Happy Birthday, Dante," Tibor said. "Enjoy your day in Paradiso." As they walked, without haste, without aim, down the Via della Lungara, Malory felt he was entering a new world—a world that was certainly new to Malory at least. In that world, Tibor had gathered the forces of the displaced and homeless of Rome to celebrate Malory's journey down to the depths of Hell and back up to Paradise. There was no room in this new world for discretion.

"It's time, Tibor," Malory said, "that I told you where I went that evening, when those men took me away from the hospital."

Malory told Tibor about the Vespa ride to the Sistine Chapel. He told him about the Turn that chose the new Pope, about his own investiture on the porphyry circle of St. Peter's as Holy Roman Emperor and King of the Jews. He told him about Isaac Newton and how the whole story boiled down to One—one rule, one god, one woman. He told Tibor about Settimio and the Driver and Septimania, the invisible country that gave him unlimited powers. He told him about the Sanctum Sanctorum. He told him about the Pip.

Tibor listened as they walked, silent, unsmoking.

"So," he said. "Septimania. In this country of Septimania, you believe that if you find the answer to Newton, if you bring all of the world's religions under your belt, then you will also buy Peace in Our Time and find your girl? The One Girl?"

He understood, Malory thought. He wasn't taking Malory for crazy or delusional.

"What about your colleague?" Tibor asked, a paw steering Malory towards the parapet overlooking the Tevere.

"She arrived this afternoon from Cambridge. With information about Louiza."

"Malory," Tibor said, "I am not a scientist or a king, only a poor, unemployed Rumanian from behind the Iron Eight Ball. But I do know that redheaded women do not come all the way to Rome to give organ tuners information about lost girlfriends."

"You're wrong," Malory said.

"Holy Roman Emperor," Tibor said, placing both paws down on Malory's shoulders. "Don't be a Holy Roman Fool."

Cristina and Dora swept by and pulled Tibor and Malory out of their conference. But Malory fell away into the backwater of the sidewalk beneath the plane trees, where he found Radu leaning against the parapet overlooking the Tevere.

"I'm sorry, Malory," Radu said.

"Sorry?" Malory asked. "That I am one year older and starting to lose my hair?"

"I imagine Tibor just told you."

"Tibor told me a lot of things."

"About Louiza?"

"Louiza?" Now it was Malory's turn to place a tentative hand on Radu's shoulder.

"He didn't tell you?"

"Radu, tell me!" Malory had just said goodbye to his Angel of an Antonella. But the sound of Louiza's name convinced him that this Divine Comedy, this divine birthday was bringing him a transcendent luck he could never imagine. The Bomb Squad had found Louiza, his prayers—such as they were—had been answered. "Where is she? At the Dacia?"

Radu took off his glasses and wiped them on a pocket of his anorak. "I can't believe Tibor didn't tell you," he mumbled into the pitted asphalt at his feet.

"Tell me what? Where is she? How is she? Is she okay? And the baby?"

"We didn't find her," Radu said.

"Oh," Malory said. Okay, he thought. The usual daily regret. A little more disappointment than usual. "But you will keep looking?"

"No," Radu said, "we won't."

"What do you mean?"

"She isn't here. Not in Rome, not in Italy, not in Europe."

"You know?"

"We know."

"Then where?" Malory was shaking Radu again. The sun was fully risen on the waters of the Tevere. The river was moving fast, swollen with the flood.

Radu shrugged. "The Bomb Squad has failed."

"But," Malory said.

"It is the first time. I'm sorry."

Malory's hand slid from Radu's shoulder.

"You better come talk to Tibor. At the party."

Malory stared out at the water.

"Let's go." Radu took Malory's elbow. But Malory had turned into a stone as rigid as the statue of Newton. He felt Radu try. He felt Radu give up and leave. He felt the eddies of the crowd from St. Peter's part around him as they headed home for Christmas lunch. When he finally began to move again, it was without compass or sense of propulsion, but only with the force of his pain now that the sedative on his lips had worn off. It drew him downriver, past the steps to Regina Coeli and the Dacia. It drew him across the Ponte Cestio to the Isola Tiberina, to the mini Albert Memorial with the Ospedale Israelite on his right and the Ospedale Fatebenefratelli on his left. The tide pulled him portside into the *cortile,* the *cortile* he had crossed countless times, where Tibor had smoked and waited for Cristina. It was there that gravity proved stronger than pain and Malory sat down on a bench, all hope abandoned.

There was a sound at his feet. Malory looked. A bag. From Heffers in Cambridge. He picked up the bag, looked inside. A binder. The binder, heavy and black, that he had been carrying all night—Antonella's translation of the Newton Chapbook. It had become such a part of Malory as he followed Tibor's production for eighteen hours that he had completely forgotten its existence.

Malory opened the cover where it lay by his feet in the *cortile*. *One tree, one garden*, he read again. He read to the bottom of the first page. And then the second. By the tenth page, he had picked up the binder and settled himself onto the bench. Noon passed. Malory read on. Oblivious to noise, oblivious to tranquility, Malory read the account of Newton's friend. He read of the travels of the pair from Cambridge to Rome, their meetings with Leibniz and a variety of princesses and abbesses.

As he read, it became clear to him that Newton's friend was not only aware of Septimania, but was himself the King. This was the journal of the King of Septimania, circa 1666, a man who had disguised himself as a student—the way Haroun had disguised himself as his own envoy—in order to travel to Cambridge to study. There he had met Newton, recognized his intellect, and encouraged him to travel abroad during the forced sabbatical of 1666. The Chapbook that his grandmother had given him in St. George's, Whistler Abbey, Malory realized, was written by one of his own ancestors, someone close enough to his Sir Isaac that Newton had felt comfortable enough to scrawl a discovery—perhaps the most important discovery in the history of science—in a margin. Antonella might be waiting for him at the party in the Dacia, but Malory had to read—it was her translation, after all.

Malory read. He read of Newton's arrival in Rome, his visit to the Church of Santa Maria sopra Minerva, his introduction to the sculptor Gian Lorenzo Bernini. As he read, he turned back and forth, searching within the daily notes for the identity of the woman in the Bernini sculpture with the floating apple. Was it the sister of the King of Septimania, his mother perhaps, a daughter of the Settimio of the time?

And then the truth walked out of the smoke, like a *djinni* from a Baghdadi lamp.

"Here are the facts," the King wrote one late night. And Malory read on:

Here are the facts, presented with a desire to bring Reason to a human act, far from cold marble.

We returned from our visit with Bernini and took our supper without conversation. Isaac repaired to his room and I to mine. My custom was to bathe and be in bed by midnight. But this evening, I sent Settimio away and took myself into the Sanctum Sanctorum, where the silence of my books, the books of Septimania, might give my mind the tranquility to listen to the beating of my heart.

And so it was in the deepest hours of the night—the clock had struck three times but I was so entwined with the words on the page that I literally defied Gravity—that I felt Isaac's hand on my shoulder. I had left the door ajar from the vestibule down the passage to the Sanctum Sanctorum, thinking none would enter but—I ask my older self—was I not nurturing an unconscious hope?

"You have kept a secret," Isaac said to me, looking around the room in admiration. He was wearing only a nightshirt. His feet were bare.

"There are secrets I must keep," I said. "It is part of my duty to Septimania."

"This room," he began.

"I can tell you a few things about this room," I said softly. "It contains seven catalogues. Grammar, Rhetoric, Logic, Arithmetic, Geometry, Music, Astronomy. Each contains seven drawers. Each drawer in turn is divided into seven sections. Each catalogue leads to a separate library, entered through one of the seven doors, although many of the volumes are not here within this building—don't ask me, please, I am not at liberty to tell you where. But make no mistake," I added quickly. "There is no special meaning to the number seven. None, at least, that I have uncovered."

"These books"—Isaac motioned to a stack upon a leather desk.

"Have only just arrived," I said. "It is part of Settimio's employ to assist me with the catalogue, although he has trusted minions to do the actual labor."

"Artephius His Secret Book," *Isaac read.* "The Epistle of John Pontanus, Nicholas Flamel, his Exposition of the Hieroglyphical Figures which he caused to be painted upon an Arch in St Innocents Churchyard in Paris. Containing both the Theoricke and the Practicke of the Philosophers Stone, Lazarus Zetzner's Theatrum Chemicum. *Are you searching,*" Isaac asked me, "*in earnest through these books for a recipe for the Philosopher's Stone?*"

"*Ah,*" I said. "*I have been pondering the properties of stone, following this afternoon's visit to Bernini. His Apollo and Daphne. That moment when the nymph turned to laurel just as the god was about to capture her, her feet taking root, branches sprouting around her girdle, fingers blossoming into leaf.*"

"*I too was thinking of Bernini,*" said Isaac.

"*You spoke this afternoon of the attraction of two bodies at a distance. What the Stoics called Sympathy. I wonder,*" I continued, "*whether Bernini could sculpt another particular moment. A moment of three bodies. The moment when the attraction of the apple to the scientist, or the desire of the scientist for wisdom, proves greater than the power of the tree over its fruit. Surely,*" I added, as Isaac's eyebrows rose on his forehead, "*if the Earth can remain suspended above the Sun, and the Moon can remain suspended above the Earth, and the Comets above all else, an apple and a genius can pull off the trick.*"

"*You are wondering,*" Isaac asked, "*if the Sympathy is strong enough, what is stopping a man from sculpting an apple suspended in mid-air?*"

"*Suspended between the tree and the outstretched hand,*" I answered. "*Yes.*"

"*I prithee,*" he said. "*Let's talk of Nature and not wax mystical.*"

"*I live in a world of mystery,*" I replied. "*Every discovery I make leads irrevocably to another mystery.*"

"*One does well, therefore,*" Isaac said, "*to choose one's mysteries with care.*"

"*Do we choose our mysteries?*"

"*Perhaps they choose us.*" Isaac sat down next to me on the bench, his nightshirt hiked up to expose one pale, chilblained knee. "*I was born on a Christmas morning . . .*"

"*You've told me the story many times.*" It was my turn to interrupt. "*Methinks it is you who is waxing mystical.*"

"Perhaps these questions of Sympathy are best left to chance."

And at that moment, I reached down, past the exposed knee and between the legs of my giant and felt Isaac rising against the pull of nature, a force that had more to do with the attraction of two bodies than the force of gravity, an obelisk rising away from knowledge. He groaned, I am forced to say, and his great eyebrows relaxed until his face took on the look of that tiny Christmas-born babe too small to fit in a pint pot.

And it was then that his own hands made an equal and opposite reaction. His hands, the hands of my Isaac, slipped down between my legs and began a search, first up, then down. A search for something that reason told him should be there, but experiment proved was not. And since our experiment was too far advanced to admit retreat, I removed my trousers, showing him that not finding the expected is sometimes the greatest triumph of Science. In recompense, I then undid my blouse, removed the pins from the bandage around my breasts and let loose the abundant secret that only Settimio and now Isaac knew—that I am as much a nymph as Bernini's Daphne. I am a woman: not the King but fully the Queen of Septimania. And since the rules that guide the attraction of two bodies are absolute, there was no stopping the congress that had been guiding me in blindness since I first set foot for Cambridge and Woolsthorpe.

And, as many as the fireflies a peasant sees on a summer's evening, so many were the Pips that rushed into me from my apple tree love in unimaginable multiplication.

Malory set the Chapbook down on his lap. He looked out into the *cortile*, full now with the casualties of Christmas night. But what he saw was the statue in the dining room of the Villa Septimania of Newton and the woman and the apple. The Queen of Septimania. Newton's friend was not the King but the Queen of Septimania in disguise. If I am descended from this Queen of Septimania, Malory thought, then I am descended from—is it possible?—from the other statue as well. I am the grandson of the man born 309 years to the day before me. I am of the seed of Newton.

Malory thought about Newton and his Queen. He thought about the red-haired Aldana. But he also thought about another red-haired woman. He thought about her faith in him, her devotion, her arm locked in his, her *zabaione* lips. Perhaps Antonella had been in disguise all this time, in front of his eyes. Perhaps it was time to search no more. Like the Queen of Septimania with her Newton, Malory had to take action if Septimania were to survive.

Malory walked out the front door of Fatebenefratelli without a glance up to the room where he had last seen Louiza. Night was fully advanced, the new day just clearing its throat at the horizon. He crossed the river at the Ponte Cestio and hugged the still-dark parapet of the river. As he descended the steps to Regina Coeli, the yellow walls of the prison were just beginning to catch the morning light. He turned down the Via della Penitenza and saw Cristina, *La Principessa*, her hair wrapped up in a kerchief, gliding towards the bus stop, on her way to the first of her three jobs—mopping up the butt ends of Christmas 1978. He opened the gate to the Dacia quietly. The courtyard, the broken-down Dacia were both empty. He walked through the front door into the living room. There was a body on each of the sofas, another curled up in front of the fireplace. None of them was Antonella. Malory climbed the stairs to the two bedrooms.

He was the great-grandson to the power of seven of Isaac Newton. He was not only King of the Jews and King of the Christians but a direct descendant of the King of Science.

And yet, as Tibor had warned him, he was also a Holy Roman Fool.

He hadn't meant to open any box, but the box was there, open to him, open to the world at the end of the corridor. In the sleepless dawn, at first Malory thought that he had found Tibor and Antonella deep in conversation about the glorious new future of their friend Malory—a new future, if he could admit the possibility, of a Roman Empire of Malory and Antonella, Tibor and Cristina.

But the cold light of morning broke the scene into other motion. The curls above were red, the tangled mat of hair and beard below was black. Together they moved with a frantic rhythm in the key of F-sharp that shook Malory and stopped his breath. Tibor had kept his promise. He had guided Malory into the depths of Hell.

Malory turned. He may have been King of Septimania, but he was no King Shahryar. He would not hack Tibor and Antonella in two. He would not vent his wrath on a host of virgins. Malory simply turned, turned downstairs, turned back across the river, up the Clivo, back into the Villa Septimania. And like Haroun al Rashid, like the *djinns* of a thousand and one other deceived cats and credulous fools, Malory climbed down the spout of his lamp, climbed back into his box, and pulled the top closed.

KNOCK.

Louiza opened her eyes.

A tree.

Louiza closed her eyes.

A knock.

Open again, a tree. A tree inside, a single pine tree standing inside a house. Above, a ceiling painted white, planks crisscrossed by whitewashed beams. One cobweb, another. A long thread of dust bobbing in the breath of the room, although it could have been just another cobweb, abandoned.

Louiza turned her head.

The back of a sofa. Soft, smelling of dust and sun. A yellow cushion embraced by passionflowers, faded, all faded.

A knock.

She turned towards the sound. A wood fire, fresh, three logs propped up like Guy Fawkes. The tree, a smell of pine.

A third knock, not the fire. Louiza sat up.

She was in a dining room—at least, there was a round table covered by a lace cloth, half a dozen willow library chairs, an open folder, sheets of paper, a pencil. Next to the table in a bay window shielded by lace curtains, a piano, a small piano. More lace on the piano, and resting on the lace a vase. Flowers. The sofa, the sofa she was sitting on, had yellow cushions. Passionflowers. The fire. Above the fire, a mantle. Marble. A pair of crystal candlesticks, old. Two plaster busts, small. On the wall above, a portrait. A man, a man from long ago, looking down on her. Not unkind.

She had no idea where she was. She had no idea why there was a pine tree inside the house. She knew something was missing.

"Lou! Lou, honey!" Three knocks. Outside. There must be a door.

Louiza stood. The heat of the fire nudged her back in the direction of the knock. She walked towards the sound, out of the dining room and into the hall. She turned the doorknob.

A man.

"Lou! Honey! Were you sleeping?"

The smile, the mouth. A map of ridges and valleys climbing up to a tree line of spiked black hair. The man pushed his way past Louiza, a paper bag of groceries in each arm. Louiza turned towards him and followed down the hall.

"Hey, Lou! Front door! It's freezing!"

Louiza turned back and shut the door. There was a window—nine panes of glass on the front door—frosted. Beyond, a veranda, snow, trees covered with snow.

Louiza had no idea where she was. She had never seen the man before.

Something was missing.

Through the vague light of the hall, through a door at the far end, Louiza saw the man set the two bags down on a table. The man disappeared. A tap opened, the sound of water in a tea kettle, the pop of a flame. The man reappeared, turned towards Louiza, smiling, blowing on his hands, slipping his arms out of his parka.

"Colder than a Siberian nun!" The man hung the parka on a wooden peg in the hallway. Something dripped onto the floor. "Hey, Lou!" The man was wearing a T-shirt, a white T-shirt. He took Louiza by the shoulders—not roughly but not with delicacy either—and drew her head into his chest.

Louiza had never seen this man. But with her cheek turned against his chest, she could see the figure tattooed into his bicep. It was a figure she recognized—the long *s* of the integral sign. The formula for the logarithmic constant of *e* to the power of *x*.

$$\int e^x$$

Mathematics. Maths. Maths she knew.

"How about a cuppa your good ol' English tea?" The man let her go. He walked down the hall and disappeared to the side across from the dining room. She heard the sound of a zipper, water splashing, a soft moan.

American.

This was not the cottage. This was not Rome. She had no idea where this was.

There was a pine tree inside the house. Something was missing.

Louiza reached up to the wooden peg and took down the dripping parka. She slipped her arms into the sleeves and zipped it shut. She turned the handle of the door. She walked out onto the veranda, yellow boards through the snow, a gable. She breathed. Her eyes opened. Cold climbed from her bare feet to her knees, rung by rung. The Gables. She took another breath.

There had been a plane. There had been a car, a ride through a city, up a river. A pine forest, a mountain, a yellow house, The Gables.

Vince—the man was Vince. American. A soldier. He taught at a place called West Point; he taught soldiers. He taught soldiers maths, he taught soldiers mathematics. He drank beer at a bar down by the river. He brought groceries and beer home in paper sacks and made tuna salad for lunch and steak for dinner. And at night he drank beer and then he came upstairs and slept with her.

Vince. Was Vince her husband?

Something was missing.

And in the morning, Vince cooked oatmeal and left a folder of maths problems on the dining room table. Just like at the cottage.

But she wasn't at the cottage. She was with Vince, who taught maths to soldiers, who brought her problems and took back the answers and drank beer. She was in America.

Something was missing. She had to go back. She stepped off the verandah into the snow.

"Good morning, Louiza."

Another man, larger than Vince. In a large parka. Much larger. And under the hood, a red beard. This man she had seen before. This man she remembered.

"Lou, honey!" Louiza turned. It was Vince, out in the cold with his T-shirt. "Where you goin'? I didn't see her go out," he explained to the man with the red beard. "Lou, what you doin' out here in the snow without no shoes?"

Louiza looked down at her feet, snow melting in the heat between her toes.

"Come, come inside, Louiza." The large man took her arm, took her by her arm in her parka and gently turned her around. His voice was deep; she knew this voice. Louiza's feet made little angels in the snow.

Louiza was sitting at the dining room table by the papers. Vince was on one side, the red-bearded man on the other. MacPhearson—that was another name, his name. She had met him at the Orchard with her mother and father. MacPhearson. She had seen him before. There was steam. There was tea. No parkas. Her feet were dry and warm in long, gray socks. MacPhearson was speaking.

"Louiza," MacPhearson said. "How long is it that you've been with us?"

With us? With whom? She was in America, now she remembered, somewhere up the Hudson—that was the name of the river. How long had she been with the Hudson? With America?

"Little over two months," Vince said. "Christmas last week."

"Thank you, Vince," the man with the red beard said. Louiza remembered. MacPhearson didn't like Vince. But Vince couldn't afford to get angry.

"You remember the cottage, Louiza?" MacPhearson said. Christmas.

"You did very good work for us back there," MacPhearson said. "Very good work."

The pine tree indoors. Christmas.

"But the last two months," MacPhearson said.

"I've been bringing the problems to her," Vince said. "I've been bringing the answers back."

"But the answers haven't made sense, unfortunately." MacPhearson took a sip of his tea. "Cookie?"

The answers. The problems.

"Please," Louiza said, "I should like to go home."

"Lou, honey," Vince said, "you are home."

"Discretion," MacPhearson said to Louiza. "Do you know the meaning of the word?"

"Secrecy," Vince added. MacPhearson held up a hand full of red-haired knuckles and warning. Vince stopped.

"You have a gift, Louiza," MacPhearson said. "A gift for solving problems in the realm of imaginary numbers that has had very real results. More," he chuckled, "than you might imagine. And more than many others might imagine. Which is why, for the immediate future, we need to exercise discretion as to your identity and your location." And then MacPhearson stopped smiling. "But lately, something is missing, Louiza," MacPhearson said, taking a bite of shortbread. "Something . . ."

"Yes!" Louiza turned to MacPhearson. He had said what she had been thinking. Something was missing. There were crumbs on his beard. And in between his upper two teeth, a piece of shortbread was stuck, as big as an apple pip.

"What is it, Louiza?" MacPhearson said. "What happened to your solutions, to your imaginary solutions?"

"The baby . . ." Louiza whispered. And she saw MacPhearson's face, with its pip-sized crumb of shortbread looking down on her. Not in that house with the pine tree inside. Not in the cottage, not in the Orchard. In Rome. In a room at the prow of a boat. And she was screaming, and he was talking in his low voice. And then she was screaming in the room at the prow of the boat.

Now she was off the boat, in the house with the pine tree inside.

Louiza jumped up. She ran down the hall. She ran into the bathroom, the kitchen, up the back stairs and into the bedroom and then into the guest bedroom, where Vince slept when she curled up into a ball and refused. Where was it? Where was her baby? Where was her baby? And she screamed. And she screamed. Vince ran up the stairs. MacPhearson looked down on her, his beard full of crumbs, his forehead heavy with sweat.

IT WAS DARK WHEN SHE WALKED BACK DOWN THE STAIRS. MACPHEARSON was gone. Vince was gone. The fire was low behind the grate, but the windows cast a light back onto the tree, the sofa, the lace tablecloth, and the folder of problems, the pencil. Louiza sat in her chair. She was wearing a woolen nightgown, a nightgown her mother had packed for her when she went to Cambridge. Her mother. She pulled her feet up and squatted on the chair below her, and buried her face between her knees for warmth, and rocked. The baby, the baby . . . where was the baby? What had happened to the baby? Baby, baby . . .

And as she rocked, she began to hear a sound. A guitar. An electric guitar, a low note, a slow trill, approaching from a distance, like a motorcycle along the Grantchester Road, or the first notes of "Foxey Lady." She had heard the sound before. But it had always receded, always driven away as soon as she turned her head. Now, though, the sound grew louder, closer. And as it grew closer, it was joined by the treble tattoo of a light stick against a ride cymbal, tinsel and sparks. And then a pulse—not too fast, slower than a heart, but insistent, warming. An electric bass pushing rhythm into song.

It was a group. Not a Galois Group, or a Langlands Group, or any of the groups of higher mathematics she had played with in Cambridge that looked only like Greek letters and played only a tune of pencil scratching on paper. But a group of human performers, four of them, standing around the table—four girls. They were Una and Dodo, Terri and Quatro—their names were as clear as their costumes. Una wore a jasmine PVC mini-dirndl over a black-and-white, horizontal-striped rugby shirt topped by a Funkadelic corduroy cap, and she played a Gibson Flying V electric guitar in shades of cardamom and curry. Terri was more conservative—pinstriped Carnaby Street suit (flared trousers, of course) with a ruffled cream shirt open past her cleavage, just above her left-handed McCartney bass. Quatro was the schoolgirl, which meant she kicked her bass drum and tickled her cymbals in a no-nonsense, Scottish-knee-sock-and-tartan-skirt kind of way, light years from Japanese anime porn.

And then there was Dodo. From the start, Dodo was Louiza's favorite. Dodo was the lead singer of the group, camouflaged to the nines in bulletproof Gore-Tex, seven-league boots, and a Kiwi Ranger's hat that disguised a meter-long plait of raven hair bound up in a double-helix with a jackknife and a bungee stick.

"Unimaginable . . ." Dodo sang, or said, or said and sang in a way that Patti Smith was beginning to insinuate into the universe. "More than imaginary. Unimaginable . . ."

"Yes," Louiza said, stopping rocking, but not moving, except for her head as she looked from Una to Terri to Quatro and back to Dodo. "My loss. My baby. Unimaginable."

"One over zero," Una sang.

"Unimaginable!" the other three joined in.

"Two over zero," Terri now.

"Unimaginable!"

"Three over zero, four over zero-o!" Dodo cried.

> *Add me to zero*
> *Subtract me from zero*
> *Multiply me by zero*
> *Divide, divide, divide me by zero-o-o.*

Ever since she was a small girl, Louiza had listened to teachers tell her, You can't divide by zero. You just can't. One divided by zero, they said, just made no sense.

"Six divided by two," one tall, rock-star of a junior teacher told the class, "equals three. And three times two equals six. There is at least one solution to the problem, therefore the problem makes sense. But six divided by zero equals?"

"Zero?" one small hand suggested.

"But zero times zero?" the teacher asked.

"Also zero."

"And *not* six. Therefore, not the answer." In fact, the teacher stated, there was no answer, no number which, when multiplied times zero equaled six. Therefore six divided by zero, any number divided by zero, made no sense.

And yet, Louiza remembered thinking, and yet—there it is. There is six divided by zero, right up there on the chalkboard, and seven divided by zero next to it—not just a trick of the light. And in later years, $\neq$ divided by zero and i divided by zero joined their sisters in the very real world of Louiza's imagination and refused to disappear just because they did not make sense. If the Imaginary System was based on the square root of −1, now she had a new system, a new group of friends. If someone could call the square root of −1 *i*, then Louiza could baptize one divided by zero as Una, and two divided by zero as Dodo. Una times zero equaled one, Dodo times zero equaled two. Simple. The Unimaginables—in vinyl miniskirts and knee-high boots—and quicker than they could kung fu a dozen gangbangers they divided by zero and multiplied times zero and came up with a whole number and rocked, far better than any junior maths teacher.

Louiza picked up her pencil and opened the folder of new problems MacPhearson had left her. She divided by zero and solved the problems, one and then another and then another. The Unimaginables, her sisters, saving her from the unimaginable.

And Malory.

"Standing on the shoulders of giants"—isn't that what he said when she opened her eyes in the organ loft? Malory told her that Isaac Newton said if he saw further than others it was because he was standing on the shoulders of giants. "I'm lucky," Malory told her, "if I even get a peek between their legs." She thought of Malory when the Unimaginables first began practicing their particular music in her brain. That March afternoon, waking up in the organ loft of the church with Malory, the infinite was in the air. "When I was a boy," Malory started, "just when my mother took ill, I had a great need to see things, to stand with the giants. I remember the day Mrs. Bogatay told us about infinity. I asked her, 'What does infinity look like?' And she answered, 'It's bigger than any other number.' And I asked, 'Is it bigger than a quadrillion?'—I was the only nine-year-old in school who knew the word, and it became my signature number. Mrs. Bogatay invited me up to the chalkboard and had me write out a quadrillion— one with fifteen zeroes after it. And then, as simple as cutting off my penis, she erased the final zero and replaced it with a one. She had found a larger number.

"Well," Malory continued—and Louiza remembered his excitement, the way he propped himself up on one elbow, but made sure to leave a leg lying over hers, "the challenge was on. I was going to write even bigger numbers. I was going to do what she said was impossible. I was going to write infinity. I wrote my quadrillion and then, with the daring of sailing off the edge of the earth, I added a comma and three more zeroes. And then another comma and three more zeroes. I refused to do any other work in maths that morning. Or any other work during my other lessons. I kept at it with my notebook. After two days of writing commas and zeroes, I came up with a genius of an idea. Instead of writing three little zeroes, I wrote one big one. And then I substituted a zero with a diagonal slash for ten groups of three, and then a horizontal slash for a hundred groups of three.

"And so on. Three weeks of substitution, a fever of filling up notebooks, ignoring my lessons, the other boys, barely eating, ignoring the world around me. Until finally Mrs. Bogatay took pity on me and showed me the ultimate substitution. The sideways eight. ∞. Infinity.

"I was furious, of course, and I fought back. $\infty + 1$, I wrote in temporary triumph.

"'Equals infinity,' she said, writing it out: $\infty + 1 = \infty$.

"$\infty + \infty$, I wrote. $\infty \times \infty$!

"'Equals infinity,' she said, 'I'm sorry to say.'

"That was the day," Malory said, putting his head back down on Louiza's chest, "that I returned home after school and found the vicar waiting for me. Two days later they buried my mother. Monday I found myself at a new school. Every hour became an infinity of seconds, every day an infinity of hours. And every night, I curled up into the sideways eight of my best, my only friend."

The Unimaginables began to play. The pine tree inside the house disappeared, the snow melted. Vince came, Vince went. Louiza solved the problems. And still there remained the pulse, the beat, the infinite, the unimaginable loss of her baby.

2/6

"THE MORNING OF MY TENTH BIRTHDAY—OR AT LEAST ON THE morning of the tenth anniversary of my arrival at the baby hatch of Santa Sabina—Sister Francesca Splendida asked me if I wanted to be an angel."

A girl. A girl stood beside the Bernini statue, speaking to Malory.

He had awakened to a brilliant late-summer morning. He had walked, as he had for more than twenty years of mornings, down the corridor, through the foyer, and into the dining room for his scones and tea, and had discovered Settimio and the girl beside the apple tossers.

"I found her in the Sanctum Sanctorum," Settimio said, "half an hour ago, asleep on the desk. When she opened her eyes, she asked for you."

The girl was even smaller than him, hair cropped in a golden helmet, almost as young as Louiza, or as young as Louiza had been twenty-three years before. Jeans, leather jacket over a white T-shirt, blue trainers—she must have been like many other girls on the streets of Rome. But Malory had met very few girls in recent years. In fact, none.

"Tibor said, 'Malory will understand.'" The girl spoke English. But the words buckled Malory's knees. He sat. The girl sat across from him. Settimio brought a cup and a plate. The girl continued her story.

A FAMOUS THEATER DIRECTOR WAS COMING TO ROME FROM AMERICA to stage a tenth birthday of his own—a revival of the *Divine Comedy* that had catapulted him to fame. He needed young things—a dozen young things—to play angels. For us damaged girls from Santa Sabina, Santa Chiara, Santa Cecilia, and elsewhere, it was a chance to run around the Circo Massimo dressed in something other than our daily uniform. And run around most of us did. I, alone among the dozen, followed directions. It was what I had been trained to do for as long as I could remember. And because I was so good at following directions and knowing where and when to go, at the end of the week Tibor and Cristina took me for a *gelato* in Testaccio.

They asked me questions—about my family, which I didn't know, about my schoolwork. They were impressed by my Italian and my Latin, my history and my geography. Most of all they were impressed by my mathematical ability, which had already outstripped what the Dominican Sisters were able to teach in Santa Sabina.

When the Dante was over and the rest of the girls went back to the convent, Sister Francesca Splendida took me aside and told me I was being sent to a school in Switzerland. It wasn't until I turned thirteen in a girls' grammar outside Lucerne that I saw Tibor and Cristina again and realized—even if they didn't say so explicitly—that they had been paying for my education and my escape from Santa Sabina. I thought Cristina was the most beautiful woman I had ever seen, a real princess—I believed it when I heard Tibor order *"thé au citron* for *La Principessa"*—so I allowed each of them to take one of my hands and lead me down to the Lake of Lucerne, buy me a stuffed zebra, feed me a cream bun as if I were Paddington Bear and deposit me back at the school before supper. Later, at the English school above Nice, Tibor and Cristina came to visit every year on Family Day when no other family came for me. And even at the A-Level crammer outside Inverness, where my only friend was a flannel-covered hot-water bottle, I answered Cristina's questions about my knowledge and Tibor's about my dreams without asking why and kept a secret scrapbook with reviews and photos of all of Tibor's productions in the bottom of a steamer trunk. "Cope-able," was what one headmistress called me; I can't remember if she was Swiss, French, or Scots—the word existed in none of the languages. "Ottavia is able to cope," she wrote, "with anything."

It wasn't until I was on the cusp of graduating from Trinity that Rix the Porter rang up to say that a Miss Cristina was calling for me at the lodge. I was a week away from receiving my degree so hadn't expected a visit. And it was immediately clear that there was something improvised about Cristina's appearance. She was in a taxi. She needed to talk with me. She had been crying.

I suggested the Orchard, just a few miles outside of town, where I used to go when I was in search of a quiet place to contemplate Fourier Series and Eigenvectors. The next week it would be full of proud parents and cream teas and jam-sotted bees. But Cristina and I had no trouble finding a trestle table in a quiet corner of apple trees with the church rising up on the other side of the road.

"Ottavia," Cristina began, dark glasses still firmly in place over the gray eyes that had first seduced me into a schoolgirl crush twelve years before. "You are old enough now that I think it is time to tell you a few things."

My scrapbook of clippings memorializing Tibor's successes also included photo features on Cristina. From the moment she strolled out of the maternity ward of Fatebenefratelli on that astonishing October evening in 1978, Cristina had found herself surrounded by a magnetic field that didn't so much open doors for her as blow them off their hinges. A job scrubbing floors for a Reuters functionary at the Vatican led to an invitation to be a sound editor in New York and a pair of green cards for her and Tibor. Within a year she was reporting traffic on the radio. Within two, isobars and satellite radar on the *Today Show*. As tanks rolled through Tiananmen Square and heads rolled over six of the seven continents, no palace leader or rainforest revolutionary was safe from the charms of Cristina. Here was one page from *Time*, Cristina at the siege of Sarajevo, here in a firefight in Hebron. There were stories from Darfur, New Orleans, Nagorno-Karabakh, Praia da Luz, Casale, Gori, Wasilla, Garoowe where, for ten days that she would be happy to forget, she was the property of the Somali warlord Jama Abduk Boosaaso. Not to mention the dinners and interviews with Clinton, Blair, Havel, Prince Bandar, and Bishop Tutu. Cristina didn't stop long enough to count, but her producers told her that she had filed more stories and won more Peabodys than Christiane Amanpour by a factor of three, not to mention a Pulitzer. And even now that she was approaching the age when correspondents with creaking knees and spreading posteriors were shunted behind studio desks in New York or London or Atlanta, Cristina not only remained in the field, but consistently placed in the Top Ten Sexiest Woman on TV. And not in the Grandma Class. Top Ten. Punto.

"Why did I come today to talk to you?" Cristina asked. She hadn't touched her tea, nor removed her glasses. Leaning back, her helmet of gray hair lying just past her ears against the canvas of the lawn chair, black linen blouse without sleeves, black linen trousers without calves, and toenails that needed no paint shining out from within her espadrilles, she seemed like a runway astronaut about to eject into the ether. "Because I may be your mother. And a mother's duty is to warn her daughter."

Even though mathematics was my strongest suit, I had, of course, created plenty of fantasies featuring Cristina and Tibor as my parents, although we couldn't have looked less alike. Where Cristina and Tibor were tall, I barely broke five feet and struggled to get my weight up to a hundred pounds. There had been a time in my first year at Cambridge when I brought cutouts of Cristina's head from *People* and *Time* to Cropper's across from the Trinity gate and asked the hairdresser to perform the impossible with my thin, disembodied hair. I tried to smoke, since I never saw either of them without a cigarette, but found it easier to imitate Cristina's preference for *thé au citron*. I had no desire to become a director like Tibor or an investigative journalist like Cristina. But they had clearly spent a lifetime coping with one thing or another. And maybe, just maybe, they were the biological origin of what the headmistress had called my copeability.

But the word *maybe* and its verbal cousin *may* awakened the part of my mathematical brain that dealt in probabilities. I *may* be your mother, Cristina had said. I could understand the uncertainty of Tibor's paternity, but with mothers . . . isn't there a higher level of probability, reaching almost to absolute certainty?

"There was confusion," Cristina went on. "Tibor and I were very poor in those days and we had just arrived in Rome." That much I knew from the articles in *Il Messaggero* and *Oggi* that celebrated Tibor's 1988 return to the Eternal City and the dinners and drinks in expensive restaurants by the Pantheon or the Palazzo Farnese that featured Tibor's face next to Laura Morante or Valeria Golino. "I was pregnant. I gave birth in Fatebenefratelli. But then . . ."

"I know," I said, wanting to save Cristina the pain of saying it but also keen to try out my pet theories, "but you didn't have enough money, the Italians were going to send you back, you had to give me up. Santa Sabina . . ."

"No," she said. "It wasn't that." Cristina looked up to the church across the road, the steeple cradled in the cleavage of the afternoon sun. "The room in the maternity ward of Fatebenefratelli was very beautiful—white light, the river just past the windows on both sides. I was there for a whole day—very quiet, very tranquil, floating on a white bed between contractions, twenty-four hours at least, totally alone. More than alone—well," she stopped and realized that she was speaking to me. "While Tibor . . ."

I waited. Behind me, I heard the rattle of a bicycle chain on the towpath by the river, a shuffling breeze through the apple trees. I tried to imagine Cristina, my mother, with the proto-me inside her, the two of us riding the raft of Fatebenefratelli down the Tevere, waving up to the girls of Santa Sabina looking down on us from the Giardino degli Aranci.

"Tibor finally arrived on the second day. He was with a strange little English man and his strange little English wife—a girl really— very pale, very blonde, very pregnant. I saw them come in. I saw them lay the girl on the bed. I wanted to speak with Tibor. But then both of us, the English girl and I, went into serious labor, and the doctor shooed everyone else from the room. When I woke up enough to focus, I was in the room again, alone. Or, to be more precise, Tibor was gone. The English girl was gone, the strange little English man was gone, the doctor was gone. The light from outside was sulfur and cold. It was all I could do to pull the blanket up to my chin. I don't know when the nurse came in, it could have been two minutes or two hours later. She put me in a wheelchair—the pain was, well, pain. She wheeled me down to where Tibor was sitting on a bench, smoking a cigarette. I was in no shape to understand much except that there was a problem. Everything was in Italian, and my Italian was still new.

But what I understood, what Tibor and I understood at the time was like this:

"The English girl and I both gave birth. Both babies were taken away in a single cradle, to be weighed and measured and registered. But when the Sister went to bring the babies back to us, she opened the cradle and it was empty. Not two babies. Not one. Empty." Cristina paused to light a fresh cigarette. The sound of her lighter shocked me.

"And one of the babies that wasn't there was me?"

"I screamed for a long time, I think," Cristina continued. "Or maybe I just think I screamed." She exhaled, smoke rose into the branches of the apple trees—had she even heard me? "Then I stopped. Tibor smoked. I smoked. It grew dark outside. We went home. Tibor didn't say anything. I didn't say anything. Tibor made up a story for our friends, about the authorities—I don't know exactly what, we never discussed it. All I had to do was smoke and accept their sympathies. Somehow—and I don't expect this will make you happy, Ottavia—we both came to believe that this was the best solution, whatever happened to you was better. I would be lying to you if I said we hadn't thought about giving up the baby every day of the nine months of my pregnancy. We spent enough of our childhood in Rumania fighting against the dictator who was calling on our patriotic souls to climb on top of each other and have children. It felt like we'd be giving in, selling out, if we actually had a child."

But there had been the anniversary production of the *Divine Comedy*, I thought, when Sister Francesca Splendida sent me down to meet Tibor with eleven other girls, and something in the way that I did something—my sense of space, of direction, the way I could find things—reminded Tibor of his own early days with the Bomb Squad and his unerring ability to sniff out the mines along the delta of the Danube that the Soviets, the Germans, or maybe the Emperor Trajan had left during one war or another. And Tibor and Cristina were convinced that one of those two babies who had disappeared from Fatebenefratelli ten years earlier was me. Maybe. Tibor had become a successful director in America. Cristina was climbing up the ladder of television journalism. They had enough money to pretend. I could be a toy, a cat they took out once or twice a year, to pet and play with when they weren't otherwise engaged. It was in nobody's interest to check DNA, to open the lid of the genetic box too wide—except mine. Maybe.

"Cristina," I asked, since the word *mother* had never gained much of a flavor, "why are you telling me this now?"

"Because Tibor—because your father—needs you to help him." She let the cigarette drop next to a forgotten crabapple. "And I don't think you should."

Cristina returned to Cambridge for my graduation a week later. Tibor too. He was playful, in manic high spirits. All my friends thought that I was the luckiest girl in the quad to have such a fantasy close at hand. The hint of a bald spot on Tibor's crown had widened into permanence. But the rest of his hair was thick and cut and shaped in a way that spoke of financial health as much as art. He had no idea that Cristina had come up the week before, that we had driven out to the Orchard and spoken. But that evening, after half a duck and two bottles of Merlot at Midsummer House, after I'd walked them back to the University Arms, Tibor stopped me under a sulfur lamp on St. Andrew's Street. The National had signed him to direct a production of Sophocles' *Antigone*. He had a concept that he knew could be extraordinary but required the kind of diplomacy and organization and sense of direction that he believed only I possessed. Might I come work as his assistant? Immediately? This clearly was the help that Cristina warned me about. But Tibor, my father! The National—how and for what reason could I say no?

Even though the National ran with strict union rules regulating hour and place, everyone involved in Tibor's *Antigone* had signed a waiver to accommodate Tibor's particular method. Every day, the entire company met in a large rehearsal room just before noon. Not just actors but designers, carpenters, seamstresses, the occasional executive, and a smattering of ushers and other front-of-house personnel. At the stroke of twelve, Tibor would appear to give a benediction to the company—a sermon that riffed on Sophocles, Dante, Winston Churchill, the changing politics of Eastern Europe, or sometimes just a comment on the hairstyle of one of the actors in the company. Eventually, the road led back to *Antigone*. And with that, Tibor would declare the workday begun. A couple of trestle tables were laden with food and drink. Most of the company would grab a salad or a Scotch egg and a coffee to fortify themselves for the day's surprises. Tibor never made a plan in advance. He might begin by gathering a covey of actors into a corner to discuss context and character, or he might spend two hours drilling a speech with the Creon in the middle of the hall while the others looked on. Or he might just huddle with the costume designer, even though everything had been sifted and sorted, for the entire afternoon.

At four, lunch was exchanged for tea. At seven, the drinks trolley appeared. More food at seven-thirty, and then the official end of the day at midnight. Everyone—particularly the actors—was expected to be present all the time, all part of the theatrical engine. "An infernal machine," Tibor called it, quoting Sophocles or Anouilh or some other aesthetic engineer.

And for the first week, the machine ran like a well-oiled Jaguar. The actors were marvelous, particularly the Welsh girl playing Antigone, the young daughter of the dead Oedipus, who defies the laws of her Uncle Creon to bury her brother, who was killed trying to restore morality to the throne. When they weren't rehearsing with Tibor, they'd go off into corners by themselves and swot the history or run lines. Fruit and bottled water were the staples of their diets that first week—I was the one on the phone every morning at eleven, calling to the buttery for fresh supplies. And so we came to the end of the sixth day and all was good.

Monday was the day of rest. Part of my job was to pick Tibor up at his over-designed hotel on St. Martin's Lane before rehearsal and deposit him there afterwards. I didn't expect to see him on Monday—frankly, I needed a day away, and there was some unfinished business with a tutor of mine up at Trinity. But at 7 a.m. my telephone rang.

"Oc-TAY-vya?" The woman on the other end was clearly not someone who knew me. "I've got a friend of yours here. In a bad way. What'd you say your name was, love?"

I took the tube up to Baker Street, to a basement flat just north of the Marylebone Road. Reshma was the girl's name—she was tall and well filled-out, roughly my age, but in different circumstances. As she fixed me a cup of instant—with a drop from the pint of milk she'd asked me to pick up along the way—she told me about her dilemma, whether to return to Bollywood or try to make it in England. She rattled off the roles she'd played in community theater in Hendon and Ealing and mentioned a couple of TV shows I'd vaguely heard of that had almost offered her a role. The TV was on low by the counter—BBC strangely enough, with Anna Ford reading the morning news. I looked around Reshma's kitchen and wondered behind which door "my friend" was hiding, or lying, or dying.

"So—" It was the door behind me, as luck would have it.

"Poor darling!" Reshma looked up at Tibor with the eyes of an actress in mid-audition. Tibor waved her off. He was dressed in the same clothes I'd left him in at the hotel the night before. If he had taken them off, it hadn't been to sleep. It wasn't particularly warm in Reshma's kitchen, but Tibor's shirt bore a stigmata of sweat beneath the arms and breasts. He was holding a water glass in one hand. The other was planted on his knee to support the weight of a back that refused to straighten. "He's been stuck like that for over an hour," Reshma said. "That's why I called you."

Tibor shook his head and waved the glass towards the TV. Anna Ford was talking about Vice President Cheney, who was preoccupied with his own stress test. But Tibor was more interested in the bottle next to the TV.

"Do you really think?" Reshma asked, not moving from the chair.

"Ottavia!" Tibor shouted in a Tom Waits whisper and shook the glass again in the direction of the bottle. I brought it over to him—a liter of Absolut with perhaps a slurp and a half at the bottom. "Pour," Tibor said. He drank, he swallowed. And with an effort that seemed to wring several slurps of sweat out of his body, Tibor straightened his back with a crack that momentarily drowned out Anna Ford. "So," he said, fully erect. "You found me. The same way you first found me and Cristina."

"Did I find you?" I asked him. "I thought it was the other way around."

"When *La Principessa* walked into my rehearsal on her wedding day," Tibor said, "wardrobed to the max in full bridal regalia and looking for the District Hall, do you think it mattered which one of us found the other? Which one of us was the Sun? Which one the Earth?"

I blushed, struck for the first time by an image of Cristina seated on a bathroom sink, her wedding dress hiked up around her waist and her second-hand heels digging into Tibor's bomber jacket.

"In love and discovery," Tibor said, looking over my head at Reshma, "there is no Fucker and no Fuckee. Only the Fuck. It's what we do afterwards," he said, striking a match, "after the cigarette and the vodka and the snoring are over and the stage lights are off, that's what matters. Action," he said, pulling on the Camel, "action is everything."

"I was just telling Oc-TAY-vya here about my dilemma." Reshma offered me a cigarette. I declined.

"Give her the address," Tibor said to me.

"Which address?" The most intelligible person in the room was still Anna Ford, and I never knew what she was saying.

"The Studio, the National . . ." Tibor waved his own cigarette at me. "My concept," Tibor said. "Cristina told you I had a concept. She warned you, didn't she?"

I didn't know that Tibor knew about my tea with Cristina, about her warning. So I said nothing. But on cue, a familiar Eastern European voice came into the room, care of Reshma's TV.

"This morning, my guest is the Vice President of the United States, Dick Cheney."

"*Fututi pizda matii!*" Tibor roared. "It's the Puli-tzarina!" A baby started crying in the next room.

"Oh shit!" Reshma said, as a wet stain began to spread over her T-shirt by her left nipple. "Pardon my Swahili and pardon my hungry monster. Won't be but a minute." And with that, she disappeared through another door.

"She follows me everywhere!" Tibor lurched around the room looking for the remote. Cristina continued to talk calmly to the vice president with authority and the charming scalpel of her Rumanian accent. I was happy to have her in the room with us, even if I could understand Tibor's annoyance. Cristina had a way of looking through the camera and making you believe you were her sole audience. Nevertheless, I reached behind the TV and pulled the plug.

I got Tibor out of the flat and into a mini-cab by Regent's Park before Reshma finished breakfasting her infant. Back at the hotel, I poured coffee and scrambled eggs into Tibor and tucked him into bed. He began to snore immediately. I cancelled my Cambridge tutor and the rest of my Monday and pieced through the hotel room *Tatler*s and *Vogue*s. Cristina was mentioned five times in the magazines, Tibor only once and then as "husband of . . ." I thought about calling Cristina but remembered Tibor's reaction to her appearance on TV. *She follows me everywhere.* I remembered her appearance just a few weeks before on the forecourt of Trinity. Was Tibor jealous of Cristina's success?

Was that why she warned me?

Was he warning me?

I thought about Reshma and her baby. I thought about the night Tibor had spent in her depressing flat. I thought about why I had followed Tibor's instructions and given her the address of the Studio. I didn't think about the bottle of Absolut.

Tibor woke around 4 p.m. He sat up in bed. He had no idea where he was. He reached out with his left hand and hit a pillow. He reached out with his right and knocked over the over-designed bedside lamp. I stood above him and handed him his glasses. He tweaked them over his ears and looked up at me.

"So."

I offered to call up some food. I handed him a glass of water.

"Go away."

"Can I call you later? See if you're okay?"

"I'm okay. I'll see you in the morning."

"Are you sure?"

He looked up at me again and blinked. Twice. Thrice. I don't know if Cristina ever got that look from him. But I understood her warning.

In the morning, Tibor was downstairs in the lobby of the hotel waiting for me. There were no signs of the previous day's adventure. If anything, he seemed more energized than he had a week earlier before the first rehearsal. As we walked through Trafalgar Square and across Hungerford Bridge to the South Bank, he talked about how the time had come to begin to unveil the new concept for *Antigone*. It was a concept he had been considering for over twenty years, since his first days in Rome.

And that's when he mentioned your name.

"Malory will understand."

I had no idea who you were, or whether the name Malory referred to a man, a woman, or a Rumanian experimental theater company. I didn't ask. But then, I didn't ask a lot of things on that late-morning walk to the Studio, and if I had, a clarification of the name Malory would have been low on the list. I was glad that Tibor was mobile. I wanted to forget our lost Monday. It was Tuesday, the beginning of a new week. We would show our passes at the stage door, take the lift to our well-lighted rehearsal room, listen to our week-two benediction from our glorious leader, and set off on the next episode of our journey towards genius.

"Oc-TAY-vya!"

It wasn't just the sight of Reshma outside the stage door. It was the sight of Reshma and five other women—Asian, Latin, African, Polynesian, and Eskimo—all yoo-hooing Tibor in ways that told me one thing. Monday hadn't been the product of Tibor unwinding at the end of a long week by drinking a bottle of Absolut and picking up an Indian prostitute. Tibor had been doing this every night since we began rehearsal. He had been going out in London with a bottle of Absolut and looking for women. A new bottle every night, a new woman every night.

"My concept," Tibor said, as he stirred the six new women into the murmuring mix that was his disconcerted company, "is that Antigone will be played not by one woman, but by seven women. Antigone is not just white, not just black or yellow or . . ." I could have supplied Tibor with the names of the seven colors of the rainbow more easily than figured out the reasoning behind his coalition.

"But why?" It was the Welsh girl, the original Antigone who asked the question. Entirely reasonable. Entirely within character, both as a Welsh girl and as Antigone.

"You should know, Antigone." Tibor smiled a dangerous smile, the warning of imminent attack. "Your Uncle Creon thinks there is only one right side to any battle, one right answer to any question, one nephew, one hero who can be buried. But you . . ."—and Tibor laid a comforting palm on her shoulder—"know that sometimes there is more than one answer, more than one hero, more than one heroine."

"Perhaps . . ." she began.

"Tell me," he said, smiling again. "How many boys have you fucked in your life?" Before the Galahads in the company could raise their voices in defense of the poor girl, Tibor held up his hand. "I don't really want to know. I suspect the number is more than one. But I'm sure you're looking for the one guy to settle down with, the one man—or maybe woman, I'm easy—to spend the rest of your life with. Aren't we all?"

The murmur dwindled to the silence of general confusion.

"On the Other Side, where I was born, One was the only number. One party, one president, one way of living, of thinking, of eating, drinking, shitting, and, when it came down to it, one missionary position for making love. I have been fighting a battle against One since I escaped from the Other Side. It is a battle I have tried to describe and explain. And now all of you—and I include our six new, professional colleagues—are here to give life to that battle. To prove once and for all that life is full of answers and origins. There are more Big Bangs, more explanations, more ways to tell where we've come from, where we're going, and why we're taking the trouble. As many, Dante would say, as the fireflies a peasant sees on a summer's evening, when he lies on his back on a grassy hill after his work is done. And you, my pilgrims, are going to bring the light of all these fireflies to the world!"

The company was made up of professionals, people who had been in the business, some of them for more than forty years. I was impressed how many of them followed Tibor's concept for the first day or so. Many of them had worked in the political sixties and sev-enties with non-professional actors—Kentish farmers and farriers in reenactments of Wat Tyler's Rebellion or Hackney undertakers reliv-ing the Great Plague of 1666. And they all had grown up in the eccle-siastical hierarchy of the theater where the Director was the One.

The problem was not the National Theatre. The problem was not Reshma and her international friends—for whom I acted as agent and intermediary with staff, and secured a pretty tidy compensation package. I suspect that at least one Antigone was keeping the Director company on St. Martin's Lane. The problem was Tibor. He was drink-ing—at least that one bottle of Absolut a night. And even though every morning when I picked him up, he was showered, shaved, and stable enough to walk the twenty minutes to the Studio, it was clear that he was stumbling in rehearsal. I became both lightning rod and the handkerchief for the individual and collective anxieties. As I waited in the lobby for Tibor on the morning of the sixth day of the second week, I rehearsed again the speech of concern I had been writ-ing all night.

Tibor didn't come down. I rang up to his room. No answer. I convinced the front desk to come up with me to the room and knock, and when there was still no answer, persuaded security to let me in.

Tibor was there. Sitting on the edge of his bed, fully dressed. Not one but three empty bottles—empty liter bottles of Absolut—stood on the console next to the TV. BBC News was playing, without the sound thankfully, and equally thankfully with no sign of either Cristina or Anna Ford on the screen. But Tibor was absent—clearly alive in body, dressed, and ready for rehearsal, but absent in mind.

I asked security to call for a doctor.

"No," Tibor whispered, from a great distance—more distant than a Tom Waits rasp. I thanked the hotel staff and assured them I'd be all right. They left and closed the door. I sat next to Tibor on the bed and took his right hand. It was huge and heavy.

"Something's missing," Tibor said. "The box is empty."

"What box?" I asked him, thinking about the vacant bassinet in Fatebenefratelli.

"Seven isn't working," Tibor said. "I was so certain!"

"Perhaps," I suggested, "we should go to rehearsal?"

He said nothing.

"Perhaps you should slow down on your drinking."

Tibor turned his face to me and gave me a look of such infernal hatred. "You are your mother's daughter," he said, with an accent on every bitter word. "You stand on my shoulders and press me down with your heels." I couldn't make much sense of what he was saying. But his hand was still in mine, my father's hand.

"What do you need?" I asked him, and stroked that hand with my other.

"The Pip," he said.

"The Pip?"

"Once upon a time, little girl, my friend Malory told me that I was out of tune. Maybe he was wrong then. He is right now."

That was the second time I'd heard your name.

"Malory will know. Malory will give me the Pip to put me back in tune. Then Cristina, maybe she will hear me."

I put Tibor to bed and stepped out into the hallway. I called Cristina in New York. I called the National. Both had contingency plans in place. So when on the third day, Tibor was still unable and unwilling to go to rehearsal, the National quietly let it be known he was being replaced. Cristina arrived that morning on a private jet loaned by someone grateful. Heels on his shoulders or no, Tibor let us guide him down to a cab and the airport. I rode with them to the airport, holding Tibor's big right hand. But when he saw the plane, he balked.

"The Pip," Tibor said, looking at the stairs up to the cabin door. "Do you have the Pip?"

And so I stayed—the only way we could get him onto the plane—with the promise that I would find Malory, with the promise that I would find you and bring you and the Pip to him.

I took the next flight to Rome. I had no idea where to look for you. But I went to see Sister Francesca Splendida—I hadn't been back in ten years. And as I entered the Basilica of Santa Sabina, I looked up at the light, translucent through the foggy marble, and knew that you were close by. I know how to find people.

Monday, September 10, is Tibor's birthday. He will turn fifty, and you must be there. He is stuck, like Dante, in the middle of the road of life, the right road lost. He has been tested by loss and has surrendered to gloom. He needs a Virgil to guide him out of the dark woods. You must come. I know you are the little Englishman with the pale English wife. I know you lost that wife and also lost a baby at Fatebenefratelli. And maybe all that loss makes it difficult for you to go to Tibor. But you must come. And you must—Tibor was very insistent—you must bring the Pip. Do you know what he means? The Pip?

MALORY HADN'T TOUCHED HIS SCONE. NOR HIS TEA. HE HAD ONE thought—it is not possible.

He had other thoughts—it will not happen.

Yet he also had a question, for himself.

How can I tell this girl, this Ottavia who somehow found her way past the doors, the gates, the walls, the alarms, the buzzers, not to mention Settimio and his invisible minions, how can I give this girl who found me the simple answer No, when I have forgotten how to speak?

In the beginning, Settimio brought me invitations for meetings with popes and rabbis, imams and lamas, politicians and supplicants. In the beginning, Settimio brought messages that came four, sometimes ten times a day, frantic messages from Antonella, from all the residents of the Dacia that through Fra Mario eventually found their way to Settimio. I ignored all news, especially news of Tibor. I had seen what I had seen—the position of Tibor's body, the position of Antonella's body beneath his, the velocity of Cristina's walking away, the futility of my own observation. On the morning of December 26, 1978, I made the calculations that anyone with basic Newtonian common sense would have made. All added up to betrayal.

"Go," Tibor told me at Fatebenefratelli and promised to look after Louiza.

"Go," Tibor told me at the Dacia and promised to look after Antonella.

I went. I trusted those promises. Trust—the One True Rule of friendship.

Not for Tibor.

The betrayal is too great.

I will not go again.

Twenty-three years ago, I climbed into my oil lamp and pulled down the lid. In twenty-three years, I have set foot outside the grounds of the Villa Septimania precisely once, spoken to no one except Settimio, and most of what I have said to Settimio required no speech. For twenty-three years I have stared at the statue of Newton, the Princess of Septimania, and the marble apple. The force of gravity that Bernini harnessed in his sculpture, the force that attracted the two lovers and their apple into a perfect balance no longer calls to me. I'd had the gall to imagine the woman as Louiza and the man as myself and to dream that such a perfect balance guided our lives. But I had been late, been off-balance. I forsook the quest for Louiza and our lost child in a misbegotten lunge for happiness and Antonella. I rejected gravity, rejected attraction, rejected all of them, including Newton.

What did I have left? Septimania.

From the depths of my lamp, I sent away for books and papers, entire libraries on Newton and science. I corresponded with super-experts in super-gravity, super-symmetry, super-colliders, cosmology, string theory, and quantum hoo-hah to such an extent that Settimio had to redesign the Sanctum Sanctorum and wire it with serious self-updating computer machinery to handle the quantity and quality of information that I collected from Feynman in California, Hawking back in Cambridge, Greene, Klebanov, Polyakov, and even Freeman Dyson whose black holes and theory of perpetual free-fall felt most sympathetic to my own state.

I built tunnels and bookshelves, dug deep and deeper, seven times seven, beneath the orange trees and Roman pines, into the hill of the Aventino. I filled the tunnels with books, with manuscripts. As Settimio brought in computers, I devised a way with him to digitize what we have and acquire what we have not with a system that receives without giving any clue of its existence. The amount of knowledge I have beneath me, beneath the Villa Septimania, would not only bury Minerva the Goddess, but Maria the Mother, and two, if not all three, of the Catholic Gods without giving a clue to the outside world.

Discretion.

Settimio passed on the key to quiet acquisition of knowledge, as I searched for what Newton knew, as I tried to put the world in tune. Discreetly. Leaving no trace.

I buried myself in everything and anything that might lead me back to Newton's One True Rule so I might begin again. I sat and thought, the way Newton sat and thought back in our frozen rooms next to the gate of Trinity College. But I couldn't will myself back to the balance of knowledge and ignorance that Newton had.

I am not Newton. I am a descendant. And even if I am not the giant that Newton was, I am standing at least several shoulder heights above the giant, and see far too far to limit my vision. My knowledge is made up of toothpaste that cannot be unsqueezed.

My memory cannot be unsqueezed.

I have sat in this dining room every day staring at this statue, contemplating the one mystery I cannot explain. I have read of Arthur and Excalibur, the Sword in the Stone, and all the tales in the Arabian Nights.

I am Malory—King of the Christians, King of the Jews, and, if the Princess of Septimania's Chapbook is to be believed, I am the Son of Newton, King of Science, King of the World, and yet I have nothing and have nothing to say. I argued that the answer was One. Tibor argued that the answer was Seven, at the very least. The answer was none of the above, neither negative nor imaginary.

The answer is Zero, terrifying and complete.

I have Zero to say to this girl. Less to say to Tibor.

On Christmas Day, I will turn fifty myself. And still I have Zero to say.

And yet, this girl found me.

Ottavia? Could that possibly be her name?

Could she possibly be Tibor's daughter?

Could she possibly remind me more completely of a day, almost twenty-three years ago, that I have worked so forcefully to forget?

And yet—if the simple really were the sign of the truth—it is clear, despite Ottavia's theatrical delivery, that if someone does not rescue him, Tibor will be dead very soon.

I will not be that someone, even though I have no wish to see Tibor dead.

And yet I do not want the girl to leave empty-handed.

The Pip. She asked for the Pip.

It is here, of course, in its canister. Behind Newton and his Queen.

POOR MALORY. I DON'T KNOW WHICH OF US WAS MORE THE GHOST. BUT while I explained myself, while I told my story, he shrank further and further into himself, as if he might disappear and leave only a pile of corduroy on the terrazza. But after I finished telling him about Tibor, after I finished telling him why I had come to find him, to bring him to the United States, to bring him up the Hudson to TiborTina, where Cristina was busy preparing a celebration of Tibor's fiftieth birthday in the hope of a miraculous rejuvenation, I waited. I waited five minutes, fifteen. I polished off two scones and three espressos.

Finally, Malory spoke, in a voice that convinced me that he really hadn't spoken to much of anyone in a long time.

"No," he said, and then began again. "I'm sorry, but no. I can't. But I'd like to give you something."

"For Tibor?" I asked.

Malory shuddered. "For yourself," he said. "You've come a long way. I don't want you to leave empty-handed."

I looked around. It was a dining room—seven chairs set around a table. Unused but not undusted. And then I saw them. At first I thought they were alive, the people. And then I saw that they were as small as me, as comfortably small as Malory, and made of stone. A statue of a man—I thought for a moment it was Isaac Newton, although he looked much younger than the statue in Trinity College Chapel— and next to him, a woman.

"That," I said to Malory.

"The whole sculpture?" Malory asked, even paler and smaller than before. "You want that?"

"Only the apple," I said. I don't know why I wasn't more surprised that the apple was floating in mid-air. Without waiting for an answer from Malory, I walked over to the figures. And whether the man on the left and the woman on the right smiled their approval to me, I can't be sure. But I reached out and took the apple, as easily as I might pick a McIntosh at the market.

"Thank you," I said to Malory. It looked at first like pain, the movement of his mouth, perhaps because he hadn't performed the action in over twenty years. But by the time Malory walked over to me and reached down to touch the marble apple in my hand, I knew he was smiling.

2/7

OTTAVIA RETURNED FROM ROME IN TRIUMPH, AND FOR THE NEXT four days, as Tibor's birthday approached, she was treated the way she imagined a daughter ought. Cristina installed her in the Yellow House down by the creek. With the antiqued brass of the four-poster and the angelic white of the sheets and mosquito netting, Ottavia was starring in Cristina's idea of an Ibsen dollhouse, in the stately pleasure dome of TiborTina—the upstate kingdom that coupled Cristina's name and Tibor's to an approximation of the Roman island of Tiberina, so central to their beginnings in the western world. Ottavia's yellow dollhouse by the creek sat below the white clapboard house of the Master and the Mistress, the red-sided barn for the Bomb Squad and the Nurses, and the host of guest cottages—the love children of Andrew Wyeth and David Hockney in bright pastels of magenta, chromium, and cobalt. All the color, all the light refracted through poplar and reflected off water and wrapped Ottavia in familial comfort and power.

She rose at dawn on Tibor's birthday, as she had each of the preceding dawns. The morning was still cool. She crossed the bridge over the creek and strode up a tractor path through the meadow and past the vegetable patch to the pond. She swam for an hour, back and forth across the water, roughly following the minute hand clockwise. By the time she'd dried herself and climbed up the wooden terraces to the back deck of the White House, Cristina was waiting for her with grapefruit juice, café crème, and a basketful of fresh breakfast. Cristina met Ottavia in a fully engaged present, full of mutual marvel and wonder at the butter and marmalade and cut flowers of her Paradiso. Ottavia had grown at least an inch and a half since repatriating

Tibor and convincing Malory to leave the Villa Septimania and fly to the United States. If Cristina was the president of TiborTina, Ottavia was anxious to prove herself a worthy secretary of state and see this diplomatic mission through to a world-changing conclusion.

Once she'd heard that Malory had agreed to come to Tibor's party, Cristina stepped into high gear. Malory's plane was due to land at Teterboro at noon. His driver would deposit him at the Blue House at two, giving him time to shower and rest. Drinks would be at five, dinner at six in deference to Malory's jetlag. Simple. Cristina had initially wanted to invite surviving Nurses, mobile remnants of the Bomb Squad, a producer or two, and a number of local neighbors to celebrate. That was Plan A. But given the unpredictable state of Tibor's storm front, Cristina had changed plans so many times she was well past the alphabet.

In the ten days since he had returned from London, Tibor had done little but sit on the deck in a wooden-slatted Adirondack chair, look down at the pine-ringed pond, and smoke himself into a fog. He wasn't drinking—there wasn't even a flip-top can of turpentine on the ten acres of TiborTina. Cristina wasn't certain this silent alternative was more desirable. But although he sat apart in his Adirondack, the white of Tibor's shirt and trousers and the gray of his hair and cigarette smoke mixed into a shade of solidity that anchored the women and convinced them that, as long as the cigarettes held out, there would be fifty more years in TiborTina of peace and hope.

Still, Cristina needed fruit and vegetables. More, she needed Tibor to show some signs of life.

"Darling," she said to Ottavia. "Why don't you drive Tibor down to the Farmers' Market after lunch and pick up a few things for dinner?"

On that Monday afternoon, there were a dozen or so cars and SUVs at the round barn of the Farmers' Market. Across River Road, two beat-up Chevy 10s stood in front of the Seven Veils Bar & Grill. An early-model BMW idled in front of Kolodney's Fish Market.

"I'll get the veg and fruit," Ottavia said, pulling the Yukon onto the grass beside the Farmers' Market. "Do you want to come with me?" she asked, turning off the ignition. "Or do you want to buy the *vongole* for dinner?" Tibor climbed down from the Yukon and headed across River Road to Kolodney's. "Do you need money?" Ottavia called after him. Tibor lifted his wallet from his pocket and walked on.

Kolodney wouldn't have known what a *vongole* was in any accent. But Tibor was able to point, pay, and walk out of the fish market with four pounds of netted clams in a plastic bag in under ninety seconds. The lunch crowd—there was a road crew painting yellow lines two miles up 9D—was long gone. But the Seven Veils still smelled of sauerkraut balls, marinating wieners, and bleach.

Tibor was oblivious to all, even the scent of stale beer that rose from the carpet on the stage. It had been well over a week since he'd had a drink, and that was in another country. Malory was coming. Malory was coming with the Pip. Malory was coming with the Pip. And although Tibor knew the hiding places of at least six bottles of vodka in the beams of TiborTina and even a stump or two around the pond, he was determined to keep his mouth as dry and receptive as possible. The Pip, the Pip that had saved him from plunging to the pavement of that drafty church the morning he'd awakened to the sound of Malory, the Pip would save him now. The Pip would save him. The Pip would cure him.

A skinny college girl Tibor had auditioned on an earlier visit to the Seven Veils, back when he and Cristina were scouting the back country of the eastern shore of the Hudson for property, was lying on the stage on a beach towel laid above the carpet in the interests of hygiene, crossing and uncrossing her educated legs.

"Hi, Tibor!" she called from the floor over the music, "Sweetest Taboo." Sade. If he didn't know the name of the girl, Tibor knew the singer, named after one of his favorite aristocrats, even if everyone pronounced her name wrong. He nodded. There was no need for more.

He was bored. Terminally bored. Neither the Indian Antigone—impossible to remember names—nor the countless other big-hipped, short-legged, long-waisted, laughing, weeping, lactating girls he had auditioned in London had managed to cure him of his boredom. They had tried, all of them—he couldn't doubt their sincerity any more than he could make fun of Ottavia's earnest pleas. They had walked him through the meat stalls of Smithfield, through the thornier copses of Hampstead Heath and the shadowy buttresses of the flyover on the backside of Westbourne Grove. They had mixed vodkas and whiskies and ragas and rap in an attempt to entertain this foreigner who wouldn't be entertained. They did it for money. He knew that. But that had no effect on his inability to find either joy or purpose, aesthetic or reason. And Ottavia. It was only to give Ottavia something else to do besides worry over his leaky pores that he told her about Malory and the Pip. He wasn't sure exactly why. But he had memories of each of them, images of tranquility before something began to piss him off, as it had done with Cristina—done so thoroughly that all former happiness was chased into some distant cell of his brain and bolted shut.

In the week since his return from London, Tibor hadn't spoken—not to Cristina, Ottavia, Nurse, Bomb Squadder, or anyone. It didn't matter. No one really wanted to hear what he had to say. College Girl was no different. Tibor sat on a stool. The bartender, who was at some kind of college himself, studying communication, reached down into the well for the bottle of Absolut. Tibor waved him away with an index finger and pointed to the soda siphon and a lime. The bartender shrugged. Tibor set his plastic bag of clams down on the bar and lowered his mouth to the straw.

"Hey, Tibor," College Girl called to him. Tibor looked up at the mirror in the bar, but the image of the bottom of the girl's stilettos crisscrossing behind the bourbon was too vertiginous. He turned. "This guy's a foreigner too. Where'd you say you were from?" Tibor looked over to his left. There was a man, the only other customer in the Seven Veils, sitting two stools away. He was sipping on a vodka and tonic and staring intently as the girl's legs exposed then hid then exposed again, as if he was studying for a final exam.

"Jed-dah . . ." the man said.

"Jed-dah!" the girl repeated. "They got dollar bills in Jed-dah?"

The man didn't understand. Tibor took out his wallet and handed him a five, making it clear with a thrust of the chin that he should carry the bill directly to the girl on the towel as Tibor had in years of defending his belief in the multiplicity of pleasure. The man hesitated. He had a bag on his lap. There was a bit of delicate negotiation before he could place the V&T and the bag on the bar and trot the bill over to the stage. He was compact—that was Tibor's thought—Malory-sized, although his hair was cropped in short Arabian curls. Tibor had cast an Algerian in his first Dante production back in Rome—as the homosexual Brunetto Latini, if he remembered correctly. The Algerian was a Muslim, Tibor recalled that much. He'd come back to the Dacia once or twice, had a perfectly good time, Tibor thought, even without drinking the vodka or eating the prosciutto. Dora, or was it Brendushka, had taken pity on the guy—Tibor couldn't remember the rest. The Seven Veils was a long way from Jeddah, so maybe College Girl would take pity on this poor schmuck.

"Wanna dance?" She'd raised herself up to a standing position on the stage and was lazily scratching an itch on her left shoulder blade with her rolled-up towel. On stage, in stilettos, she towered over the man from Jeddah, who held Tibor's five in embarrassed supplication. "Whaddya doin in the Seven Veils if you don't wanna dance?"

"Give him a dance, Rache," the Bartender called out. "I saw his wallet. Full of Benjies."

"Aha!" Rache—was that really a name? Tibor wondered—said. "A rich guy from Jed-dah! Where is that? Somewhere in Es-PA-ña?" She stepped off the stage and nudged the man with a practiced fingernail back onto his stool.

"Saudi," Mr. Jeddah said, still wondering what to do with the five.

"Live around here?" She nudged his knees apart with both of hers.

"Boston," the man said.

Tibor turned back to his water. He knew that in seven and a half minutes, College Girl would have the guy's passport number and two, if not three of the hundred-dollar bills the Bartender had so expertly spied. Except for the Algerian, Tibor couldn't remember knowing any other Arabs, any other Muslims. Rumania in the days of the Sheikh and Sheika Ceaușescu wasn't comfortable with any show of obeisance except to the holy couple. There had been a few Iranian refugees in Rome before he and Cristina left, but then, they weren't really Arabs, were they? He had been happy in Rome, hadn't he? Cristina had been happy too, even with her mopping and dusting and burping babies that belonged to other people. And she had been happy again when he'd discovered Ottavia in the godforsaken icebox of Santa Sabina. There had been chances—even after he had run off to an organ loft to hide from a terror worse than any he'd felt searching for mines in the delta of the Danube. There had been chances, even after Fatebene-fratelli, even after the red-bearded doctor lost their child and disappeared. Malory would bring another chance. After all this time, maybe Malory was right and he was wrong. Malory would bring the Pip. The Pip would show him the answer.

"We Muslims believe," Mr. Jeddah said, with a muffled sound that told Tibor exactly where his mouth was. "We believe there is a body and there is a soul."

"Really?" Rache said, and Tibor could hear her voice descend in pitch and placement. But the man continued.

"The soul is connected to the body in four different ways: as a fetus in his mother's womb."

"Ah . . ."

"After birth."

"Mmm . . ."

"When a person is asleep."

"That's three . . ."

"And . . ."

"And . . . ?" Tibor could hear the rustle of money exchanging hands.

"And on the Day of Resurrection, soon to come, *insha'allah*, after the Caliph of all Islam reveals himself."

"But tell me, Mister Jed-dah," Rache went on, "in case I missed something. If I'm not mistaken, at this moment, you aren't being born or sleeping. And the Mahdi isn't hanging around this joint. Am I right?"

"Yes," the man said, with a glance over his right shoulder at Tibor. "That is correct."

"So while the soul is AWOL, whaddya say we take a trip back into the VIP room and check out the body?"

Tibor continued to stare at the water. But he could tell that the man was standing, the man was walking.

"Let me just clear out the mop," the Bartender said, and ran down the far end of the bar and out the back.

Tibor looked down the bar. Rache had locked her arm in Mr. Jeddah's—these may have been the first V&Ts in his life—and was whispering something in his ear that Tibor was sure signaled the exchange of a few more hundred dollars.

And then Tibor saw the bag.

The man had left his bag on the bar, the plastic bag he had been cradling in his lap until College Girl came along and began her dance. And through the opening of the bag, Tibor could see a barrel, a handle, a trigger. Mr. Jeddah had a gun. Tibor thought of saying something—to the Bartender, to Rache, to Mr. Jeddah himself. But that would involve speaking.

He also thought about taking the gun.

He looked back at his water glass and up to the bottles of liquor ranged along the mirror at the back of the empty bar. He looked up into the mirror. And that's when he heard the music change.

A guitar. An electric guitar, a low note, a slow trill, approaching from a distance, like a Ducati along the Lungotevere, or the first notes of "Foxey Lady." As it grew closer, the guitar was joined by the treble tattoo of a light stick against a ride cymbal, tinsel and sparks. And then a pulse—not too fast, slower than a heart, but insistent, warming. An electric bass pushing rhythm into song. Tibor looked up into the mirror.

There were four of them, on the stage where Rache has been crossing and uncrossing her legs, four girls. The guitarist was a very young Charlotte Rampling starring in *The Sound of Music*—all dirndl and translucent eyes. The bass player was a female David Hemmings—Carnaby Street cream shirt open past her delicate cleavage. The drummer was knee socks down to the bass pedal and tartans past the snare—the kind of Japanese anime porn outfit that always made Tibor's visits to Ottavia's Scottish academy more interesting.

And then there was the bulletproof lead singer of the group, Ramboed to the nines, booted to the max, with a hat from a lost Ark big enough to disguise a meter-long plait of raven hair bound up in a double-helix with a jackknife and a bungee stick.

"Unimaginable . . ." she sang, or said, or said and sang in a way that sounded like Patti Smith cynicism. "More than imaginary. Unimaginable . . ."

ACROSS RIVER ROAD, IN THE FARMERS' MARKET, LOUIZA SAW THE GIRL and something gave out inside her. Or maybe something gave out even before she saw the girl, something that made her just want to fold her knees and settle on the hard earth of the round barn. Louiza steadied herself by one of the six poles that held up the roof of the shed and focused her eyes on what she was certain had sent a wave, a field, a beam of particles, a message of some sort to her and caused her to lose balance. She saw the girl from her right side. The girl was in profile, short fair hair hanging straight down to her earlobes, cut in a saw-tooth fringe at the forehead. She was filling a paper bushel sack with apples. She was wearing linen in a canvas color, a long-sleeved smock over rope-colored moccasins, no jewelry, no makeup. The canvas, against the yellows and greens and spotted browns of the late summer apples, was almost mathematical in the way it divided what the girl was examining from what was behind. Louiza stared.

"Hello," the girl said. Louiza said nothing, but continued to stare. "Hello," the girl said again. Other people turned to look. This was Louiza's cue that she was back in the real world and that she could safely speak without being taken for a madwoman. The Unimaginables had been playing louder in recent months. Vince came to her more and more frequently with problems to solve. Mr. MacPhearson spoke to Vince in a way that Louiza wasn't supposed to hear. There had been an exponential rise in the chatter on the Internet, on mobile phones, and even hidden within the print of major newspapers. With the help of the Unimaginables, Louiza was taking the chatter from all these key sources and from a significant number of insignificant ones as well, and with her elegant method of dividing by zero, focusing the messages into a lyric that Dodo could sing in her crystalline voice. Only Louiza could hear Dodo, of course, since Dodo was Unimaginable. But the woman speaking to her now was very real.

"Hello," Louiza said. "Do I know you?"

"That depends," the girl said. "Have you ever been to England?"

England? Louiza thought. What an odd thing to ask.

"No, I guess not," the girl said. She smiled. Imperfect teeth, Louiza noticed, but a perfect smile. "Do I know you?" the girl asked. She lowered her sunglasses—Louiza realized that the girl was wearing sunglasses, very large sunglasses—and looked at Louiza. Her eyebrows were straw, almost canvas-colored themselves, but her eyes were a pale blue that . . . yes, perhaps Louiza did know her. The accent. The girl was a foreigner like her, but not from one nation in particular, an equation with more than one solution.

Unimaginable, she thought. Was this girl one of her Unimaginables? Louiza had lived alone with her girl band of zero-dividers for so long that she was less than completely surprised to find one of them buying Granny Smiths at the Farmers' Market on River Road. She tried to make sense of the girl's pale blue eyes, match them with the appropriate electric instrument, match the sound of the girl's voice with the Unas and Dodos of the Unimaginable world. But it wasn't the name of a girl that came out of her mouth but, unbidden, the name of a city in which she had once experienced, or so she thought she remembered, the unimaginable.

"Rome," Louiza said. "I know you from Rome."

Now it was the girl's turn to stare. It didn't bother Louiza. It had been years since she had a chance to look at anybody. The one photograph she had of her mother among the sugar beets on the farm in Norfolk had long since stopped looking back at her.

"I grew up in Rome," the girl said, "on the Aventino."

"Malory," Louiza said. "Malory," she repeated. "Do you know someone named Malory?"

"Lou, honey?"

"Malory?" the girl said. And suddenly something in the entire shape of the girl aligned itself into an equation that Louiza recognized.

"Lou?"

Louiza felt the grip on her arm. She closed her eyes and opened them again, hoping the nightmare wasn't real. But it was Vince and the smell of his aftershave and the pitted hollows of his cheeks.

"You'll excuse us," Vince said to the girl, "we have to get home."

"Please," the girl said. "We were having a very nice conversation."

"I'm sorry," Vince said, with his military politeness that ended all conversation. "But my wife hasn't been well, and we're pressed for time." And quickly the world turned and River Road was in front of Louiza and they were walking to the car.

"Wait!" Vince was just buckling Louiza into the passenger seat when the girl ran up, sunglasses back in place. "You forgot your apples." She handed Louiza the bag. Vince smiled and closed the door. Louiza couldn't tell what the girl was thinking on the other side of the glasses. But Louiza was as certain it had something to do with Malory as she was certain that she hadn't bought any apples.

Poor Malory, Louiza thought, as Vince turned the car and headed back up River Road. It was a combination of words that often came to her even after all these years, remembering how touched she had been, waking to the Vespers bells with her head on his chest, remembering how he'd carried her in his arms from that cold church down the streets of Rome, yes Rome! The more that Louiza lived with Una and Dodo and Terri and Quatro and all the Unimaginables, the more she began to imagine another universe in which, strangely enough, Malory continued to appear. Not as her husband, per se, although she had only the vaguest idea—no fault of Vince's—of what a husband might be. But as a presence, a presence not always separate from her. She held conversations with the Malory in her mind, not just about Schrödinger and not just about cats, but about bare feet and snow and catching fireflies in an empty jam jar. There were long periods of the day, long days, maybe long weeks, when she heard organ music—not just faint, imagined music, the way just the buzz of electricity in the walls can make one imagine a little bit of Bach—but full-throated St. George's, Whistler Abbey, organ music with stops out and pedals blazing and Louiza giggling, giggling—something she hadn't done in years—with the Pip in her hand.

Louiza could barely remember Malory's face. She could remember Malory's number, −78, identical to hers. She could remember the sound of Malory's voice, curled on her chest, resonating inside her like a sideways eight with its infinite regret—the regret of not saying goodbye after that day in the organ loft of St. George's, not turning back to explain why she was leaving, why she was accepting the invitation of the Americans, why she was taking that red hand with the red hairs and stepping into that car, stepping into that Morris Minor, and then onto a plane, first to Rome—she was certain of it—and then across the Atlantic to this only imaginable world where everyone, from the beige-suited men to Vince, Mr. Kolodney, herself, and all the cats, were half-dead and half-alive.

Vince walked Louiza from the car across the porch and into the kitchen before returning outside. She heard voices. Vince was scolding somebody, many somebodies. Louiza took off her cardigan and hung it on the hook. She reached into the bag the woman gave her and bit into an apple. Uninvited, her hand began to stroke her belly. It was true what she remembered, she thought as she chewed. Her belly had once been bigger. There had been a time—she wiped the apple juice from her chin. There must have been. Rome. The woman with the gray eyes on the other bed. The giant with the beard and the strange accent. And life. There had been life—she took another bite—there had been a child growing in her, a child born, unimaginable if not. There had been Malory, –78, carrying her across the river, over the bridge, up the stairway of the hospital. And a child, their child, her child, Malory's child, no other possibility, but a girl? A boy? What was it Malory had said about cats? Don't look, they told her in Rome. A girl? A boy? Don't look!

Louiza couldn't resist. She looked into the paper bag. There was something on top, not an apple. A slip of paper, a phone number, a name. She looked. TiborTina.

"TIBOR!" OTTAVIA HAD NEVER BEEN INSIDE THE SEVEN VEILS, NOR IN any place resembling the Seven Veils. But it was quickly apparent to her that there was a man at the far end of the bar who was very angry with Tibor, and another man with him who was equally determined to keep the first man from attacking Tibor. Much closer, Tibor was sitting on a bar stool staring at a glass of water, while a girl—possibly the same age as Ottavia but wearing considerably less—was whispering something in a consoling tone of voice in his ear and trying to encourage him to stand. "Tibor," Ottavia said again, and everyone stopped for a moment.

Tibor swiveled his head to the left.

"Tibor, it's all right." Ottavia touched his wrist.

Tibor picked up his clams and walked out the door and into the light. It took a moment for his glasses to darken. He saw the Yukon. He followed Ottavia across the street. He climbed into the passenger seat and placed the plastic bag next to him, buckled his seat belt. Ottavia opened the driver's-side door, threw a paper bag from the Farmers' Market and a plastic bag onto the seat between them, and then jumped up behind the wheel. She sniffed the air.

"Clams," she said, somewhat mollified. "Water?" she said, sniffing Tibor's face, "with a piece of lime? Well, now I expect Cristina will only half kill me."

Ottavia pulled out and past the Mobil station, the culvert. Tibor looked forward through the windscreen as a late-model BMW did a U-turn and headed south on 9D. A roar of noise—music maybe—came out of the back seat or the exhaust pipe of the car. Behind the BMW, another College Girl followed on a red Vespa, a guitar strapped across her back. And then another, in a vinyl minidress on a lime-green Vespa, and then a third, a fourth—the entire band from the Seven Veils. The music was coming from the band, not the BMW. But when Tibor swiveled to follow their progress, they had disappeared, and the music was gone.

He swiveled back and looked down at the little girl, Ottavia, behind the wheel. Ottavia felt his look and turned to him. She smiled, she couldn't help it, and looked back at the road. Tibor looked down at the seat—the paper bag of corn and apples, the plastic bag of clams. And another plastic bag. Ottavia must have taken the man from Jeddah's plastic bag. Tibor raised his chin to look down beneath his glasses inside the bag. Squeezing the top of the bag closed, he placed it slowly into his jacket pocket. And for the first time in more than a week, in perhaps a month, he smiled.

WHEN MALORY SHOWED INTEREST IN CRISTINA'S INVITATION, SETTIMIO—ancient though he was—took on a tone that reminded Malory of their first meeting, twenty-three years earlier, in the corridors of the Ospedale Fatebenefratelli.

"There has been chatter, *mio Principe*."

"Chatter?"

"Conversation, both vocal and electronic, across the Internet." Over the phone lines, in cafés and airports and docks and markets and ice cream parlors around the world. It was chatter that grew louder over the summer, chatter reported by Settimio's channels of contacts who owed allegiance to Septimania in ways that Malory happily kept beyond his learning. "They say that the United States is a prime target for attack. No one knows precisely where, no one knows who or how or why. But might I advise," Settimio said to Malory on the afternoon of Ottavia's visit, "that the *Principe* avoid public celebrations and pass the autumn here in Rome?"

Malory had to acknowledge Settimio's clarity. And his own reluctance.

"You might recall what His Holiness told you, early in your reign. Anonymity is a blessing." Both men were right. No one recognized Malory, no one knew who he was. No one came at him with a baby to kiss, a car to bless, or a gun to discharge. Leaving Rome, leaving the Villa Septimania was putting that anonymity at risk.

Settimio insisted—and Malory didn't object too strenuously—that the Driver accompany Malory to the United States. The three of them rode together in a simple Lancia, driven by the Driver's twenty-three-year-old son, to Ciampino, where Settimio had arranged for a private jet. Although a Saharan wind was blowing into Rome from the south, Settimio was wearing a winter overcoat of midnight blue. It had been twenty-three years since he had first accosted Malory in the corridors of Fatebenefratelli. Malory then thought he had been old, but now age was showing its conquest.

"Will you be all right, Settimio?"

"Excuse me, *mio Principe*?"

"While we are away?"

"No one is searching for me," Settimio said. "No one is searching for Septimania."

"No chatter?" Malory smiled.

"No one sees Septimania for what it is," Settimio smiled back at him. "It is a trick of the light." The Driver's son pulled the Lancia up to the curb and left the engine running. The Driver jumped out and retrieved Malory's bag and his own and held the door for Malory.

"Hercule!" Settimio rolled down his window, and Malory walked around the car. It was the first time Settimio had called him by name.

"Be careful, Hercule," Settimio said. "Discretion."

"Thank you," Malory said. And then Settimio reached up, the way Suor Miriam had reached up to him all those years before. Settimio reached up with his gloved hands to Malory's shoulders, and Malory bent so Settimio could kiss him, on one cheek and then the other.

IT WAS PLEASANT TO LAND IN A PRIVATE AIRPORT IN THE NEW YORK countryside. The view from the chartered jet as they bisected New York Harbor between the Twin Towers and the Statue of Liberty and headed up the Hudson—Malory had flown only two or three times in his life and then only to France so had little to compare—was extraordinary. The walk directly from the airplane into a comfortable and discreet vehicle with the friendly face of the Driver at the wheel felt as comfortable as crossing the Ponte Palatino. They crossed a bridge, they crossed a river, the Hudson he believed, although he wasn't certain whether they were crossing from New Jersey to New York, New York to New Jersey, or none of the above. Both banks of the river were dripping the bacchic green of late summer into the water. There were boats, a sun. Malory had seen the sun, every day for the past twenty-three years, from the garden of the Villa Septimania. But with all the time he'd spent down in the Sanctum Sanctorum, all the time he'd spent reading and then thinking and then reading and thinking some more, he'd forgotten almost completely about the horizon, about the curvature of the Earth, about nature.

The Driver made a left turn onto River Road. At the crossroads, a bar, a few shops. On the other side, a round barn was set back from the road down a dirt drive. In front, a host of young girls in overalls were selling corn and pumpkins and apples and pies and ragdolls. Past the market, low fieldstone walls in brown and off-brown flanked the road. To the left, a man jumped a horse over a pair of crossed timbers. There was nothing Italian about it. Nor English, nor Rumanian.

"*Mio Principe.*" The Driver turned left onto a dirt road, marked by yet another pair of fieldstone fences, then downhill to a creek, and stopped the car by a gate. "*Eccoci qua.*" A woman approached the car, raised her sunglasses.

"*Buona sera,*" Malory heard her give a few instructions to the Driver. She opened the rear door and climbed in next to Malory. "Hello, Malory," she said, with a kiss on either cheek. And then, for reasons more complex than Malory could follow, she grabbed Malory tight away from his seatbelt and held onto him. "Thank you," Ottavia said. "I'm so glad you are here. You have no idea."

"Thanks," Malory said, thinking it had been an extraordinary day to have his cheeks kissed twice.

"Shall we walk?" Ottavia asked, and exchanged a few more words in Italian with the Driver.

Malory stepped out of the car and blinked three times.

"Come with me," Ottavia said. She opened the gate for the Driver, and then, linking her arm in Malory's, she led him down the road. Malory looked back. The Driver smiled and waved as he straightened the car and followed. How wonderful, Malory thought, that there is someone in the world who has to stand on tiptoe to reach me. Arm in arm, Ottavia led Malory onto the bridge across the creek and then off the road and onto a track across a pasture, rutted with the marks of tractors and horses and rimmed with the late summer weeds that Malory knew only from the Cambridge Arts Cinema.

"I've been thinking about Rome," Ottavia said, slowing down her footsteps to extend the moment. "A lot."

Malory said nothing, but squeezed her arm tighter with what biceps he had and looked at the small rocks in the tractor path in the hope they might dilute his embarrassment but not his pleasure.

"Do you know what my favorite moment was?"

Malory thought about the dinner Settimio had served, their stroll out in the garden to peek down on nighttime Rome—the first time

Malory had strolled in the garden or much of anywhere with anyone. And the apple, of course.

"That night," Ottavia said, quick and bright, knowing that Malory was too confused to reply, "when you tucked me into bed and read me a story. No one has ever done that."

Nor to me either, thought Malory. Not in a long while.

"I slept so well," Ottavia said. "I felt safe. Not managing, not coping, not worrying about Tibor or Cristina or my own sorry life, but safe."

"I'm glad," Malory said. "The villa is really quite extraordinary."

"It was you, Malory." Ottavia stopped and cupped a small Malory elbow in each of her smaller hands.

"I only read you something that was written a long, long time ago."

"But there was something in the way you read. The tone of your voice."

Once upon a time, Malory had thought about the tone of his own voice. Once upon a time, Malory had tuned organs.

"I don't know anything about music," Ottavia continued, "except the chants and hymns I had to sing from Santa Sabina to Trinity. But I know there have been times, very rare times, when I've been sitting in a particular niche of a chapel or above a Scottish loch at sunset and the sound of a distant boat comes to me. And all feels . . ."

"In harmony?" Malory asked.

"If that's the word," Ottavia said. "It's like the moment before I find the solution to a particularly thorny mathematical problem. Even though I can't yet see the answer, I can hear the sound of its perfection coming from a distance. That's the sound I heard as I closed my eyes that night in the Villa Septimania."

"And the answer?" Malory asked. "Did that come to you later?"

"Malory," Ottavia said, "do you remember the story you were reading to me that night? About the first meeting between Haroun al Rashid and the daughter of Charlemagne?"

"Aldana?" Malory asked.

"Do you remember how Aldana was flirting with Haroun?"

"Would you really call it flirting?" Malory asked, suddenly aware of Ottavia's hands still on his elbows. "She was a young girl. He was, well, he must have been close to fifty."

"Do you remember how, at the end, when Aldana was called upstairs to join her father and the others, Haroun promised to come back?"

"Yes, why?"

"Did he?" Ottavia's hands moved up to Malory's shoulders. "I've been wondering since that night in Rome. Did he come back? Is there more?"

"Just a polite visit eleven years later," Malory said. "When Charlemagne was crowned Holy Roman Emperor in 800, Haroun returned."

"Disguised as his envoy?"

"It's not clear. I remember there was a note about the visit in the *Complete History*, but it was written by a ten-year-old boy."

"Aldana's son?"

"And Aimery's. The boy was the son of Charlemagne's daughter and the King of the Jews. He was the eldest grandson of Charlemagne and heir to the throne of Septimania. He wrote about standing on the circle of porphyry in St. Peter's after the coronation. Next to him was his grandfather, Charlemagne, and his parents. And there was another man, a friend of his father's, who had traveled all the way from Baghdad."

"So Haroun kept his promise and came back!" Ottavia walked a few steps down the track and then turned back to Malory full of light. "And why do you think he did that?"

"For Aimery, his old friend Gan, of course," Malory said.

"But couldn't it be that he came back for Aldana?" Ottavia asked. "That he kept his promise to Aldana and came back to see the boy. Isn't that possible? Isn't that the answer?"

"To what question?" Malory had an uncomfortable feeling, a residual pain like a rope burn on the back of his skull.

"Haroun didn't come back for Aimery. He came back for Aldana."

"Why? Because he promised?"

"To see his son!" Ottavia's exasperation with Malory was real, but charming, Malory thought, which relieved his discomfort a touch.

"You're saying . . ." Malory corrected himself. "You're suggesting that perhaps it wasn't Aimery who was the father of the boy, but Haroun?"

"Oh, Malory!"

"And that the line of the kings of Septimania, and queens for that matter, descended not from the line of King David, but from the Caliph of Islam?"

"Why . . . ?"

"And that therefore I, Malory, am not King of the Jews after all?" Malory knew he was lecturing, but the rope burn drove him on. "But as a consolation, I am the Messiah of the Muslims?"

"Stop, Malory!" Ottavia said. "I didn't mean to get you so upset. But can't you see that sometimes people celebrate uncertainty?"

"What uncertainty?"

"The boy," Ottavia said. "Aldana knew that his father was either Aimery or Haroun . . ."

"But didn't know which?" Malory asked.

"Aimery was born in the same fertile crescent as Haroun," Ottavia smiled. "Olive skin, curly hair—Aldana probably didn't have much to go on to identify the boy as the son of one or the other. And in those days, millennia before DNA testing . . ."

"Nobody knew how to open the box, or even which box to search," Malory said. He didn't expect Ottavia to understand, but she smiled. "Here, Ottavia." Malory reached into his jacket pocket and pulled out a small flash drive. "I had Settimio scan the *Complete History of Septimania* onto this for you. You can open the box yourself if you want and search for an answer. Or at the very least, it's a lifetime supply of bedtime stories. I suppose you have a computer of some sort?"

"Malory," Ottavia said, "I don't care whether you are Holy Roman Emperor, King of the Jews, Caliph of the Muslims, or all three rolled into one. I'm glad you're here. With Tibor. With me."

The force of Ottavia's hug, her arms around Malory, her cheek next to his, stopped him from nattering away. When she was through she said nothing, just took Malory's arm and led him to a building at the edge of the field.

"This is the Blue House," she said. "There is a room upstairs for you and a room downstairs for the Driver, as well as a garage for your car, although the space is tight next to the firewood. Cristina and Tibor are up the hill in the White House. The Nurses and the Bomb Squad are usually in the Red Barn. But it's only the four of us today."

"The Nurses and the Bomb Squad?" Malory repeated, suddenly struck with a terrible thought. "You aren't one of? You haven't become?"

"A Nurse-in-Training?" Ottavia laughed again, but the laugh wasn't quite as melodic as before, and Malory immediately wished he could undo the question and tune away the pain he detected behind the dissonance. "Never. No," she said, leading Malory up the blue staircase at the side of the house.

And before she left him, another hug. No matter what, Malory thought, I am glad.

Malory's room was simple. An iron bed stood at the far end, a mosquito net draped from a serrated crown above its center. Malory wasn't certain whether there were curtains for the windows. But there was a Shaker hook rug on the painted blue floor, and a bathroom whose fixtures were so intricately designed that Malory, while ignorant of their function, understood that they were of the same high quality as the hair creams and skin emulsifiers and loofahs and face cloths and bathrobes and even the tarantula-shaped juicer that shared the bathroom with him.

"I'm giving you fifteen minutes to wash your face," Ottavia said, as the Driver set Malory's suitcase on the wicker bed stand, "then I'm coming to get you. Cristina's so excited she'll kill both of us if it's any longer."

"Ottavia . . ." Malory called to her.

"Yes?"

"Promise me you'll come back? To Septimania?"

"Only if you promise to read me another bedtime story and tuck me in." A final peck on Malory's cheek and she was gone.

The air was appreciably cooler when Malory opened his eyes and realized that the peck had carried a charm. Somehow, he had showered and climbed into a bathrobe before navigating the mosquito netting into an hour of dreamless sleep.

"Feel better?" the girl asked. She was nestled into the cracked leather of a Morris chair in a still-sunny corner of the room, legs folded beneath her. She smiled, and the mole at the top of her left cheekbone reached towards heaven. Malory blinked. "Coffee?"

"Actually," Malory said, "just some water would be lovely." Were there two heads he saw through the curtain? He hadn't remembered the mole on the girl's cheek.

"I found him." The two heads separated.

"Cristina?" Malory pulled himself up on the bed and adjusted his robe.

"You did. You found him." Cristina leaned down and brushed Ottavia's forehead with her lips. "Why don't you get the Driver a cupcake and a Cosmo and let me have Malory to myself for just one minute?" Ottavia smiled and hopscotched out the door. "I love that girl," Cristina said to Malory. "She makes me happy."

Truth be told, very little made Cristina happy any more. She would be happy, more than happy if all the Nurses went away. And the Bomb Squad. And the celebrities and the interviews with presidents and ministers and actresses and dictators and flying to Libya and flying to Chile and flying to Ascot on the private helicopter of someone who wanted to be richer and more famous than he was and thought that Cristina's presence in a hat—no matter how gorgeous it was—in his private box, within four feet of the Queen would further that ambition. What she wanted was an old story, but one that still made her cry when she stayed up alone late at night wrapped in her shawl, drinking still water from a blue bottle and watching any one of a number of movies that celebrated the days of innocence when apples were still black-and-white.

She wanted Tibor back. Back to before, before the flight to Rome, before the flight to Fatebenefratelli, the flight to America. There were things Tibor knew. He knew her blind father, her Jewish grandmother, the way her parents' apartment smelled when Tibor bartered a few smuggled strands of copper wire for two kilos of bacon and a dozen eggs, the school where she was the top student from age eight to seventeen, and the way she looked in a bikini the summer after she graduated. He knew about the abortion and he knew about the birth. And although they slept in separate rooms more often than they slept in separate countries; and sometimes in his separate room there were separate girls and separate sounds and separate activities that he sometimes insisted, awash in a haze of vodka and creation, that she enter and join; he was the only one who knew how to stop her from shaking when she saw things in the dark that threatened to separate her from sanity. In spite of everything, more times than not, she wanted Tibor back. And the curious man in the bathrobe on the bed, the curious man she hadn't seen in twenty years, who had been avoiding her and Tibor for who knew what imagined or unimagined slight—and there were slights that Tibor had inflicted on Cristina that were worse than unimaginable—might make that happen. Malory had brought Tibor to her in Rome. Malory might be the only one now who could bring Tibor back.

"Hello, Cristina." Malory tried to maneuver himself off the bed without dropping the robe or ripping the netting. But at the sound of his voice, all of what Cristina had built to make Cristina *Cristina* gave way and she ran to the bed and grabbed Malory in a hug that was anything but controlled and photogenic. "Are you all right?"

Malory's voice was unchanged from the first night she met him in Fatebenefratelli, when all she had wanted was to crawl onto Tibor's lap in their claw-footed bath and have Tibor soap away all the longing while she scrubbed away all the guilt. She held Malory's shoulders and looked past her own reflection at her old friend. There was something more formed about Malory, not exactly chiseled, but defined nonetheless. The universe had cooled in the past twenty years, and the softness of the young Malory had hardened into someone Cristina felt she could grab onto, small as he was, and not fall over.

"I'm happy you invited me," Malory said, looking out the window for a moment towards the pasture. But her hand on his cheek was too present, the scent of Cristina—he hadn't remembered it over the years, or it had changed, or his nose had simply gone into hibernation for two decades—too strong. It was the same scent, he was sure of it, that Isolde dabbed behind her Celtic ears when Tristan rowed over to Ireland and lost his mind. The smock she was wearing was of the same unbleached linen as Ottavia's blouse and trousers, but softened and rounded in the places where Cristina softened and rounded, and led his eyes forgivably down to the breasts that sloped as gently as her nose and her chin, as dark and warm and inviting as the Pyrenees of Malory's childhood. Malory was well aware of the vows of Perceval, Galahad, Roland, and all the other neo-Arthurian virgins who had, literally, lost their lives in just such a pass. But at this moment, with her hand on his cheek and his eyes deep within her cleavage, Malory was powerless to refuse her anything.

"Tibor couldn't turn fifty without you," Cristina said. But it was obvious—wasn't it?—that Malory didn't know the first thing about Tibor. About Tibor's public successes, his public performances, maybe he did. But about Tibor's private disasters, it was clear that Malory knew nothing. And she was glad. Not because she could still feel shame, but because, in some way, she wanted to protect the innocence in this strange Englishman who had brought Tibor back to her on that terrible day when she had the baby. The baby. The baby.

"It's six o'fuck!" The shout came from outside, through the wall of the Blue House. "Is Sleeping Beauty awake?" Malory knew the voice, gone badly out of tune.

"Take your time getting dressed," Cristina said. "Tibor can wait." And Cristina was gone.

When he'd pulled on the trousers, shirt, and vest that Settimio had packed for him, Malory opened the door at the top of the outside stairs. Tibor was at the bottom, turned away, smoking. From the rear, he looked well-dressed at least, in a loose cashmere sweater the color of horse chestnuts, tight-fitting jeans, and kid-glove moccasins that Malory reckoned meant Cristina had burned the rest of his clothes. But as he turned, and the two looked at one another for the first time in twenty-three years, the view was different. Malory wasn't surprised that Tibor had lost his hair, or at least enough of it to give him a vaguely Capuchin look at the crown, while the rest ran as long and gray as the Tevere after a bad rain, when plastic bags and bottles gargle in the eddies below the Isola Tiberina. It was the absence of Tibor's beard that confused Malory. When had Tibor shaved? It was a face as smooth and round and devoid of life as any of the holy fools Malory had seen in the badly smoked portraits of saints beneath the organ lofts of Rome. It was the face of a man who had discovered either infinity or zero, when neither was an enviable choice—spooked, desperate, untuned.

But then there was Tibor's palm. Malory descended the stairs, and Tibor's palm landed on his shoulder. It pushed Malory up now, up the slope from the Blue House to the pond below the White House, the way the palm had guided him through the streets of Rome twenty-three years before. They walked in silence, slowly. But Tibor's palm registered a real warmth. If the sum of the workings of Tibor's brain no longer passed through his shaven and barren face, its heat still found its way somehow down a hidden channel in the neck and out the shoulder and arm to this one palm. Through this palm ran a trickle of confidence, a bond that had once been forged between them—if only to be fractured—twenty-three years ago.

"Tibor," Malory began.

"Shh, shh," Tibor waved the cigarette in front of his face, launching fireflies of ash and spark.

"Tibor," Malory insisted. "How are you?"

Tibor stopped. He didn't look at Malory, but he withdrew his palm.

"Is that a scientific question?"

"That morning," Malory said, realizing that this might be his only chance to broach the inevitable subject. "That Christmas morning. Antonella."

"Antonella?" Tibor repeated. "Who the fuck is Antonella?"

"My colleague from Cambridge? The Christmas party after the Dante? The redhead? The one you promised to protect, but instead . . ."

"The Pip, Malory," Tibor said. "Did you bring the Pip?"

Malory stopped walking. And in one lung-squeezing moment of degutted breathlessness, Malory realized that what he had seen that Christmas morning—the image of Tibor making love to Antonella, an image of horror and beauty and infinite betrayal—didn't exist, no longer existed, perhaps had never existed for Tibor. The stone that had lodged in the tightest corners of Malory's intestines was rock of his own invention—or if not invention, then preservation. Tibor, or Tibor's memory, or perhaps all the alcohol that Tibor had swallowed in the past twenty-three years, had excavated the memory of that night, that action, that betrayal as completely as ten thousand Dacian slaves had torn down a mountain of volcanic rock to create room for a column to the memory of their own defeat. Malory looked at Tibor's face, a face that even in its bearded tangle once had a power and conviction that had made Malory feel safe and honored by its friendship. That face was blank, dry, begging for something from Malory. With the tip of his smallest fingernail, Malory poked the column of his twenty-three-year-old memory of betrayal, and it fell to the ground in ash and blew into the pines.

What it revealed was a light that shone back into his face.

"Stay," Louiza had told him all those years ago as he left the maternity ward at Fatebenefratelli.

"Stay," Antonella had told him as the Rumanians had carried her off to the Dacia.

Louiza had trusted him to return, Antonella had trusted him.

But Malory had been late. He had been curious. He had betrayed them both.

But that wasn't it.

Gone was his anger at Tibor. Gone his disappointment with Antonella. Instead a vision rose up in front of him, behind him, refracted in all the shades of the rainbow as his memory fed freely on the months and the years. It was the vision of his own betrayal.

Malory had ignored the simple, he had slipped off the towpath. Malory had betrayed the obvious, the gift that had climbed the ladder to the steeple of St. George's that March morning. Malory had betrayed the gift that Louiza had brought him, the vision of what he could become. He had committed that crime alone, without the help of Tibor, Antonella, or Settimio. He had hidden it behind a veil of red hair and Rumanian beard. And for that, he had served a sentence of twenty-three years in Septimania.

"The Pip, Malory," Tibor repeated. "Did you bring the Pip?"

"Why?" Malory asked. The vision slunk away into the trees around the pond. The air grew light. Malory breathed. "It's only an apple pip."

"Then you won't mind giving it to me?" Tibor asked. "If it's only an apple pip."

"Why the Pip?" Malory said.

"For a performance." Tibor squeezed Malory's shoulder with a pressure that seemed both kinder and more insistent than before. "A performance tonight. One show only, I promise. You'll get it back."

"Tibor"—Malory surprised Tibor with the shift of register and cadence—"there was a baby. Back then. In Rome." Malory had one more question before he could feel entirely free. "A few years later, Settimio told me that the press, the public thought Cristina had a stillbirth in Rome, a miscarriage, uterus ravaged from Bucharest abortions. But that isn't the truth, is it? Cristina had a baby. That day I met you. She did, didn't she?" The Ospedale Fatebenefratelli. Louiza. Cristina. Images that hadn't faded during his hermitage. "There was a baby. Is Ottavia that baby?"

"Has it occurred to you, Malory," Tibor said, his hand dropping from Malory's shoulder, "that maybe Ottavia is Louiza's baby?"

"Louiza?" Malory repeated. Of course the thought had occurred to him, in that fraction of a moment when Ottavia first found him in the Villa Septimania. But he had filed it in the cabinet where he kept similar thoughts, like waking up one morning ten inches taller or with a PhD.

"Who had a baby in Fatebenefratelli, Malory? Cristina? Louiza? You? Me? Who are the fathers? Who are the mothers? 'Oh the streets of Rome,'" Tibor sang:

> *are filled with rubble,*
> *Ancient footprints are everywhere.*

Malory remembered Sasha and his guitar, the Dacia, the first warm night of Rumanian friendship in Rome. And Tibor's voice, if not completely in tune, still closer than ten minutes before:

> *You could almost think that you're seeing double*
> *On a cold, dark night on the Spanish Stairs.*

"And the baby?" Ottavia appeared. Had she been standing with them all along, hidden by her smallness? "Who was the baby?"

Tibor laughed—impossible to know what image from what Fellini that laughter hid. "You, Ottavia," he said, "were the one we pretended was our daughter. When it was convenient."

"On Family Days," Ottavia said.

"And other days. Ones you didn't see."

"But not when I needed."

"No," Tibor said quietly, "maybe not. Maybe I have been wrong. Eternally wrong."

"What's the matter, Tibor?" Malory asked.

"I lack the Pip," Tibor answered.

"Why the Pip?"

"You told me the story of how your Virgin Louiza, your mathematical Eve, found the Pip and not only tuned your organ, but tuned your organ!"

"Tibor, Ottavia is . . ."

"So . . . isn't it possible that there is a power in that Pip? Isn't it possible that, if you are descended from King David and Charlemagne and who knows how many other Grand Poo-Bahs, that your Pip is the great-grandson of that original apple from that original tree? That your Pip holds the sum of all human knowledge? And isn't it just possible that if I swallowed the Pip with a glass of the purest rainwater, I will not only find out why I make *La Principessa* and Ottavia and everyone around me—and I'm including you, Malory—so unhappy? But maybe, as a bonus, the Pip will raise my pickled limp *puli* like Lazarus from the dead and I'll get laid once more before I die?"

"Tibor," Malory said, "it's just an apple pip. If it had been able to solve anyone's problems, don't you think it would have solved mine?"

"The Pip, Malory. I need the Pip." Tibor placed both his paws on Malory's shoulders. There was such a frightening lack of harmony in his voice—not even close to the F-sharp of twenty-three years earlier, a far more desperate sound oozing from Tibor's throat.

I have come so far, Malory thought. I have left the Villa Septimania for the first time in decades. My anger is gone, my sense of betrayal is gone. Who knows where Louiza is, if she is even alive. If I need to bring any part of the world into tune, the way I had promised my mother long ago, it is this part, this TiborTina, with Tibor, Cristina, and their daughter, my wonderful new friend, Ottavia.

And the Pip is in my pocket. What harm could it do?

"Here you are, Tibor," Malory said, pulling the old 35-millimeter canister out of a vest pocket. He shook the Pip. A dry rattle in the throat of the canister. Malory couldn't bear to open the top and look.

Tibor stepped back, releasing Malory from his grip. With one shaking hand, he took the canister from Malory, with the other he opened the top.

"I will not turn fifty, Malory," Tibor said. "*Je refuse.*" And with that, he tipped the canister to his mouth and swallowed the Pip.

Malory couldn't move. Tibor couldn't move—although Malory's paralysis was due to shock and Tibor's due to the explosion he expected would release his body from its pain. Only Ottavia realized that performance was just that—performance.

"Tibor," Ottavia took his elbow. "Are you okay?"

"I suffer," Tibor whispered. A large patch of sweat had gathered below his right breast. His entire face was wet. "I suffer from Septimania."

Malory looked at Tibor breathing heavily, two, perhaps three inches away. He wondered whether anyone had been as close to Isaac Newton—at the end of his life or ever—as he was at this moment to Tibor. And he wondered—was he right to give him the Pip?

"Come. Let's prepare the *vongole*," Ottavia said, looking up at both men. "Go to the kitchen, I'll pick some parsley and pepperoncino and meet you there." The girl stared into Malory for a moment. Malory felt there was a message he was missing, but by the time he thought to ask for a translation, she had run up the steps of the terrace and around the far side of the house.

"Twelve steps," Tibor said. "How easy she makes it seem."

Malory looked after Ottavia, and looked at Tibor looking at Ottavia.

"When Dante was up the *culo* of Satan, all Virgil had to do was show him a secret tunnel, and twelve lines of *terza rima* later he was back in the land of the living."

And then Malory saw the plastic bag sticking out of Tibor's pocket. And out of the opening of the bag, a handle of a gun.

"Tibor," Malory said, "what's that?"

"A bag," Tibor said, taking it out of his pocket. "A gun. Here . . ." Tibor handed the gun to Malory. "I don't imagine you've ever held one."

Malory had no idea that a gun was so heavy. But he knew that he must not give it back to Tibor.

"Don't worry, Malory," Tibor smiled. "Ottavia is safe. We are all safe. I'll put the gun inside the house." Tibor began to reach for the gun, but stopped as he saw Malory flinch. "Or if you prefer, you can hold onto it."

Malory set the gun carefully back into the plastic bag Tibor held out to him, and put the bag on a low table by the pond.

"So," Tibor said, his hands resting with their accustomed weight on both of Malory's shoulders. "Now we are fine. We are all fine. I will put the clams in to soak and start chopping the garlic." Tibor turned Malory towards the water. "Look at the sunset on the pond. Count to ten minutes, then come on up. I promise I'll be ten minutes wiser. The Pip, you know . . ." Tibor tapped his throat. "The Pip will help me up Dante's twelve steps."

Malory felt Tibor's hands leave his shoulders, listened as Tibor moved away through the grass, to the sound of his shoes climbing the terrace. He squatted at the edge of the pond and looked into the water, at the reflection of a ceiling as ornate as any of Michelangelo's. The Pip was gone, his last link to Louiza swallowed by Tibor. With that swallow, all air was sucked out of the evening. Malory felt he would never again take a breath.

The next moment, something loosened. Malory stood. His windpipe opened and, in that intake of breath, while the bellows were drawing the wind and the pollen and the feathers and the dust and the mayflies and the pips of the world towards him, a face appeared across the far side of the pond. A face backlit by the last rays of the sun, so that age was softened into something still recognizable. A golden head. A pale chin lifted upward, still scenting the air twenty-three years later. A body, a woman rising up from the meadow like a lost deer in the last light of day, as pale as she was the afternoon she crossed from the Orchard to St. George's Church, Whistler Abbey.

If there had ever been a doubt that he should dedicate his life to finding the woman he had twice lost so long ago, that doubt had been replaced with a certainty that here, only a pond's width away, was the real Louiza, unboxed, alive, as beautiful as his uncased memory could have painted her.

At the far side of the pond, the taste of apples grew rich in Louiza's mouth and the haze of late afternoon lifted from her eyes and the warmth of the sun on her hair pushed her towards the water.

"Malory," she said.

Malory was amazed—amazed that the simple act of giving away the Pip had brought Louiza back to him. As all the loneliness and research of the past quarter century faded into the forest, the pond began to glow in the light it reflected from the woman moving towards him from the far side of the water.

Louiza awoke—perhaps for the first time since she had given birth in the Ospedale Fatebenefratelli. She saw Malory by the edge of the water and the girl from the Farmers' Market halfway up the terrace. And she knew, even as Una and Terry and Quatro and her beloved Dodo began to pick their ways over the stumps and the fallen branches into the woods, that the music of the Unimaginables was fading away forever, and that here were the real solutions she had been searching for. This small man, this small girl.

Ottavia, from the herb garden on the side of the terrace, saw the pantomime down below her and understood—although there wasn't time for her to construct an entire bedtime story out of it—that this man she had found in a strange villa above Rome and this woman she had found in the round barn of the Farmers' Market on River Road were bound to each other as tightly as the statues of the man and the woman in the Villa Septimania. She belonged with them as much as the apple she had taken belonged with the statues.

But as she began to walk down the terrace towards them, she saw two other men approaching Louiza. They were running—at least the one with the crew cut, the one she had seen at the Farmers' Market taking Louiza away from her, was running. The other man, old and hobbled, followed with difficulty up from the Blue House, sporting a cane and the graying remnants of a red beard. She saw Malory notice the men and turn back from the pond, searching for something on the low table, something he was desperate to find. Ottavia gathered her breath within her to shout a warning to Malory, to Louiza, to all of them.

Then the shot rang out.

It seemed to Malory—like Dante's Tuscan peasant on the side of a hill at the time of day when the sun turns his face and the woman he loves lifts her chin across the pond to call him home for supper—that all the fireflies of the world had come to illuminate TiborTina, to show in a single, pitiless flash the solitude of Ottavia and Cristina, the paralysis of Malory at one edge of the pond, of Louiza at the other. In the light of that big bang, Malory saw the sorrow, the seven-sided confusion of Tibor blown into as many memories, although he had no way of recognizing the faces of all the women—not just the Indian Antigone with her crying baby but all the women: women of memory, women with memories—who paused as they heard the blast on their own private hillsides far away. All paused, at TiborTina and beyond, and smelled the air, touched their hearts, glanced around, as if a universe had just disappeared and their lives weighed a fraction less than they had a moment before.

Up on the porch of the house, above the terrace abandoned by *La Principessa* and her court, all the countless bits of what had been Tibor's childhood and adolescence and hopeful struggle and boundless energy, all the memories of the actresses of Tenth Avenue and the ballerinas of St. Petersburg and the demimondaines of Paris and nights sleeping rough in Rome and cracking a vertebra or two leaning over the parapet of the organ loft of Santa Maria sopra Minerva, all these bits went flying through the nighttime air towards the half-roof above the terrace, towards the top branches of the three protective birches, towards the quivering underbellies of the leaves, and lit up the night with a light as sharp and ambitious as the flames of hell; all strove with a last muscled flicker of energy to become a part of the great Tevere of stars that twisted across the heavens.

The bit of Tibor that flew the highest, attached for a moment as brief as that timeless instant at the beginning of the beginning to a still-intact apple pip, was his first memory of a rising sun in the depths of a Bucharest winter; of hair dark, years away from the merest hint of gray; and the two eyes, gray, even silver, interrupting his rehearsal, looking for a bathroom, drawn to his—eyes pure and clean and full of a saving innocence in a time before knowledge, before the wisdom of Minerva overran them both. That final spark of Tibor's compounded, complex, unimaginable love for Cristina released its forgotten energy and lit up the sky above the Red Barn and Cristina's gray head.

And then, since these countably finite memories—each attached to a portion of swiftly cooling brain—had been forcibly exiled from any connection to heart and lung, all that remained was the echo of the pistol that Mr. Jeddah had left in the plastic bag on the bar of the Seven Veils, the bag Ottavia had so thoughtfully retrieved for Tibor. Then came a silence and then the prayers of the crickets and the mantras of the bullfrogs, as the fireflies—whose memories are the merest fraction of their brief lives—lit what was left of the world, until, giving way as it must to the law of gravity, the light circled back upon itself, licked its paws, crept into a box, let fall the lid and seal, and settled cold, extinguished, irreversible.

PART THREE

If I have seen further it is only by standing on the shoulders of giants.

—Isaac Newton

3/0

11 September 1692

Dear Mr. Newton,

      I regret to inform you that, on the night of 10 September, after consuming a light supper with a bottle of claret, Her Royal Excellency, the Queen of Septimania, retired to the Sanctum Sanctorum for the last time. Enclosed, please find a letter in her hand addressed to you. I rest

your most humble & most
obedient Servant,
Settimio

3/1

LEEPLESS, BUT NOT DREAMLESS.

Sleepless in the Good Knight's Inn in South Hackensack.

The digital alarm blinked out the minutes of the early hours with a spastic colon. Malory reckoned he had been awake for every one of those indigestible blinks. But sometime in the darkness a vision came to him—perhaps in the way the Arabian Tales revealed themselves to restless storytellers over a thousand and one insomniac nights. Water—an ocean, or maybe just the pond at TiborTina, water lapping the grassy shingle like a lukewarm summer's bath—pole pines, shadows, evening fog muting all sense of space. Sitting at the edge, shoes off, trousers rolled below the knees, toes deep in loamy mud, a bamboo pole and shop-bought string for a fishing rod.

"So . . ." Malory knew Tibor was behind him, could smell the tobacco and the vodka merging with the fog. "Do you promise to tie my legs?"

Malory tried to answer, tried to ask, but in his half-sleep couldn't move his lips.

"Tie my legs," Tibor continued, "tight at the ankles. Tie my wrists behind me. Tight. Toss me into the pond and count to thirty. If my hands come up first, waving, fish me out and dry me off. If my feet come up, bound and lifeless . . ."

Malory knew the story, knew how it would end. He knew the Tale of Judar, the tale that Haroun al Rashid had told Aldana in the stable below the *shochet's* house in Narbonne. He knew the story of the three brothers from some distant Arab land—Morocco was it? Tunisia?—the three brothers who approached a young fisherman named Judar on the shore of Lake Karoon. They had made the same request as Tibor—bind my wrists behind me, bind them tight. Toss me into the water and count to thirty. Two of the brothers drowned. The third rose to the surface hands first and led Judar to unimaginable treasure.

Malory didn't want to tie up Tibor, couldn't imagine unimaginable treasure—certainly didn't need it. But in his sleep, he felt bound—yes, he remembered thinking that word—to bind his poor, sick, drunken, sweat-soaked friend. He reached into his Kit Bag and pulled out a meter's length of laundry cord. He began to wind the cord around Tibor's arms, but Tibor's elbows kept slipping the knots.

"Sorry," Malory said. He reached again into the Kit Bag and pulled out a coil of grapevine, the leaves and grapes still hanging ripe and heavy. But tying knots in the mess only made the job more difficult. Malory reached into the Kit Bag a third time and found a cello string, the low C-string, a length of steel-wrapped gut thicker than the grapevine but less complex. With the C-string, Malory was finally able to tie Tibor's arms behind his back and bind his ankles in a rough imitation of a Transylvanian martyr.

"Now what?" Malory asked in his half-sleep.

"The rules," Tibor said, with a long sigh. "Just follow the rules, Malory." And although Malory had no idea which rules, or who else was following the same rules, Malory lifted Tibor over his head with a strength that he hadn't manifested since he'd carried Louiza from Santa Maria sopra Minerva to the Ospedale Fatebenefratelli twenty-three years before.

"Now!" Tibor commanded.

With the heave of a Hercules, Malory launched Tibor towards the Sun. And as Tibor descended towards Earth, as the rules mandated, and the full force of his turkey-trussed, balding frame hit the water, the explosion—unlike anything Malory had heard, even from the sixty-four-foot contra-trombone stops of the cathedral of Narbonne—shattered whatever sleep had brought on the dream.

The clock flashed 05:34, September 11. Malory found the light.

WHEN MALORY HEARD THE GUNSHOT AT TIBORTINA THE NIGHT BEFORE, he first thought that he had been hit and then feared it was Louiza.

But as he was running to her and she to him, he realized that the sound must have come from elsewhere and been directed at somebody else. He was happy—he remembered that sentiment—happy that it was not them, that he was close and closer and Louiza was also running.

And then he was stopped.

"*Principe!*" The Driver grabbed Malory around the waist in a manner both respectful and determined. "I apologize, but we must go."

"Let me go, please," Malory said.

"I cannot," the Driver said. "My instructions are to protect you."

"I," Malory began, as the Driver pulled him towards the car, "I command you . . ."

But clearly Settimio's commentary of twenty-three years before, that Malory was the one who made the choices, was the Chooser-in-Chief, did not apply to this situation. There were other rules that Malory couldn't understand, rules that overruled Malory's rule. And as the Driver firmly, but respectfully, shoved Malory into the passenger's seat and locked the door, Malory saw the man with the brush cut follow Louiza up the hill to the pond. He saw the brush cut lead Louiza away.

What did he know?

He had heard a gunshot.

And after?

He had seen Louiza, alive thankfully, but in the grip of the brush cut.

He had seen Ottavia—yes, he was certain of it—running up the hill from the herb garden to the White House.

He hadn't seen Cristina. He hadn't seen Tibor.

Except in his dream in the Good Knight's Inn. He had tied up Tibor in his dream. He had lifted him over his head and tossed him into the pond. And then an explosion.

And now he was awake at 5:34, sitting on the edge of the bed, bound in the vague motel smell of cigar and mold on an unwashed scrim of plastic and foam. His suitcase was open—had been opened by the Driver the night before. They had arrived—or, more precisely, the Driver had ceased his tour of the smaller roads of New York and

New Jersey—well after midnight, many hours after the flight from TiborTina. A fresh pair of corduroys and a cotton dress shirt hung from the closet door. Malory's toiletries—bypassing the Good Knight's Inn bar soap and packet shampoo—had been neatly laid out on a towel covering the broken bathroom shelf. It was 5:34, and Malory was sitting at the edge of the bed. When the Driver knocked on Malory's door, the digital alarm clock showed 7:30 and Malory still hadn't moved.

"My lord," the Driver said softly from outside. Malory stood and padded across the carpet to the door. The morning air was cool, the sun already risen, the car already humming. If the Driver was surprised at seeing Malory undressed, he had the grace not to show it. He merely guided Malory through the bathroom into his clothes and out into the car in under seven minutes. The ride to the airport was even shorter. And as the Driver had doubtless been in communication with Settimio, the private jet that had brought Malory from Rome to the United States the morning before was refueled, repiloted, and waiting for them. The Driver carried out whatever formalities were necessary to assure the U.S. government that Malory was a safe bet on a private plane. A flight attendant, a young Italian woman who identified herself as Maria Grazia, brought Malory a cup of tea with a choice of two scones—the Driver took only water—as the plane taxied towards takeoff. And at 9:15, Malory pulled his seatbelt tighter as the engines revved, or did whatever they were supposed to do, in preparation of takeoff.

Malory didn't want to go.

What he wanted was to return to TiborTina. What he wanted was to find Louiza, to find Ottavia, to find out what he could about the explosion, about Tibor and Cristina. He had no cell phone himself, of course, and was barely aware to what extent Settimio or the Driver or anyone else might be able to find out what had happened at TiborTina the night before. The Driver and Settimio knew he was concerned. They were concerned. Everyone was concerned.

So when the engines on the plane suddenly revved down, or whatever they were not supposed to do, and Maria Grazia answered a call from the pilots over the intercom and then said to Malory in lightly accented English that she was very sorry but the flight would be delayed, that the pilot was turning the plane back to the terminal and would he like another cup of tea, Malory began to plot how he might drive, as quickly as possible, to TiborTina and find out what had happened.

It was easier than he'd thought. While he was pondering a strategy, the Driver and Maria Grazia chatted in a rapid, half-whispered Italian that was full of concern, but which Malory imagined had to do with liaisons either past or future and didn't concern him. So when they returned to the terminal—although shortly thereafter things would be forever changed in airports public and private after this moment—it was only a matter of a quick trip to the bathroom and a mistaken turn to the left, and Malory was in a New Jersey taxicab heading north to River Road.

The cabdriver was a heavyset Kodiak bear of a man, who made no attempt to help Malory into the taxi. A full pelt of hair pressed his head onto his chin and his chin onto a chest wrapped in a multi-pocketed vest full of pens and pads and things covered in feathers and fur that Malory couldn't begin to identify from the back seat. The cabdriver was playing a CD on his audio system—*La Chanson de Roland* by Louis Couperin—which meant that he and Malory could travel the roads up the Hudson unencumbered by knowledge of events only a few miles to the south.

"Like music?"

"Sorry?" Malory thought he had heard.

"I asked if you like music," the cabdriver said again, with a punctuated crescendo on every syllable.

"Mmm," Malory answered, since an explanation would be too long.

Malory not only knew the piece, he knew the recording—E. Power Biggs on the organ of Saint Sulpice in Paris. *Baroque Biggs* was one of the few treasures left behind by his mother, a gift for his ninth birthday. The Couperin was not a difficult piece—he had persuaded the organist in Narbonne to teach it to him that next summer. His favorite part was towards the end when Roland calls for help. He blows his horn of elephant tusk so hard—the young Malory had to stand up on the pedals and reach high with both his arms to produce the effect on the organ—that his brain explodes and he dies on the spot. But another memory struck Malory with greater force as the taxi headed up the river. When Haroun first met Aldana in the stables below the house of the Jewish *shochet* Yehoshua, he had spoken of the death of Roland, Charlemagne's cousin and best friend. Roland had stayed at the rear of the retreat of the Franks from Spain. He had died in the Battle of Roncesvalles deep in the Pyrenees, cut off from the rest of the troops by the betrayal of one of his kinsmen. Was Malory himself guilty of such treachery? He had left his own friend behind, if not the night before, then twenty-three years of nights before. And if a large part of Malory knew that Tibor was already dead, an equally large part was determined to return to TiborTina and at least put the body to rest.

And find Louiza.

And Ottavia.

If not the Pip.

"I began to dig organ back in the Navy," the cabdriver said.

"Mmm," Malory said again, not convinced he understood but certain he would find out.

"Moms put me in Language School. Keep me from going to Vietnam. Spruce Cape. Alaska. Not much to do up there except throw rocks at seagulls and study Russian. One of the SEALs training for cold weather combat had a Nakamichi reel-to-reel and about a hundred hours of tape—Karl Richter, Olivier Messiaen, that showboat Virgil Fox and the blind Kraut Helmut Walcha. But my favorite was Edward George Power Biggs. Man, I couldn't get enough of E. Power."

Malory thought about telling the Driver that he had met Biggs once, had taken him on a tour of the Father Smith organ in Trinity, with its forty-two ranks refurbished by Metzler Söhne. One ear was listening to the *Chanson de Roland* and the other for clues as they drove onto the toll bridge across the Hudson.

"Listened to so much E. Power," the cabdriver said, as he threw some change into the basket, "that I failed my language exams. They stuck me in a booth with a set of headphones and played a tape— a simulation of a couple or three Russian MiGs in attack mode.

The back and forth of the voices, the hiss of the switches going on and off. Lots of Russian. And above everything, the sound of air, like a giant bellows. Something about the voices reminded me of E. Power's recording of the Bach *Toccata and Fugue in D minor*, you know, the second section where everything goes haywire. And then suddenly—silence. 'Hey' I told the examiner, 'your tape broke.' 'Nope' the guy told me. 'My tape didn't break. Your fighter just got shot down.'" The cabdriver turned the wheel to the left by the round barn. Malory looked out through a window, greasy with New Jersey. Half a dozen people were gathered around a TV plugged into one of the lights in the parking lot. "So I came back here and started driving."

They stopped at the fieldstone fence at the top of the dirt road that led down the hill to Ottavia's yellow cabin by the creek. Malory handed the cabdriver his wallet, furnished by Settimio with enough American money and discreet identification to last him several days. It was almost noon, less than twenty-four hours after Malory first strolled with Ottavia down the road and up the tractor path to the Blue House. Malory was returning to TiborTina. For Louiza? Did he really expect she would be there? For Tibor? Did he really believe he was still alive? For Ottavia? She had spoken to Malory of Haroun and his own return to Rome for the coronation of Charlemagne. Haroun came back for Aldana, Ottavia told him, for the daughter of the Holy Roman Emperor, for love. The driver took what he needed and handed the wallet back to Malory. The Couperin had trickled down into a runnel of sixteenth notes, a soothing anesthetic for his arrival. The driver backed into the dirt road, turned the way he came, and drove off over the last of the organ.

It wasn't until Malory crested the hill to the pond that he saw any signs of life. There were no cars parked by the Blue House, none by the Red Barn. The pond at noon was still and gray and nearly invisible. Whatever traces Louiza had left in the loam around the edges were merely the residue of his imagination. Malory turned. He hadn't climbed up the terrace the evening before, hadn't been invited yet up to the White House. Tibor had left him by the pond while he went to cook dinner, Ottavia had run off to pick herbs, and then there had been Louiza and the explosion and all that followed.

Had the explosion come from the White House?

Nothing was out of place. The potted pines or ferns or whatever Cristina had set in whitewashed uniformity on the steps of the terrace were as Malory remembered—as he remembered as Ottavia ran up the steps of the terrace to pick herbs for Tibor's pasta. Only the gun was gone—the gun Tibor had handed to him and that Malory had placed back into the plastic bag and set on the table by the pond. And there was a yellow ribbon, barring the way up the first step of the terrace. A plastic yellow ribbon with writing.

When he thought back to the terrace—the lifting of the yellow ribbon, the walk up the steps, the arrival at the top, the discovery of the table holding the half-drunk glass of red wine, the wire-rimmed glasses he had first seen Tibor tweak over his ears twenty-three years earlier as he emerged from the organ case in the loft of Santa Maria sopra Minerva, the Adirondack chair that must have held Tibor in the final moment before he shot a bullet through the roof of his mouth and spattered the ceiling that overhung the terrace and parts of the deck with what had once been his divided mind—Malory couldn't remember reading the writing on the yellow tape: its warning, its infernal admonition from the police to abandon hope all ye who cross this line. All he remembered was the pull, the pull up the steps. And the music, the noise, the hum, the buzz, the ascent and descent of thousands of flies from roof to deck, from deck to roof, thousands of tiny angels, like the Jacob's ladder of dust motes he had seen in another organ loft in another lifetime. The message of the flies—this was clear, this he understood.

"Hey, Mac!"

"Hello?" Malory wasn't certain where the sound came from. He turned to the pond, but the gray surface was level and quiet.

"Hey!" An American voice, followed by the squawk of something electronic. "What're you doing here?"

Finally Malory saw it, saw the man. He was sitting in a car parked on the driveway just to the side, between the trees that screened the view down to the Blue House. It was a car painted black and white, with a light on the roof. And although the light was unilluminated, Malory was fairly certain that the man at the wheel of the car was a policeman.

"I'm sorry," Malory said. "I just came back to look."

The man opened the door to the car slowly and swung his legs and his belly and then the rest of his body out into the open. There was also a mustache and a hat and a badge and a uniform.

"C'mon down from there," the policeman said, drawing his fingers into his palm as if he wanted Malory to throw him something. Malory looked back at the table with the wineglass and the spectacles, and up at the ceiling. He walked down the steps of the terrace empty-handed and over to the policeman by the patrol car. "Now," the policeman said, "what were you doing up there?" And although Malory's answer could have been what he told Louiza in the loft of St. George's, Whistler Abbey, or what he told Tibor in the loft of Santa Maria, he decided against a frontal response and instead followed the advice of Settimio. Discretion. He was no Roland. TiborTina would not be his Roncesvalles.

"I'm sorry, officer," Malory replied. "I came back. Yesterday, I was here as a guest. But then there was an accident and I had to leave."

"Didn't you see the tape?" the policeman asked.

"Sorry. I'm not from around here," Malory said. "I don't know the customs."

The policeman spoke into his walkie-talkie and passed these bits of information, along with Malory's name and vitals which he gleaned from items in Malory's wallet, to someone far away, Malory imagined, someone perhaps with Cristina, perhaps not. Malory looked around in the silence between crackles. He saw that the driveway beyond the patrol car bore the impression of a caravan of tire prints. He tried to imagine what had gone on after the Driver had taken him from the scene of the accident. The ambulance, the police. Cristina in her Yukon, Ottavia he hoped with her. And how had Louiza gone? In another vehicle. How many other vehicles had come and gone in search, in delivery? When had this patrol car arrived to keep watch? To keep watch over what?

"Mr. Malory," the policeman said to him after the last squawk, "would you mind coming with me? They've got a few questions for you."

"Excuse me?" Malory said. "Who is they? Where do you want me to go?"

"Just get in the front. Don't worry, you're not under arrest, just a few questions."

"But where?"

"Don't worry," the policeman said again, "I'll bring you back for your car."

"I don't have a car," Malory said. "I came by taxi."

"Well then," the policeman said, "that'll make life a whole lot easier. Now if you don't mind . . ." And the policeman lifted Malory's arms and methodically searched him for weapons.

They drove through the Farmers' Market intersection and turned off River Road into the woods above the Hudson. Malory thought about asking to call Settimio—he wasn't entirely certain how to contact the Driver. But he was more curious than nervous—he wasn't under arrest, after all, and that must mean something. He had run from his own Driver in order to find out what had happened to Louiza and Ottavia, and he was still not entirely clear what had happened to Tibor and Cristina, despite the passacaglia of the flies. The policeman claimed ignorance and disinterest. But the drive beneath the screen of American leaves was pleasant. The dappled light of noon wrapped him in a camouflage that felt—despite the discomfort of ignorance—coddled and warm.

The police car pulled up to an iron gate. Through the windshield, Malory saw a pair of men talking into more walkie-talkies. Behind them, a yellow house. Clapboard—that was the word that came to Malory's mind as the gate opened and the policeman drove through. Clapboard, like the White House at TiborTina. This is America, Malory thought. Clapboard. I like it.

"Wait a minute here, Mac," the policeman said.

"Of course," Malory said, thinking, what a wonderful clapboard house.

The policeman closed his door and locked Malory in. Malory watched him walk up the steps to the veranda that led to a sheltered front door flanked by a window checkerboarded into wooden sashes. A cluster of dried flowers and variegated corn hung off one column. The front door opened and the policeman disappeared. Malory looked up: above, a second story window nestled beneath a peaked gable, a gentle wooden drapery imitating the lace curtain that sat patiently just behind the glass. Malory looked up to that window. He wanted to be there. He hoped, although he didn't know why, that the policeman would reward his own patience and invite him inside and he could explore that room.

The front door opened again.

"Okay, Mac," the policeman came around and unlocked Malory's door. "C'mon in. You're just in time for lunch." With a hand on Malory's elbow, persuasive but not in menace, he helped Malory up the steps of the veranda and served him through the front door.

"Thank you," Malory said.

"Don't thank me, Mac," the policeman said, "I wasn't invited," and closed the door.

Malory found himself in a narrow corridor. At the far end stood what looked like a kitchen. There were a few hooks on the wall, jackets and scarves—a woman's, he thought—hanging even though the day was warm. The corridor smelled of beeswax and sunshine. Malory didn't know where to go, but for the moment he didn't mind.

"You can come in here," a voice called out. It was a male voice, not dissimilar from the policeman's but with a tone that compromised Malory's sense of contentment. "First on the left."

A sofa with faded yellow cushions. A fireplace, unlit, and above it the portrait of a man who might have been a contemporary of Isaac Newton, perhaps another young scientist who had sat for the portraitist, Keller or Kneller—Malory had lived in the land of Bernini long enough to squeeze these Germanic names out of his memory.

"Over here."

Malory turned away from the portrait. A man was sitting at a round dining table. Behind the man, the midday light set a lacy screen that made it difficult to separate the man's features from his outline. Malory walked to the table. The man didn't stand up to greet him, but there was a chair at Malory's side of the table and a cup of tea and a plate. With a scone.

"Sit down, Mr. Malory." At this distance, Malory guessed the man was no larger than him, perhaps his age, although with more nose and less hair, and what there was of it was as pale and flat as the midday light. The man had a folder open in front of him in place of tea and scone. Some type of pocket recording device sat at the center of the table. Malory wondered what local police force kept such detailed files that a brief call on a walkie-talkie could identify him as a tea-and-scones man. But he knew it was in Settimio's nature to anticipate his needs. And he knew that the reach of Septimania was longer than he had interest or ability to understand. "Please," the man said. "Sit."

Malory pulled out his chair. And as he did, he saw the piano tucked next to the table in the bay window giving out to the veranda. A baby grand with a light cherry veneer, probably nothing important. But its very lack of importance gave Malory a feeling of security, of nestled comfort. Whatever he was about to learn, whatever had happened to Tibor, to Louiza, to Ottavia couldn't be that bad if there was music nearby.

"First," the man said, "let me offer my condolences on the death of your friend Mr. Militaru."

Malory heard the name, Tibor's surname, for perhaps only the second time in his life.

"From all appearances, Mr. Militaru died from a self-inflicted gunshot that separated the greater part of the upper half of his skull from the lower. Death was immediate. Please, try the scone. It's from the Farmers' Market. They tell me it's fresh."

Malory listened as if deciphering an equation in a foreign language. But it was enough to settle the question. Tibor had shot himself. Tibor was dead.

"Where?" Malory began, but the man held up a hand.

"That is all the information I have."

"Surely," Malory said, "you can tell me where I am, who you are."

"You'll have a chance," the man replied, "to ask questions. And maybe there will even be someone who can answer them. Someone else. Right now, I'm the one asking. So drink your tea and eat your scone. And then you can tell me why you left Mr. Militaru's house so quickly yesterday evening."

"Of course," Malory said. The man pressed a button on the recorder and waited. Malory spoke. He spoke of his friendship with

Tibor, his invitation to Tibor's birthday, his position in Rome—as the director of a private foundation—and the security requirements surrounding that. His hasty departure was not of his own volition, but company policy. But as Malory spoke, his explanation played back into his own ears as something entirely tuneless and unconvincing. Backlit as he was, the man's face was impenetrable. Perhaps there was no need to plumb the man's private reaction. Perhaps all was for the recorder. But as Malory spoke, Malory wondered. Who was listening to the recorder?

Malory finished speaking. The man turned a page in his folder. He turned another. Malory took a bite of the scone. Tasteless. A sip of tea, cold.

"Can you explain," the man said, turning a third page, "why we found your fingerprints on the gun that killed your friend?"

Malory could explain. Of course he could explain. Tibor had handed him the gun. He had put it back in the plastic bag as quickly as he could and then left it on the table. But the memory of what he had done, or hadn't done, what he hadn't prevented, made explanation seem imprecise, perhaps even false, ultimately useless. So this time, Malory chose another option and said nothing.

"Can you explain why, Mr. Malory, in addition to your fingerprints and the fingerprints of your headless friend, we found another set of prints? A set of prints a whole lot smaller? Maybe a girl? Maybe you know of whom I speak?"

Of whom he spoke? Ottavia? Malory thought. Maybe the man knew and was just feeling Malory out. Discretion. He felt Settimio just out of sight behind his right ear, whispering the word. And he said nothing. But he wondered who was listening.

"And finally," the man stood and walked to the piano by the bay window, unmoved by Malory's silence, "can you explain why we found a fourth set of prints on the gun, a set that is a perfect match with a man who, at a quarter to nine this morning, flew an American Airlines 767 into the North Tower of the World Trade Center?"

"Excuse me?" Malory said, unable to say nothing to a sentence so foreign in tone and meaning. "Can you repeat your question?" And although, at the beginning, Malory's disbelief was far greater than the man's, as the man explained the events of the morning—the four planes, the attack, the collapse, and all that followed—ten minutes of back and forth was enough to transfer that incredulity across the table.

"You really don't know?" The man—who Malory thought was incapable of surprise—was clearly thrown off balance. "You didn't see the TV, didn't hear the radio, run into people on the street?"

"I'm sorry," Malory said finally, the sound of E. Power Biggs on the taxicab sound system loud in his memory, the soundtrack of his ignorance. "Nobody. I wasn't."

"Come with me," the man said. And something in the atmosphere changed. Malory still didn't know what the man was talking about. But as he followed the man up the narrow staircase off the front hall, he felt for the first time not only that the man believed him but the weight of his own ignorance.

"Sit down," the man said. Malory sat. The bed was soft and warm from the morning's heat. It was covered with a quilt that broadcast an America of film and history to Malory's untrained vision. But his fingers picked up another personality from the cotton squares, a familiar, downy heat that reminded him of the woman he had seen less than twenty-four hours before across a nearby pond. This was the room beneath the peaked gable he had seen from outside, the room he had wished to see. There was a bed, a dresser, and on top of the dresser, a television set.

"Here," the man said, flicking on the TV. "Why don't you look at this while you're waiting? It'll be an education."

All afternoon and into the night, Malory sat on the bed and watched the TV. He watched the day rewind, replay. He watched the planes turn and return, the towers, the dust, the flames and bodies go in then out, down then up. After an hour he turned off the sound. But the images repeated themselves like the loop of Couperin's Chaconne in a dance that accumulated force and power with each repetition. And each repetition brought an added understanding. Because of this, his plane was turned back at the airport. Because of E. Power Biggs, he hadn't heard the news on the radio. Because of the walk to the pond, the talk with the policeman, the drive over to The Gables, he hadn't seen the collapse, heard the name Osama, or seen the first tentative photos of the suspects. The hand that clutched the steering wheel—or whatever it was they had on airplanes—had, only a few hours earlier, left an impression on the gun Malory held by the pond of TiborTina. I danced with the man who danced with the girl who bombed the Prince . . .

And more. In between the videos, in between the lines of the newsreaders and the speeches of the experts and the disbelief of the witnesses, their chins lifted up to a sky that was raining the B-movies of their darkest imaginings, Malory heard the word *caliph*. It came in the middle of what sounded like a meaningless incantation, "the return of the Caliphate . . . restore the Caliph of all Islam." But Malory felt its force. What if Ottavia were right? What if Aldana had borne a son of this Caliph-in-disguise? What if I am descended from Haroun al Rashid? What if all this destruction is to restore me to yet again another throne I never dreamed of, never desired? If there is one rule that explains everything, is there also one ruler to blame? Is this all my fault?

As the light of September 12 began to sift through the lace curtains of the upstairs room, Malory stood. Unable to turn off the image, he pulled the plug from the wall and held its prongs in his right hand as he pushed the curtain aside with his left. There were two men below, smoking in the near dawn by the gate. Even with the TV unplugged, the sun continued to rise. Without untying his shoes, without removing his jacket, Malory let the plug drop and gravity carry him towards the bed and a comforter that smelled of time before.

Although he slept, and his dreams were free of Tibor, he found himself walking across the desert of the Maghreb, hand in hand with Judar and the Moorish brothers he had thrown into the pond. And he wondered whether that was Louiza's hand behind him like Eurydice's, and whether that was the hijacker's fingerprints leading him on in front, and whether there really was a treasure at the end of the journey. Or simply a punishment for all he was, for all he stood for— Holy Roman Emperor, King of the Jews, Caliph of Islam.

When Malory awoke, it was to Bach, the music of Bach, the theme to the Goldberg Variations. Malory stood up from the bed, walked out into the hallway and down the stairs. The music was coming from the parlor, the baby grand. Another man was sitting at the piano, a broad expanse of tweed, the back of a head gone gray with only the memory of red in thick, polished staves running down to the back of his neck. The man was much larger than the man who had sat across the table from him asking questions the afternoon before. There was a walking stick propped up against the bass end of the keyboard. Malory had seen the man before, at TiborTina, climbing up towards the pond behind a man with a brush cut.

"I only play the Aria," the man said without turning, without stopping. "Never bothered to practice enough to learn the variations." The notes came out in measured doses. Measured, Malory thought, watching the hair on the man's knuckles rise and fall in the morning shadows of the bay window, but not music. What the man was playing was Bach but was not music. It was a study for music, the notes leached of color as thoroughly as the cushions on the sofa. Nevertheless, the man played through, played through to the end of the Aria before he turned to Malory and stated his theme.

"Louiza," the man said. "Shall we talk about Louiza?"

Malory washed quickly in the bathroom off the corridor and joined the man on the veranda. Another cup of tea, another scone. Malory was too keen on talking about Louiza to wonder whether these men had a greater variety of culinary information on him.

"My name is MacPhearson," the man said. He was sitting back in his own wicker chair, his red knuckles wrapped around a mug of coffee. He made no attempt to rise, to shake Malory's hand, or even to look at him, but Malory recognized the gift for what it was—a name he could attach to memories that dated back several decades. "You may remember meeting me on several occasions in the past. Cambridge, Rome."

"Of course," Malory said, trying to match MacPhearson's professional coolness and masking his own eagerness with a bite of scone.

"As you are no doubt aware, I hired your friend Louiza straight out of Cambridge. She's been working for me—doing excellent work, you can imagine—for all these years."

"Twenty-three," Malory said. "Nearly."

"You're also a numbers man," MacPhearson said. Malory couldn't tell whether MacPhearson was smiling beneath the mustache and beard, but he saw teeth stained with coffee and age.

"Yes," Malory said, taking a sip, the tea too hot to say any more.

"The number of disasters your friend Louiza has prevented—do you have any idea how high it is?"

Malory set his cup down on the arm of his chair.

"But yesterday," the man said, "she was on to something. Maybe she knew. When you saw her, maybe she was coming to tell you."

"Tell me?" Malory said. "I hadn't seen her in almost twenty-three years."

"Maybe not. But she was looking for you. No question, case closed."

"Are you certain?" Malory knew that his face was showing warmth and behind that warmth was pleasure, but he was incapable, at the moment, of discretion.

"The only thing we're sure of," MacPhearson said, "is that we don't know where she is. When your friend Mr. Militaru shot himself . . ."

"Tibor," Malory said.

"Tibor," MacPhearson said. "When Tibor shot himself, all hell broke loose."

"But wasn't there a man with her? I saw someone chasing her, someone with you, with a brush cut?"

"A crew cut?" MacPhearson frowned.

"Yes!" Malory said, recognizing that his excitement was all about pleasing the red-headed man before him, even though this might be precisely the man who had been keeping him from Louiza for all these years. "The man with the crew cut. I saw him. I saw him with Louiza. At TiborTina, at Tibor's house, just before." Surely, Malory thought, this bit of information would buy him some reward. But Malory had spent the past quarter century studying physics and the internal workings of pipe organs and watching very few movies.

"I'm afraid that man is dead," MacPhearson said, and took a sip of his coffee.

"But," Malory said, "just the other day, the day before yesterday. At TiborTina."

"He was in the North Tower," MacPhearson said.

"The World Trade Center?"

"The first one to collapse."

"He went from TiborTina to the World Trade Center?" Malory asked. "Right after Tibor?"

"He was following Louiza."

Malory felt ill. Was this what the conversation was about? Had MacPhearson come to tell Malory that Louiza was dead?

"No," MacPhearson said, in answer to the unasked. "We think Louiza was not in the towers. Maybe Vince was wrong."

"Vince?"

"Louiza's husband," MacPhearson said, and watched Malory's confusion with interest. "Ah," he said, "she never told you?"

Malory said nothing.

"There's no time to weep for poor Vince," MacPhearson continued, far from tears. "Louiza. We have to find Louiza."

Now it was Malory's turn to be discreet. Louiza had married. Louiza had not married Malory. Louiza had married Vince. But Vince was dead.

"$i = u$," Louiza had told Malory in the beginning. "The implications are potentially dangerous." Vince was dead, but Malory was alive. Louiza was alive. Malory had a thought. "Mr. MacPhearson," Malory said, and for the first time stood, "why is Louiza so important to you? What does she know?"

"We don't know exactly who you are, Mr. Malory. I suspect we will find out, sooner or later. We know you are a physicist. We know that you know that 80 percent of what exists in the universe cannot be seen. But it's what makes the universe stick. It's what gives us weight, what gives us gravity. Our search used to be the same as yours—for that dark matter. But now we know that there is another force—a dark energy, an anti-gravity—that is dedicated to sending out its armies of galaxies on an endless jihad to the far corners of space, dedicated to blowing things up, as you saw yesterday, exploding towers, tumbling bodies in a perpetual freefall.

"For 13.8 billion years the universe has been expanding. And in that darkness we have never seen, sits the pitiful dribble of galaxies and stars and planets and mosques and churches and skyscrapers and gabled Victorian piles that we spend 99 percent of our time rebuilding and redecorating. But within that visible matter is one person who has a glimpse into that darkness. We have to find her."

"Louiza?"

MacPhearson nodded.

"You think that what happened yesterday, the attack against the Twin Towers, the Pentagon, is the fault of dark matter?" Malory's disbelief had given him a voice. "You think dark energy applies to the motives of people as well as the motions of stars and subatomic particles?"

"Do you think there's anything else?" MacPhearson asked, and hummed the Goldberg Aria. "Come, Mr. Malory. I know who you are. I know what you've been looking for. I need your help."

"My help?" Malory said. "You have been keeping Louiza away from me for twenty-three years and now you want my help?"

"Yes," MacPhearson said. "I want your help. We are looking for the same thing."

"And if I refuse?"

MacPhearson set his hands on his cane and shrugged. "You're free to go." He pointed to the far side of the gate. The Driver, Malory's Driver, was standing at the passenger door of the car that only a few days before had driven him to TiborTina. "Your driver knows how to find me, if you find Louiza."

Malory walked off the veranda and down the gravel path to the gate. He felt larger, taller than when he'd awakened to the sound of the Goldberg Variations. MacPhearson knew something, but Malory knew more. Without turning back, he sat in the car and waited as the Driver closed the door and returned to the wheel.

"Oh, and Mr. Malory." MacPhearson hobbled up on his cane and motioned Malory to lower his window. "Mr. Malory," Mac-Phearson said, leaning heavily on his stick to bring the remains of his red beard and his coffee-stained teeth to window level with Malory. "If you find that girl, please let us know."

"Which girl?" Malory said, willing the Driver to back up and leave as soon as possible.

"The girl who left that fourth set of fingerprints on the gun."

"Yes?" Malory said, thinking of those fingers wrapped around his arm in the innocence of the pasture below the Blue House, her excitement about the stories of Haroun and Aldana and the remarkable treasure of Judar Son of Omar.

"We ran a quick DNA test on all your prints."

"I see," Malory said.

"Of course science requires a little more patience than just a day, but I thought you might like to know."

"Know what?"

"The girl, you know who I mean," MacPhearson said. "That girl—well I suspect you suspected."

"Is my daughter?" Malory asked.

"And Louiza is her mother, yes," MacPhearson said.

"But a funny thing," MacPhearson interrupted Malory's vision, leaning down to the window of the car. "There's more to the genetic test. It appears that your friend Tibor was her father, too. It all depends on how you look."

The Driver pulled away from the yellow house with the gables. Malory heard the sound of a guitar, the voice of Dylan, or was it Tibor:

> You could almost think that you're seeing double
> On a cold, dark night on the Spanish Stairs.

Two fathers. Malory looked up at the sky. As MacPhearson saw it, there were big things and there were little things. Big things like galaxies, little things like the color-coded quarks that make up the cozy bits of atoms. But that only accounted for a fraction of the stuff that was maybe 5 percent of the universe on a rainy day. The rest was dark matter or dark energy. And Louiza.

3/2

IT WAS A MONTH BEFORE I CAME OUT OF THE WOODS, BEFORE GRAVITY proved stronger than fear and I fell to Earth. My memory of that month includes water—streams, creeks, not all of them the same, a few ponds and September puddles, a lake perhaps. Above all, my memory includes the water that penetrates the forest in the slimmest of trickles, that blackens the bark of maples and birches, and mulches the leaves to an oaken rot that ferments into the colors of nightmares dripping onto softer wounds. My memory includes bugs and beetles, ants and earwigs, small things that wash in acorn cups, things that I followed at night into hollowed trunks, where I folded myself into knotholes, contracted into the shelter of a single leaf to escape the harsher elements and memory herself. Malory believed in One, Tibor in Seven. But the things I saw were beyond number.

I did my best to shut out memory. But at night the music came at me. And it came not just with electric girls in polyethylene thigh-highs and strap-on Fenders, but in a hail of falling leaves, falling branches, falling limbs more present, more horrible than any memory of Tibor's exploded mind. The unimaginable had happened, although I couldn't have known it at the time. Unimaginable not just to me and Tibor and Cristina, but to the world outside the forest. And the music of the unimaginable drove a wedge between sleep, thought, and imagination itself.

I don't know how I coped that month, but cope I did. I swallowed bugs and mushrooms, licked the nighttime moisture from the naked trunks of my fortress. One tree at a time, I began to wander away from my knothole. One dawn, one week—although it could have been two or twelve—after the explosion, I found myself sitting at the edge of my creek, a hundred yards from my cabin, watching the water carry bits of TiborTina to me. I watched as cars came and went, up and down from River Road, policemen, others. And I waited. I don't know how long I waited—hours, days, with the music louder, if that were possible, than it had been deep in the woods—sitting there on a boulder on the far side of the creek, through the sirens of the day and the Stratocasters of the night. Until one morning . . .

"So."

I opened my eyes and looked around. No one. Across the creek, the morning had risen halfway to noon.

"So." I didn't turn around this time. "Did you find it, Ottavia?"

I didn't need Tibor's voice, real or imagined, to remember when I'd first heard that question, the day when Sister Francesca Splendida led us down past Mussolini's Rose Garden to the Circo Massimo. There were twelve of us, hopping like sparrows behind Sister, down the granite steps and across the dusty oval. Along the middle of the Circo stood a crane with a cameraman on a seat. Below the crane, the most wonderful women—gowns, faces painted brighter than any in the frescoed chapels of Santa Sabina. And in front of them all, black and as large as a statue, sat a man. Sister Francesca Splendida led us up to him and stood to the side to present us for inspection. Immediately he looked at me. I knew he was looking at me.

He was different from the few men I had seen in my ten years at the convent, in spite of the black. The hair on his head was pulled back behind his ears. His beard climbed high up to his cheekbones. The whites of his eyes shone clear and direct. None of us could look away as he spoke, as he told us of seven treasures that were buried in the Circo Massimo—seven treasures that only we could find.

"Girls," he said, "you have grown up your entire lives here in Rome, no?"

We all looked at Sister Francesca Splendida for guidance and nodded our heads.

"And you are good girls, no?"

Again a look and a dozen vigorous nods.

"But Sister Francesca Splendida and your other teachers have told you about sin, haven't they?"

We were used to nodding by now, but did so with a little more hesitation.

"I am directing a spectacle in Rome, beginning right here in the Circo Massimo. It is a spectacle about sin, about a man in despair." He saw our puzzled faces. "A man," he explained, "who is confused. A man who doesn't know which way to go. And so a teacher, someone perhaps"—and his eyes grew whiter—"like Sister Francesca Splendida, takes him on a walk. He takes him to a very special place where he sees all kinds of sin. But really, when it comes down to it there are only a few major, a few deadly sins."

"Seven!" I didn't raise my hand—I rarely did. Sister looked back at me fiercely, but Tibor smiled.

"So," he said, "so small and already you understand the connection between sin and mathematics." I didn't understand what he meant until years later, when he repeated the story to others in an effort to make me blush. But that day, I was guilty only of the sin of pride. He was looking at me, talking to me. "Seven sins," Tibor said. "Seven deadly sins. So girls. I need you to help me. I need you to look around the Circo Massimo, go exploring if you must. But come back to me once you've found an example of . . ."

"Lust."

"Gluttony."

"Greed."

"Sloth."

"Wrath."

"Envy."

"Pride."

One by one, seven girls counted down what they had learned by rote rather than experience—although later I discovered that many of them had experienced much in the days before they had been rescued and brought to Santa Sabina.

"Ready?" Tibor asked us.

Twelve vigorous nods.

"Go!" he said. And with that, eleven girls ran off. Only I stayed, looking straight up past the beard and the hair into Tibor's eyes.

"Didn't you understand?" he asked me, speaking more distinctly, kindly even. I nodded again, and he turned to one of the women at his flank. But I stood there, and the woman signaled to Tibor. Now when he turned, the kindness turned to impatience.

"What?" he asked.

"I have found them," I said. "You asked for an example of the seven deadly sins. I have found it."

Tibor's first reaction was incomprehension. I'm not sure that at ten years of age I understood completely. All I knew was that all the human frailties that Sister Francesca Splendida and our other teachers had warned us against were bound together by spiderweb and spit and the glue that holds together bird's nests and the insides of atoms, bound inside the dark, dark energy of the dark, dark man sitting in front of me. Tibor understood. I saw the moment when Tibor understood. It was a moment of fear, a moment of discovery. But once discovered, once uncovered, Tibor smiled. It was a smile of recognition. Recognition of his sinful frailty. Recognition that I was someone who knew him, who, perhaps, was even a part of him, a potential companion in sin, a comfort.

"So." The voice came to me thirteen years later, as I stood on a flattened boulder at the edge of the creek, mumbling past the first chirps of the morning birds as the air began to resuscitate the waking forest. "So." I knew he was dead. I had seen the body before I ran, had seen it at least up to the lower jaw, the loose linen trousers and shirt, the empty tumbler, the specs sightless on the arm of the Adirondack chair, and above a darkness more complete than his beard and hair had ever been. "So." I knew he was dead, but still the voice, the breath. "Did you find it, Ottavia?" Another treasure hunt. But what was I hunting?

While Malory was sleeping on that afternoon a month before, I took the gift he had brought me from Rome—the flash drive containing *The Complete History of Septimania*—and plugged it into my laptop in the cabin by the creek. I read again the Tale of Judar that Haroun had told Aldana. Like me, Judar was good at finding things. He found the three Moorish princes by the edge of Lake Karoon. And when the last of the princes survived, he traveled back to the Maghreb with him and found the treasure of Al-Shammardal, including the Magic Bag that held all the foods one could ever wish for. What did Tibor want me to find? The Magic Bag? I turned to ask him, but he was gone. He didn't want to be found, or at least it wasn't time.

I walked from boulder to boulder down the creek towards my cabin. Birds, early-morning shadows, water flowing slowly, still warm, even if the sun had passed into October. I opened the door and looked around my room. Muddy boot prints on the floor, powder and dust on all my books, the handles of my few pots. My toothbrush was missing. Someone had come searching for me, searching for my things.

I remembered the wheel.

Ten feet along the far bank of the creek, the shell of a Chevy 10 that had spent the past thirty years rusting into the leaves, stood wedged between a willow and a birch. Soon after I arrived at TiborTina, I realized that I needed a secret storage away from Tibor's unexpected curiosity—the back rear wheel well of the rusting Chevy 10. The wheel was untouched, the leather pouch still there. I emptied the few contents onto my desk inside my cabin, the few things I valued—my passport, the marble apple from the Villa Septimania, a mosaic tile from Santa Sabina, the flash drive with *The Complete History of Septimania*.

But strangely, the treasures refused to stay still. As flat as my desk was, the flash drive slid down towards the floor, the passport flopped open, and the apple I had taken from the Villa Septimania resisted my attempts to set it down but rolled towards me, like a kitten insisting on being picked up. Only by securing them back in the leather pouch could I keep them from falling off onto the floorboards and through the cracks into the water. My treasures, I thought. Were they urging me to get out of the cabin, moving me away from the water as surely as Judar had moved away from Lake Karoon to a greater treasure? Were Judar and I adept at finding things, or were the things we'd found using us for their own purposes?

Holding the leather pouch, I crossed the meadow and went up the hill to the pond. The policemen, the others were long gone. I walked up the terrace. The wind had eddied the fallen leaves of the overhanging maples into hassocks along the steps. Some battered yellow police tape still cleaved to the rails. Everything had been cleaned at some point, cleaned of the worst before being abandoned once again.

I looked up. Or to be more precise, something made me look up, an unfelt hand that lifted my chin, until my eyes saw the spot, the spot on the overhang of the terrace, a single spot that must have missed the high-power hoses.

How many wonders happen as if by magic? I don't know whether it was gravity or another force—the apple in the leather pouch that had only recently been suspended between the figures of the man and the woman in the Villa Septimania, the attraction of the treasure and the seeker, but a moment later the Pip separated from whatever bit of Tibor had glued it to the overhang and was in my hand. Was it the Pip I had seen Tibor swallow at the edge of the pond? The Pip that had found its way upward out of Tibor's blasted head to the roof of the overhang of the terrace? The Pip that, as far as I could tell, had waited while I hid unconscious in the forest, until I rewired myself and returned to find it?

But as it fell into my palm, as I closed my fingers around the Pip, I saw something else. I saw what my nightmares in the forest had been telling. I saw the airplanes, I saw the towers, I saw the flames, the ashes of incinerated words, the falling bodies. I saw the man I had seen at the back of the Seven Veils, the man who had wanted to attack Tibor. And I saw other men, other women, hundreds of them. I looked down from the terrace and I saw what Tibor must have seen in his final moment—an entire history, an entire empire. Thousands of people, perhaps more, filling every edge of the TiborTina, ordinary men, ordinary women, children ranked as neatly as convent girls singing back-up to the Rolling Stones, standing waist deep in the pond, perched on trees, spreading into the shadows of the forest, nested atop isolated columns above the crumbling ruins of ancient cities like seagulls awaiting the decline and the fall, circle after circle, as many as the fireflies. And in front of me, as an invisible DJ rode his volume pods up to eight, four unimaginably kick-ass girls in thigh-high boots and PVC mini-dresses pounded out the opening chords to a song whose lyrics I didn't know but in a key I recognized, as unimaginable as that might be.

"So . . ." the voice said behind me. "You found it." I reached back without looking, unwilling to see the half-face I was sure would greet me. I grabbed a microphone from his hand and stumbled forward, still unclear, wondering what I was meant to sing. I looked up towards the audience of thousands and saw her. There she was in the front row, the blonde woman from the Farmers' Market, the woman I had seen talking with Malory by the pond. She smiled at me and the Pip grew warm in my hand. The apple glowed in my leather pouch. Her head swayed, her shoulders rolled softly to the music. She knew the girls in the band and she knew the words. She was my mirror and my teleprompter. Microphone gripped tight, I stepped forward as the spotlight picked me out from an impossible angle on the rising moon and I sang.

ALORY STOOD AT THE GATE OF TRINITY AND WONDERED.

It had been twenty-three years since he last walked through Cambridge.

He had walked from the station, the towers of Addenbrooke's Hospital at his back, dodging bicycles on Parker's Piece—academics in their daily migration and townies on an early-evening forage for bitter and crisps. He had pulled his suitcase, his worldly belongings, down St. Andrew's Street, through Lion's Yard to King's Parade. Malory had thought very little over the past quarter century of the hours, years he had spent with Chelsea buns and Cumberland sausages in the tea rooms and butcher shops, in the tie-dyed emporia or at the fruitmonger's buying organic papadums or bruised Prince Williams. Gone, all of them. Gone were the stalls in the market, where E. Power Biggs rubbed vinyl with Billy Preston, and Telemann shared a rack with Telephone Bill and the Smooth Operators. The ghosts of the Taboo Disco Club, the Whim, the Eros had taken up residence in Topshops and H&Ms. Malory's own back was scarred from his journey. His feet shuffled down Trinity Street thanks only to the motor of memory, his suitcase trailing like a minor moon.

Malory stood at the gate of Trinity and wondered whether he dared go inside. Henry VIII still guarded the entrance with a stone sword or chair leg or hank of mutton in one hand. The remnants of Newton's garden sat between the gate and the chapel. Above and to the right, his windows—Newton's windows, Malory's windows, inset between the chapel and the bay window that had once been Newton's loggia—still looked out on Trinity Street, still felt the shade of the anniversary apple tree. For seven winters and seven summers, Malory had sat behind those windows. He had read and he had thought. He had written nothing. Seven autumns of wood fires and moldering leaves, seven springs of thaw. Seven years of paths worn between those rooms and the chapel, the tea room of the University Library, the weekly bicycle ride to Whistler Abbey, and the occasional journey to organs on other greens, in other fens. There had been the High Tables, of course, and pints in the Portland Arms and the Eagle, Sunday lunches at the Spade and Beckett, long afternoons cross-legged on the carpet at Heffers or eating buns in the steamy intimacy of The Whim, and Saturday night Herbie Hancock marathons upstairs on Rose Crescent—the naïve entertainments of a student who might have had a special facility for organs and the history of science, but was otherwise just a normal lad who wanted to fit in, to be coupled to other pipes and sing less solo.

Newton, of course, was a resident of those windows for much longer than Malory—over thirty years, even if one subtracted the months that Trinity closed for the Plague and Newton traveled with his friend, the King, the Queen of Septimania. For the first time Malory wondered—was it mere coincidence that had brought him those two windows in Trinity? Or were all the other tenants, from Newton through the eighteenth, nineteenth, and much of the twentieth centuries also direct descendants of the Great Sir Isaac? Were they all kings of Septimania? Had they all been expelled from Paradise?

It had been seventy-two hours since Malory flew back from New York to Rome. International flights began again on September 15, only four days later than Malory had intended to return to the Villa Septimania. But intention no longer had much connection with what Malory experienced. For three days and three nights, Malory sat in the Good Knight's Inn, fed, watered, and generally supervised by the Driver. During the days, the image of Louiza's face from across the pond seemed no farther than the other side of the motel window. Malory felt certain that all he needed do was open the door to the room and she would be on the other side. But every time he turned the deadbolt with the intention of stepping out to find Louiza, to rescue her from whatever terror or loneliness she was facing, a magnetic force, as strong as the one that had pulled him to her that afternoon so long ago in the organ loft of St. George's, turned on its pole and pushed him back into the room. Don't, it said. Stay away. And at night, the red-bearded face of MacPhearson would blink with the regularity of the digital alarm clock. I'm watching you, Malory, it said. If you look for her, if you find her, I will take her from you. For three mornings, Malory awoke convinced of an awful truth—as long as he didn't look, Louiza would stay alive. And Ottavia. Was MacPhearson looking for her too?

On the fourth day, the Driver drove Malory to Newark. He saw him up to Security, handed him his ticket and passport. Private planes were still grounded, but the Driver, on instructions from Settimio presumably, was able to find a seat in Business Class, if only for Malory himself. It was the first flight back to Rome. From his seat in the relative tranquility of the front of the plane, Malory could see lower Manhattan still smoldering below. Tibor was dead. Louiza, Ottavia, and perhaps even Cristina had disappeared. Smoke covered New York, clouds covered the Atlantic, and even gatekeepers like MacPhearson were confused.

But Malory hadn't expected the destruction to reach as far as Rome. Outside Customs, he waited ten minutes, an hour for a driver, any driver, even Settimio. He joined the queue in the September heat and sat in the back of a Roman taxi for the first time in his life. Ruins. All he saw from the back seat were ruins, from the aqueducts to the Aurelian walls. The taxi drove past the *Mattatoio* in Testaccio, the crumbling slaughterhouse along the river, where once upon a time all the cattle of the Romans were carved and sliced to feed the imperial belly. There too smoke, if only from the afternoon dust. The taxi driver deposited Malory at the base of the Clivo di Rocca Savella. Malory pulled his suitcase up the cobblestones between the high walls that hid the villas on either side from the alleyway. He hadn't walked up the Clivo in many years, had never noticed the scars of ancient wounds, the bricked-up archways of centuries, the rubble-filled omegas that had once led to other villas, other gardens perhaps. He passed a pair of Japanese girls heading down from the Aventino to the Tevere, to the Bocca della Verita, most likely, to pray to the goddess Audrey Hepburn. At the *cancello* to the Villa Septimania he stopped and rang the bell. He rang again. All was dark.

Malory sat for a good hour on a bench beneath the bitter oranges of the Giardino degli Aranci above the Villa. As the lights came on in St. Peter's, he stood and wheeled his suitcase over to the parapet and looked down on the Tevere. The view wasn't dissimilar from the view from the hidden garden of the Villa Septimania below. Except the view was public, open to anyone who turned right in front of the shaded portico of Santa Sabina and followed the gravel past semi-spliced teenage lovers and the occasional grandmother looking for a bit of orange zest for a *torta*. Below Malory, the late-summer plane trees shaded the sidewalk by the river. To his right, the Ponte Rotto and the arse end of the Isola Tiberina. How many times had he looked down at the hospital from his garden, the hospital where Louiza had given birth to their daughter? And for how many years had Malory neglected to see what was behind him—the massive buttress of Santa Sabina, whose cloister had housed that daughter, their Ottavia, for her first ten years.

Depending on how you looked.

Wasn't that the way that MacPhearson had put it? Depending on how you looked, Ottavia was either his daughter or Tibor's. Did that mean either Louiza's or Cristina's as well?

Was anything that MacPhearson said to him worth believing as gospel? Or was MacPhearson willing to say whatever if only Malory could lead him to the lost Louiza?

Wouldn't Malory do the same?

An hour's walk later, down from the hill of the Aventino, Malory sat in Santa Maria sopra Minerva—the church that the Dominicans had raised above the ancient Roman Temple dedicated to the Goddess of Wisdom. He took a seat in the second pew away from the altar— the nineteenth-century loincloth still hiding the operative bits of Michelangelo's Savior from the worshippers—and thought about all the knowledge spinning away from him like the blades of so many windmills. Louiza gone, MacPhearson using him as bait to find her when he hadn't the slightest clue where to look. Septimania dark and barred, no sign of Settimio—and he didn't have the slightest idea why.

"*Signore?*"

"*Sì?*" Malory looked up. A white-robed friar, possibly the same age as the long-gone Fra Mario who had greeted Malory when he first walked into Santa Maria twenty-three years earlier, possibly wearing Fra Mario's steel-rimmed glasses.

"*Siamo pronti.*"

"*Pronti?*" Ready for what? Malory was grateful, at least, that someone recognized him, that the past twenty-three years hadn't been a tale within a dream within the filigreed lantern of some Arabian *djinni*. He picked up his suitcase and followed the friar past the Michelangelo *Salvatore,* past the tomb of headless and thumbless Santa Caterina into the Carafa Chapel. All was familiar. Filippino Lippi's *Annunciation*, with Thomas Aquinas introducing the scrofulous Cardinal Carafa to the Virgin Mary. Above, the angels greeted the rising Virgin. To the right, Thomas Aquinas gently but firmly defeated a rogue's gallery of heretics. Here in a yellow robe was Arius who said there was only one God and Jesus was just a very talented little boy. There in scarlet was Sabellius who preached that Jesus was just one of many blinks of God's eye. Between them Mani, a Persian in the days before the Shah and Khomeini, who believed in Good and Evil, which was one god too many for some. Dante led a chorus of others who denied the laws of the Church and the truth of the Trinity as strenuously if with less discretion than Isaac Newton. Chief among them—the real serpent that Aquinas had to crush beneath his feet— was a white-haired, white-bearded old man holding a scroll. "*Sapientia vincit malitia,*" it read—Knowledge conquers evil. His entire mission, the mission of the Dominicans, was to show that knowledge alone was powerless against evil. There was something greater than knowledge.

"Bernini's elephant knew, Minerva knew, before they dropped a basilica down on top of her." Tibor had jerked his chin in the direction of the piazza on Malory's first trip to the chapel many years before. "There's knowledge and there's knowledge." Malory's mission at the Villa Septimania, and perhaps even before, was to prove Aquinas wrong. There was a knowledge, hidden somewhere in the trinity of Newton, Louiza, and the Pip, that would—if not raise the dead and the Twin Towers—show the One True Rule that guides the universe.

Two pews had been set up for a service. The friar showed Malory to a seat in the second, his back to the altar. With the *Annunciation* on his left, the *Triumph over the Heretics* rose directly in front of him. Malory wondered whether any of the kings of Septimania thought of the *Triumph* the way he did. Not just as the triumph of the Dominican way of thinking over the Arian Heresy, the Gnostics, the Manicheans. It was the triumph of the artist, the triumph of Lippi—the illegitimate product of a friar and a nun. It was the triumph of perspective—the desire to fit within a single frame both the big picture and the little, the cosmology of galaxies millions of light years in diameter and the quantum theory that mumbles about things too small to mumble about. It was a two-dimensional solution to a three-dimensional problem, a painted path to distant solutions that one could enjoy from the comfort of a bum-polished pew. Perspective was the discretion that Settimio had preached to him for more than two decades. For several minutes, Malory let himself relax beneath the illuminated splendor of the fresco of his friend Aquinas, with all its little details and symbols that made it feel like a member of the family—as complex as that concept might ordinarily seem to Malory.

And then Malory noticed other people in the chapel.

Malory noticed the coffin.

Malory thought back to the last funeral he had attended—twenty-three years before in the Church of St. George, Whistler Abbey, the moment before the adventure began, when he was still so full of the discovery of Louiza that he had improvised a love duet on the organ at the funeral of his own grandmother. And although he wondered—perhaps for one of those unmeasurable quantum moments—who was in the coffin beneath the fresco of Thomas and the Heretics, in short order he knew. No driver at the airport, a locked gate at the Villa Septimania.

Settimio was dead.

Settimio, who had guarded almost every movement since Malory first straddled the Driver's Vespa for his extraordinary maiden voyage from the Ospedale Fatebenefratelli to the Cappella Sistina. Settimio, who had awakened Malory and bid him goodnight for twenty-three years. Settimio, who had fed him tea and scones for breakfast, who had ordered books and computers, had overseen the cooking and the cleaning, the weeding and the waxing of Septimania.

Settimio who had devised his own algorithm to filter out the unnec-
essary and bring Malory only what he wanted before he knew that
he wanted it. Settimio, who had imported the distant world into Malory's Sanctum Sanctorum.

Settimio who had kissed him on both cheeks only the week before.

Malory's world was losing perspective.

In the pew in front of Malory sat an old woman, a younger man,
and his wife and young child. Settimio's family? Had he never wondered whether Settimio had a family? Would this young man be assum-
ing Settimio's duties? From his quarter-sided, rearview angle, Malory
tried to read the grief on the face of the wife and the son. But much
had been hidden from Malory for the past twenty-three years—perhaps for much longer. I want to tune the world, he had told his mother
before she died. What had he told Settimio? Settimio was as far from
the father Malory believed he'd had, that amorous Irish sailor with
more passion than perspective. Settimio was perhaps the only father
Malory had known. And yet what had he known? Looking at the
family, Settimio's family, so close, so perfectly attuned to their grief,
Malory realized that no matter how much he knew about music, he
knew little about harmony.

There was no music in the ceremony. Few words were said,
and all of them by the white-robed friar in a Latin pitched at too
low a volume for Malory to make out much. The family rose and
left the chapel. Malory thought about approaching them, thought
about giving his condolences, asking about their welfare, taking the
young man aside and ensuring that he knew Malory, Septimania
would provide for them. But the coffin, or maybe it was merely the
presence of Settimio, even dead inside the coffin, reminded Malory
that discretion would be the best way he could memorialize Settimio.
And he sat.

"*Signore?*" The white-robed friar returned to the chapel. He
took a seat next to Malory on the pew and looked forward.

"I didn't know," Malory said. "It must have happened when I
was in the States."

"There was something that Signor Settimio wanted me to give
you," the friar said, even more discreetly, "if you did not return in

time." He handed Malory a package wrapped in brown paper, no heavier than a suit and a change of shirts.

"Thank you," Malory said. So it was true. Settimio was dead.

The friar stood.

"One more question."

The friar stopped.

"The family, Settimio's family. Will they, will the son be at the villa tonight?"

"The villa?" the friar asked. In the dim light of the chapel, Malory had no way of telling whether he honestly lacked knowledge or knew more than Malory or Thomas Aquinas for that matter.

"Thank you," Malory said again, "for the package."

The friar descended the steps into the nave of the church. Malory was alone with Settimio and Lippi. And the package.

He separated the tape from the paper. Malory. He saw his name, his father's name, stenciled along the flap. The Kit Bag. The Kit Bag with his name. He hadn't seen the Kit Bag in many years. He'd had little use for the Universal Tuner inside. And since he had used Antonella's English translation of the Newton Chapbook, the Italian original had remained semi-forgotten, tucked away in the central pocket next to Malory's own Book of Organs. There was only one reason why Settimio would want Malory to have the Kit Bag. Twenty-three years before, Malory had brought the Kit Bag to Rome. It was the sum total of what had belonged to Malory before he arrived, before he was crowned King of Septimania. Settimio had left him a final message. It was time for Malory to go.

On top of the Kit Bag sat a first-class train ticket from Rome to Cambridge, departing that night—Rome to Milan; Milan to Paris; Paris to London; London to another garden, another life. Malory thought back to the vicar of Whistler Abbey and another funeral. He had been sent to Rome by train twenty-three years before. Now, with the world falling apart and the Villa Septimania dark and shuttered, he was being sent back home without so much as a *panino*? And why? Because Settimio had died? But Malory was alive. Why would they crown a new king of Septimania to go along with a new majordomo? Did the choice of a new caliph of all Islam depend on the life of the butler? It was all a little too ornate to be the punch line of a rather extensive joke.

Malory stood and walked over to the coffin. Discretion be damned. He wanted to pound on the lid and get a few answers from Settimio. Or better yet kick the coffin down off the trestle and trample it beneath his feet in response to this heresy! A butler dictating to the King of Septimania. That is not how it works.

But Malory didn't. He pulled the strap of the Kit Bag over one shoulder. He wheeled his suitcase out Santa Maria sopra Minerva. The elephant was gray. The train departed from Termini at 8 p.m. And now Malory stood at the Gate of Trinity College, Henry VIII holding his stony sword like the angel at the eastern gate of Eden, and thought about his own expulsion, and wondered would they let him back in?

"Excuse me?" Malory stood at the counter of the Porters' lodge. Pigeonholes and bulletin boards had been replaced with computer terminals and stainless steel, but the hat stand next to the desk still sported a pair of bowlers, and the porter on duty still wore a tie. "I was wondering whether I might speak with Mr. Rix? Is he still the Head Porter?"

"Rix?" The porter looked carefully at Malory. "Did you ask for Mr. Rix?" He couldn't have been much older than Malory, but his hair had already turned the color of a dishwater that Malory associated with his Trinity hallmate and his baroque cooking habits.

"Yes," Malory said. "I am a member of the college, but it's been quite a few years."

"Would you mind waiting a moment," the porter asked, "Mister . . . ?"

"Malory," Malory said.

"Ah," the porter's eyes lit up and he disappeared for a moment into the back room. When he returned, it was in the company of a younger woman, one of those bright-cheeked, sensible women of indeterminate post-marital years that Malory always associated with biology degrees and children who played field hockey.

"Mr. Malory!" The woman walked around the counter and gave Malory a hug, which surprised him, even if it was an eminently sensible hug. "I was hoping you might come."

"I'm sorry," Malory said. "You are?"

"Sybil," the woman said, "the eldest."

"Ah," Malory said.

"Would you mind doing the honors?" She took his arm.

"I'll look after this, sir," the porter said, taking Malory's suitcase as Sybil led Malory out of the Porters' lodge and towards the chapel.

"Honors?" Malory said, but the woman was walking so quickly that he wasn't able to make out much of anything except that she was hoping Malory might be willing to play the organ. Malory looked up at a statue of a second king, the stony Edward III with his scepter and orb, as he passed beneath the arch into the chapel. *Pugna pro patria,* read the challenge beneath the king's feet—fight for your country. Edward had been king of his country for fifty years—Malory had seen his own kingdom locked and barred after a mere twenty-three. What kind of king was he? But even Edward, conqueror of Scotland and France, had seen his England pustulate and crumble beneath the buboes and inky gangrene of a Black Death that recognized neither scepter nor orb. Now it was September 2001. The whole world was falling apart. And though the King of Septimania at one time could crown a pope, what was that against planes from above and guns from below? Perhaps the best Malory could do for his *patria* was to pull out all the stops and play the Trinity organ, the organ he knew more intimately than he knew Louiza, than he knew his mother, or even poor, dead Settimio, his most constant companion in life.

Sybil led Malory into the forechapel, past the statues of Tennyson and Bacon, with barely any time for Malory to genuflect to the odd French statue of the old Newton, a man so full of himself in the world that he had been caught in the act of stepping off the pedestal and onto the shoulders of ordinary mathematicians. She stopped at the door to the staircase up to the organ—the Metzler Söhne–refurbished Father Smith organ Malory knew so well—that stood above the arch to the chapel proper, opening its pipes both to the fleshy congregation inside and Newton and his marble companions frozen in the forechapel. Sybil turned to Malory and pressed his hands. Hers were wet—with what Malory couldn't properly tell.

"Father always said that he missed the sound of your playing. 'There was none like Malory,' he said. He waited twenty years, you know," she added, "until he couldn't wait anymore." And with a final press of the palms, Sybil left Malory to climb alone and she joined the mourners at the coffin at the altar-end of the chapel.

Now Rix, Malory thought. Dead from waiting for the *Toccata and Fugue in D minor*—which sat open on the music stand. The hired organist slid aside to make room for Malory. Malory was late again. He was as late as he had been for Settimio, for his grandmother, for his thesis, and above all for Louiza. When had he forgotten how to tell time? When he climbed onto the back of the Driver's Vespa, or long before, when he invited the pale, fair-haired girl up to the organ loft of St. George's, Whistler Abbey? Or perhaps even at birth, three months too late to know his father. Fifty years ago, Malory thought. Fifty years ago the other Malory, the elder Malory, had drowned, knocked into the water by his eagerness, by the ferry that was bringing his young bride, the pregnant Sara, to him. In three months I shall turn fifty, Malory thought and remembered Tibor's last words before he swallowed the Pip—I will not turn fifty. *Je refuse.*

Over the top of the music stand, Malory looked into the forechapel. There was Newton, walking off his pedestal towards him. It was the short-haired Newton, the fifty-year-old Newton. A Newton backed by a marble plaque memorializing the War Dead, the Trinity fellows who gave their lives for the England of Edward III, for principles as ingrained into their patriotic hearts as the cosmic laws of gravity. A Newton who looked, with his half-open mouth and firm step, as if he were ready to lead them like Edward III to victory over the French or the Nazis and maybe even smother Thomas Aquinas under the banner *Sapientia Vincit Malitia*—Knowledge Conquers Evil.

But Malory knew better. Malory knew this was the fifty-year-old Newton of 1692. The Newton of that lost year, when he didn't eat, didn't talk, didn't sleep. This was the Newton conquered by a sorrow impervious to the remedies of science, the Newton who wrote to his best friends, John Locke and Samuel Pepys, that if he ever saw them again he would kill them. The Newton of 1692, the last date in the chapbook that Malory's grandmother, Old Mrs. Emery, had given him; the same Chapbook that was the diary of the Prince, of the Princess of Septimania.

I will not turn fifty—*Je refuse*. Tibor's words came at him again. He tried to look at the music, to turn to the Bach. But no turn was possible. Newton fixed him with his marble glare. I shan't turn fifty, Newton said to him. I shan't turn fifty, Malory answered. I shan't turn fifty, Malory knew. *Je refuse*.

Master's Lodge, Trinity College
24 December 1692

y *Dear Pepys,*
     This evening I abandoned Lady Montague and the children and took myself across Great Court to Newton's rooms. Christmas Eve, as you well remember, is a muffled holiday at Trinity—the fellows deserting the stairwells for more familial climes. But at noon, the Head Porter informed me that Newton was still in residence, although the man himself had not been sighted in some days. I climbed the stairs and knocked on Newton's oak to convey not only your but also my best wishes on the eve of the anniversary of the birth of Our Saviour and the eve of Newton's own fiftieth birthday.

     "Go away!" Newton shouted at me.

     "My dear Newton," I said, "I hate to see you suffer so."

     He opened the door with one mad pull. He stood wigless, without a jacket, his boots unlaced, a sheet of foreign paper dangling limply from one hand. "What do you know of how I suffer?" I looked into his rooms. Since he made no effort to block my entrance, I walked in. The disorder was indescribable, the stench even worse.

     "I know," I continued, opening the window onto Trinity Street, "that you have not touched food these four days and that the porters say you have neither ventured forth from your rooms nor extinguished your candle this week. I dare say you are not sleeping."

     "You are correct," Newton said, in a somewhat more placatory manner. "I have not slept for close on eighteen months."

     I was too astonished to carry on this line of inquiry. Newton continued.

"For these past twenty-five years," he said, speaking as much to the letter in his hand as to me, "I have been thinking, at various times, on the attraction at a distance between two bodies, and from thence, the attraction between three."

"And for this reason," I asked, "you neither eat nor sleep?"

"The force, for example, that the Earth exerts on the Moon and the Moon on the Earth. And then the force that the Sun exerts on the Earth and the Moon and the force those two exert on the Sun."

"Or the force," I tried to lighten the conversation, "you exert upon those like myself who are worried about the effects this study is having on your body."

"Yes," Newton replied, vaguely. I knew he was not fond of metaphor. But I had a sense that I was not far off by bringing the conversation down to Earth. I doubted that the affairs of the cosmos could produce such a calamitous effect in our most gifted fellow.

"My dear Newton," I said, gripping his shoulder. "It is fast approaching the dinner hour. Lady Montague and I are entertaining some friends at the Lodge. There will be music, dancing, children. We would be delighted to count you among our guests in, say, an hour's time? Tonight, after all, is the eve of the birth of Our Saviour."

"Yes," Newton replied, just as vague but with the hint of a smile. "And mine."

"What?" I feigned. "You were born on Christmas Day?" Newton nodded. The smile remained, but his eyes wandered over to a portrait above the mantle. It was a sketch in brown charcoal, a sylvan scene, a man and a woman tossing a ball, the ball suspended between them, the motion caught in flight.

"Septimania," Newton said.

"Excuse me?" I replied.

"Septimania," he repeated. "It is the reason, Lord Montague, that I must decline your generous invitation. Please tender my best wishes to your gracious wife."

"If I cannot persuade you," I said, "please allow me to send over a tray. You must eat something. And certainly," I added, "you must celebrate your own birthday with a slice of my wife's Christmas Pudding."

"I have made many calculations in my life, Master Montague," Newton said. "I have read the Holy Scriptures," he continued, "and I *have calculated that the Battle of Armageddon will bring the Universe to a violent end less than four centuries from now."*

"By that time," I began—and I must confess I was at a momentary loss for a riposte—"you and I shall certainly be long gone. Although my wife's Christmas Pudding may still be edible. Let us gather our rosebuds, as Old Herrick suggested . . ."

"I can calculate the motions of heavenly bodies," Newton went on, "but not the madness of people."

"I don't follow you, dear fellow," I told him, brought up short by that word.

"I shan't turn fifty," Newton mumbled, folding the letter carefully and placing it into an envelope on top of his papers. He was smiling so benignly, Pepys, and the disorder of his countenance had realigned itself into something so delicate and determined that it wasn't until I awoke this morning that the words took on a more terrible meaning. I called on the Porters, however, who told me that Mr. Newton had been in and out of college all day, preoccupied, yes, but as was his wont.

My dear Pepys. Perhaps it is indeed time to take firm action to save this noble mind. Might you ride up to Trinity before the New Year? I believe Newton will follow your counsel. I understand he still has property in Lincolnshire. A small farm might be just the thing. Beets. A few sheep.

Yours,
Montague

3/5

OW DID YOU LIVE?

I find people, Cristina. That's what I do.

I remember. You found me and Tibor.

Or did you find me, all those years ago on the Circo Massimo?

Maybe. You were such an attractive little girl.

Attraction works in two directions. It's what brings us food and shelter and, when we need them, a car, a plane.

How did you decide where to go?

At first, there was some question. Louiza told me she used to wake up every morning—had spent the past twenty years waking up every morning—with a fresh set of problems laid out next to the orange juice. Orange juice was not my strong suit. And for the first few days, as we wandered from Motel 6 to Waffle House, our days were vague and Louiza withdrew in a way that made me nervous.

One night I woke up cold, what passed for a blanket on the floor. The draft came from the open door of a TraveLodge near Tuxedo, New York. I heard voices, Louiza's. When I walked outside to see if she was okay, she was alone, in a thin slip, standing with her left foot flat on a plastic deck chair, while her right index finger drew shapes and numbers in invisible scrawls on her exposed thigh. I looked around. No one else. I led Louiza back to bed. I chained us in. When I woke up, it was daylight. Louiza was showered and dressed. Her eyes, her hair, the skin from her cheekbones to her collar was brighter than I'd ever seen.

"I was sleepwalking," she said.

"Yes," I said, "I heard you last night."

"Not last night," she said. "For years."

Where did you go, Ottavia? After Tibor shot himself.

The first month, we walked and talked. Louiza told me about her childhood, imaginary numbers, her mother. She told me about the day she passed her *viva* at Cambridge, how she met a strange little man in the organ loft of a church. She told me about following him to Rome, about finding him in a church and how he carried her to a hospital. And how she never saw him again until that day.

That day?

Twenty years ago. I saw them by the pond that day. I saw the way that Malory grew into another human, another body, more powerful, more massive, an altogether larger person in the range of Louiza's orbit. It took much longer for Louiza to tell me about the dark matter. The years in The Gables, Vince, MacPhearson, her father, negativity.

Where did you live? After that day.

We couldn't stay at TiborTina, of course, and it was getting cold in the woods.

Where did you go?

Louiza followed the girls, I followed Louiza.

The girls?

At first, I could only hear them, and I'm sure that the music I heard was different from the music that moved Louiza. She called them the Unimaginables. Sometimes there were four, sometimes six, sometimes more. They weren't real in the sense that you and I are real, but products of the far reaches of our imaginations, if not beyond. Their music came to my ears in a style and a rhythm past what Louiza could imagine. Louiza described them to me, Una and Dodo and Terri and Quatro. But since we shared the language of mathematics, it was on the long nights of walking, following Louiza following the Unimaginables, that Louiza told me about dividing by zero.

Dividing by zero?

There's no point in talking about that now, trying to explain how Louiza had discovered not only ways but benefits of dividing by zero, how to manage the Unimaginables. Old news. After Tibor's death and Malory's disappearance, it was no longer enough to divide by zero. We were past that. Oh, occasionally the girls played an oldie or two, or invited another group to sit in on an encore until some producer pulled the plug or a groupie got stomped. But the girls played newer and newer combinations and Louiza and I danced past velvet ropes of mathematics my tutors could never have imagined.

So you joined forces with Louiza?

Joined forces? No. There was a sympathy that joined us, that joined us together.

A sympathy?

When I was little, Sister Francesca Splendida at Santa Sabina took us into the Giardino degli Aranci at night and showed us the stars above St. Peter's. She taught us that there was a sympathy between heavenly bodies, a mutual attraction, the same way there is between human souls. Isaac Newton called it attraction at a distance, since it didn't require that the two objects touch or even be in the same city. The boys guiding rocket ships from Houston, the boys with their fingers on buttons or joysticks guiding bombs or drones know a great deal about power operated at a distance. But Sister Francesca and Sir Isaac were talking about something else. They were talking about the way that an orange or an apple pulls the Earth at the same time as the Earth pulls the fruit. It's the same sympathy that drew Louiza to me that morning at the Farmers' Market on River Road, that led me to scribble an invitation to Tibor's party and drop it into a bag of apples for her. Malory was the name she mentioned then, and perhaps Malory was the link. But there was a force that drew us towards one another and all the adventures that followed.

The adventures, yes. That's what I want to hear about. Where did you go?

Do you want a list? We went to Minsk, to Benghazi, to Baghdad. We went to Beirut where I danced on rooftops to R.E.M. and Fairouz, to underground temples in Malta where it was David Bowie and Croatian cello duos playing Guns N' Roses. But most of all, we went where the answers took us. The answers to the problems that came to Louiza in the middle of the night, the ones that she solved with her right index finger on her left thigh or drawing equations in the air.

What were the answers?

What were the questions?

Did it matter?

I knew where to go. That's my talent. I know how to find people. That's what I do. That's how I found him.

Him?

It was easy. But it wasn't from any lesson I'd learned at the feet of Tibor or the Bomb Squad, or any genetic talent deep in my DNA. I simply followed Dodo, the leader of the Unimaginables. I left Louiza sleeping in a stone hut outside Tora Bora and followed Dodo, as completely camouflaged as my raven-haired supergirl. Over rocks, through the wind, picking my way around Improvised Explosive Devices made of sheep bladders and shrapnel, down, down. Dodo, hard-edged against a sky more purple than black, luminescent for my eyes only. I followed Dodo and walked into his cave with a cadre of *mujahedin.*

But the Americans say they found Osama in Abbottabad, and not in the caves of Tora Bora.

Years later. Many years later. They never asked me.

Would you have told them?

After Baghdad and Kabul, Helmand and Tora Bora? After the mass slaughter, the gang rapes, the multiple manias of Sunnis and Shi'ites, Kurds and Pashtuns, Alawites and Maronites, Israelites and Philistines, Episcopalians and Mormons? I had seen the apple tree. I had talked to the gardener. I had spoken with the apple. If talking to the Americans would have prevented that, why not? But they didn't ask, and I didn't see any point in volunteering the unbelievable. I followed Louiza, and she followed Dodo and the answers to her equations to Serbia to Karadžić and Mladić, and then to the Sudan for Omar al Bashir, and Burma for Than Shwe, North Korea for Kim Jong-Il, and Venezuela for Ingrid Betancourt.

And nobody followed you?

If they did, they didn't do anything about it.

Didn't you wonder why?

Of course. I read the papers, I scanned the Internet from the cubicles and cafes around the globe. One night, it was in a roadside shack near the Salt Cathedral outside Bogotá, I finally heard a plausible explanation. I left Louiza inside our hostel and went looking for something to eat. An Australian surfer bought me a steak at a roadside shack out in the country, a pair of cows grazing in the parking lot. He was full of insight and stupidity, and I was grateful for the silence when he excused himself to go to the bathroom. But as soon as he had gone, the silence gave way to another voice. Maybe I was drunk on the altitude and the slab of meat I'd swallowed and a couple of *mojitos* served in a gourd the size of a goat skull. It was Tibor.

You spoke with Tibor?

Tibor found me. "It's all hide-and-go-seek, Ottavia," he said, the smell of Absolut wafting in from just outside my vision. Tibor was dead, of course, thankfully with his head intact and spine straight enough to sit on the stool beside me.

"I know, Tibor," I said. "You always told me, success is based on the willingness to open the wrong cave, to look for the cat in the wrong box. But I've been successful. I found the cats. Every time!"

"Maybe," Tibor whispered, and the smoke from his eternal Camel mixed with his vodka breath, "your American dogs are following you. They just don't want to kill their pussies."

They didn't want the answers. They didn't want the answers to the equations. That's what Tibor was telling me. No one wanted the answers, not even Una and Dodo and the Unimaginables—they were guides, not executioners. When the Americans found Saddam, when they shot the Old Man and dumped his body at sea, it was an accident, a mistake. Everybody was having too much fun with their beheadings and their stables of torture. They were slitting throats and sacrificing cattle to their own gods. But they drew the line at sacrificing the gods themselves, even if they were the other chap's gods. Where's the fun in that? Game over.

But while they weren't finding the gods I found, the gods I found were killing real people—other men, other women and children. I saw them, too, homing in on our rearguard with their Stingers, blowing off the legs of our Rolands with their landmines and Improvised Explosive Devices. The ritual slaughters. Abrahams beheading their Isaacs, Ishmaels beheading their Abrahams, with no angel or *djinni* to stop their hands. Charlemagne only lost Roland in the Battle of Roncesvalles. But we were dying—not just Americans but we, we— by the hundreds, by the thousands, headless, limbless bodies with names and histories and families, Tibor after Tibor after Tibor. I tried to connect the dots, to understand the picture that I was helping to draw. But the freckles kept moving. And moving. And moving. And the roar of Charlemagne in pain only grew louder.

"Get out," Tibor said from his stool, "before your Australian comes back from the bathroom. Just walk out. Get Louiza and go back into the forest."

Did you?

I stood, as Tibor suggested. I started walking out. But then I looked up at the TV over the door and I saw you.

You saw me?

You were talking to Hillary about her campaign, something about following Obama. And that look, seeing you. Another force.

Another force?

Yes, Cristina, another force. Different but just as strong as the force that joined me and Louiza. It was a force that reached out of your studio and through the radio waves across half the world to me. It was a force that said keep moving, Ottavia. Keep moving. Move forward.

. . .

Are you still there?

. . .

Cristina?

I've had a long time to think, and not just in the twenty years since Tibor's fiftieth birthday surprise, but before. The long hours, the plane rides when I should have been preparing questions for a foreign minister or a warlord. The thoughts weren't complicated—I don't do complicated, that was Tibor. I'm the one who is prepared. I am the one who is never late. Long before Tibor and I climbed onto the plane out of Bucharest to Rome and he gave me his New Wave lecture on the smallness of the Earth, the absurdity of human ambition, and perspective in general, I realized that being on time, moving forward was the only reason for moving at all. When I was dying for a pee and left my first husband standing on the steps of the National Theatre on our wedding day and came out on the arm of Tibor, that was moving forward. When I persuaded a variety of commissars and less—I don't need to go into detail—to sign exit visas out of that shit hole for me and Tibor, that was moving forward. And when the nurse

*came back into my hospital room and told me in the fading light of
that Roman evening that my baby had disappeared, well . . . I had a
choice. Move forward or die. Tibor tried to move with me, but he
used up his energy moving in too many directions at once and never
achieved escape velocity. He was too democratic or too much of an
anarchist to accept that forward is forward and backward is backward. All roads lead to Rome, he used to say, blah blah blah. Well,
news update—they don't.*

*I moved forward. I found you. And I saw that you too were
moving. And I let you keep moving, without forcing you to pull us,
to pull us forward with you. I warned you about Tibor, about allowing him to deflect your motion. But you were free to ignore me. So
. . . as Tibor used to say. Which means absolutely nothing.*

You can stop.

I have stopped. I've been stopped.

By what, Cristina?

You still won't call me . . .

Please.

But Ottavia . . .

Cristina, stop. Please. The only person in the world who ever
treated me like a parent was Malory. He read me a goodnight story
the first night I met him. About the crowning of King Charlemagne.
How the Caliph of Baghdad, Haroun al Rashid, returned in disguise
to Rome—although he had never been in Rome out of disguise—
dressed in the uniform of his own ambassador. He was in love with
the daughter of Charlemagne, but she was married already to the King
of Septimania, a Jew.

Ah, Septimania . . .

And there was a child. Both the Jewish father and the Muslim
lover were olive-skinned, and in those days there was no DNA testing.
So not even Aldana knew who the father was.

That was the story?

It's the story of the history of the kings of Septimania. It begins
with doubt. If Septimania can survive with questions of origin, I can
survive without a mother.

Origin? That's a cold way to speak of a mother.

Malory was curious about origins. I'm not. I'm moving forward. Like you.

Malory. He told me my voice was out of tune.

He told me something else. That your voice sounded one way in his left ear, another in his right—like a Tibetan throat singer or maybe some Balkan peasant woman who could sing two notes at once. I always thought it was the cigarettes, the endless cigarettes refracted into gray, into your voice.

I like that. Those endless cigarettes have turned me into a Balkan throat singer who no longer has a throat.

We can live without voices.

And type messages, like we're doing now, on a keyboard to a face on a screen for the rest of my life?

. . .

What was it that Tibor said? "I won't turn fifty. Je refuse." Well, Ottavia, I was always younger than Tibor, until. It wasn't fair that I turned fifty before he did, that I grew older than him. But I won't make sixty-five.

I know where you are, Cristina. Even without your telling me.

The hospital hasn't changed very much. Perhaps the Roman pines outside the windows, the palm trees are a little taller, the sun a little older, the water of the Tevere a different water than the one that flowed past Fatebenefratelli the afternoon you were born.

The day Malory named the Pope.

Only one person is missing.

Would you like me to get her to the keyboard?

Louiza?

Hello, Cristina. I never knew your name. But I've never forgotten the mole on the crest of your cheekbone or your hair, gray in the afternoon light of the hospital window.

I wish, Louiza. I wish we could have met again. I wish I was still someone. I wish I was still working. I wish I could interview you, ask you questions. It would be very big, very important. Not just to me.

You can ask me now.

What do you have that no one else does?

I have the Unimaginables.

Ah yes, the invisible women.

Not invisible, just unnoticed since unimaginable. They're here just like you and Ottavia and I are here. Like the neutrinos that pass unfelt and unseen through the Earth, that pass in the billions every day, like the dark matter that makes up the lion's share of the universe. You just don't know how to look for the Unimaginables. And when we are singing with them, you don't know how to listen to us, so we pass unnoticed.

And you have Ottavia.

Yes. I have Ottavia.

And the Pip? Tibor mentioned the Pip. Ottavia said it holds all knowledge like a crystal ball, like a computer searchable in every possible language.

The Pip. There was a church outside Cambridge. A steeple, a young organ tuner.

Malory?

Ottavia told me she visited Malory. She told me that his Villa Septimania was sitting on the world's biggest computer network, connected according to the principle of Maoist cells or Cathar cabals—no person or part knew the identity of more than six others. It was disconnected from the public Internet, entirely untraceable. The sheer information Malory had acquired would have made Mr. MacPhearson so happy, not to mention poor Vince.

But whom did it serve, all that information?

Ask Malory. He's the one you want to interview.

But the Pip, Louiza? I need to understand before I die why Tibor did what he did. I can't help blaming the Pip.

You think the Pip has that kind of power?

I saw Tibor. I saw what the Pip did to the top of his head.

One night, Ottavia and I found ourselves outside Baghdad, perhaps on the very spot where Haroun al Rashid had his palace. Perhaps the Pip was being pulled by the memory of that first apple tree. But even the Pip didn't have all the information. The ground had been laid waste, many times. Many, many times. Sometime recently it had been a Toyota Dealership—the crumpled remnants of a pole and a sign still remained, along with a few burnt-out Corollas and Land Cruisers.

Information is only . . . what would you call it? Stuff? Noise? What computers have is the ability to collect stuff, to sort through chatter. But does a computer guide the Moon around the Earth, the Earth around the Sun? Ottavia and I, and I suspect Malory too if he only knew it, are drawn together by something else. Call it a sympathy, the same rule of attraction that guides everything in the universe, from the tiniest pip of a sub-pippic particle to the galaxy of Pippa Major and all the stars that astronomers, with much more knowledge than I have, say are older than the universe itself.

But you and Ottavia are guided by this sympathy. You've caught dozens, perhaps hundreds of criminals, bad men, over the decades.

We haven't caught anyone. For a while, I answered problems that Mr. MacPhearson and Vince gave me. Who knows what they did with the answers? Vince died. And MacPhearson, he may have died by now as well. I am not sad, even if that sounds terrible. I imagine my mother, whom I loved dearly, and my father, whom I loved not at all, have died by now as well.

And Malory?

What about Malory?

All those years, all those men. Surely if you could find all those men, couldn't you have found Malory?

On one of our journeys, Ottavia met a young physicist. We were somewhere in Switzerland or France outside Geneva, I think. There were mountains, snow, the kind of padded silence I remember from that day you and I spent in hospital in Rome. The young physicist was very excited that Ottavia was paying attention to him—his eagerness reminded me of Malory the first time I met him. He had a key to some super-powerful analytic equipment—scanners and computers. I don't know anything about these machines that dissect reality. Ottavia had been keen—keen for years—to peer into the depths of her treasures—and not only the Pip, which she carried around in a leather pouch, but a shiny marble apple that was another of the gifts she'd taken from Malory.

The young physicist asked me if I wanted to join them to take a look, but I told him it wouldn't be necessary—Ottavia could be my eyes. He smiled in the patronizing fashion that I've been used to for so long, not understanding that the sympathy between me and Ottavia is such that I do, indeed, see what she sees—although not, perhaps, in the way that young physicists might imagine. I sat on a leather sofa in a conference room outside the lab, one of those butterscotch modernistic sofas that make the Swiss feel more Italian and up-to-date. For the first time in a long time, I felt strangely but comfortably alone. The Unimaginables had stayed outside for a little snowboarding. Ottavia was inside the lab with her man and his equipment.

But as I sat there alone, I felt—I don't know how else to put it—as if a series of switches were clicking on, a series of lights shining at different angles within me. And whether this is what Ottavia saw at the center of the apple, at the center of the Pip, I don't know. But as each light clicked on, I saw a pyramid. And then another pyramid and another, attaching themselves to one another in a giant crystal. And then I was inside the crystal, as if inside the Cathedral at Ely, with the Norman arches and arcades and chapels multiplying and stretching away, and producing with each generation of crystals more altars and statues and, one by one, the pipes of a giant organ. Long pipes, short pipes, wooden and metal pipes, bent and fluted. And as the crystal structure grew, I felt myself shrinking smaller and smaller, like Alice in Wonderland, until I was cocooned within the center, surrounded above and below in a crystalline transparency. I was alone, all alone at the heart of something.

Was it the Pip, was it the apple? I don't know. There are only two things I knew about this place at the center of the crystal. It was a place where distance didn't matter. As vast as it seemed, I could reach out with my hand and touch the other side of this infinite cathedral without having to stretch. But more, it was a place where what seemed possible was beyond imagining—was greater than I'd been taught in all the books and articles and parental speeches going back to Vince and MacPhearson and my father. I was at the center of the secret and I was dying to tell someone what I saw. But I was alone—Ottavia was gone with her young man. And then I thought—Malory should see this.

And then he was there.

He was sitting next to me, as if he were sitting in that conference room on the butterscotch sofa. He wasn't exactly the Malory I'd first met in the organ loft, or the one I'd seen in Rome, or the one who was at your party that terrible day. He was an older Malory, a Malory of less hair and worn elbows. But he was also a younger one, a boy in short French trousers and knee socks, who very patiently took my hands and placed them on a crystalline keyboard in front of me. And as I did, Malory stood at full height on a pedal—did you know, Cristina, that organs had pedals? And the music! The music that I heard!

And then?

And then, of course, Ottavia came back. Without her man. I stood up. We went back out into the snow.

Without Malory?

Don't you understand, Cristina? Newton found the equation to describe the attraction between two moving bodies at a distance. But three bodies in motion—that was too much for his mathematics. For anyone's mathematics.

What does that have to do with Malory?

I met Malory the day that I was awarded my PhD. It wasn't much, my thesis, just a simple equation: $i = u$, an identity, a relationship of two bodies. Ottavia and her young physicist pointed their equipment at the Pip, believing, in this digital century, that we can be quantified, boiled down into numbers that are the sum totals of all the little packets of information of the things we Google or Like or the keys we touch when we send the private messages of our unconscious wishes as we shop on Amazon or flirt on our cell phones. But that's not why $i = u$ is so powerful. That's not why we aren't with Malory.

What happened?

A third element entered the equation.

Ottavia, Malory, and me. It's a Three-Body Problem. There is so much to tell Malory, so much I want to tell him, waking up after all these years. But Malory has to open his eyes, listen to the music. Malory has to follow the unimaginable.

3/6

PHYSICISTS, MATHEMATICIANS, AND A HANDFUL OF ARTISTS MAY have the luxury to dream about alternate universes of dead cats and live cats and ten-dimensional cats of many colors. But Antonella returned to Cambridge in the middle of January 1979 with a job that was balancing on the precarious edge of her visa. She had dreamed about Malory, she had boiled kettles and asked impertinent questions to porters and junior faculty. She had traveled on her infrequent holiday and scanty budget to Rome for Malory. But she had blinked. She had blinked when Tibor confused her one Christmas morning. And although that blink spawned many tears, eventually her eyes opened back onto the damp on the skirting of her bedsit and a series of days measured out more in chocolate biscuits than in mathematical units.

For her own preservation, she succumbed to one of the up-and-comers in the Faculty—a willowy, insinuating statistician who wore his confidence in orange and honey patterns of tweed and persisted in following Antonella with a patience not dissimilar from her own with Malory. Antonella gave in. The two children she bore him gave in. And by the time the willowy cad succumbed to a shoddy death, hushed up during a conference on fractals in Málaga, the boy had escaped to study trees in Zambia and the girl to parts unknown—which Antonella believed to be the cottage of a gardener on an estate just outside of Newmarket. She was alone in the flat she had dreamed into being on Cranmer Road, with souvenirs of a family and the *Times* of London on her doorstep.

The flat on Cranmer Road was the garden level of one side of a freestanding two-story building, with a semi-circle gravel drive in front guarded by two stone lions and a gardener's shed in the back that her late husband had imagined stocking with wines and their associated machinery if he ever won the Fields Medal. As English as the garden flat was, Antonella over the years filled the vacuum of her family's negligence with strings of garlic and pepperoncino, fruit bowls from Deruta, and five-liter drums of olive oil. And she continued to be useful. Organizing guest socials for the Maths Faculty, teaching romantic Italian conversation to ambitious Girton girls intent on trading their sensible cardigans for a Palermo fling with the Alain Delons or Vittorio Gassmen they were certain were pining for a pale British hand.

Old Rix, the Head Porter of Trinity, adopted her, both after Malory's initial disappearance from Cambridge and especially upon her return from Rome. When Sybil Rix returned from her own failed marriage to her father's home, she and Antonella took it in turns to prop up the old man as age fought with his sense of duty and decorum. There was nothing surprising about Antonella's presence at Rix's funeral, and indeed something natural about her rescue of Malory, frozen on the bench of the organ in Trinity Chapel.

The current Organ Scholar had stepped in and played the service as Antonella, with the aid of a junior porter, escorted Malory down the steps from the loft and to a folding chair in the antechapel. Malory let her lead him, let her bring him a glass of water. After the service, Antonella sat with Sybil and Sybil sat with Malory, touched by the depth of feeling she assumed had overwhelmed Malory at the shock of her father's death. Yet as they walked under the Wren Library and across the Trinity Bridge, the first autumn acers in the Clare Gardens beginning to turn, there was no sign that Malory knew who Antonella was. And when they'd pulled Malory's suitcase up Burrell's Lane past the familiar bulk of the University Library and the unfamiliar wall of Robinson College, when they'd turned into the house at the end of Cranmer Road and Antonella had sat Malory down at her kitchen table, not even a cup of tea broke through the cuirass and buckler and greaves and helmet of resignation that Malory had donned in that single moment of commune with Newton in the organ loft of the Trinity Chapel.

Sybil rang at nine that evening to see how Antonella was getting on. Malory was unchanged. He sat where Antonella led him. He ate the *carbonara* she placed in front of him. He followed her to her son's bedroom—or at least the bedroom she had reserved for her son if he ever decided to come home to a Cambridge that was free of the sarcasms of his father if not the memories of childhood. He sat contentedly, or at least without complaint, at the edge of her son's bed as she opened up Malory's suitcase and laid out his toiletries and took away the dirty laundry of his journey. She would put him up for the night, she told Sybil. In the morning, she was certain he would be fine.

But the morning was the same. Antonella opened the bedroom door at 8 a.m. and found Malory lying on his back with the covers pulled up to his chin, eyes open and fixed on the infinite space between his nose and the ceiling. She spoke to him, asked how he had slept, what he wanted for breakfast. Without an answer, she left the door half open and went into the kitchen. She put a flame under the *macchinetta*, scrambled some eggs, toasted some bread, set out butter and jam— she hadn't been prepared for a guest, after all. When she went to find Malory, she found him dressed—clearly he had lain down the night before without removing a single piece of clothing. She led him to the bathroom. He knew enough to stand, to sit, to unzip and relieve himself. She put soap in his hand, toothpaste on a fresh toothbrush she kept because she had more hope than company, and made certain that whatever part of Malory's brain was still functioning knew how to brush teeth. The eggs and the toast were cold, but that didn't bother Malory. He ate, he drank tea. He sat.

Antonella cleared the dishes, washed them in the sink, set them in the rack. She was just drying her hands on a Florentine dishtowel— there had, in the past, been family trips, presents, affection once bottled if long uncorked—when he spoke.

"Biscuit?"

"Excuse me?"

"Might you have a biscuit?" Malory asked. His voice sounded strange to Antonella, touched with an Italian precision; she would not have recognized it over the telephone. "A chocolate biscuit?"

With each bite, with each dip of Antonella's hand into the tin for another biscuit, and another, the old Malory returned, the Malory she had remembered loving in a time when she was very young and very foolish. And as the bites turned into days and the days into weeks, Malory, against the odds of Tibor, against the marble stare of Newton, turned fifty. And fifty-one. And two.

Still, for Malory the world of Cambridge was encapsulated in a crazed and greasy globe of Perspex. There was a film over all his senses, and trying to rub it away only moved the streaks from one quadrant to another. He began to tune organs at two churches, then a dozen. He ate two, sometimes three meals a day with Antonella and watched the *Nine O'Clock News* with her on an ever-renewing range of television sets. He spoke, he heard, he saw. But he made little attempt to pop his ears or adjust the aperture of his telescope. And on the few occasions he did—when he found himself by the front gate of Trinity College, or on the towpath by the river—a sharp tweak of the lens only brought his pain into focus with the force of a light from a distant galaxy and warned him away from even thinking about Louiza, for her own safety.

From time to time, Malory believed that people were watching him. Occasionally he thought he recognized one or two of the Americans from The Gables. But no one was stopping him from doing anything, perhaps because he was doing nothing. No one came for Malory—on a Vespa, in a police car, or with the stealth and ingenuity that followed the marriage of technology and suspicion in the new century. Whether Malory's interest in the world died before the world's interest in Malory, or whether both died from the removal of whatever had nurtured their ambitions, it was impossible to say. But to all appearances, Malory returned to the same unremarkable counting of time that had preceded the afternoon when Louiza found him in the organ loft of St. George's Church, Whistler Abbey, with little left of his ambition to tune the world.

From time to time, Antonella persuaded Malory to climb into her car—an updated cream-colored Cinquecento—to drive for an afternoon, to walk in the gardens of Anglesey Abbey, or shop for a skirt in Bishops Stortford or a jumper in Saffron Walden, or eat cakes at the Old Fire Engine House across a damp field from the isolated Norman pile of Ely Cathedral. Occasionally Antonella would invite a pair of undergraduates home for Sunday dinner, and occasionally one would get into conversation with Malory about Newton which would, on rare occasions, lead to more teas and lunches and a semi-official advisory capacity for Malory over the student's studies, with the benediction of the Maths Faculty. It was Antonella's way of bringing Malory back into the world.

The world assumed that Malory and Antonella were married or, even better, living in the presumed excitement of sin at an age when mystery existed only in sixty-minute segments on television. They kept their separate bedrooms, although Antonella was convinced that, if she had climbed into Malory's bed with the red-haired fullness that had lost nothing to the birth of her two children and gained something with widowhood, Malory would have done whatever she asked of him. But the thought—the one or two times she allowed it—filled her with a horror: not that she would be making Malory do something unpleasant, but that the patience of all those years of waiting for Malory to come to her would be shot as full of holes as that poor Aldo Moro in the boot of the Renault 4.

It was enough to bring Malory into the world, to return him into the tuning, the tutoring, the Saturday morning organ lessons at Impington Village College for the children of the fens. More than to her bed, she craved to take Malory back to Rome, or rather have Malory take her. They had walked there only once, the night of the *Divine Comedy*. She wanted to walk through the Christmas fun fair at Piazza Navona and eat roasted chestnuts and lentils at New Year. She wanted to take him down to the open-air cinema along the river in July, to the Celimontana, to Villa Ada with its smell of citronella and cardamom, for jazz and reggae and bad Italian pop stars at the PalaLottomatica. Antonella wanted to feed *cacio e pepe* to Malory at Felice's in Testaccio and to watch him eat chocolate cake with *panna* in the driveway of Augustarello, where the plastic chairs and tables migrated every summer in flight from the oven. Most of all, she wanted to take him up to the Giardino degli Aranci, the Garden of the Oranges, where, as a young convent girl, she had first developed a love of mathematics, counting the fallen fruit and measuring it against the future harvest. Antonella was convinced with the smattering of maths she'd picked up in her years of service at the Faculty, that more than any theoretical notion of forgiveness or forgetting, a positive Roman Holiday was needed to cancel out the negative of that Christmas Roman mistake.

Even without Rome, Antonella was more than content with each new year to have Malory in her life, in her flat, at her table, even if much of the day he pedaled away from her bay window out the Coton footpath to nowhere in particular. She was hardly a victim of the centrifugal motion of the Earth. But similarly she never pretended that anything she might do would sway its course or align it into more perfect motion.

On the day that the *Times* announced Cristina's death on page five, Antonella made no attempt to hide the news from Malory.

"The paper mentions Tibor," Malory said—and Antonella noticed, with mixed emotions that he didn't look over at her with either censure or memory—"but it doesn't mention her daughter."

"There was a daughter?" Antonella asked. "Back in Rumania or later?"

"In Rome," Malory said, eyes still on the photo of Cristina. "They gave her up for adoption, but then found her again later. Nice girl. Read maths at Cambridge, I think. Maybe you ran into her. Must have been twenty years ago."

"Militaru?" Antonella didn't remember any Militarus. Although the Johnsons and Davidsons and Georges and Wilkinsons passed through her mind without leaving a trace, the foreign names—the Selasis and Szegeds and Algaríns and of course the Antonellis—remained with imported postcards and stories of distant relatives who couldn't understand why their children thought they could feed a family with the study of mathematics.

"I don't know what surname she used," Malory said. "She was brought up by nuns in Rome. Santa Sabina, I think."

"Ottavia?" The name came out of Antonella's mouth uncalled by memory.

"Yes, Ottavia," Malory said, looking up. "Did you know her?"

"Santa Sabina," Antonella said. "Of course my Malory remembers nothing about his Antonella. But that is where I went to school, although of course I had a home to return to at the end of every day." And indeed, Cranmer Road had served as an occasional home for Ottavia during her studies, so thirsty was Antonella for any news of her Rome that didn't come over the television, even though Ottavia's news was removed by a generation from her own childhood. Antonella put away the tea and biscuits and served Ottavia espresso and baked her a *crostata* and listened to her problems with boys and England, even as she wished her own son might take interest in this underfed girl.

"Ottavia is Cristina's daughter," Malory said.

"That's impossible," Antonella said. "Look at Cristina, Malory. Ottavia was a little mouse, not this high-cheekboned, gray-haired movie star! Who told you she was Cristina's daughter? Tibor?"

It was that red-haired old man. The one who had asked him all those questions the day after. The one who had been in the Ospedale Fatebenefratelli, who might even have been at the Orchard. Malory couldn't remember his name. But he remembered something he had told Malory, something Malory had stored in a box he had been afraid to open for twenty years.

"She's your daughter," the red-bearded man had told him. "But she's also Tibor's."

Malory had ignored the first statement for the second. He had assumed the man had corrected himself. How was it possible, after all, that any creature could have two fathers, two origins? Did she have two mothers? Did she grow in two wombs? There was the story he'd heard from Cristina years ago at a party in the Dacia—about how the nurses had produced only one baby after she and Louiza gave birth; how Cristina had given that baby away to keep Tibor from doing something unspeakable. But the credibility of Malory's paternity was as low as the credibility of what the red-bearded—MacPhearson, wasn't that his name?—MacPhearson had told him. Two fathers, two mothers? Why not seven to fit into Tibor's multi-headed cosmology? Impossible. Unimaginable.

But the moment the breath cooled into words, the moment Malory said that Ottavia was Cristina's daughter, he knew that the sentence was out of tune. There was Cristina, on page five of the *Times*, in a quarter-page photo from an era more recent than the death of Tibor, but looking no less glamorous. And although he hadn't seen Ottavia in all that time, Malory couldn't conceive of pale, golden-haired, comfortably small Ottavia being the issue of Cristina. Malory knew immediately that Antonella had touched on the truth. Ottavia was not Cristina's. She was not Tibor's. She was Malory's daughter, the daughter of Malory and Louiza. For the past twenty years, he had allowed himself to live in a world where he refused to see his daughter—that his daughter was his daughter—refused to believe that she even existed. For twenty years, Malory had bottled, boxed, trapped, hidden, disguised so many memories. To protect Louiza, surely. To keep the red-bearded man and who knew how many others from taking her away. And into that box, Malory had also stuffed the information that red-bearded man had given him.

Ottavia was his daughter. Ottavia was Louiza's daughter, the daughter, the child who had pushed her tiny hand from within Louiza's womb to meet his in the drafty October cold of Santa Maria sopra Minerva. Ottavia was the lost girl, the girl who had disappeared along with her mother. He had thrown into the storage bin his memories of that little girl, Ottavia, her miraculous appearance at the villa, the way she sat upright, hugging her knees beneath the duvet as he told her about Septimania and the Caliph Haroun al Rashid and read to her the same goodnight story about Judar the Son of Omar that Haroun's ambassador had read to the Princess Aldana in the court of Charlemagne. The way Ottavia so naturally linked her arm in his as they walked through the pastures of TiborTina. The way Ottavia so simply and delicately removed Bernini's apple from the Newton statue. Ottavia was his daughter and she was also the once and future Queen of Septimania.

These stored memories added up to loss. Boxes full, tunnels full, libraries and mountains full of loss. But instead of the stale taste of outdated regret, Malory felt joy. It was a joy he had known only at those brief moments when he had drawn together with Louiza and Ottavia. But now, here with Antonella, the patient nurse who had cared for him with biscuit tin and copper curls for twenty years, Malory felt a joy with this woman who had removed the glaze from his eyes and given him back his sight, given him a family.

That night he bicycled down to the Off-License and brought back a bottle of a Cahors from the Pyrenees. There wasn't much in the pantry she could throw together to fit the moment. But she lit a pair of candles and she talked with Malory; Malory talked with her, about her, asked her about her own children. Antonella looked at the Malory before her, the smaller Malory, the still mobile Malory, the seventy-year-old man, more tonsure than hair, but still the comfortably lost Malory, and she talked about her own lost Matteo, the lost Anna, all the lost years of her marriage. There were tears and there were kisses, their dry, unpracticed lips moistened by Cahors and years of tacit intimacy. And when the time came to separate for the night, Malory took Antonella by the hand to lead her into his room. But neither his bed—her Matteo's bed—nor Antonella's own seemed a comfortable option. So they lay in the candlelight in the bay window. And Antonella removed the copper curls that disguised the chemical savannah of her scalp, unzipped and exposed the runnels of operations and rough edges of tests and countless medical ravages she had hidden and perfumed away from Malory's sight over all these years. For the first time, Malory looked at Antonella. He looked and he saw past the scars, past the gravity that had drawn the skin to the bone and the bone closer to the Earth, the time and the time that had thrown its own disguise over the eternally young Italian woman who loved him. He saw what Antonella had been and what she had grown into. He saw the copper Tuscan curls and the full curves of the Antonella who first opened her biscuit tin to him in the Maths Faculty. And Antonella discovered that, late though he was, barely imaginable as it might seem, her Malory had finally returned.

The next morning was a Saturday. From that same bay window, Antonella watched Malory bicycle off to Histon to teach his seven-year-olds about the pedals. The view out the Coton footpath had changed over the years as Corpus Christi sold land to a developer who shot up a constellation of seventy-two prefabricated cottages that seeped off the Barton Road to the edge of their sports grounds. And if she looked out the right panes of the window, she could see the towers of the Newton Institute, where for more than thirty years she had looked after her mathematicians when the university booted them out of their cozier home at the Sidgwick Site, where the one piece of Antonella that remained was the biscuit tin she had donated to the Faculty. But the view from the center of the bay window was of the Coton footpath. And as Malory bicycled away, the perspective of his diminishing form—as ideal as in any late Renaissance painting—gave her a sense of balance and tranquility.

As soon as Antonella could see no more of Malory out the window, she went to her closet. There, from the carton she reserved for her marriage license, the children's birth certificates, and two cameos of a pair of dead Romans, she took out a faded envelope holding two more ancient sheets of paper. They had been folded in the Chapbook that Malory had given her to translate. As they were written in English, Antonella had put them aside in this envelope all those many years before and had forgotten to bring them with her translation to Rome. They were Malory's, of course, and she should have given them to him before. But now was as good at time as any.

They were both written on the same quality paper smelling of comfortable age, embossed with a seven-sided S.

The first:

11 September 1692

Dear Mr. Newton,

I regret to inform you that, on the night of 10 September, after consuming a light supper with a bottle of claret, Her Royal Excellency, the Queen of Septimania, retired to Sanctum Sanctorum for the last time. Enclosed, please find a letter in her hand addressed to you. I rest

your most humble & most
obedient Servant,
Settimio

And the second—although written the day before the first:

10 September 1692

My dearest Isaac,

What we did was simple. Simplex sigillum veri—*the simple is the sign of the truth. Isn't that what you said, twenty-odd years ago? And yet, for twenty-odd years, my letters to you have remained unanswered, my envelopes returned unopened.*

Yet what could be simpler than two hearts, two bodies joining together in science and in sympathy? When I left Rome and traveled to Cambridge, I knew that the future of Septimania was beyond my sole power. I needed a second body. And when you left your mother's garden to travel with me, you knew that your own quest, your own questions were beyond the capabilities of any one man.

You never knew your father. I never knew mine. Yet we solved problems, Isaac, we created life—a child I'd hoped you might lift onto your shoulders the way Aeneas or the giant Hercules bore their futures. Our son of flesh and blood, our twenty-odd-year-old son lives to carry on the line of Septimania. And he will have daughters and they will have sons, and doubtless there will be others who will stand on our shoulders and solve problems which exist beyond our horizons.

I have little faith that you will open this letter, the most recent in the series. If you do, you will understand it is the last, that I have reached my limit.

If you do not, I live still.

Antonella laid the envelope flat upon Malory's pillow, with a fresh sheet upon which she wrote the single word—Malory.

And then, because she knew it would be her last time at Cranmer Road and worried that Malory might not have taken his key, she left the door unlocked and made her way by foot out Grange Road to the Fen Causeway, past the train station to Addenbrooke's Hospital.

THERE ARE CERTAIN MOMENTS IN THE YEAR WHEN ROME—A CITY that has seen its share of awakenings and slumbers—is so deserted that a traveler might imagine that the buildings are equally hollow, a set for a warehoused opera, and that a quick dash behind the Baths of Domitian or the Palazzo Massimo would reveal plywood and braces stenciled with the name CINECITTA in capitals. Only a few other travelers stepped down from Malory's train, testifying to the emptiness. For all he knew, they might have been choristers on the way to an early morning rehearsal of *Tosca*. The fountain at the center of the Piazza della Repubblica was dry, the roundabout empty, the newspaper kiosks and bookstalls shut tight. The first light of mid-August picked out the *sanpietrini* in such pockmarked detail that Malory wondered how the stagehands, the grips, the best boys, or whatever the movie people called them—Antonella always insisted on staying in the Cambridge Arts Cinema to laugh at the credits that, even after decades in England remained exotic—could lay them all down in this brief moment when Rome was deserted. Was this a national holiday, a saint's day, Malory wondered? Was there a crucial football match or rugby or whatever they played in the summer that had kept the entire population off the streets? Had he purchased a special out-of-class fare that had switched him onto a siding that led to a private Rome? Had it been this quiet when Newton first entered Rome and rode with his college friend up the Aventino to the Villa Septimania?

Malory saw Rome with a transparency and the sensation of a twinkling dark matter, as a breathing city that he hadn't experienced in the forty-three years since he'd first arrived with only his canvas Kit Bag, his toiletries in Tesco's plastic, and the letter from his grandmother.

He walked along the Via Nazionale, past the English church, the Irish Pub. He crossed by the Palazzo delle Esposizioni, where the street sloped down to its medieval level at the Basilica of San Vitale. He knew there was something Roman below the church, and below that something Mithraic, and so down and down, each blind stone trusting the shoulders of the ones beneath it. He walked past the massive flanks of the insurance agencies that backed onto Trajan's Forum, past the lonely column graffitied with the Emperor's conquests over Tibor's ancestors from which he had long ago surveyed a kingdom of hopeful actors. He crossed Piazza Venezia, turning left at the Palazzo Caetani, where Aldo Moro was found crumpled in the trunk of a red Renault 4 to the horror of Anna Ford and Antonella and half the citizens of Italy. And though Malory knew no more about that mystery than he had all those years before, the transparency with which he walked through Rome assured him that he had chosen correctly. Rome. This was where Antonella wanted Malory to bring her.

Antonella was more Roman than Catholic, after all. None of the few members of the Cambridge Maths Faculty who came around to Cranmer Road to give their condolences objected or even noticed when Malory arranged for the Huntingdon Road Crematorium to handle the funeral. Malory couldn't imagine Antonella imagining a ceremony at Our Lady and English Martyrs, which was such a pale imitation of the churches of her hometown, with none of the Lippis or Caravaggios that made the worm-eaten relics and the waxy air of the altars manageable. He gave no thought to contacting Antonella's invisible children. Nor did he believe he would stay much longer by himself in the house at the end of Cranmer Road. His decision to bicycle out to St. George's Church, with what remained of Antonella in the blue marbled biodegradable cardboard box that Huntingdon Road had so solemnly handed over to him, was made in the sincere belief that Antonella had become part of the family, part of Malory's family, and that it was fitting to scatter her on the ground that held Old Mrs. Emery and in the air that had borne the Pip.

Malory hadn't visited Whistler Abbey, hadn't chosen to tune or play its organ since he had returned to Cambridge, hadn't seen the church since the day of his grandmother's funeral. Nevertheless, the bicycle path by the river was where both had always been. It was older, much older, as was he, and had resisted the improvements and regulations that generations of planning councils had brought to the Coton and the Histon footpaths. He negotiated its summer dips and baked ridges more nimbly than he had years before. Antonella's box rode secure inside his Kit Bag, which rested snugly in the basket on his front handlebars. He dismounted in the garden of the Orchard and walked the bicycle across the Cambridge Road, up the ramp to the wooden gate of St. George's. He had thought of taking Antonella inside, even of carrying her up to the steeple and scattering her ashes through the slats that not only brought air into the bellows but breathed out into the fens beyond. But Malory knew enough physics to know that even if he were fit enough to climb the ladder to the organ loft, there was no going back in time to the afternoon in 1978 when he had been surprised to see a young girl crossing the Cambridge Road from the Orchard, entering the church and climbing the ladder only to see him, Malory.

Instead, Malory wheeled his bicycle around the back of the church and propped it against the yew, unchanged in the brief span of yew-years since Malory had last stood in its shade at the grave of Old Mrs. Emery. The grave itself had been well-tended—he could only imagine the arrangements for its manicure, made long ago by Settimio. Surely this was a safe and comforting place to scatter Antonella, perhaps the one place I might return at least occasionally, Malory thought, although he wondered how much returning there might be for him, how much longer he might be able to straddle a bicycle.

He opened the flap of his Kit Bag, the stenciled letters entirely faded, the strap more hole than canvas and restitched several times, most recently by Antonella herself. The blue marbled box was a simple thing of cardboard, large enough for a cat, small enough to fit in a Kit Bag, but entirely inappropriate for a woman as generous as Antonella. Malory hadn't been shocked by the phone call from Addenbrooke's. He had felt the force of Antonella's goodbye that morning as he'd cycled away up the Coton footpath, even if he hadn't understood all its applications. What surprised him, when he was left alone with Antonella's body after signing the papers set in front of him, was how warm her hand was in his. It was the same warmth, in the same key, as the warmth he had felt when he read the letters she had left on his pillow. It was the warmth of the Queen of Septimania. It was the warmth of the woman who had loved her Isaac enough to disguise herself more completely than Haroun al Rashid, the Caliph of Baghdad, himself. It was the warmth perhaps of Aldana, daughter of Charlemagne, who had cloaked her heart in memory and the thousand and one stories she brought to her bed every night. Natural causes. Malory had no idea from what the Queen of Septimania had died. But he imagined it was from the same "Natural Causes" on the certificate Malory signed below the signature of some anonymous Addenbrooke's doctor. Antonella had been a queen, was a queen, would always be a queen in whatever part of Septimania still survived in Malory's universe.

"You know the church, I believe?"

Malory turned. A man, in that confident age between thirty-five and forty-five, before the thinning above and the thickening below signal beginnings of endings.

"I used to tune the organ. Years ago. Many."

"Ah." The man squinted up at the steeple, but not even in the vague direction of the organ. "Ten days and she'll be down."

"She?" Malory looked at the man.

"The church. Parish raised the funds to knock her down to the ground and build me a new one. Splendid, don't you think?"

"Knock the church down?" It was late enough in the day that Malory doubted most of what passed through his ears. "And you are?"

"The vicar," the vicar said, squinting up at the vault again.

"And you intend to knock down St. George's Church, Whistler Abbey?"

"Knock, knock, knock," the vicar smiled. "What the church eats up in heating bills alone."

"You can't be serious?"

The vicar turned and focused on Malory for the first time. "You're not one of those university preservationists, are you?"

Malory wasn't certain what he was. He never had been. But he thought back to MacPhearson, to all the red-haired, red-bearded questers devoid of doubt.

"It's a Norman church," Malory said. "I've seen the entry in Holinshed, it's been around for . . ."

"Eight bloody hundred years. Don't quote the vicar, chapter and verse," the vicar quoted at Malory. "Eight bloody hundred years old. And the electric is eighty, and the plumbing over a hundred, and the drafts have been around since Noah built his bloody ark. 'It's a Norman church,' he says." The vicar simpered. "Well so are fourteen hundred other Norman churches in East Anglia alone. I believe we might spare this one and build ourselves a church where elderly gentlemen won't catch their deaths of colds in the bloody springtime!"

Malory put the box back in the Kit Bag, the Kit Bag back in the basket of the bicycle, and pedaled back to Cambridge. He booked a train ticket the same afternoon—he was too fixed in his ways to approach the city otherwise—a train ticket to Rome for a final visit with Antonella. The transparency of his sight allowed him a view into the depths of his regret—late once again—that only now was he bringing Antonella back to the city she ached to visit on Malory's arm while she was alive. Still, she was there with him, in a box, as safe as any cat, snug within the sturdy canvas of Malory's ancient Kit Bag.

Malory walked from the Palazzo Caetani through the Ghetto to the Tevere, the same path he had run with another woman in his arms long before.

"Biscuit?" Louiza had asked then.

Biscuit.

Had she thought of that jog, that walk since then? Had she remembered through the pain of delivery and loss and all those years, how Malory had followed Tibor down to the Ospedale Fatebenefratelli, carrying her in his arms? Malory looked over the parapet to where the Tevere spilled over the smallest of waterfalls as it passed the prow of the island, and the plastic bottles and cartons and floating debris of decades was caught in the bubbling eddies at the downriver end, floating in an endless balance between water and gravity.

He left the Isola Tiberina, left the square hulk of the synagogue behind him and walked, slower now, past the Temple of Hercules, the Temple of the Vestal Virgins, survivors of that religious fervor to knock, knock, knock to the ground. Crossing the empty slip road off the Lungotevere, Malory found the shaded entrance to the Clivo di Rocca Savella. The *sanpietrini* looked no more moss-covered, the pines, the bougainvillea no older or less colorful. The Clivo was empty, the medieval brick walls bare of even a midsummer gecko. No *cancello,* no entrance, not even a fig leaf or a turban to disguise the identity, no omega of a bricked-up arch to suggest that once, long ago, there might have been a hidden door and a villa and a kingdom.

At the top of the Clivo, Malory turned towards the rising bulk of Santa Sabina and in through the iron gate of the entrance to the Giardino degli Aranci. The sun was fully risen, and the odor of the bitter oranges gripped his nostrils. It had been a full day since he had eaten. He set his Kit Bag down upon a concrete bench and picked a piece of fruit from one of the lower branches. The peel came away slowly—he was hot, he was tired, and the skin beneath his nails stung from the juice. He sat on the bench and ate the orange, section by bitter section. The juice ran down his lip and hung suspended from his unshaven chin. He was alone in the garden.

Beneath him lay what remained of Septimania: the bedroom of the portraits of his ancestors; the scarlet cap and cape of the secret cardinal hanging in the wardrobe; the *majlis* of Haroun, all cedar and cushions; the marble Bernini of Isaac Newton and the Queen of Septimania eternally without the apple; the Sanctum Sanctorum, where Newton and the Queen had made their discoveries, where the Queen had written her lonely letter to the lonely Newton—all of them, Antonella, Malory himself alone in these words; and beneath the words, the kilometers upon miles upon light years of tunnels holding books and wires and information that was declining into antique and ruin with every passing moment. Twenty-three years of his own life passed down there below, eating scones, wandering in the garden, and searching for an answer to a question he may never have understood. Searching for what it meant to be King of Septimania, Holy Roman, Jewish, Muslim, heir to the throne of Science, as if the sum of those titles would add up to One.

What he was, what Malory was, was something else. He was the Hercule of his mother, dreaming of a father and a giant buried beneath the hills of the Pyrenees. He was the organ player of Narbonne, long before he had any notion that the Old Lady up the hill was Mrs. Emery, that Mrs. Emery was his grandmother. He was a seventy-year-old man with a corduroy suit too warm for midsummer Rome and a Kit Bag containing . . . He opened the flap and set the entire inventory on the bench beside him. A bag of toiletries, including a razor and soap, a toothbrush, and toothpaste with perhaps one good squeeze left. The Book of Organs and the Newton Chapbook—the meager remains of his once infinite library. The Universal Organ Tuner, with its memory of thousands, perhaps tens of thousands of pipes, but at base only a piece of bent and rusting metal. And finally, the blue marbled box holding what once was a young Italian girl with a biscuit tin, a few kilos of dust.

Malory sat on the concrete bench with his belongings beside him, as lost as the old men he used to see camped out beneath the bridges by the Tevere with their possessions spread out on a muddy piece of tarpaulin, knowing less—if that were possible—than when he'd first come to Rome. He sat, and the day turned into evening and the evening turned into night. Malory sat all night in the Giardino degli Aranci. Beneath him and his concrete bench and the contents of his Kit Bag, there was only dust. And beneath that, the center of an Earth that was same size as the point at the center of the Sun, ninety-three million miles away. In all the years since he had been crowned on the circle of porphyry in St. Peter's, the Earth had traveled thirty billion miles around the Sun. And yet the Sun's two-hundred-fifty million-year journey around the center of the Milky Way during that time barely registered on any calendars, Julian, Roman, Arabic, Biblical, or otherwise, even less the motion of the Milky Way around the center of the universe, and the universe around whatever collection of other universes unimaginable to a species that had been around for only a few hundred thousand years. What would it mean to discover Newton's One True Rule that guided everything? Would it explain all that? It was all that Malory could do to imagine scattering Antonella's ashes here in the Giardino degli Aranci, behind the Basilica of Santa Sabina where she had spent her girlhood, where Ottavia had spent her early years. Scatter Antonella, turn her into an orange tree the way Ottavia had been the product of a pip. Dust to dust, ashes to oranges.

As the rays of the sun rose and touched the round dome of St. Peter's, the square dome of the Great Synagogue across from the prow of the Ospedale Fatebenefratelli, Malory took the box, took what remained of Antonella from out of his Kit Bag, and placed it on his lap. He was alone in the Giardino degli Aranci except for a few early morning ancients—he was now one of them—walking alone or with caretakers. One old man—could he possibly have the faded memory of a red beard?—in a wheelchair, a plaid flannel across his lap, watched his movements carefully from the shade of a Roman pine across the gravel path. But who would notice, who would mind the sentimental sprinkling at this early hour?

Malory set his thumb against the lid of the blue marbled box to pry it loose. He thought of the box on the seven-sided desk of the Sanctum Sanctorum that Settimio had shown him on his first morning in the villa. He thought of the villa itself, perhaps only an immeasurable meter or two beneath his feet. This box, this marbled box, he would open. But search as he did, turn the box and turn again, Malory couldn't find an opening. Had there been a list of instructions from the Huntingdon Road Crematorium that he had carelessly discarded? He searched again in his Kit Bag but came up empty-handed. He tried again with his thumbs, but the top wouldn't budge. He set the box down next to him on the bench, defeated even in this one simple task. Yet as he did, the light reflected off the metal of his Universal Organ Tuner. Picking it up, he wedged its bent and mottled tip under the forward edge of the top, and in one easy motion pried off the lid and opened the box.

There she was, his Antonella. He thought of her biscuits. He thought of the first kiss in a Rome of another era. He thought of Tibor and the weight of his hand on Malory's shoulder. He thought of gray-eyed, gray-haired Cristina and the Nurses and the Bomb Squad, of Settimio and the Driver and the poor Pole whose funeral he had missed while he was in mourning in England. He thought of Rix. And he thought of that last kiss at the door of Cranmer Road, tasting of coffee and comfort, and a memory of copper curls.

Malory reached his hand into the ashes, as warm in the morning light as Antonella's hand in the chilly ward of Addenbrooke's. But as he did, his fingers touched something hard. They had told him at the Crematorium that sometimes pieces of bone remained, resistant until the end against the flames. But what Malory pulled out from within the ashes was something more solid, something heavier. It was a pen. A simple ballpoint pen. Silver, if coated with a dull layer of ash. Had a careless attendant dropped it into the box? Had Antonella managed to leave it for Malory as she had left the letters from the Queen of Septimania? He clicked the butt-end. It had a point. Malory set down the blue marbled box of ashes for a moment and picked up the Book of Organs and turned to an empty page. "15 August," he wrote. The pen wrote.

With the pen in his hand, an understanding came to Malory, borne by the light of the sun. It wasn't that he had read the letters too late—the letter from his grandmother, the letter from Settimio, the letters that Antonella left on his pillow that signified that he was too late to kiss her goodbye. It wasn't that he realized too late that Mrs. Emery was his grandmother, that Louiza loved him, that Ottavia was his daughter, that Tibor, Settimio, Rix, Cristina, and Antonella would die. He realized that what he had failed to do was what all had been urging him for more than fifty years. He realized that Louiza with her $i = u$, Newton with his One True Rule did not merely describe what existed but gave birth to a new creation. Newton, for all his inability to acknowledge the love of the Queen of Septimania, had created something extraordinary beyond a mere line of heirs. Newton had spent years, after all, experimenting with alchemy, calculating the End of Time using the Bible as his slide rule—activities and obsessions that would have got him laughed out of the least academic of pubs. Such a small portion of Newton's life had been spent with the science that history remembered. But perhaps it was all tied together in this marginal note, this one rule. Newton was looking, as Malory was looking—as perhaps the rocks, the planets, the stars, the oranges on the branches of the trees of the Giardino degli Aranci were looking—they were all looking for sympathy. For sympathy. For love. And that creation, that equation, that identity of Louiza's, the $i = u$ that described the attraction of two bodies at a distance—what was that if not love? The same love that broke

Newton when he learned of the death of his Queen—that fractured, marble look that paralyzed Malory on the bench of the organ loft of Trinity College.

"The applications are extraordinary," Louiza had warned him, "and quite possibly dangerous." Malory knew nothing. He had spent forty-three years searching without looking.

The first rays of light of the new mid-August day began to ripple the tips of the Roman pines. Malory saw that all the colors of light that he had so carefully separated into files, that he had collected onto shelves through the prism of all he had learned were as useless as when Richard Of York Gave Battle In Vain. With that first light, Malory let go of all that he had gathered beneath him for seventy years and picked up a second prism. Malory saw the answer approaching nearer and incalculably nearer, understood what Newton knew, what Newton had learned, not by standing on the shoulders of giants, but by falling into the arms of his Queen. The One True Rule that guides the universe. Armed with that prism—not the scepter of Charlemagne or the orb of the treasure of Al-Shammardal, but the pen he had drawn from the ashes, a simple biro—Malory intercepted all those infinite rays and concentrated them into a single beam. *Forse oggi*, forty-three years after the Master of Trinity yanked away the lever from beneath Malory's fellowship, Malory began to write.

He began at the beginning with that first day: the shaft of light, Louiza's golden head around the side of the Orchard, Louiza's pale chin lifted in the balmy air of mid-March forty-three years past. He wrote through the morning and into the afternoon. He wrote as the clouds above the Tevere draped a modest loincloth over the savior of an evening sun. He wrote as the shadows deepened, shaped and reshaped, tuned and retuned into ever-modulating harmonies, as swarms of starlings chased their own invisibles, beaks open in reckless hunger. Malory wrote. He wrote in the Book of Organs. Sometimes he picked up the Chapbook and wrote in the margins, in the spaces between the lines of the Queen of Septimania's journal, in and around and astride the shoulders of Newton's triumphant footnote. As he wrote, the fig leaves fell away, and he began to understand how little he had understood the signs of simple love that Louiza, Ottavia, Antonella, and even Tibor and Old Mrs. Emery and Settimio, had shown him, given him, tried to teach him all these years.

Although he couldn't see it, the bitter oranges in the trees of the garden began to fall and the air was rich with their bruising, and the sound of the little girls released by the nuns for their afternoon freedom like starlings themselves, chasing the living cats that hid in the ruins of the garden walls. And as he wrote, two women entered the garden from the gate behind Santa Sabina, lifting their pale chins in the late-summer light, walking slowly—out of choice, not out of need, although one of the women, the taller one, was clearly as old as Malory and the smaller, while not in her youth, looked as if she could fly to the top of Trajan's Column at any moment.

Malory wrote. And what he wrote was Newton's solution—the answer, what Newton had found, what Haroun had found, what he, Malory, was slowly, slowly discovering. All difference is merely a disguise for the One True Rule that guides everything. And even as the light began to fade, Malory continued to write with a strength and a determination that came not from an anxiety of being late, but from an understanding that, with the approach of the two women, this was the time. That he could not have made this discovery until now. Even if all the ink of the Queen and all the ink of Newton and the new ink that Malory joined with theirs, full of his Mother and his unseen Father and the unknown Old Mrs. Emery; even if all this history and science and philosophy and dreams and truth and imagination and what is unimaginable, even if all this melted into one indistinguishable paste. Maybe, just maybe, with this new pen that mixture could be unsqueezed back into a tube, a tube that contained all the dishes, all the desires, all the *djinns* as handily as the Magic Bag of Judar, the one tube, the single tube that mattered—or at least mattered to those who mattered to Malory.

When Malory had finished writing, when he'd followed the alphabet in the negative path of Louiza from the bricked-up arches of the omega back to the alpha of the apple of that first Pip, Malory laid down his pen and took up the box with Antonella's ashes. In the fading light of the Roman evening, the two women approached the bench. Malory looked down into the box. What he saw was alive and it was dead, it was life and death, lives and deaths, Antonella and Louiza, Ottavia and Cristina, Tibor and Mrs. Emery, his Mother and Father, and as many as the fireflies that a Tuscan peasant saw in the imagination of a Florentine poet on a summer's evening so many more years ago.

Malory looked up. The women sat on the bench beside him, Louiza on his left, Ottavia on his right, Antonella in the blue marbled box before him.

"Hello, Malory," Louiza said.

"Hello, Father," Ottavia said, "may we come up?"

And Malory felt that he had grown. In the fading light, he looked down at the uplifted faces of Louiza and Ottavia. Had he risen from the bench, or floated up like Bernini's apple, balanced by the force of the two women—the scientist on one side and the Queen on the other? In the deepening dark, it was impossible to say whether the old man with the faded red beard and the tartan flannel across his lap might roll in his wheelchair towards Malory and break the ascension. But for a moment, all laws, all rules were suspended. Sometime very soon, perhaps, others would stand on his shoulders. Ottavia, her daughter, others would straddle a Vespa and ride into their own Septimanias, away from their Louizas, towards their Louizas. But for now, he was on the topmost layer with no need of religion or science. Malory, his world, his universe, were in tune.

ACKNOWLEDGMENTS

SEPTIMANIA TOOK ROOT AT THE BEAUTIFUL ROCKEFELLER FOUNDA-tion villa above Bellagio, Italy, where I spent a month of tranquility and creation with ten other fellows in late 2007. Down the hill, the Foundation was simultaneously hosting a conference on developing low-cost drugs to battle African diseases. One evening, our two groups came together for cocktails, and I spoke with a young doctor—a genuine hero from a small village in Mozambique—who had traveled out of Africa, out of his country for the first time in his life. He told me why he was in Bellagio; I told him why I was there. But even after I had told him twice, he couldn't believe that I was being housed and fed and supported in order to write a story.

It is extraordinary. And I have received extraordinary support from many sources. My editor Allyson Rudolph championed my book to Overlook Press and its celebrated owner Peter Mayer. My agent Ayesha Pande guided me with elegance and acumen through a marathon of rewrites in unerring belief and affection for *Septimania*. The poet Robert Pinsky not only introduced me to *The Inferno of Dante,* but also generously gave me permission to incorporate freely his extraordinary translation.

But it is the unquestioning belief of my family—of my children, Rebecca, Gabriel, and Mimi, of my wife, Stephanie, and my parents, Judith and Isaac, who have followed the changing fortunes of Malory and Louiza with patience and the advice of their wider lives—that has sustained me the most and has taught me the true meaning of copeability.